Queen of Dreams

Also by Chitra Banerjee Divakaruni

The Unknown Errors of Our Lives
Sister of My Heart
Arranged Marriage
The Mistress of Spices
The Vine of Desire

Poetry

Black Candle
Leaving Yuba City

For Young Readers

The Conch Bearer
Neela: Victory Song

Chitra Banerjee

Divakaruni

Doubleday

New York London Toronto
Sydney Auckland

Queen
of Dreams

A NOVEL

PUBLISHED BY DOUBLEDAY
a division of Random House, Inc.

DOUBLEDAY and the portrayal of an anchor with a dolphin are
registered trademarks of Random House, Inc.

This book is a work of fiction. Names, characters, businesses, organizations, places, events, and incidents either are the product of
the author's imagination or are used fictitiously. Any resemblance
to actual persons, living or dead, events, or locales is entirely co-
incidental.

Book design by Maria Carella

ISBN 0-7394-5306-8

Copyright © 2004 by Chitra Banerjee Divakaruni

All Rights Reserved

PRINTED IN THE UNITED STATES OF AMERICA

for my three men

Murthy

Anand

Abhay

dreamers all

ACKNOWLEDGMENTS

My deepest thanks to:

My agent, Sandra Dijkstra, for the many ways in which you keep
helping;

My editor, Deb Futter, for your wise questions;

Kim Chernin, Deepika Petraglia-Bahri, and Lawrence Hogue, for
your comments;

My mother, Tatini Banerjee, and my mother-in-law, Sita
Divakaruni, for your blessings;

Murthy, Anand, and Abhay, for love and understanding;

Baba Muktananda, Swami Chinmayananda, and Gurumayi, for
your presence in my life.

What we know and what we don't know are like Siamese twins,
inseparable. . . .

Confusion, confusion.

Who can really distinguish between the sea and what's reflected
in it? Or tell the difference between the falling rain and
loneliness?

Haruko Murakami, *Sputnik Sweetheart*

We say *America you are
magnificent* and we mean
we are heartbroken

Reetika Vazirani, "It's a Young Country"

2

FROM THE

DREAM JOURNALS

Last night the snake came to me.

I was surprised, though little surprises me nowadays.

He was more beautiful than I remembered. His plated green skin shone like rainwater on banana plants in the garden plot we used to tend behind the dream caves. But maybe as I grow older I begin to see beauty where I never expected it before.

I said, It's been a while, friend. But I don't blame you for that. Not anymore.

To show he bore me no ill will either, he widened his eyes. It was like a flash of sun on a sliver of mirror glass.

The last time he'd appeared was a time of great change in my life, a time first of possibility, then of darkness. He had not returned after that, though I'd cried and called on him until I had no voice left.

Why did he come now, when I was finally at peace with my losses, the bargains I'd made? When I'd opened my fists and let the things I longed for slip from them?

His body glowed with light. A clear, full light tinged with coastal purples, late afternoon in the cypresses along the Pacific. I watched for a while, and knew he had come to foretell another change.

But whose—and what?

Not a birth. Rakhi wouldn't do that to herself, single mother that she is already. Though all my life that child has done the unexpected.

A union, then? Rakhi returning to Sonny, as I still hoped? Or was a new man about to enter her life?

The snake grew dim until he was the color of weeds in water, a thin echo suspended in greenish silt.

It was a death he was foretelling.

My heart started pounding, slow, arrhythmic. An arthritic beat that echoed in each cavity of my body.

Don't let it be Rakhi, don't let it be Sonny or Jonaki. Don't let it be my husband, whom I've failed in so many ways.

The snake was almost invisible as he curled and uncurled. Hieroglyphs, knots, ravelings.

I understood.

Will it hurt? I whispered. Will it hurt a great deal?

He lashed his tail. The air was the color of old telegraph wire.

Will it at least be quick?

His scales winked yes. From somewhere smoke rolled in to cover him. Or was the smoke part of what is to come?

Will it happen soon?

A small irritation in the glint from his eyes. In the world he inhabited, *soon* had little meaning. Once again I'd asked the wrong question.

He began to undulate away. His tongue was a thin pink whip. I had the absurd desire to touch it.

Wait! How can I prepare?

He swiveled the flat oval of his head toward me. I put out my hand. His tongue—why, it wasn't whiplike at all but soft and sorrowful, as though made from old silk.

I think he said, There is no preparation other than understanding.

What must I understand?

Death ends things, but it can be a beginning, too. A chance to gain back what you'd botched. Can you even remember what that was?

I tried to think backward. It was like peering through a frosted window. The sand-filled caves. The lessons. We novices were learning to read the dreams of beggars and kings and saints. Ravana, Tunga-dhwaja, Narad Muni—. But I'd given it up halfway.

He was fading. A thought flowed over my skin like a breath.

But only if you seize the moment. Only if—

Then he was gone.

Rakhi

My mother always slept alone.

Until I was about eight years old, I didn't give it much thought. It was merely a part of my nightly routine, where she would tuck me in and sit on the edge of my bed for a while, smoothing my hair with light fingers in the half dark, humming. The next part of our bedtime ritual consisted of storytelling. It was I who made up the stories. They were about Nina-Miki, a girl my age who lived on a planet named Agosolin III and led an amazingly adventurous life. I would have preferred the stories to have come from my mother, and to have been set in India, where she grew up, a land that seemed to me to be shaded with unending mystery. But my mother told me that she didn't know any good stories, and that India wasn't all that mysterious. It was just another place, not so different, in its essentials, from California. I wasn't convinced, but I didn't fret too much. Nina-Miki's adventures (if I say so myself) were quite enthralling. I was proud of being their creator, and of having my mother, who was a careful listener, as my audience.

When the story was done my mother would kiss me, her lips as cool as silver on my forehead. Sleep now, she whispered as she left, shutting the door behind her. But I'd lie awake, listening to the soft cotton swish of her sari as she walked down the corridor. She'd stop at the door to my dad's bedroom—that was how I thought of the big, dark room in the back of the house with its large, too soft bed and its tie-dyed bedspread—and I'd hear the companionable rumble of their voices as they talked. In a few minutes I'd hear his door closing, her footsteps walking away. She moved quietly and with confidence, the way deer might step deep inside a forest, the rustle of her clothes a leafy breeze. I'd listen until I heard the door to the sewing room open and close, the sigh of the hinges. Then I'd let go and fall into the chocolate-syrup world of my dreams.

I dreamed a great deal during those years, and often my dreams were suffocatingly intense. I'd wake from them with my heart pounding so hard I thought it might burst. When I could move, I'd make my way down the dark corridor by feel. Under my fingers the walls were rough and unfamiliar, corrugated like dinosaur skin, all the way to the sewing room. I didn't know why she called it that; she never sewed. When I opened the sighing door, I'd see her on the floor, face turned to the wall, covers drawn up over her head, so still that for a moment I'd be afraid that she was dead. But she'd wake immediately, as though she could smell me the way an animal does her young. I'd try to crawl under her blanket, but she always took me—firmly but kindly—back to my own bed. She lay by me and stroked my hair, and sometimes, when the nightmare was particularly troubling, she recited words I didn't understand until I fell back into sleep. But she never stayed. In the morning when I awoke, she would be in the kitchen, making scrambled eggs. The sewing room would be bare—I never knew where she put her bedding. The carpet wasn't even flattened to indicate that someone had slept there.

My discovery occurred on an afternoon when I'd gone to play at the home of one of my classmates. This was a rare event because, in spite of my mother's urgings, I didn't tend to socialize much. Children my own age did not seem particularly interesting to me. I preferred to follow my mother around the house, though she didn't encourage this. On occasion, I listened from behind a door as she spoke on the phone, or watched her as she sat on the sofa with her eyes closed, a frown of concentration on her forehead. It amazed me how still she could be, how complete in herself. I tried it sometimes. But I could keep it up for only a few minutes before I'd get pins and needles.

I've forgotten the girl's name, and why in the course of the afternoon we went into her parents' bedroom, but I do remember her telling me not to jump on her parents' bed, they didn't like it.

"You mean your mom sleeps here—with your dad?" I asked, surprised and faintly disgusted.

"Sure she does," the girl replied. "You mean your mom doesn't?"

Under her incredulous eyes, I hung my guilty head.

"You guys are weird," she pronounced.

After that afternoon, I undertook a course of serious research. One by one, I went to the homes of the children I knew (they were not many) and, between games and snacks and TV, checked casually into their mothers' sleeping arrangements. Finally I was forced to conclude that my family was, indeed, weird.

Armed with the statistics, I confronted my mother.

That was when I made the other discovery, the one that would nudge and gnaw and mock at me all my growing-up years.

My mother was a dream teller.

The discovery did not come to me easily. My mother disliked speaking about herself and, over the years of my childhood, had perfected many methods for deflecting my questions. This time, though, I persisted.

"Why don't you sleep with Dad?" I kept asking. "Or at least with me, like Mallika's mother does? Don't you love us?"

She was quiet for so long, I was about to ask again. But then she said, "I do love you." I could hear the reluctance in her voice, like rust, making it brittle. "I don't sleep with you or your father because my work is to dream. I can't do it if someone is in bed with me."

My work is to dream. I turned the words over and over in my mind, intrigued. I didn't understand them, but I was in love with them already. I wanted to be able to say them to someone someday. At the same time, they frightened me. They seemed to move her out of my reach.

"What do you mean?" I asked, making my voice angry.

There was a look on her face—I would have called it despair, if I had known to do so. "I dream the dreams of other people," she said. "So I can help them live their lives."

I still didn't understand, but her face was pale and tight, like a cocoon, and her hands were clenched in her lap. I didn't have the heart to badger her further. Hadn't she admitted to the most important thing, that she loved us? I nodded my head as though I were satisfied with her explanation.

Her smile was laced with relief. She gave me a hug. I could feel the remnants of stiffness in her shoulders.

"Why don't you decide what you want for dinner?" she said. "You can help me cook it, if you like."

I allowed myself to be diverted and asked for ravioli. I'd had it for the first time on that fateful afternoon in my classmate's house. At home we rarely ate anything but Indian; that was the one way in which my mother kept her culture. She had never made ravioli before, but she looked it up in a cookbook. We spent the rest of the afternoon rolling, crimping, stuffing dough with cheese. The ravioli turned out lumpy, and the kitchen was a disaster, sauce smeared everywhere and shreds of cheese underfoot, but we were delighted with ourselves.

In the middle of boiling the ravioli my mother turned to me and said—though I hadn't shared my classmate's words with her—"Rakhi, remember this: being different doesn't mean that you're weird." She startled me in this manner from time to time, referring to things she couldn't possibly know. But her clairvoyance was erratic. It would create problems for us over the years, making her ignorant of events I expected her to know, secrets I longed to tell her but couldn't bear to speak of.

For example: the reason why I left Sonny.

At dinner Father admired the creative shapes we'd made and said it was a meal at once delicious and instructive. He cleaned up the kitchen afterward, humming a Hindi song as he scrubbed the sink with Comet, his hands encased in neon yellow rubber gloves. He was the tidy one in our household, the methodical one, always kind, the one with music. My mother—secretive, stubborn, unreliable—couldn't hold a tune to save her life. I wanted to be just like her.

Years later, after she died, my father would say, "Not true. She didn't love me, not really. She never let me get that close. The place right at the center of her—that was reserved for her dream gods or demons, whoever they were. She never shared that with anyone. Not even you."

And I would be forced to admit that he, too, was right.

3

She's thinking of green. Deep-forest green, gold-gray green, green tinged with the foggy silver of dawn, edged with the brittle brown of time passing. All the colors of the eucalyptus grove she walked to earlier this morning. She's thinking of the colors she will have to mix in order to re-create that green, colors that are not green at all. It is the closest thing she knows to magic in a world that has disappointed her over and over with its mundane worka-day habits. Even its terrors are predictable ones; its disappoint-ments mark the air with their distinctive, unmistakable odor long before they come to pass.

She takes out the big clear-glass plate that serves as her palette as she thinks this; she takes out a new, primed canvas. She feels its spackled surface; its smell is as familiar to her as Jona's breath. She squeezes out Naples yellow and yellow ochre, cobalt and cyan and burnt sienna, a bit of Prussian blue for the shadows, and considers the unfamiliar geometry of foliage. Her thick black hair, tied back mercilessly with one of Jona's old ribbons, threatens to escape and curl around her face. Deceptive, those baby curls. Along with the ridged planes of her cheekbones, her high, unlined forehead (which is shiny right now with concentration), and the small mole in the exact center of her lower lip, they charm strangers into believing that she is innocent and high-spirited and optimistic, and that this is so because nothing bad has ever happened to her. If they looked into her eyes, wide, with a depth in them that is almost purple (like night, like a new bruise, like the aparajita flower that her mother has never described to her), they would see that this is only partly true. But few people care to do that—and of these even fewer know how to go about it. Rakhi is not unhappy about this. As she told Belle once, she prefers to remain misunderstood.

The eucalyptus grove was wet when she got there this morning, a fact that surprised her. It hadn't rained near her house, though it was misty the way it usually is in Berkeley. But in the grove there were puddles of water. She had to step around them to keep her shoes dry. And then another surprise: there was a man in the eucalyptus grove. A rare occurrence, so early on a weekday. He was practicing Tai Chi.

She had come to the grove because she planned to paint it, and this made her nervous because she'd never painted trees before. Until now, most of her paintings had been about India—an imagined India, an India researched from photographs, because she'd never traveled there. She'd painted temples and cityscapes and women in a marketplace and bus drivers at lunch, but never trees, not as her main focus. But last night it had struck her that she needed to do something new, something challenging. It was a thought she was already regretting.

She was annoyed when she first saw him. She had wanted the grove to herself, its energies undisturbed. But he was far enough away that after a while she did not mind. She watched his clean underwater movements and thought, This is how people were meant to use their bodies. From where she stood, it seemed to her that he had beautiful hands. He was dressed in loose-fitting white clothes, and the sun, filtering hesitantly through eucalyptus branches, lent iridescence to his black hair. She could not see his face clearly—just a hint of olive skin and high cheekbones. For a moment she wondered who he was. If he was Indian. She wanted to walk up and look into his face. There was a tingling in the soles of her feet, precursor to desire, which she'd thought she had put away after things went wrong with her marriage. She shut her eyes to control it. She was older now; she was a mother. She knew from experience that the tingling pointed the direct route to trouble, and she'd had enough trouble in her life already.

She fastens the canvas to the easel, tightens the screws to hold it steady. She loads a brush with color and makes that first pure sweep across the virgin background. This is the moment when anything is possible.

The phone rings.

Annoyed, she wonders who it could be. Belle knows not to disturb her in the morning, which is her painting time. Her mother would be busy with her clients. Her father would be at work. Besides, he calls her only when he is drunk, on weekends.

She waits impatiently through the rings for the machine to turn itself on. A voice begins to leave a message. The phone is shut in a closet at the other end of the apartment (she puts it there at painting time), so she cannot decipher the words. But she knows the voice.

Sonny.

She should have guessed it! She feels herself tensing, a tightness that starts in the backs of her calves and moves up her body into her fingertips. She grips the brush more firmly. *I refuse to stop for him.* But the truth is that she can't stop for anyone, not right now.

She tried to explain this to Sonny once. How at a certain moment the colors take over the eyes, the hands. How she must surrender her body to their rhythm. How, until the movement is done, nothing else matters.

She had not expected him, who was not an artist, to understand.

They were at the table, finishing dinner. He was eating and flipping through a music magazine. She can never remember the names of his magazines—except *Playboy,* over which they once fought. He took small bites of the sandesh she had made. This was when she still cooked elaborate meals—appetizers, rotis rolled out fresh, rich curries in almond sauce, traditional Indian desserts that required hours of culinary acrobatics. He was careful to brush the sweet white crumbs from his fingers between bites. It never ceased to amaze her that a man like him, so Dionysian in his other appetites, should have such dainty table manners. He didn't say anything for so long that she thought he had not heard. He was often off in places in his head. Or perhaps he had nothing to say. But as she was taking the dishes to the sink, he murmured, "It's like being in the middle of lovemaking, isn't it?"

She had been silenced by the exactness of the comparison. He humbled her like that from time to time, making her see invisible things about herself, articulating what she had no words for. It was one of the things she had loved in him before the night that had spoiled everything.

As soon as she thinks the words, she knows they aren't true. A relationship doesn't spoil in one night, like milk. There had been hints for a while, but she had chosen not to see. She had gone around and around the millstone of her life that she was so in love with, like the blinkered bullocks she had seen in a photograph of an Indian village.

Bulls can be forgiven their blindness. She had never forgiven herself for hers. That is why her calves grow tight when Sonny calls, and there's a pain like a stuck fishbone in her throat.

She finishes a set of strokes, drops the brush into a jar of turpentine, and picks up another. She adds colors, shapes. She thins the paint carefully with linseed oil so that the lines of objects grow fluid. When their edges bleed into each other to form unplanned-for designs, her scalp prickles with pleasure.

But the phone is ringing again, just when she needs all her concentration.

If it's Sonny calling back, he's going to be one sorry puppy.

But this time the voice is female. Muffled and closeted as it is, she can't quite place it, though it is tantalizingly familiar. She registers the gritty purple anxiety of the tone. The whole world, yin and yang, is conspiring against her today. Well, this woman will have to wait, too.

She's halfway into the first layer of the painting, which is a close-up of a tree, texture of leaves and peeling bark. Sunlight glints at its edge like an uncertain memory. A breeze shakes the chunky eucalyptus blooms in the left corner free of their pollen. She stares at the easel, trying to feel the life behind the brush-strokes. Below what she has made, there are other layers waiting. New colors to introduce. Ivory, black, vermilion, a hint of sea salt heavying the air. She touches the lower right corner tentatively. She needs something more here. Perhaps—? She hadn't planned on it, but suddenly she decides to paint in the man with the beautiful hands.

The phone calls have done their job, though, waking the whisper voice that lives inside her skull. What if Sonny was calling about Jona, who's staying with him this week? it asks. What if that second call was from Jona's school? What if something terrible happened to her? *If you were a good mother,* it says with disapproval, *you'd stop right now and check.* The whisper voice calls up catastrophes behind her squeezed-shut eyes. It makes her hand shake.

If she paints any more now, she'll ruin the entire composition.

She abandons the painting and goes to the closet where the answering machine waits, winking its malicious Cyclops eye. She jabs the replay button. A line from a movie she once saw flits through her mind: *Life gets in the way of art.*

That pretty much sums up my existence, she thinks.

But as she's told Belle, she's not complaining. Compared to how things were three years ago, when she'd just moved out and was waiting for the divorce to come through, her life is roses, roses all the way.

Sonny called her apartment every morning those days. His messages, excruciating in detail, were always the same. He didn't understand why she was doing this to him. Whatever she thought he'd done, he was sorry for it. They (he really meant *she*) had made a terrible mistake, they needed to get back together. He adored her. He used his most helpless, guilt-generating voice.

"I wouldn't pick up," she told Belle, "but he knew I was there, listening. He knew I wouldn't be able to paint anything decent the rest of the day. After a month of those calls, I was ready to kill him."

"Then what happened?" Belle asked.

"He stopped."

"Just like that?"

"Yeah," she said, but inside she wondered, as she had often before, if her mother had had anything to do with it.

Sonny's message says: Dearly beloved Riks, this is just to inform you that Jo and I are taking off up the coast for Mendocino. Paul says there's a bunch of whales up there, some blues even. He says we can bunk with him for a couple of days, maybe go out on the water in his boat. Jo'll miss a bit of school, but I'm sure you won't mind. She'll be learning more important things from the great university of life.

She hates it when he speaks in clichés like that. He knows this. That is why he teases her with them. Here are some other things he knows: She disapproves of Jona missing school—her daughter has little enough stability in her life. She disapproves of Paul, who's an okay photographer but who smokes far too much pot to be trusted with a boat or a child. She hates it when Sonny upsets the routine she's worked so hard to establish for Jona and herself, and exposes her daughter to dangers both physical and moral. And all without asking her permission.

Okay, okay, she tells herself. Let's not get melodramatic.

You're just afraid Jona will have too much fun with Sonny, interjects her whisper voice, which never misses an opportunity. *You're afraid she won't want to come back to you.*

I'll deal with you later, she tells the voice.

The second message is from Belle. It says, "Rikki, please please please come down to the shop right away. Something terrible has happened."

She sighs. She loves Belle (a.k.a. Balwant Kaur, though not even her parents are allowed to call her that) and always has, ever since they were roommates during their freshman year at Berkeley. They've nursed each other through romantic troubles, failing grades, bouts of flu and the pressures that only Indian parents know to apply to their offspring. They've loaned each other money and underwear, courage and lipstick, and held each other's heads when they threw up after drinking too much at parties to which they shouldn't have gone. They've confessed to each other things that they've never dared to tell anyone before, and seen themselves newly through each other's eyes. They've stayed up nights talking about how Rakhi sometimes feels too American, how Belle would love to shed the last vestiges of her desi-ness. Without Belle, Rakhi doesn't think she could have survived her divorce. Belle knows her weak points, her stubbornness, her suspicions, her passion for her art, and her fear that she'll never be good enough at it. How hard it is for her to change her mind once it's made up. How she can't bear to let a mystery be. How much she hates Sonny and loves her mother. How much they both aggravate her. Rakhi accepts Belle's wildnesses, the way she's often restless, as though something's gnawing at her insides. The way she moves from boyfriend to boyfriend, never letting them become important. Her constant fights with her parents, good country folk bewildered by their hummingbird daughter who refuses to let them pull her back into their safe Sikh nest. She knows how Belle loves the store and how she loves drama, a combination that often lures her into exaggeration.

It's probably the espresso machine broken down again, she thinks. Still, she pulls off her painter's smock and pauses only to soak her brushes in a jar in the sink.

The small kitchen is in its usual disarray of good intentions gone awry. The dinner dishes haven't been washed. The mung beans she soaked with virtuous resolution three days back, intending to cook dal, have begun to sprout. She'll have to call her mother and find out what one can make with mung that has sprouted already. The table in the dining alcove is piled with library books and art catalogs and a big blue bowl filled with apricots from the landlady's tree—and unpaid bills. (Ah, the banality of bills, another curse in the artist's life.) Leaning on the western wall is an oil painting, almost done: sunset on the peaks of Kanchenjunga. She has left it there so she can examine it from time to time and ascertain what needs to be added. Jona's discarded tights and ballet slippers lie by the window, next to the avocado plant she's been trying to grow in Rakhi's favorite mug. The eastern wall has been given over to Jona's artwork, rainbow drawings of dwarflike people with intense black-markered eyes.

Rakhi likes the comfortable clutter of her life, the things she loves gathered around her like a shawl against the winterliness of the world. It surprises her (when she thinks of it, which is deliberately not often) that she used to be such an anxious housekeeper when she was married to Sonny, arguing with bitter fervor about picking up wet towels from the bathroom floor and replacing caps on toothpaste tubes. She feels a certain pity when she thinks of that time, that self. Such an earnest wife-self, wanting so much, her stance one of perpetual leaning forward, as though perfection was a town just a little farther down the road. She didn't know then that perfection had nothing to do with happiness.

And now you've learned that happiness lives in messy rooms? her whisper voice taunts.

Tomorrow, she tells herself as she makes her way to the door, wincing as she steps on a sharp piece of Lego camouflaged by carpet. I'll clean it all up tomorrow. Be a good example to Jona. I'll even vacuum.

Yeah, right, says her whisper voice.

4

In the night I dreamed of a golden chain breaking. I could hear the links, snap-snap, like chicken bones. When I woke it was three A.M. The tendons in my back ached with my attempts to hold the chain together. I knew I wouldn't sleep again.

I went to the landing and looked out on the sickle moon. When I opened the window, the night was full of the smell of wild fennel, which doesn't grow anywhere near our house. The elders used to say fennel healed internal wounds. We cultivated it in the caves and gave it to the dreamers who came to us. Could I take it as a hopeful sign?

But as I stood there the wind turned, and now the smell was of salted fish. I went and sat on the empty bed in Rakhi's room, where she sleeps with Jonaki when she comes to visit. I touched the pillow to gain a little comfort. It was hot to my hand. In troubled moments, the elders would recite from the *Brihat Swapna Sarita*. I did the same now, though I have forgotten many of the cantos:

The dream comes heralding joy.
I welcome the dream.
The dream comes heralding sorrow.
I welcome the dream.
The dream is a mirror showing me my beauty.
I bless the dream.
The dream is a mirror showing me my ugliness.
I bless the dream.
My life is nothing but a dream
From which I will wake into death,
which is nothing but a dream of life.

But in the morning, after my husband has left for work, when the woman comes (as I knew she would), it makes it no easier to tell her what I must say.

She's older than I thought she would be, with gray woven into her short, curly hair and crinkles cut into the edges of her eyes.

She says, We're thinking of having a baby. We've been married just a year now, but we met late and we're not getting younger. That's why I came to see you. People say you can tell if this is a lucky time for me, or not.

Have you had a dream recently? I ask. One that you remember?

I dreamed of a hillside twice, she says, grasses swept by wind.

I ask what color the grasses were, were they dry or living, but she cannot remember.

Far away there was a light. She knew it to be the light of her home. It glimmered welcome, but she couldn't find the path to it. There were thorns; they pricked her feet.

Was there pain?

But no blood, she says. Her voice pleads for me to say something hopeful.

Then, halfway up the hill, her husband appeared. He held out his hand. From the concern in his eyes she could tell how much he loved her. Her voice grows shy and grateful as she says this.

She put out her hand and miraculously, their fingers touched. But it wasn't her husband anymore—the face was a stranger's, dangerous and attractive.

What was he wearing?

Her brows crease. Maybe a coat, or a shawl.

Was it gray, like fog? Was it white, like bones?

Maybe, she says doubtfully. Then she lowers her eyes.

I wanted that man more than I've ever wanted anything. I was ready to leave my husband and follow him. The longing was like someone had thrust a knife into me. My stomach ached even after I woke up.

How can I tell her of the cancer that has started spreading its web through her? Soon the pain will be so bad that one half of her will long for death while the other half struggles to escape it. And her husband, paralyzed by his own misery—he won't be strong enough to help her.

Who *is* that strange man? she asks.

The elders, who believed in saying the truth whole, would have told her. But I broke from their ways long ago. I say, The dream is a warning to take better care of your health.

It is? she says doubtfully. That's what those images meant? But I *do* take good care. Exercise, vitamins, soy powder, breast self-exams—you name it. I feel pretty healthy.

I'd advise you to make an appointment with your doctor right away.

But what about what I asked you? The baby? Should we try for one now? Is this a lucky time?

She holds my hands in hers. I look down at them. Pale, bloodless, cold as coffin earth. But only I can see this.

I make myself smile. I make myself say, No point worrying, and no point waiting.

Let the closeness bring them some joy. Who knows, perhaps it will strengthen the bond between them so it won't snap as quickly. I have been wrong in reading dreams before, though not often.

But make that doctor's appointment anyway. Make sure you get everything checked. Promise?

You're as bad as my mother! Okay, I promise. Thank you. Thank you so much. At the door she turns, diamond-eyed. If it's a girl, we'll name her after you.

5

Rakhi

I can sense Belle's anxiety even before I enter the Chai House, even before I see her face. It's written all over her back, the way she's stiffened it like a threatened animal. The way her hair, which is usually gathered into a sleek ponytail, snarls over her shoulders. Even so, she's careful with the muffins she's setting out on their tray. Chocolate chip, blueberry, bran, carrot, almond. They form a warm mosaic of browns and oranges, dotted with the astonishing purple of the berries. Next to them are lemon-glazed Danishes, and then a plate of the crumbly sugar-and-cinnamon cookies we've christened Delhi Dietbusters. The smell of strong coffee spills out onto the street. And freshly baked bread.

Once I said to my mother, As long as there's fresh bread in this world, things can't be beyond repair.

She nodded. But I could read her eyes. *My poor Rakhi, to place so much belief in bread!*

I've never worked out the following: am I naïve, or is my mother cynical?

I draw in a deep breath. Naïve or not, I love this place—and I'm fortunate to have it. Because if it weren't for this store, I might not have Jona today either.

It had been touch-and-go while we were battling for custody—with surprising fierceness. I hadn't thought Sonny would want the bother of caring for a three-year-old who wasn't quite toilet trained yet, but he'd surprised me. Sonny's lawyer had argued eloquently that, as the number one DJ of a popular nightclub, he would be a far better provider for Jona than I would. But the Chai House had swung the balance in my favor. Otherwise Jona would have been spending three weeks out of every four under the care of Sonny-the-infuriating.

I stand for another moment outside the store, enjoying the view. Belle and I had put everything we had into the Chai House— all our creativity as well as whatever little money we possessed— and converted a run-down establishment into something special. We painted the walls ourselves in shades of peach. The carved chairs (practically antique, according to Belle) we found at a warehouse sale. I was the one that discovered the twin maple rockers, each with its matching footrest, at the Ashby flea market. Placed in a nook, they're a favorite with customers who come in alone. But I never sat in them myself. I'd refinished them in the long evenings that followed my divorce, and it seemed to me that they still smelled of that time, that sad mix of freedom and fear.

In an alcove was our free "Leave one, take one" bookshelf, where Paul Auster and Dean Ornish rubbed shoulders with Mary Higgins Clark and Salman Rushdie. Beside it a rug formed a children's area strewn with blocks and hand puppets made from old silk saris (my mother's contribution), for which Jona still made a beeline each time she came into the store. By the door was the bulletin board where customers advertised dancing lessons, garage sales, animals in need of homes, and humans in need of mates. On strategic spots on the wall, I'd hung my own paintings. Light fell on them, making jewels out of Mughal gardens, making water drops glisten on the hides of bathing elephants. Huge glass jars of coffee, each with its name stenciled on—Sumatra, Ootacamund, Peruvian Organic, Jamaican Blue Mountain—gleamed behind the counter. On the large boards that hung above, Belle wrote the menu each day in her best cursive.

"Homestyle, but with more style than home ever had," she was fond of saying. I'd laugh at her, but secretly I agreed.

There's another way in which the Chai House saved me in those dark months after the divorce when I couldn't stop wondering if I'd really made a terrible mistake, as many people were quick to inform me. If I'd ruined Jona's chances of a happy childhood by separating her from a loving father. I'd tell myself they didn't know the whole truth. They didn't live with Sonny, they didn't know the way he'd raised his face that night at the party and looked at me, eyes glazed, without recognition. But then I wasn't sure. So many people loved Sonny—even my own mother. How could they all be wrong, and I right? Through those restless midnights of doubt, the Chai House gave me something tangible to hold on to, something that was exactly what it appeared to be, nothing more and nothing less. Taking care of it was a way to make at least one part of my life turn out right.

Perhaps it's significant that the first thing I managed to sketch after my divorce was a scene of the store's interior. It took me an excruciating three months and it wasn't very good, but at least I completed it without throwing it away, like I had done with all the others. I pinned it on my bedroom wall next to a sketch of Jona, and on bad days I drew comfort from its solidity. On those days the only thing that got me out of bed was knowing that without me they might not survive, my store and my daughter.

The chime at the door signals my entrance, and Belle whirls around.

"Oh, there you are, Rikki! Finally! Thank God!" She wipes her hands on her apron and hurries over to grab my arm. "I'm *so* sorry to disturb you like this—I know mornings are important to your painting—"

This is not a good sign. The last time Belle apologized to me was when she borrowed my one and only evening dress to go dancing in and ripped it all the way up the side. This had happened the night before my big date with Sonny, the one where he was going to propose to me. And even that wasn't a true apology. Because later she claimed she'd done it on purpose, in a vain attempt to save me from myself.

"It's okay," I say cautiously. "What's the problem?"

In response Belle drags me over to our front window and points. Her finger, tipped with frosted fuchsia nail polish, quivers eloquently.

I move aside the fronds of the many overly healthy houseplants that live on our windowsill—gifts from customers over the years since we opened—and peer out across the street. There's Easels, where the owner, Mr. Jamison, gives me a good-neighbor discount on my art supplies. Estrella, the Mexican restaurant run by the Soto family. And Purple Jam, which sells used tapes and CDs and is always overcrowded with young people who are outrageously dressed and coiffed.

Belle had rolled her eyes when I'd told her that.

"You're getting old," she'd said. "Besides, they probably think you're the outrageously dressed one. Outrageously old-fashioned, that is."

What else could I have expected from someone whose favorite outfit was a red sequined halter-top mini, and who had recently double-pierced her navel?

On the pavement directly across from us is Marisa's flower stall, which today has a display of tulips in stunning yellow. Three students, armed with dark blue cups of coffee (ours!) are waiting at the bus stop for the 51 to take them to campus. Two mothers in jogging suits chat as they push strollers. At the crosswalk, a man is handing out pink flyers for some event or other. Marco, the homeless guy who lives over in People's Park and comes in at the end of the day to buy our leftover Danishes at a discount (he refuses to take them for free), is setting up his guitar case.

"God's in His heaven, as far as I can see," I say. I like the way Marisa's tulips have formed a lemony wedge against the warm beige of the restaurant wall, the way the early sun has brought out the texture of the bricks, the subtle shadows. I begin to put together a composition in my mind.

"You aren't paying attention," Belle accuses. "You're thinking about painting something, aren't you?" She jabs at the glass with her finger. "There, look on that side!"

This time I see it. The store on the corner—a coveted spot—which had stood empty since Mrs. Levy had closed her deli to retire last month, isn't empty anymore. The front is still unchanged, but there are people inside—uniformed people, cleaning and setting up. The uniforms—an elegant olive green—tug at my memory. Where have I seen them before? As we watch, a truck drives up. Men start unloading tables and chairs, crates of various sizes. One of the women from inside steps out to supervise. She's tall and willowy, with arresting cheekbones and frost-gold hair, and the olive uniform fits her like it had been tailored for her. Which of course it wasn't, because—it comes to me suddenly—it's standard issue for the fifty-five thousand employees who work for Java nationwide.

"That's right," Belle says with grim satisfaction. "There was an article about them in *Business Week* last month, remember? I read parts of it to you." She recites, " 'Java is the fastest-growing café chain in the country, notorious for its policy of opening new stores in the vicinity of existing coffee shops and luring away their customers with low-priced specials and freebies. Within three years of its inception, it has captured sixty-seven percent of the U.S. market. "That's nothing," claims CEO Jeff Norfolk with characteristic modesty. "We're aiming for one hundred percent." ' "

Belle has this dubious talent for perfect recall. I, on the other hand, believe in forgetting unpleasant facts as soon as possible. The more you think of them, I've told her, the more psychic power they suck from you, and the stronger they grow.

But even I can't be an ostrich about this situation.

"We might as well throw in the towel right now," Belle says gloomily. "Sell before we're forced out of business. Seven years of backbreaking, heart's-blood toil down the drain, but I guess that's how it goes."

I consider reminding Belle that we've only had the Chai House for five years, then think better of it. Besides, she's right about the toil.

"I guess I could always go back to Turlock," Belle continues. "Help Mom and Dad with the produce store. They'll be happy enough. They never were convinced that living in the Bay Area was good for me. They'll probably arrange my marriage to one of those upright young Indian farmers they buy their supplies from. They're always trying to get me to meet them—"

"Let's not get all worked up."

"I can just see myself ten years from now, shrouded in fat and a polyester salwaar kameez, a passel of snot-nosed brats hanging onto my dupatta, rolling out makkhi ki rotis for all my in-laws—"

"Belle, you don't *know* how to make roti—or any Indian food, for that matter. And I've never seen you wearing anything remotely resembling a salwaar kameez—"

"Exactly," Belle says. Then she bursts into tears.

"Calm down!" I say sternly, but I can see that under all the theatrics this time Belle is really worried. The Chai House means even more to her than it does to me. She was the one who dreamed it into being. I remember the day when she came over to my house—I'd still been married then—waving a stack of sheets excitedly. She'd gone over the ideas while I nursed Jona. Cocooned in domestic bliss, I'd been doubtful. I had my hands full taking care of a husband and baby, I told her, not to mention my art. I didn't need the hassle of trying to manage a business on top of that. But she'd kept at me. *Think how much fun it would be, not having to work for anyone else. I've always wanted that.* She'd cajoled her parents into letting her have the money they'd been saving for her wedding to use as a down payment for the store. They gave it—but with great reluctance. They didn't quite believe that Belle (or I) had enough business sense to keep from going under. Even now, when they call us, there's apprehension in their voices as they ask how we're doing. Maybe that's why Belle works so hard, to prove them wrong.

Sonny wasn't too happy either. He didn't want me starting something that would require so much of my attention when Jona was still a baby. I'd expected my parents (my mother, really; my father rarely expressed his opinions on matters pertaining to my life) to support him. But my mother surprised me. Women need something of their own to make them independent, she said with unexpected vehemence. Something to give them a sense of self. Something to fall back on, if necessary. Had she sensed, somehow, what was to come? She'd given me a large sum of money, never explaining where it came from—enough to buy all the equipment we needed to get started—and offered to babysit Jona.

Panic is contagious. What if we do lose the Chai House? I find myself thinking. My mouth fills with bitter fluid; my palms are clammy. All that time and money, all my hopes gone. But that's the least of it. I'll never be able to hide something this big from Sonny-the-hawk. It'll give him what he's been waiting for all this time—the chance to take Jona away from me.

Belle dabs at her eyes. She's struck by an idea, I can tell.

"Let's call your mom!" she says. "She'll know what we should do."

"No!" I say, grabbing for the phone, but she's already dialing.

. . .

The line is busy.

A disappointed Belle hands me the phone with strict instructions to call every two minutes until I get through. Then she goes to put away the rest of the muffins.

Belle has been a great fan of my mother's—maybe *devotee* is a better word—ever since my mother deciphered a dream for her. (I never knew the details—my mother maintains strict confidentiality about the people she helps. I suspect it had something to do with Belle's beau of the moment, a young man who sported green hair, a razor earring and a perpetual scowl, and who shortly thereafter exited her life.)

My mother had a similar mesmerizing effect on Sonny. At their very first meeting—long before he officially became my boyfriend—he decided that he was going to adopt her. (Or, more accurately, that she was going to adopt him.) He proceeded to worm his way into her heart by shamelessly using his charm (with which commodity he is excessively endowed) and bringing her gifts of exotic organic vegetables from the farmers' market in San Francisco. He continues to visit her every week to have dinner and to tell her his many tales of woe (self-created woe, in my opinion), to which she listens with far too much sympathy. He brings back care packages filled with his favorite gourmet dishes—palak paneer, tandoori chicken, pooris—items that take hours of preparation time. I know this because he makes sure to call and tell me.

When I go over, she makes me Chinese stir-fry, fifteen minutes from start to finish.

Sonny and I have had a few altercations on this subject.

"She's *my* mother, in case you've forgotten," I said to him once, after a call where he'd waxed eloquent about the wonders of my mother's fish kurma. "Now that you and I don't have a relationship anymore, don't you think you should back off a little?"

"Why?" he asked, all hurt innocence. "She's still my mom, as far as I'm concerned. She's also the best cook in the world and one of the few people who understand—and appreciate—me."

"Sonny, you wouldn't recognize appreciation if it came up and bit you on the nose."

"Besides," he continued with a dramatic sigh as though I hadn't spoken, "in my heart, you and I will always have a relationship."

I hung up in disgust.

Soon after, my mother phoned. She was angry, which was rare for her. "I can't believe you're jealous of the poor boy, lonely as he is. I can't believe you want him not to see me."

"That tattletale! Just wait till I—"

"There you go, jumping to suspicious conclusions. I'd like you to know Sonny didn't say a word to me."

"Uh-huh, sure," I said, using my best ironic voice, but strangely, I did believe her. My mother has a way of knowing things.

"I don't want him sponging off of you," I added. I had to bite my lip to stop myself from adding, And how is it you cook him all that fancy stuff you never make for me?

"He doesn't sponge off of me. He brings your dad and me something every time he visits." Here she paused meaningfully— to help me realize, no doubt, that I could show some improvement in that area. "He does a lot of things for me, in fact. Last week he took me to the doctor for my checkup."

"But you always go on your own——"

"I don't like to drive so much nowadays," she said.

"What do you mean? Are you sick? Why didn't you ask *me* if you needed——?"

She changed the subject deftly. "And he brings over the latest Hindi movies and watches them with us, the ones with all the hit songs. Your father really enjoys that. You know how he loves music——"

"Since when did you start watching Hindi movies? You never let *me* watch them when I was growing up. You called them brainless, sexist fluff."

"Since when did you start wanting to eat my Indian food?" countered my mother, who believes in offensive play. "It was always pasta and pizza and *Oh mom, not alu parathas again!* when you were growing up." Then she added, "I love you both, you should know that. You're not in competition, even though you did decide to get a divorce."

My mother has never made a secret of her utter and irrational fondness for Sonny. I can't figure out this aberration in a woman who is otherwise one of the most intelligent people I know.

Maybe there's another Sonny, Belle told me once. A kinder, gentler Sonny that only your mom can see, the way she sees her dream people.

Yeah, I said. A kinder, gentler Sonny. That would have to be a dream for sure.

To give my mother credit, she never tried to pressure me into staying with Sonny once I'd decided to leave. Even though I could never bring myself to tell her why.

But here I am, obsessing on ancient history when I should be tackling the problem on hand. This has always been my shortcoming, one more way in which I'm different from my mother, who is the original Do It Now poster girl. Perhaps this is why she dreams and I paint. Because dreams look to the future, and paintings try to preserve the past.

We watch from the window of the Chai House as movers unload another truckload of expensive-looking equipment and wheel them into Java.

Belle gives me a you'd-better-get-back-to-the-phone-and-make-that-call look.

I give her a why-do-we-have-to-drag-my-mother-into-this look.

"Rikki, this is not the time to indulge in false pride. We need your mom's help."

"We can handle it ourselves," I say in my most confident tones.

But inside, I'm afraid. I've never been a planner. Mostly, I've fallen into things that life has swept up against me. Going through with the divorce is the only difficult decision I've made. My mother, now: she's the fighter in the family. Once she decides on a goal, she never lets go. "Like the tortoise," my father would say, "in the tale of the hare and the tortoise." With a wry smile and a wink, he'd add, "And guess who's the hare?"

I was never sure if he meant himself or me.

But there were races my mother didn't win. She never could get my father to stop drinking, though periodically she'd get mad and throw out his bottles.

"Why should I quit?" he told us once. "It gives me happiness—or keeps me from sorrow, the same thing. And I'm not harming anyone, am I?"

His drinking was erratic. I could never understand what brought it on. Sometimes he'd go for a month without touching alcohol. Other times he'd start drinking on a Friday night and continue through the weekend. He only drank red wine—he claimed it was good for his heart—and was never abusive when he drank. He sat in the corner of the living room and played songs by dead people on his antiquated stereo, mostly love songs by Sehgal or Rafi or Kishore Kumar, though sometimes he'd surprise me by playing Lady Day. From time to time he would sing along—he had a powerful baritone—a rapt and distant smile on his face. When he got too drunk to sing, he'd curl up on the couch and cover himself with a blanket he kept ready for that purpose, and go to sleep. On Monday morning he'd go off to work, apparently unaffected by his weekend escapade.

I never hated him for drinking. Not until my mother died.

My mother tried to stop him every way she knew. After the binge was over, she'd cook his favorite dishes. She'd stand behind his chair, massaging his neck. "You're going to kill yourself, drinking so much!" she'd say. She'd make her voice light. Only I, glancing across the table, would see the troubled look in her eyes. I waited for her to ask him why he did this to himself, but she never did. She did beg him to go see someone—a doctor, the priest at the Shiva Vishnu temple, an AA counselor. But he never listened.

"As long as I don't kill you," he'd joke, "you shouldn't complain."

"Maybe you'll do that, too, one of these days," my mother would say, annoyed.

"Where'd you get that? In one of your dreams?"

Her face would lose all expression whenever he said that, as though she'd shut something off inside. She didn't like either of us mentioning her dreams.

"Okay, okay," my father would say. "I apologize. Forgive me—please?" He'd go down on one knee in front of her and throw open his arms, Bollywood style. "Mere sapno ke rani," he'd sing in his husky voice until she smiled and said, "Oh, stop it, you ridiculous man!" His words—my Hindi was spotty at best, but I think they meant *queen of my dreams*. Or was it *my queen of dreams*?

6

Rakhi

There were two kinds of interpreting that my mother did, though there may have been others. My knowledge of this facet of her life is furtive, fragmented, gleaned through eavesdropping.

The first—as she had reluctantly told me—was when someone came to her with a dream, and she explained to her what it meant. (But why do I say *her?* I suspect that men came to my mother, too, though I imagine them to be more awkward about it.)

"A dream is a telegram from the hidden world," I heard her say once. "Only a fool or an illiterate person ignores it."

The second kind of interpretation was more complicated. I'll get to it later.

I learned early not to question my mother about her work. Though she talked freely with me about matters that were taboo in Indian families—boyfriends, bodily changes, bad things that happened at school—she was silent on the subject of dreams. If I brought it up, she would look distressed. Sometimes she'd leave the house. Once she took the car and didn't return for hours. I was beside myself with worry, certain she'd had an accident. I think it was soon after that that I stopped asking questions. Or maybe it was after she'd given up on teaching me.

. . .

Let me not misrepresent facts. My mother wasn't the one who wanted to teach me to interpret dreams. I was crazy for it myself.

As far back as I can remember, I wanted to be an interpreter. But when I turned twelve, I grew obsessed with the idea. I saw it as a noble vocation, at once mysterious and helpful to the world. To be an interpreter of the inner realm seemed so *Indian*. (In thinking this, of course, I deluded myself. Weren't the American papers filled with advertisements about psychics?) I hungered for all things Indian because my mother never spoke of the country she'd grown up in—just as she never spoke of her past. But if I could be a dream interpreter like her, surely I would understand her without the need for words.

Not all my motives were so pure. I daydreamed sometimes of how my talent would make the more popular girls in the school befriend me, how it would force Elroy Thomas, who played drums in Band, to notice me at last. I imagined running my hands over his hair, its tight, springy curls.

When I asked my mother, she shook her head. "First, you can't give this knowledge to people who might want to use it for selfish gain." (Here she looked at me until I looked away.) "And second, you can't give this knowledge, period."

I wasn't convinced. "How did you learn, then?"

"I have to make dinner."

I caught the edge of her sari as she tried to escape to the kitchen. I told her I wasn't letting her go until she told me the whole story.

"There's no story to tell. I had a gift. A distant aunt who was a dream teller recognized it when she came to visit."

"But how?"

"I don't remember very well. I think she made me sleep in the same room. Anyway, when she left, she took me back to live with her."

I stared at her, trying to imagine how it must be to leave everything you love behind and go off with a stranger. "You left, just like that? Didn't your mother stop you? Didn't you miss her?"

She stared down at the backs of her hands. Her unhappiness was a tangible thing. I could have held it in my palm, like an injured bird. I'd never noticed before that the ends of her nails were ragged, as though someone had been biting them. My mother, biting her nails? It shocked me so much, I said, "Never mind. Tell me what your aunt taught you. Did she give you lessons?"

"I guess you could call them lessons." She spoke slowly, the words sleepwalking through her mouth. "But they came later, and only because I already had the gift."

"And I don't have it?" I tried to make my voice nonchalant, but it cracked a little.

She hesitated. "I don't know for sure. I haven't sensed it, that's all. Maybe I'm just too close to you to see it."

I knew what she was saying, under the careful kindness. But I couldn't bear to give up yet.

"I want you to try, Mom," I said. "Really try, one more time. Let me sleep with you."

She drew in her breath to say no—I could see it in the set of her mouth. But then she agreed. Was it because she loved me? Was it some deep, chromosomal guilt, for not having passed on the gift to me?

I slept deeply that night, waking in the morning with a slight headache. My mother's face was drawn, her eyes rimmed with dark circles.

"Do you remember anything? Anything you saw?" she asked. She sounded hoarse, as though she were coming down with the flu.

When I shook my head, she looked disappointed and relieved at the same time. "It didn't work," she said. "I'm sorry."

Her words were like a door closing, with her on the other side, beyond my reach.

"It's all right," I said, turning away, my voice as casual as I could make it. "It doesn't matter. Thanks for trying, anyway."

I've never been able to fool my mother. I could feel her eyes on me, sharp and sad. But she only said, "Maybe it's for the best. Being a dream interpreter isn't as glamorous as you think."

A year later, I would learn how right she was.

The second kind of interpretation occurred when my mother dreamed. These dreams were not about herself, or us, or anyone she knew. All the people in these dreams were strangers, and usually they didn't believe in dreams. Or they believed—but in spite of themselves. Which was worse, because when you're forced to believe in something you wish you could dismiss, it makes you an angry person.

My mother's duty was to warn these angry people of what was about to happen to them.

. . .

This particular morning my mother had a migraine. She'd get a blinding headache once in a rare while—though looking back, I think it was probably more often than my father or I realized. She wasn't the complaining type. Or maybe she kept deliberately silent because she didn't want us to realize that the headaches occurred whenever she'd had a stranger-dream.

But this morning the headache must have been really bad, because after she'd made my father his breakfast and he'd gone off to work, she lay down on the living room carpet and asked me to bring her a blanket and a bottle of aspirin. She swallowed a handful of the white pills and asked me to tuck the blanket around her. I did so uneasily—her limbs felt slack and heavy. In a raspy voice that didn't sound like hers, she added that she wanted me to stay home from school.

This was unlike my mother, for whom school was up there next to God. It scared me. What she said next scared me more.

"I need your help," she said.

My mother was always asking me to help—to wash vegetables, to make a bed, to mail letters, to take a bag of ripe oranges from our backyard to the Yangs, who lived down the street. When I was younger, it had made me feel indispensable, but recently I'd realized that everything I did for her, she could have done herself in half the time. She asked me only so that I'd learn what I needed to know before she launched me into my adult life.

But today, for the first time, she really did need me.

I sat there by her, wondering if I should call the doctor. But which doctor should I call? I knew only the pediatrician she took me to see. Did my mother even *have* a doctor? My heart thumped guiltily, out of rhythm, as I realized how little I knew, or had cared to know, of my mother's life.

As though she sensed what I was thinking, my mother opened her eyes—they were veined with red—and shook her head slightly. Then she beckoned me close. "Go to the sewing room," she whispered with effort, "and look in the closet. Under the extra pillows, there's a plastic box with a blue lid—"

I waited for her to say more, but she'd closed her eyes again. Her breath came in gasps.

I ran to the sewing room, to the big closet that took up one of its walls. I tried to slide the door open, but it got stuck on something partway, so that I could barely wedge my body in through the opening. I'd never paid much attention to the closet before this— it was the place where household odds and ends were stored. But today as I peered in, it seemed very dark, and larger than it should be. Maybe it extended on and on, beyond my seeing? (I had read the Narnia Chronicles.) I put out a hand, my heart beating rapidly. But here was the back wall, disappointingly solid. In the living room I heard my mother cough. Abashed, I dug through the pile of pillows and found the box. It was a Tupperware box, and not very large, though it was quite heavy. I opened the lid—I couldn't resist. It was filled with little rows of glass bottles, each the size of an index finger. The glass was a dark brown, so I couldn't tell what was inside.

When I brought her the box, my mother gave a wan smile. I waited to see what she was going to do with the bottles, but she sent me to look up a number in the phone book. She spelled out the name I was to look for: Raghavendra, S. P. It wasn't a name I'd heard before. By the time I located it and copied out the number, she'd finished with the box.

"Put it back exactly where it was," she said. "And then get your shoes on. We have to go out."

"But you aren't well enough," I protested.

She didn't say anything, just pushed herself off the floor. She held on to the wall and walked with faltering steps to the shoe closet. I helped her find her chappals and locked the door behind us. The sunlight made her wince and press her hands over her eyes.

"Do we really have to go?" I asked anxiously. "You're too sick to be driving—"

"No driving," said my mother. She took my arm and, leaning heavily on it, started walking.

In about ten unsteady minutes, we'd reached the corner gas station. My mother walked around to the side, where the public phone was located. She gripped the telephone and asked me to dial the number I had copied down.

"Are you sure?" I asked, worried at the turn things were taking. "Do you even know this guy?"

My mother shook her head. I could hear the ringing through the receiver. A gruff voice said, "Raghavendra speaking."

"Mr. Raghavendra," my mother said, "I'm calling to inform you that your life is in danger. One of the people living in your house is planning to kill you."

There was a silence at the other end. Then the voice, hissing and heavy, yet small and tinny at the same time, said, "Who is this?"

My mother didn't say anything.

"Is this a crank call? I'm going to phone the police, have you traced—"

"Mr. Raghavendra," my mother said, "you have to believe me. It's probably your cousin, whom you sponsored from India six months ago. He's been living in your house since then, right? Does his name start with the letter *H*?"

Silence again.

"I think he's developed a—relationship—with your wife—and wants you out of the—"

"How do you know this?" He sounded oddly calm.

"I can't tell you that."

"Someone's put you up to this, yes? A practical joke, yes?"

"No joke," my mother said.

"Then you're crazy!" He was shouting now. "Completely nuts! I'm going to have you committed. I'm going to come after you personally and—"

I found myself sobbing. I wasn't sure what I was more scared of: that the man would somehow learn who my mother was and find her—and by extension, us—as he threatened. Or that he was right, and she *was* crazy.

"I did my best, Mr. Raghavendra," my mother said sadly. "Now it's up to you."

And while the man ranted on about what he would do to her once he found her, she replaced the phone with shaking hands. She started off blindly across the parking lot, unaware of a delivery truck that had just turned the corner.

I screamed. There was a shrieking of brakes. A large, red-faced man leaned out from the truck window and yelled. "Stupid broad! Ain'tcha got eyes in yer head? Coulda gotten killed!"

My mother didn't seem to hear him. She made her way to the bushes on the street corner and threw up there. I'd reached her by then. I held her head as she heaved and retched. I glared at passersby who gave us distasteful looks, and wiped her face the best I could with a piece of tissue I had in my pocket. I was ready to run back to the public phone and open the yellow pages and call a doctor—any doctor—but my mother held on to my arm.

"I'm better now," she said. And she was. I could see it from her eyes, which were clear again. Whatever had made her ill had left her, now that she had passed on her dream.

A few months later I gathered my courage and asked my mother about what had happened that morning.

She looked at me with a small frown and said, "What morning, shona? I don't know what you're talking about."

I looked at her guileless gaze. She wasn't lying, I could tell that much. My mouth went dry. Was that part of the dream teller's gift, this ability to erase something once your duty to it was done? Would she erase us like this one day, my father and myself?

Or—but no. I didn't imagine the incident. I'm sure I didn't.

I think sometimes of how strongly a person would have to believe in herself—and the truth of her dreaming—to do what my mother did that morning. And many other mornings, I'm sure, though she never again asked for my help. I remember the thick rage in the man's voice and think, I couldn't have taken on such a task.

Thank God my world is simpler. Even my tragedies are simple ones, colored in commonplace hues.

But here's what's crazy: I'm thankful, and then, the next moment, I'm filled with regret. Because I'll never enter my mother's underground domain, those caves peopled with possibilities, what may or may not come to pass, where one plus one can equal one hundred—or zero.

7

Her mother's line is still busy. Rakhi is annoyed at this, but not surprised. Her mother spends much of her day on the phone, probably because her clients prefer not to meet her. Perhaps she prefers not to meet them, too. It would be awkward, dangerous even, if they came across each other later—perhaps at the grocery store or a social event, except her mother no longer attends those. This much is definite: Rakhi has never met any of them.

She listens to the short beeps. Impatience pricks her skin like darts, enters her bloodstream. Like always, her mother's busy with someone else, she thinks, then is ashamed at the lie. All through her childhood, her mother was careful to ensure that her dream work didn't disrupt her family's life. And so she slipped it into pouches, bottles, cracks in the wall not visible to her husband or her daughter. (Only once was there an exception, down by the 7-Eleven, smell of vomit and diesel fumes and crushed oleander leaves—) Maybe that is what Rakhi resents: that her mother, with such meticulous motherness, kept her out of the place she wanted most to enter. That she denied her her birthright and doomed her to the bland life of suburban America.

. . .

When Rakhi finally gets her on the line, her mother seems disoriented. "Who is it?" she asks, sounding breathless. "Who?"

"Mom, it's Rakhi! Your one and only daughter, remember?"

"Sorry, shona," her mother says, her voice contrite, but they both know she's not really apologizing. "What is it?"

Rakhi feels a familiar twinge of jealousy, that suspicion of being less important than *them* that stalked her through childhood. She pushes it aside and tells her mother about the new store, attempting to speak in an efficient, adult fashion. It's a little difficult, with Belle hyperventilating in her other ear, prompting her in loud whispers.

Her mother says nothing. She never responds to bad news the way Rakhi imagines other mothers must, with horrified exclamations or coos of sympathy. She is not sure if she should be thankful for this or resent it. Today her mother's silence annoys her. Perhaps she's the same way with her clients, but as her daughter, doesn't Rakhi deserve at least an exclamation or two of dismay? How can she be so unnaturally self-possessed, so different from everyone else? Is it because she already knows what people are telling her?

Her mother is still silent, but there's an intensity to her silence now. Rakhi pictures her standing in the kitchen, the way she's seen her so many times. She'd be leaning against the wall, threading her fingers through her long black hair. (There's no white in her mother's hair, a fact that disconcerts Rakhi, who has recently plucked a few offending strands from her own head.) Her mother's eyes are closed so she can focus better on what she's hearing. Her face is abstracted and emotionless, like the faces of the goddess statues Rakhi remembers from her infrequent childhood visits to the Vedic Dharma Samaj. She wouldn't answer if Rakhi happened to speak to her at such times. It's different now, Rakhi thinks with an ironic smile. This time I'm the one getting her full attention.

She has a great relationship with her mother, she knows that. They're happy whenever they meet, and they enjoy talking to each other. Her mother would do everything possible to help Rakhi if she were in trouble. She'd go beyond what Rakhi asked. Perhaps that's why Rakhi is reluctant to bring her problems to her. Or perhaps it's because her mother never talks about her own sorrows. Rakhi has no idea of what might keep her mother awake at night.

But maybe thinking that is her first mistake. Maybe dream interpreters don't ever sleep.

She remembers something her mother said to her when she was about ten years old. It has stayed in her mind because her mother so rarely gave her advice. They'd been in the garden, planting chili peppers. Her mother lowered a seedling, its boll of hairy roots, its chilies like tiny red bird beaks, into the hole that Rakhi had dug.

"Shona," she'd said in her burnt-sugar voice with its slight, delicious rasp, "the best way to love people is not to need them. That's the purest love."

Rakhi didn't quite know what her mother meant. But for years after that, she tried to love people in that need-less way. And failed. Sometimes she wonders if those words were one reason why things broke down between Sonny and her. Was it because he'd grown accustomed to her not needing him that he couldn't come through when she finally did require help?

Act like a grown-up! she thinks angrily. Take responsibility for your own mess.

But she allows herself this much: those words were the reason why, on that night when Sonny let her down so completely, she didn't go to her mother.

"You were just too pigheaded," accuses Belle (who knows only a fraction of what happened). "You just wanted to prove to her that you could make it on your own."

Rakhi doesn't know how to explain, even to her best friend, that what she was really trying to prove was that she loved her mother with the purest love.

Rakhi finishes up the phone conversation by informing her mother that she didn't want to disturb her. "Belle made me," she says.

"Damn right I did," Belle calls out, loud enough to make sure Rakhi's mother hears. "Rikki's in her usual denial mode, but I know an emergency when I see one."

Outside the new store, two workmen have unpacked a large Java sign in a jubilant, ominous orange.

"I know this isn't exactly a dream, Mrs. Gupta—though it is kind of a nightmare," Belle is saying into the mouthpiece, which she has grabbed from Rakhi. "But I felt you'd know what to do."

Rakhi didn't allow her mother to accompany her to the divorce proceedings, though she offered. She didn't tell her about the bitter custody battles. Afterward, she shared only the barest details of the settlement with her. Her mother probably doesn't realize what losing the business would mean for Rakhi, what greater losses it could lead to.

There's a long silence, all of them waiting for something, though it's not clear what that is. When her mother speaks, her voice startles Rakhi. "It *is* a situation, isn't it," she says. (Her mother prefers not to use the word *problem*.)

"It sure is," Belle says. "And we're counting on you to give us the right advice."

Rakhi glares at her and grabs the receiver back.

"You must act fast," her mother says, "before they expect you to. They're going to try to steal your customers, lure them with deals you can't beat. You can succeed only if you do something different. Create a special attraction, something that means more to people than money."

Belle, who has her ear glued to the outside of the receiver, bobs her head up and down in emphatic agreement.

"What do you mean? What kind of attraction?" Rakhi asks, but her mother is silent.

"Maybe she'll come in and interpret dreams for us!" Belle whispers. "We could take out an ad in the *Berkeley Voice*—"

Rakhi puts her hand over the mouthpiece and gives Belle her stop-it-right-now look.

Belle sighs. "I guess it wouldn't be proper to ask her to prostitute her genius for commercial purposes. Even if it does mean saving the life of her daughter and, more importantly, her daughter's best friend. I bet she's never taken a penny for all the wonderful things she does for people—"

Belle's probably right. Rakhi doesn't think her mother charges a fee for what she does. But she suspects that grateful clients give her thank-you gifts, including money. How else had she managed to keep the household running smoothly all those times when Rakhi's father was laid off? Rakhi has seen the jewelry—her mother has a whole drawer full of it, though she never wears any. They're mostly trinkets, but it wouldn't surprise Rakhi if there were expensive items there as well. For a whole year when she was in high school, a box of fresh produce was left outside their door every Sunday. Rakhi never saw who delivered it. Once her mother received a state-of-the-art food processor in the mail; once she was sent a $500 Neiman Marcus gift card (she gave it to Rakhi); and once when Rakhi was little, she opened the front door to find a cage containing a cougar cub, which, to her lasting regret, her mother donated to the Oakland Zoo.

Belle's right, too, in that she'd be a great Special Attraction.

But here's Rakhi's shameful secret: she doesn't want her mother in the store. The Chai House is her sanctuary, the one place she has made her own. Much as she loves her mother, she doesn't want her taking it over—the way she (effortlessly, without a single word, without even wanting it) dominates other areas of Rakhi's life.

Her mother gives a small laugh, as though she knows what Rakhi is thinking. "Tell Belle I can't do that, and even if I could, having me there wouldn't solve things. You need to find something authentic to offer your customers, something that satisfies a need in them that's deep and real. I know you'll figure it out. I have full confidence in the two of you."

Rakhi looks morosely out the window, wondering what she

means by *authentic*. The Java employees are out on the street, watching the workmen put up the sign. They cheer and clap when it's in place. She can hear them all the way in here. The blond manager seems to be dauntingly good at motivating her staff.

"You're just giving us a motherly pep talk," she grumbles.

"Well, what do you expect? I am your mother, after all."

"But Mrs. Gupta," Belle says, wresting the phone from Rakhi again, "can't you give us a little hint as to *what* we should do? Maybe it'll come to you as you sleep—"

"It may—or it may not," Rakhi's mother says. "I don't control my dreams, Balwant."

Belle begins to apologize, but she goes on. "If I did, they wouldn't be of use to anyone." In a lighter tone she adds, "If I can help you in any way, I'll do it—you know that! Meanwhile, I wouldn't be surprised if one of you hears some good news soon."

"Wait a minute." Rakhi leans over Belle and shouts into the mouthpiece. "Did you get that from a dream, or is it just a motherly feeling?"

"It's one of the primary laws of the universe," her mother states. "*There is no darkness but light follows.* Haven't you heard of it?"

She hangs up, leaving Rakhi to wonder if this is ancient Indian wisdom or New Age Californian.

8

FROM THE
DREAM JOURNALS

Once my daughter came to me weeping, and I couldn't help her.

You don't love me, she accused me later. You do it for everyone else, but you won't do it for me.

Impossible to prove your love to someone who doubts it.

The warnings of the elders came back to me. *Those you love the most, you'll help the least. You'll be defeated by the oneness of your blood.* I'd thought, What do these dried-up old women know of love? If love is strong and pure, it can overcome all barriers. That's the kind of love I'll possess.

Rakhi was thirteen that year, a young and worshipful thirteen. She was so unlike other girls her age. Her Indian classmates wore tank tops and tight-fitting jeans. They smoked and wanted to go to Madonna concerts. They hated anything to do with their culture—or their parents. My daughter came back from the library with a stack of books on India. She observed me from behind doors. She started Freud's *Interpretation of Dreams* but lost interest because it focused too much on Western methodology. I tried to turn her attention from the long ago and far away, to get her to focus on her American life, but she continued to believe that what I did was amazing and wonderful.

In these pages I can admit what I'd never tell her. It was a disappointment to me, too, that she couldn't decipher dreams. To have had her company on this path would have eased my loneliness. I'd wished for it when I was pregnant with her. But that gift wasn't mine to give.

The night I'm writing of, she came crying to where I slept on the floor of the sowing room, where the seeds of dreams fall into me. It was two hours past midnight. She was sobbing so hard that I could barely understand what she was saying. I held her and stroked her hair, and slowly I gathered that she'd had a dream. She didn't tell me any more, and I didn't ask. I took her back to her bed, and when she fell asleep, I returned to my sleeping mat. But an hour later, she was back, crying again. She'd had the same dream, only more of it.

In the first dream, she told me, she was walking through a crowded department store. She was alone, but she thought nothing of it—there were so many people around her. She was looking for a mirror. She asked a saleswoman where she could find one. The woman pointed her in a direction. She moved past lingerie, lots of lingerie, hanging from racks placed so close she had to push through them to move ahead. She was sweating. She couldn't see any other shoppers. Then she heard the footsteps. They were so heavy they made the floor creak. She was sure they weren't a woman's. What would a man be doing in the lingerie section? She spun around, but there was nothing. Or almost nothing. She thought she caught a blur, like a hand pulled back fast. She knew that if she turned away, it would be back. She was afraid of what it would do. That's when she woke up the first time.

The second time she fell asleep, she was already in the lingerie section, pushing through nightgowns and camisoles. They crowded around, their slippery silkiness pressing against her face. She couldn't breathe. She tried to go back to the entrance of the store. But her body moved onward, as though it had a will of its own. She knew what was coming—the footsteps, lurching around the corner of her vision. She saw the hand more clearly this time. No, it wasn't a monster hand, just an ordinary male one. No, it didn't hold a weapon. She looked past the hand to the arm, the torso encased in a white shirt. She couldn't see the man's face—it was hidden behind a rack of slips. She didn't know why his hand, reaching out to her through gauze and silk with its neat, blunt nails, should frighten her so much. The hand came closer; she was frozen with fear; the index finger touched her wrist. Then she woke up.

Now she clung to me, refusing to go back to her bed, refusing to sleep again. "He'll be waiting there," she kept saying. "He'll do something terrible, I know he will. And the worst thing is, a part of me wants him to do it." Then she asked, "Why do I keep dreaming this dream? What does it mean?"

There was a threat in the dream. It radiated heat, like a burner someone had forgotten to turn off. But I couldn't gauge its nature, or where it might come from.

She said, "Help me, Mom."

I tried to remember what I'd been taught about recurring

nightmares. What to do about them. But none of the answers seemed to fit. The only way to help her was to see the dream for myself.

I lay down beside Rakhi and put my head on her pillow, though I'd promised myself I'd never try that again. I kept thinking of what had almost happened the last time, when I'd been trying to teach her to read dreams. How I'd almost lost her. Yet how could I abandon my daughter to her terror?

I closed my eyes and willed my breath to slow, my conscious mind to fold itself inward. I could feel heat pulsing from my daughter's head, her frantic thoughts whirling like broken glass. I loosened my hold on my body and dropped into that whirlpool. I'd done something similar once or twice, with clients I couldn't help in any other way. I expected the same pull into the vortex, the images slowing down and becoming clearer, myself passing through the whirlpool into my daughter's dreaming eye.

But it wasn't so. I passed through the whirlpool, yes—but when I emerged on the other side, I was swathed in a veil. I could see nothing. I could only hear. I heard Rakhi push through the racks of clothes, the satiny swish of them closing behind her. The man's footsteps were cautious at first, then fast and sure. He knew she couldn't get away. He was saying something, but the words came to me only as gutturals. I knew she heard them differently. To her they were full of promise. I heard her turn toward him. I tried to tell her no, but the veil had blocked my mouth. A sharp, delicious intake of breath, a sound a girl might make before she's kissed for the first time. But I couldn't be sure if that was what I heard. Through the veil, all was uncertain. I couldn't decipher what the man symbolized. When in her life he would appear, or where.

When Rakhi awoke weeping, I was weeping, too. It was a hard fact to come to terms with—that I, who interpreted dreams for a worldful of strangers, would never be able to explain to my daughter what her dreams meant. I'd never be able to warn her away from the disasters of her life.

In the morning, I did the only thing left to me. I bought the dream from Rakhi. I bought it for a dollar bill, since I didn't have any cowrie shells. I'd read of the ritual in the *Brihat Swapna Sarita*, but I'd left before I had a chance to see it done. Learning from reading isn't the same as having an elder teach it to you. So that, too, I botched.

I would realize this only later. But already I sensed that my efforts were as useful as a thumb pressed over a torn artery.

I'd been defeated by the oneness of blood.

9

Rakhi

Belle and I have been driven to break one of our cardinal rules: never snack during working hours. We munch gloomily on Delhi Dietbusters and watch the GRAND OPENING!! banner across the street. It flutters merrily even though there isn't a breath of breeze anywhere. I am about to remark on this fact when the phone rings.

Belle reaches for the phone with a listless hand. But then she perks up. "It's Kathryn," she announces, "from the Atelier!"

I rush to the phone, my heart thudding.

"The board has reviewed your portfolio and has agreed to hold a show of your paintings," Kathryn tells me in her white-wine-and-black-evening-dress voice. "There was a cancellation, and a space has opened up in two weeks' time. Do you think you can have your paintings ready in a couple of weeks?"

Can I! I've been waiting for over six months to hear from the Atelier, considered the most prestigious gallery on this side of the bay. I curb my inclination to let out a wild whoop and inform Kathryn that I'll be able to bring the bulk of the paintings into the gallery by next weekend. We agree that the opening reception will be held on a Friday evening two weeks from now.

As soon as I hang up Belle flings herself at me and hugs me tight. "Congratulations! Your first show—and at the Atelier, too! Rikki, I'm so proud of you!" She kisses me loudly on both cheeks, then pulls back, eyes wide. "Why, it's just like your mother predicted! It hasn't even been an hour since she said one of us would receive good news!"

"It could be chance," I say drily.

Belle shakes her head. "You can say what you like, but you're one lucky girl to have a mother like that." Another thought strikes her, widening her eyes further. "Maybe she made it happen! You think she could have—"

I roll my eyes. "Is it so impossible to believe the board reviewed my work and decided I'm a good painter?" But inside, I have my own doubts.

I call my mother to tell her the news, and listen carefully as she says how delighted she is. She sounds surprised and excited and a little teary, just like any normal mother would—or is she a better actress than I suspect? I ask her to keep the evening of the reception free. Not that I expect my parents to be busy with another event. I can't remember when they last had a night out, or invited friends over. Do they even *have* friends? But this is too significant for me to take any chances.

"Of course, dear," my mother says. "I wouldn't miss it for life or death." There's the slightest hesitation. Then she adds, "Nor would your father."

But I've picked up the tension in her voice. "What is it, Mom?"

"I wish it weren't a Friday, that's all."

I know what she means. My father's binges always begin on Friday evenings, and he hasn't had one in a while.

"He's been laid off again," she adds. "The company's down-sizing. He's been going to the agency every day, but no one seems to be hiring—especially older people. He's taking it hard."

"I'm sorry to hear that," I say, but I don't give it too much thought. My father—a hazy presence in my life at the best of times—has been laid off before this, and he's always managed to find something. Right now, selfishly—I admit it—I'm more concerned with my own problems. "You'll just *have* to keep him from drinking," I tell her. Anxiety makes me sharp. "Just for this one night. It's really important. Can't you do this much for me?"

"I'll do my best," she says, but her voice wavers. I know we're both thinking the same thing: so far, in almost three decades of marriage, she hasn't been successful yet.

The week passes in a blur. I agonize over which paintings to choose for the show. Half a dozen times I begin dialing my mother's number, then hang up. She'd be glad to give her opinion, and so would Belle, but they wouldn't know what's right. Only I can know that. And so I pick and reject, pick and reject, lining up paintings along the wall and staring at them until they all look flawed and hideous. In between, I worry about Jona.

I haven't heard from her—or Sonny—since he left me that message a week ago saying he was taking off for the wilds of Mendocino. I imagine them lost in the forest, starving. I picture boats capsizing. Grizzlies. Hypothermia. Cobras. (Half of my mind insists that cobras do not live in Northern California, but the other half will have none of it.) Finally, I break down and call

Sonny's number. I'm ready with a scathing message, but his machine informs me that his phone mailbox is full. I'm left to seethe and wonder who's been calling him so many times.

Things are not going well at the Chai House. There's been a sharp drop in customers, especially after the new café put up a sign advertising student discounts. Sometimes an entire hour goes by with no one coming in—something that has never happened before this. I spend a lot of my store time at the plate-glass window, watching the hordes jostling under the awning of Java. Masochism pure and simple, but I can't seem to stop myself. Two of the philodendrons in our window box died recently, no doubt as a result of the jealous poison-air I was breathing on them. The only person who is benefiting from all this is Marco. We have so many Danishes left at the end of the day that he's able to pick up enough for all his homeless friends.

Once I asked if he'd been inside the new place.

He tugged at his scruffy beard. "Um—yeah, I went in last week—just to check out the place, you know."

"Was it pretty?" I asked against my will.

"Pretty?" He wrinkled his forehead. "Tell the truth, I can't exactly remember. There was lots of shiny stuff. But I sure remember the manager. I wanted some coffee—I had money, even—but that manager, she was one cold bitch. She has these pale blue eyes, almost white, that never blink. Like a robot's. Her mouth's like a robot's too, looks like it's made of metal. She told me, I don't want you coming in here again. Then she said, like she was doing me a favor, I don't mind if you go to the Dumpster in the back and pick stuff out of there, as long as it's after hours.

Serves me right, I guess, for going there instead of coming to nice young ladies like you two. But don't you fret about them. They ain't gonna last long on this street with that kinda attitude."

I smiled and put an extra muffin in his sack. "That would be good, wouldn't it," I said. But I didn't really believe it would happen. Nor did I quite believe Marco's description of the manager-as-robot-woman. But I appreciated the fact that he had lied in an attempt to make me feel better.

The only thing that takes me out of my miserable self is the painting I'm doing of the eucalyptus grove. It's still not completed, but I'm determined to have it ready for the show. I stay up late, working on it until my eyes turn bleary and the colors get muddied from reworking the strokes. I've sketched in the man I saw at the grove practicing Tai Chi. I'm pleased with my decision, though so far he's only a blur of white against the greens. When I glance at the painting edgewise, craftily, he seems to be moving. But something's still out of balance—only I can't figure out what. The not-knowing lodges inside me, irritating as a mango fiber caught between two teeth.

Sunday night, when I've given up hope, the bell rings. A long peal, then two short ones—Jona's signature. I rush to the door, ready to tell Sonny exactly what I think of his behavior. But Jona's the only one standing there, gap-toothed and grinning and grimy with dirt. Even as I stare, Sonny's Viper disappears around the corner with a roar loud enough to wake the entire neighborhood.

"How could he just leave you on the doorstep!" I fume. "What if I hadn't been home?"

"Sonny and me saw your shadow against the curtains," Jona says, her tangled hair spilling out around her face. "You were painting, we could tell." She wrinkles her nose and gives me a crooked smile that's so like Sonny's that for a moment it leaves me speechless. "Are you angry?"

I manage to shake my head as I reach for her. She suffers a hug, then squirms away. "What's there to eat? I'm starving."

I knew you wouldn't feed her right, I say triumphantly in my head to Sonny-the-irresponsible as I carry armloads of food to the dining table.

"Mmmm," she says, "peanut butter and jelly sandwiches, tortilla chips with hot salsa, oranges, cookie-dough ice cream! Mom, you're the best."

"Just this once," I say in my strict-mother voice, but I can't suppress my smile. *You're the best!* I like that! "Didn't your dad give you any dinner?"

"Actually, he did. We stopped at this really neat Italian restaurant just before we crossed the Golden Gate Bridge. Sonny said it was one of his favorite places to eat. They have foot-long French-bread pizzas with so much cheese that it just drips over the side. I ate four pieces. Really, Mom, it was the best!"

So much for my unique bestness. Trying not to feel let down, I ask, "What's this *Sonny* business? What happened to *Dad?*"

"Sonny says I'm all grown up now, and we're friends more

than father and daughter, so I can call him by his name," she says, maneuvering a dangerously wobbly spoonful of ice cream into her mouth.

I want to tell her to wash her hands, take off her muddy shoes, take smaller mouthfuls, and not listen to her father's subversive ideas. Using supreme self-control I manage to stay silent.

She goes through an entire box of Cheez-Its in record time, inhales two glasses of milk, and then turns to the easel. "Mom! You've started a new painting."

"What do you think?" My heart speeds up absurdly as she cocks her head and stares at it. Jona has a surprisingly acute eye for a six-year-old, and she's often given me good advice.

"I like it," she says, finally, and then, "It's different from all your other stuff."

"How?" I ask, intrigued. "Is it because it's set here in Berkeley?"

Jona shakes her head. "Nope, that's not it." She gives a huge yawn. "Tell you tomorrow. Hey, Mom, can I sleep with you tonight?"

"Not until you take a shower," I say, attempting sternness. "You've probably got ticks." But she's already curled up in my bed, her eyelashes dark against mud-streaked cheeks. And I didn't even get a chance to ask her about her trip.

The morning, as always, is a mad rush of brushing-teeth, getting-into-clean-clothes, finding-matching-socks, and eating-breakfast-without-spilling-it-on-above-mentioned-clean-clothes. Things are complicated further by the fact that I have to bathe Jona (grime comes off her in black streams) and wash her hair (I don't even consider detangling it). Finally we're in the car, speeding to Mariposa Montessori. Not that one can actually speed through the nine A.M. Berkeley streets, filled as they are with students who believe it's their God-given right to cross when and where they wish.

"So, what did you mean when you said my painting was different?" I ask Jona.

"What? Oh, I don't remember," she says, leaning out the window to watch a young man with impossibly spiky hair whizzing by on a skateboard.

So much for wisdom from the mouths of babes. I decide to follow another track. "What did you do all week?" I'm afraid she'll say she's forgotten this, too, but suddenly she's full of animation.

"We drove up to Uncle Paul's, then we went boating on the ocean, then we ate pizza, then we slept in the cabin in our sleeping bags, then we saw whales with their babies, then the whales went away and we went hiking in the forest, then we cooked hot dogs on a fire, then we slept in two tents for two nights, then we didn't see bears though we looked, then we came back to Uncle Paul's cabin where the toilet wouldn't flush, then we went to a music place where people played trumpets, then we ate more pizza—"

It sounds pretty much like I'd expected. "Two tents?" I ask as we pull into the Mariposa's parking lot, which is milling with harried parents as usual. "Did Paul go hiking with you?" In my mind I cast about for discreet ways to ask Jona if Paul and Sonny had been smoking marijuana. They'd better not have, if they value their lives.

"Yup," Jona says as she unbuckles herself and opens the back door of the car. "Uncle Paul came with us and told stories at night. I didn't understand them, but Sonny and Eliana thought they were funny—"

"Eliana?" Paul must have a new girlfriend.

"She's my friend, except she's a grown-up lady. She's very pretty, with long brown hair and blue eyes like the flowers on that plant you used to keep on the windowsill until it died. She stayed in the tent with us and sang songs for me to sleep—"

I take a deep breath and try to keep my voice calm. "She stayed in the same tent as Sonny and you?"

"Uh-huh. She wore a dress with flowers and sang in a different language. Oh, there's Keysha waving at me. I gotta go. Bye, Mom!"

"Wait! Did this Eliana drive up from the Bay Area with you?"

But my daughter is gone in a flurry of pigtails and backpack, leaving me to realize that one can be shocked and seething at the same time.

I drive around for an entire hour in an attempt to cool down before I call Sonny. But whatever control I've gained evaporates as soon as I hear him growling a sleepy hello in what certain people (Eliana, perhaps?) would describe as his sexy bedroom voice.

"How could you?" I scream into the mouthpiece. "How could you be so crass and irresponsible as to expose my daughter to your perversions?"

There's a moment's silence, then a deep-throated laugh. At

one time (I'm ashamed to remember) that laugh used to make me go weak at the knees. Now it only infuriates me. I take a lungful of air and hold it in, hoping to calm myself. Sonny likes nothing better than making me lose my temper.

"I should have known it was you, Riks!" he says. "You missed me, didn't you? No one to call up and yell at for a whole week, no one to blame for all your—"

"Yelling at you is not my activity of choice—"

"Could have fooled me—"

"—but in this case, even you have to admit, I have good cause."

"Because we didn't call you from Mendocino? Sorry—Paul's phone was down."

"There were other phones in town, were there not?" Then I realize what Sonny-the-master-tactician is doing. "Don't try to sidetrack me," I say acidly. "Irresponsible as that was, that's not what I called about. God knows I'm used to your irresponsibilities—"

"Ah yes, you called about my—how did you put it—crass perversions! Well, I'd like you to know that Paul and I only smoked after Jona fell asleep." Sonny's voice drips virtue. "And we went outside to do it—even when it was raining."

"And Eliana? Did Eliana go outside to smoke with you, too?"

"Who?"

"Sonny, please don't insult my intelligence by pretending you don't know what I'm talking about."

"I'd never dare to insult you, Riks! You'd probably sic Belle on me! Besides, wasn't it I who once told you that you were too intelligent for your own good?"

"Quit joking. Who's Eliana?"

"I don't know anyone by that name. Honest!"

He sounds so sincere, so not guilty, that I'm taken aback—but only for a moment. Sonny-the-sincere-sounding—I've heard *him* before.

"Let me give your memory a little nudge. She's the woman you took up to Mendocino with you. She stayed in your tent. Your tent—with *my* daughter! Eliana—long brown hair, flowery dress, foreign accent. Is it coming back to you now?"

A silence. Then: "And just how did you get to know about uh—Eliana?"

"Jona told me!" I say in triumph.

There's a moment of silence. "Jo told you that?" Sonny asks. From his tone I can tell he's shaking his head in that disbelieving way he has, as though the world has just pulled the rug from under his feet again. "Amazing!"

"Why should it amaze you that she confided in her own mother? Unless you asked her to keep it a secret? You did, didn't you? Sonny, how could you do such a low-down—"

But he's laughing, great roars of laughter, so unfeigned that I get confused.

He pauses long enough to say, "She'll go far, our daughter! What was that name again? Eliana—with flowers in her hair? Wow! What an imagination that kid has!"

He's still laughing when I hang up.

It's evening, the blue hour of gathering shadows. It used to be our busiest time, when even with Marcia and Ping helping us, we could hardly keep up with orders. Today the only person in the place—other than Belle and myself—is my daughter, sprawled across a table at the other end of the store, drawing.

I practiced various sentences in my head as I picked Jona up from school. *Did you just imagine that woman? Your dad said there wasn't anyone there except the three of you. You've got to learn to separate make-believe from real life!* But they all sounded accusing or prissy, so finally I didn't say anything.

"Don't worry so much," Belle says when I describe the morning to her. "We all used to imagine things when we were kids. It's a part of growing up."

"The problem is, I'm not sure she imagined it. Sonny's lied to me before—"

"Come on, Rikki! Sonny would never take a woman along when Jona was around."

"I can't believe you're defending Sonny! Didn't you once name him Public Enemy Number One?"

Belle grins. "Actually, it was Private Enemy Number One—as in your very own private enemy." She shakes her head. "I can't believe I'm defending him either. But you've got to give him credit—he's a good dad."

"I'm not sure about that either. Believe me, I wish I could be. It would give me one less thing to worry about."

Not true, jeers my whisper voice. *You know that what you really want is for Sonny to prove himself completely and criminally irresponsible so you can gain full custody of Jona and never let her see him again.*

I can't deny it.

"You could always call Paul and ask him."

"Paul and I are not on speaking terms. Also, his phone is out of order. And even if I broke down and called him, you think he'd tell me the truth? Especially if it incriminates his buddy?"

"Well, then, I suggest you save your worries for what you know for sure," Belle says. "Namely, this shop is done for. Another couple of weeks of business like this, and we'll have to close down. We've tried everything—slashing prices, putting up promotional posters outside, having Marco distribute coupons at the street corner. And that horrendously expensive ad we put in the *Berkeley Voice*. No results. Even our Book Club members didn't come in this week. And look at *them!*"

We gaze dispiritedly across the street. From what little we can see, past their huge GRAND OPENING banner, Java is chock-full of customers, and every few minutes their door swings open to admit more people.

"We've got to figure out their secret—there's got to be something!" Belle says, pacing restlessly, running her fingers through her disheveled hair. She looks like she's lost weight. She opens up in the mornings (we've let Marcia and Ping go) but usually stays on with me until closing time in spite of my protests.

"It's like they have a giant invisible people magnet!" she bursts out. "I've been watching all afternoon. Even folks who are striding along as though they're in a hurry to get someplace come to a stop once they see that sign—and then they go in there, like they're sleepwalking."

"You'd better go home and catch some sleep yourself," I say. "You're beginning to sound like a voice-over from *Invasion of the Body Snatchers*." But I can't help peering out suspiciously. The way my world is tilting, people magnets don't sound so impossible. All I see, however, is a gaggle of executive types, power-tied and leather-briefcased, coming out of the café, laughing uproariously as though they've been drinking something far more potent than coffee. Their laughter brings back the memory of my morning's call to Sonny.

"Auntie Belle," Jona calls. "See, I've finished my picture of our camping trip."

She holds up a brightly crayoned drawing. Purple sky, orange trees, yellow grass, two polka-dotted tents. And four people.

"Who are they, sweets?" Belle asks.

"That's Paul, that's Sonny, that's me holding Sonny's hand, and that's Eliana, holding Sonny's other hand."

I crane my neck over Belle's head to see better. I recognize Sonny's picture right away. Jona has drawn him as she always does, with his blue-black hair shiny as a bird's wing, his sharp, distinctive nose—and sun rays emanating from his head like a halo. Sonny-the-angel. Another item to add to the long list of unfair ironies that made up my life. Next to him is a tall woman in a blue dress with brown hair all the way to her waist. She has what looks like a crown of feathers on her head.

"Tell me about Eliana," Belle says, sitting down next to Jona. "I don't think I've met her before."

"Of course you haven't," my daughter replies. "I just met her during this trip myself."

"Where does she come from?"

"Czechoslovakia," Jona says without missing a beat. Over her head Belle and I exchange a look.

"Is she a friend of your dad's—or Paul's?" Belle asks.

"She's everyone's friend. But most of all, she's my special friend."

"Um—what do you mean, special? Is that like an imaginary friend?"

"Really, Auntie Belle!" Jona says with dignity as she rolls up her drawing. "Only babies have imaginary friends. She's special because she sings me songs, and tells me stories of how she grew up."

"In Czechoslovakia?" I ask.

Jona nods. "She told me how there were witches—good ones—in the village where she used to live." Then she loses interest in our conversation and goes over to check out the puppets.

In the car, as we drive home, I send covert glances Jona's way. She is examining her drawing, her dark head bent over the stick figures. It strikes me suddenly that I don't know her as fully as I thought I did. She who had come out of my body, tiny and crumpled and containable—even she now has parts to her life that I can't enter. It doesn't matter whether they're real or imagined. I feel excluded all the same. Like the rest of my family—my mother, my father, Sonny—she too has become an enigma.

Later that night, lying sleepless in bed, thinking of all the things that were going wrong in my life, I'd realize I'd included Sonny in my family list. And with chagrin I'd admit that he was still family, much as I wanted to disown him. Because only family filled you with such exasperation. Only family could irritate you like a hangnail that you couldn't chew off, no matter how much you tried.

When we turn into the apartment's parking lot, Jona is singing something under her breath. They sound like nonsense words. But who knows, maybe they're Czechoslovakian.

10

She has been trying for days to complete the painting, but she hasn't had any success. She's pleased with the foliage, the sky, the quality of light. It's the man that's giving her trouble. His body seems stiff and posed; there's something fake about the angle of his neck. And his face—she's been unable to draw it at all. Sometimes, frustrated, she's tempted to cover him over with a rhododendron bush. But that would mean a major defeat, and she isn't ready for that, not yet, even though the show opens in three days.

Things are getting worse at the Chai House. Stragglers wander in every once in a while. But it seems to her that they look around in surprise, as though taken aback at finding themselves in this place. As though they had meant to go somewhere else. They buy take-out coffee and leave as soon as they can. Even Belle's offer of free Dietbusters (they've stopped stocking other snacks) isn't enough to hold them—or to entice them back.

Where are their regular customers, Rakhi wonders. What has happened to Mrs. Locklin? To old Professor Rogers? To the Laurel Street Book Club members, who used to come in every Wednesday and fill the corner nook with the intense electricity of their arguments? She thinks of them all with bafflement and concern—and a sense of betrayal.

Last evening she walked into the store to find Belle poring over the accounts. Belle beckoned her over to her laptop computer and jabbed at the screen, at the column with the minus numbers. They'd been running at a loss for weeks. Now there wasn't enough left to pay for next week's supplies.

"Rent's due in two weeks," Belle said. The skin around her eyes looked raw, as though she'd been rubbing at it. In the weak well of light from the laptop screen, her lips were blue. "Where are we going to get the money?"

They weren't savers; their own bank accounts were too slender to last them more than a month or so. They couldn't go to the bank. They already had an outstanding loan. Their parents, never wealthy, had helped them as much as they could already.

"I guess we couldn't ask Sonny, huh?" Belle said. "He *is* the richest person we know. Doesn't that nightclub pay him an obscene amount of money—?"

"Belle!"

"Okay, okay, forget I mentioned it."

"Give me a little time," Rakhi said. "I'll come up with something." But all she had managed to do as she lay in bed that night, staring at the crisscrossed pattern of light and shadow thrown on her ceiling by the streetlamp, was to dislodge the rock she'd positioned so carefully over the snake hole in her memory.

She is back in college, in the classroom with large, green-shuttered windows where she first met Sonny. It's a literature class on modern Indo-Anglian writers, and by this she knows she's in a dream, for the university had never offered such a class when she was there, and she's not even sure what the term means.

(But perhaps this is something else, a not-dream that we choose to misname because we all love dreams. Dreams that are like kites cut free from cause, from the ground-glass-dipped string of guilt.

Also: she hasn't had a single dream since her early teenage years, since those recurring nightmares that her mother finally bought from her with a dollar and a string of Bengali words she didn't explain to Rakhi.)

She's sitting in the back of the classroom, near the window, her usual spot. She looks out on the confetti of humanity on Sproul Plaza—old hippies with guitars and bandanna-necked dogs; earnest students in Birkenstocks handing out Earth Day flyers; people queued up at the burrito stall; evangelists, fervently sweaty in black, describing with relish the torments of hell that await un-believers, among whom, surely, Rakhi is included. Spring is in the air, a faint throbbing, like the drums people sometimes play in front of Zellerbach Auditorium. She thinks she smells hot-and-sour soup from the Chinese cart on Bancroft Way and decides she'll go there after class.

She doesn't see him come into the room, but she feels it—a tingling at the base of her spine. Though why should this be? It's the middle of the quarter already; he must have entered the class many times before this. Still, with her shoulder blades she senses him checking out his seating options. There's a chair next to a blonde in the second row, and there's one next to her. He makes his choice, and her life changes.

Even in her not-dream she is amazed at how exactly she remembers certain things about him. He was wearing a faded black
T-shirt with Carlos Santana's face on it. His hair fell over his forehead as he bent to write in his notebook. Good Indian hair, thick
and glossy and true black. It was clear he had not combed it that
morning. A little shock ran through her as she realized this. In all
her sheltered life (the adjective rises in her, unexpected—already
he's started unpacking her so she can see herself better) she hadn't
known anyone who came to class so unashamedly uncombed. He
wrote without stopping through class, but when she sneaked a look
over his knuckles—solid and a little battered, like a carpenter's—
she saw that he'd filled the page with squiggles from a green fountain pen. Later he would tell her they were notations for a bhangra
remix he'd been hearing in his head. He was taking the lit class to
fulfill a requirement, but he was really a musician. He couldn't afford to be interested in anything else.

"Not even me?" she'd say, greatly daring, her heart beating
fast. She wasn't used to flirting—she'd always been a serious girl.
And he would dip his face toward hers—. But all this would be
much later. Weeks? Months? Time blurs into Before and After
when she thinks of Sonny.

Sonny is the one who made her take her art seriously. Until
then, she'd puttered around. But seeing his passion made her want
to have something like that of her own. And he'd encouraged her.
He'd been the first person she believed when he said she had something special.

But she's jumping ahead. On that first day, he didn't even
notice her, caught up in the web of sound in his head. Or maybe
he did. Because he sat in the same place next time, and the next,

and the next, and then he asked her what she was doing for lunch.

Dreaming, she wonders what it was that drew them to each other. Was it their similarity? They were both of Indian origin, though he never spoke of his past—parents, hometown, high school, habits. (In this he was like her mother. Was this core of secrecy the reason they'd taken to each other right away when Rakhi introduced them?) She didn't even know if he'd been born in America, like herself, though she could tell he'd lived in it long enough to be uncomfortable anywhere else. (She wanted to ask him if he longed for India like she did—India, which she'd never seen but had every intention of visiting next year. She didn't know then that next year would turn into the next, that she'd never go.) They both loved spicy food, preferably Asian. They'd drive his car (a battered Mustang at the time) up to Tilden Park and eat takeout with their fingers from bright cartons. They'd watch the sun set over Angel Island and feed each other pad thai noodles or Szechwan beef with extra red chilies. The stars would come up one by one; he would worry an old tune out of a guitar, a song she'd heard on her father's record player. But in his hands it became something quite different. Listening, it was hard for her to breathe. She loved watching his face, intent, oblivious, as though she weren't there. No, as though *he* weren't there. It was the way she hoped her own face might be when she was painting.

Or was it their differences, the opposed poles of their longings that fascinated them? He was a night spirit, with impulsive, uneven, boyish generosities. He loved the smoky camaraderie of clubs, though he didn't smoke (not cigarettes, anyway). He'd have bought the whole world drinks if she didn't stop him. He loved to be in crowds, jostled by strangers. Loved the desperate trust of raves. He understood how people needed to have a good time, and what they were prepared to do to get it. Understood the complexity of the enterprise. He scorned Valentine's Day, then brought her flowers for no reason. Nothing trite like roses. Instead: bearded iris, anthuriums, snowdrops, even orchids, though he wasn't rich, not by any means. He loved late-night jam sessions with the band he played in sometimes. He kept loaning his musician friends money. (They never returned it; he never expected them to.) Playing made him restless. I'm high from the music, he'd say. (Later, she'd wonder if that was all he was high from, and later still, she'd begin to get angry. But that was in the future, a lifetime away.) They went to a bar or an all-night café to talk, and even if she was bleary-eyed next day in class, or had a hangover and missed class altogether, even if sometimes her hand shook from all that unaccustomed caffeine when she painted, it was okay, it was fun, artists grew as they had new experiences, he was her new experience, and she was growing.

After she'd passed from that life into a different time, something spackled and gray, like the inside of tunnels, she'd realize you couldn't build a relationship on a new experience. Because one day it wasn't new anymore, and what were you left with?

In the classroom, months have passed, maybe years. Sonny leans toward her—they are studying Borges, or is it Bauhaus architecture? He wears a Pan-like beard now, and an earring. You loved me because of the dimple just below my lower lip, he says, speaking loud enough to make the professor raise her eyebrows. You loved me because I was the first one. You loved me because I was as risky as jumping off a speeding train. He takes off his earring and reaches for her hand—he's going to slide it onto her finger, and it will become her engagement ring, her favorite piece of jewelry. (When he starts making big money he'll buy her a diamond ring, but she'll put it in the bank and continue wearing the thin hoop on her finger.) Things will speed up after this day, will blur like a film that's being projected too rapidly. She'll bring him to meet her parents—her mother, really, who was the one that counted—but no, that had happened already, hadn't she already gathered him to her as though he were her long-lost firstborn? They'll be married in a month, in a year they'll move into the beautiful pink Victorian house in Oakland, bought for (literally) a song, under circumstances that she'll begin to question—but not until it's too late. Jona will be born. The American public will learn what a bhangra remix is, and it will electrify their souls. Sonny will make more money, and more. More than she can imagine at this moment. His name will snake its way up the charts. His fans will adore him, men and women both. Oh, how they'll adore him! And then—

But the movie reel has stuttered backward somehow. She's in the classroom again, Sonny holds out the ring. She's going to say yes, but first she wants to ask him why he loves her. She who has no dimple under her lip, she who isn't his first, she who's as risky as instant oatmeal. But he's frowning, impatient. Everyone in the room is frowning at her, even the professor, they're all waiting for her to put on the ring that will brand her as his. Never mind, she thinks, extending her left hand. There'll be time enough later to ask him everything she wants to know.

Wait. Something is wrong with this dream-or-not film—a

defective frame, maybe. Because in this scene she has no hand—no arm, even. She looks around, baffled, then apologetic under the glare of the class's eyes.

It's okay, Sonny says. Give me the other hand.

But that too is gone. She's only a torso now, a chipped piece of statuary, cracks spreading at temples and collarbones, pitted scars along the column of the throat. Surely no man would want to marry her now, maimed as she is. Tears flow from her stone eyes as she thinks this.

But look: Sonny leans forward, a glittering that might be compassion in his eyes. He slips the ring between her parted stone lips, gives her torso a shake. She feels the ring begin to slide into her mouth, her throat, down, down, until it gets lodged in her chest somewhere. She'll never be able to return it to him now, she thinks, and feels a moment of despair. But perhaps she shouldn't be despairing. Doesn't this mean she'll be his forever? That he'll always take care of her?

He nods at her as though he's read her mind, and leans forward. He kisses her. It's a long kiss. The class applauds and whistles, the professor quotes Marx, *What man most loves about woman is her dependency on him,* and someone throws rice grains for luck.

In the morning, it is raining. She drops Jona off at school, then stares dispiritedly at her half-finished painting. No solutions have come to her in the restless night. She has roughly seven hundred dollars in the bank, and a few pieces of jewelry. (Not the diamond ring, which she returned to Sonny a long time ago even though he said, *Keep it.*) In any case, jewelry never fetches much—

she knows this already, from things she's had to pawn. Just like the equipment in the Chai House will not fetch much if they shut down.

She decides to walk to the eucalyptus grove. It's unlikely that the man in white will be practicing in all this rain, but the walk might clear her head. And who knows—maybe he will be there. Maybe she'll walk up to him and ask if he'd like to invest in a café. The ridiculousness of her daydreaming makes her laugh out loud. She's shrugging on her blue poncho when the phone rings.

It's her mother. "I haven't seen you in a long while," she says. "How about I take the BART up so we can spend a little time together."

Rakhi feels a warning buzz along her daughter antenna. Her mother rarely comes to Berkeley (she calls it Berserkley)—and never on the train, because the station is a long way from both the shop and Rakhi's apartment. Then she remembers her mother mentioning she doesn't like to drive as much, now that she's getting on in years. (Her mother's words had depressed Rakhi. Somehow she'd believed that a dream teller's powers would have protected her from the banal infirmity of aging.)

"Are you sure?" she asks. "It's so rainy today—and you've been fighting that cold. Why don't you wait till Friday—you'll be coming up then anyway for the opening of the show—"

"Don't worry!" her mother says. "I took a megadose of vitamin C. Besides, the rain's going to let up in just a while."

How can she know that? Outside Rakhi's window, the rain beats down in determined, opaque sheets. It doesn't look like it's intending to let up anytime soon. Do her mother's powers extend to the interpretation of meteorologic phenomena?

"I heard it on the Weather Channel, silly!" her mother says. "I'll be at the Chai House around noon. Don't rush if you get busy painting. I'll be happy to chat with Balwant until you come."

"Painting!" Rakhi gives a snort. "I wish!" Then, impulsively, she blurts out, "Mom, we're in big trouble."

"Yes, shona," her mother says. "That's why I'm coming."

As she walks to the eucalyptus grove through rain that has obligingly reduced itself to a drizzle, a new uneasiness pricks at Rakhi. Their situation must be far worse than she has gauged; otherwise her mother would never involve herself in it.

FROM THE
DREAM JOURNALS

Notes, Lesson 17: The Meanings of Things

If you dream of a closed door, you will ultimately be successful in gaining what you desire, but it will take much effort.

A dream of milk means you are about to fall ill.

A mirror stands for a false friend, a pair of scissors for a break in a marriage, a double-ended drum for recognition and renown, an iron wheel for ill fortune coming at you from every direction.

If you dream you are grinding salt, you will solve the problem that is overwhelming you—but you must be ruthless in your pursuit of the solution. In your dream if someone presents you with sugar, beware. Such a person is not to be trusted.

Remember that these are only the basic meanings, which will change their significance depending on each situation. In the telling of dreams, as I have said before, context is everything.

For instance: If a man dreams of a thorn, he will move ahead in his career. If in his dream he removes a thorn from someone else's foot, he will turn an enemy into a friend. If a virgin dreams of a thorn, she will marry into a distinguished family. If a woman who is not a virgin dreams of a thorn, she is (though she does not know it yet) pregnant.

Likewise, if a man dreams of a monkey, he will face challenges in business, which, if handled well, will lead to great benefits. If a woman dreams of the same monkey, she will give birth to a deformed child. For those who are single, a monkey dream means that they will marry a person with a terrible temper.

You asked about the cockatoo, which occurs often in dreams. It is a symbol of luck for men, foretelling the end of a long-drawn family quarrel. For women, however, it foretells the birth of a girl-child, which may become the cause of new contention in a household.

You must wait another month for a full lesson on the meanings of animals, for there is much subtlety in them. Think, for instance, of all that may happen if a man dreams he has killed a dragonfly, or a woman of a cat that has entered the kitchen.

A special lesson will be dedicated to animal guides who come to us at times of great danger or great joy. Enough now for you to know that the eagle, the deer and the snake are the most important of them all.

Listen then to the significance of trees: A tree with glossy green leaves means a patient's health will improve; a tree that is cut down in a dream means a big expense is about to fall upon you. A palm tree presages good luck, especially if you are climbing it. If you climb down with the fruit of the palm in your hand, you will be eminently successful. A banana tree will bring you an inheritance. A date tree warns you that you must undertake a pilgrimage.

A banyan will face you with a complicated moral decision. If you see an oleander in your dream, be prepared to mourn.

You asked, What if your fortunes move you to lands where men and women dream of other trees? Of apple and pine, ginkgo and persimmon and cherry blossom, which are not written of in our ancient books. Further, what if they dream of cell phones, toll-booths, electric saws? Of roadways in the sky, of machines that whisk people from one time to another?

Do not despair. Reach into the well of yourself and draw up the necessary meaning, for the meanings of all dreams are ulti-mately inside you, and not in the words I speak. That is why, as I warned you in the beginning, I cannot teach anyone who is not al-ready a teller of dreams. And that is why you will realize one day that everything I am teaching you is most crucial—and most use-less.

You asked, What does it mean when a man you have dreamed of appears in your life? And what should you do about him?

Such an event is extremely rare and will come to you only at moments that hold within them the possibility of great change. Therefore, listen well. First, follow this man, for he is either a spirit guide or a demon. In either case, trick him into speaking to you. That is how you establish power over him. Ask him the question foremost in your mind. His answer may transform your life. But most importantly, do not lose him. More instruction on this matter will be given to you next year, when you have learned enough to understand such subtleties.

Next week you will be tested on body parts, with special em-phasis on appearances of the ear, the foot, the shoulder, the brow and the breast. Be prepared.

12

Rakhi

Armed with my sketchbook, I make my way to the eucalyptus grove. A few fingers of rain brush my face when I look up from under the hood of my poncho, but mostly it's clearing up. A wash of light blue, so typical of our Bay Area, appears here and there. I love that blue. Not that I know any other sky. Though I've wanted to travel all my life, each time I planned a trip, some obstacle would trip me up. Mostly I would get sick. Once someone snatched my purse with my newly issued passport in it as I was getting on a bus. Another time, walking down a perfectly ordinary San Francisco street, I stepped into a pothole that I hadn't realized was there and broke my ankle. This happened the day before Sonny and I were supposed to leave for Brazil to attend a music festival. I was disappointed—I'd been daydreaming about Rio for months—but Sonny was downright angry. His theory was that I subconsciously made these "accidents" happen because deep down I was terrified of trying something new. We had a huge fight over that one, but maybe he was right. Because soon there would be other new things he'd want me to try that I would shrink from. I'd claim moral outrage, but maybe it was only fear that made me refuse.

He went by himself to Rio and had a great time, and the next time he had to go out of town to attend a DJ convention, he didn't ask me to accompany him. I didn't say anything. I was afraid of revealing how hurt I was. But the jagged edge of that silence caught at our marriage and caused it to unravel a bit further.

Once I asked my mother what she thought of my accidents.

She said, "And what is an accident?"

My mother likes making statements like that. She does it well. In spite of myself, I'm impressed by them.

Then she started telling me the story of Shangri-La.

"I know about it, Mom. We saw the movie together, remember?"

It didn't stop her from repeating the entire plot—the stranger who comes to the magic valley in the Himalayas, the beautiful young woman who, in leaving it, loses her youth and her life.

I waited for the moral, but she had started chopping mustard greens. "I'm going to make saag," she said. "If you want some, I'll put in an extra bunch."

"Mom! Why did you tell me that story?"

She gave me a surprised look, as though it were obvious. "Sometimes we, too, live in Shangri-Las," she said finally, "but like the woman in the movie, we don't realize how special they are, or what they're protecting us from. We're too busy hankering after what we don't know."

"I don't understand what you're getting at."

My mother washed the saag and dropped it into boiling water. She waited until it turned bright green. Then she said, "Maybe someone's telling you to stay right where you are."

"That's so completely superstitious," I said, feeling angry and scared and unaccountably claustrophobic. "Are you telling me

I shouldn't leave California? How can you believe something so il-logical?"

She smiled a little. She rarely took offense at what I said (a fact that frustrated me through my teenage years). "Firstly, I didn't mention California, did I? Secondly, logical things require no be-lief—they're there for everyone to see," she said. She put on the kettle and went to the pantry to get a packet of the Brooke Bond tea, wrapped in its thick silver foil, which she favored. It was one of the few habits she'd carried over from India. Just as I was re-signing myself to the fact that our conversation was over, I heard her add, "But this one I don't need to believe. This one I know."

I longed to ask her what she meant by that, but she must have regretted letting even that small crack appear in the wall behind which she hid herself. She kept me busy fielding questions about Jona's activities until it was time for me to leave.

In the eucalyptus grove, I take in a deep lungful of damp air. I pick up a sloughed-off piece of bark, crumble it and hold it up to my nose. I love the smell of rain, of straggly growing things. " 'O let them be left, wildness and wet,' " I quote to Belle on seri-ously rainy days.

"Yeah," she says. "And fungus and mildew and wood rot." Some people have no romance in them.

When I got to college, I borrowed, from the South Asian li-brary, a tape with songs about the Bengal monsoons: how the skies grow into the color of polished steel, how the clouds advance like black armies, or spill across the horizon like the unwound hair of beautiful maidens. I loved that tape, even though I could understand only about half the words. (Fortunately, it came with a pamphlet that provided translation.) I listened to the songs over and over, until Belle threatened to inflict violence on me. For months afterward, I found myself daydreaming about the storm-whipped palm trees, the red-breasted bulbuls taking shelter among the hanging roots of the banyan. The lightning was silver combs decorating the rain maidens' hair. The rain was warm, like human tears. One of the singers had compared her heart to a dancing peacock. Was there some truth to that, or was it merely a poetic trope? Confronted by a direct question, my mother grudgingly admitted that there were peacocks, and that from time to time they did dance. My father informed me, with gruesome glee, that Calcutta flooded with every big rain, and decades-old muck (and worse) came up out of the sewers, and people died of cholera. But I was not fooled. They were hiding things from me, beautiful, mysterious, important things, as they always had. But why? Belle had told me that her parents—and the parents of the other desis she knew—loved to go on and on about India, which in their opinion was as close to paradise as you could get.

What cruel karma had placed me in the care of the only two Indians who never mentioned their homeland if they could help it?

"When I was little and didn't know any better," Belle told me once, "my parents would give me an extra two dollars per week to go to the language class at the gurdwara."

I sighed. "I'd have been happy to give up my allowance for a chance to learn more Bengali—"

"You need help," Belle said. "You are one sick person."

A couple of times when I was in college, I tried to plan a trip to India. But it never worked out. The fellowship I applied for didn't come through. The group I was going to travel with decided to go to Peru instead. My parents didn't say anything, but it was clear they disapproved. Perhaps it was their silence that frightened me into giving up. Or perhaps the fear came from someplace inside me, as Sonny would later claim.

I no longer yearn for travel in the same way. Jona's birth anchored me; the breakup of my marriage made a hole in my hull, imperfectly patched. I am moored to the Chai House by hope and responsibility and, increasingly, anxiety. Still, I think that before I die I would like to go to India—if only to lay to rest the ghosts that dance in my head like will-o'-the-wisps over a rippling sea.

I tromp through mud into the interior of the grove. Away from the trails to where the trees grow thickest, where the air is so wet you can almost see it, where I can pretend I'm in a real forest. It's easier on a day like this when the grove is drenched and deserted. I sit on a fallen trunk and close my eyes in order to pretend better. This is my other fantasy, to live alone in the wilderness. (Belle says it's the same fantasy because India is a jungle.)

When I open my eyes, he's there.

No. Let me rephrase that. I don't want it to sound like cheap magic, or a foolish fancy. He was there already—I just hadn't noticed him. Over on one side, in a hollow, his back toward me, practicing. He's been at it for a while—even from a distance I can tell his clothes are wet. Here's a rain lover of an even greater magnitude than myself. Emboldened by our common passion, I'm tempted to approach him. But I don't. There's an aloneness to him, an absorption in the moment that I don't want to disturb. Instead,

I sketch his movements, which remind me of the flights of egrets. But I'm having problems. Sketch after sketch turns out wrong, wooden, spiritless. Why is this happening? It's not as though I haven't sketched people before—I did a whole series of Bharatnatyam dancers once, in charcoal, and they were good! Frustrated, I tear the sketches into pieces and look up, but he's— and this time it's really that way, sudden, soundless—gone.

He's left something behind in the grove, though—an energy of some kind. I see an orchestra of movements in the emptiness, the shape of his body carved into the space between the tree trunks. Presence and absence, they form a flickering pattern. I stare at them a long time. It begins to rain again. The cold numbs my fingers, which lie still in my lap, drawing nothing. But the seed of an idea is beginning to form. A perhaps.

We're sitting at a bright orange table inside Java, Belle, my mother and myself, waiting for our order to be served. I glance around furtively, feeling like an undercover agent. "We have to venture into the enemy's terrain," my mother had said, "if we are to discover their secret." So far the secret, if there's one, seems to be in their newness. Everything in the café seems as though it were manufactured just a few hours ago. A synthetic brilliance shimmers over it all, unreal like a mirage: the yellow and orange countertops, the sharp-cornered steel napkin holders on each table, the espresso machines hissing like monsters from some futuristic world. The light from the overhead fixtures (which are shaped like flying saucers) has a hard, alien cast to it. I imagine it burning geometric patches into my skin.

Belle wrinkles her nose in distaste as she leans close. "I can't understand how people can actually prefer this place to the Chai House," she whispers.

Her words startle me. For a moment, I'm disoriented, as though awakened from a trance.

"The Chai House?" I repeat, stupidly. I know what she's talking about, of course. Our store, which is going out of business even as we sit here reconnoitering. But for some reason I'm having trouble visualizing it. There's something about this place I'm sitting in that makes it hard to imagine other places—as though nothing else existed. For a moment panic trails its icy fingers along my spine. I close my eyes and concentrate. The Chai House *does* exist, I insist to myself. But my mind is like a sodden paper, its newsprint of memories run together. Finally, shakily, I pull up an image: a maple rocking chair in an alcove, its rich, polished wood gleaming in the light of the old, goosenecked floor lamp I rescued from a garage sale. From the thankful solidity of these objects come others, until I've re-created my teahouse sufficiently to let out a breath of relief.

"Can you?" Belle is asking. When I give her a blank look, she repeats impatiently, "Can you understand why anyone would come to this place rather than to our store? They must have about as much taste as a box of instant mashed potatoes."

I look around to see who these mashed-potato people are. There are quite a few customers in the café, though it's not as crowded as I'd expected it to be. I'd been afraid that I might run into some of our old regulars, the pained awkwardness that would ensue. But I don't know any of these folks. Where did they come from? They look ordinary enough, though, as they sip their coffees and munch their muffins while shuffling newspapers. No zombies here as far as I can see, lured in by the machinations of evil beings from another planet.

Suddenly I *can* understand why these people—and many others like them—might prefer Java to Chai House. Java demands nothing from them except their money. It allows them to remain unknown. No conversation, no contact, nothing to look at or discuss, nothing of themselves exchanged or exhaled. And yet they have community, too, as much of it as they want: the comfortable company of a roomful of nameless, faceless folks just like themselves, happy to be left alone, to gaze into the middle distance, to notice no one. For a moment, I become one with them, feeling my muscles relaxing into the slouch of anonymity.

While we, with our homemade cookies and custom-ordered coffees, our hand-finished furniture and silk puppets, our bulletin board chronicling our customers' lives—we've insisted that the Chai House be noticed. That our customers allow us into their lives just as we've invited them into ours. That our shop stay with them even after they leave it. We've believed that places shouldn't become clones of other places. We've believed that it's important for people to have a venue to enjoy intelligent conversation and a well-brewed cup of tea. Have we built our entire business on an illusion? Have we wasted our time in creating a refuge when all people want is a stop-'n'-go?

But I'll have to deal with these perplexities another time, because here comes our order, carried to our table by the manager herself. This is the first time I've seen her up close, and I can't help staring. She's gorgeous, from her seal-sleek blond hair to her perfectly manicured nails. As she walks to our table, she looks like a movie star playing the part of a coffee-shop manager. Even her smile is just the right mix of charm and efficiency.

"Ladies," she says. "Here's your tea with lemon"—my mother inclines her head—"your espresso"—Belle raises a finger—"and this latte must be for you!" She sets the cup down in front of me and looks at us appraisingly. "Your first time here, right? I can always tell!" She raises her voice. "Zelda, bring over a plate of our complimentary new-customer cookies." Then she narrows her sapphire-blue eyes at me. "Aren't you the woman who owns the tea shop across the street? I've seen you standing at your window." The smile appears on her face again, sharp as crystal. "Checking out the competition, huh?"

My face is hot. I look down and pull my cup toward me. But before I can take a sip, my mother puts her hand on my arm.

"Dear," she says. "I've changed my mind. I think I'd rather have coffee today. Would you care terribly if I took yours and gave you my tea?"

I stare at her. My mother isn't a coffee drinker. She claims it gives her a headache. And she knows I hate lemon in my tea.

"Oh, you don't have to do that," the manager says to my mother as she puts a plate of large chocolate-chip cookies that look unpleasantly delicious on our table. "I'll bring you another latte, no charge." Her smile would do a toothpaste ad proud. "Think of it as professional courtesy!"

"Thank you," my mother says in her formal voice, "but it's not necessary. My daughter and I are used to exchanging things."

This is somewhat less than true. In all my life, I can remember only one instance of us exchanging things. A dream for a dollar. And even then I'm not sure one could call that an exchange.

The manager glances at me expectantly, as though waiting for me to deny my mother's statement. When I don't oblige, she gives a small, elegant shrug. "Enjoy!" she says, with an expansive wave of her hand.

My mother stares at her thoughtfully as she walks away. She takes a sip of my coffee and makes a face, then drinks the rest very fast, as though it were an unpleasant but necessary task. She shakes her head very slightly when Belle picks up a cookie. "I wouldn't if I were you," she says.

Belle drops the cookie as though it were radioactive.

"Let's go," my mother says. "We've seen enough."

As soon as we step outside, Belle bursts out, "What did you see, Mrs. Gupta?"

I wait for my mother to tell Belle what she says (I know this from eavesdropping) to her clients: she's a dream reader, not a fortune teller.

But she only says, "Patience, Balwant. Not until we're back in our own territory."

Once we are inside the Chai House, she places the SORRY WE'RE CLOSED sign on the door (not that we need it), gets a cup of warm salt water and goes into the bathroom. I can hear her gargling and spitting. Finally, she comes out and gestures for us to join her at a table. When we're huddled together like modern-day Machiavellis, she says, "Don't go in there again."

"But why not?" I ask. "And why did you take my coffee? And why didn't you want us to eat the cookies?"

"The cookies I can explain a little more easily," my mother

says. "In life, it's best not to take anything for free—unless it's from someone who wishes you well. Taking places you under obligation. And the coffee—well, maybe I'm just suspicious. But I didn't like the way the manager brought our order over herself. She didn't do it for any of the other customers, if you noticed—"

"You think she put something in Rikki's coffee?" Belle breaks in.

"Oh, please!" I burst out. "You're making her sound like Lucrezia Borgia."

Belle ignores me. "Something bad luck, isn't it?" she says to my mother. "It happened like that once in Turlock to a new bride—my mom told me about it. This woman's husband's old girlfriend sent her a gift, a gorgeous silk sari. The bride, who'd come from India and didn't know any of the history, wore the sari and got so sick she nearly died."

"That's crazy!" I say. "It could have been a coincidence."

The two of them look at me, identical expressions on their faces. I can almost hear what they're thinking. *And what's a coincidence?*

"You're both getting carried away," I say. "And even if it were true, why would the manager want to harm me?"

"Perhaps she sees you as a threat," my mother says.

"She sees *me* as a threat? When *she's* the one destroying our business? But in that case, wouldn't she want to harm Belle, too? You didn't stop Belle from drinking her coffee—"

"It was an instinct," my mother says. "I can't really explain it. But it's clear now that the situation is serious. I did what I could, but it won't help in the long run. You've got to find a whole new

angle for the store, something with spirit and energy to bring people back in. And you must do it quickly, before you grow weaker."

"But what kind of new angle, Mrs. Gupta?" Belle cries.
"We've been racking our brains for weeks and can't think of a
thing. Can't you help us?"

My mother looks tired. There are smudges of black under her
eyes; her collarbones push out from under her skin. "The reason
you don't have enough power to fight that woman there is that she
knows exactly who she is, and you don't. This isn't a real cha
shop"—she pronounces the word in the Bengali way—"but a
mishmash, a Westerner's notion of what's Indian. Maybe that's the
problem. Maybe if you can make it into something authentic, you'll
survive."

Heat floods my face, years of anger, a sensation like falling.
How dare she accuse me! "And whose fault is it if I don't know
who I am? If I have a warped Western sense of what's Indian?"

Belle gives me a shocked look. She's never heard me speak
this way to my mother. My mother bites her lip, something I don't
remember her ever doing. Her teeth are small, with serrated edges
like a child's. How is it I hadn't noticed this before? When she
replies, it is in Bengali, so that I have to really concentrate to understand. "You're right. It is my fault. I see now that I brought you
up wrong. I thought it would protect you if I didn't talk about the
past. That way you wouldn't be constantly looking back, hankering, like so many immigrants do. I didn't want to be like those other
mothers, splitting you between here and there, between your life
right now and that which can never be. But by not telling you about
India as it really was, I made it into something far bigger. It

crowded other things out of your mind. It pressed upon your brain like a tumor."

After she leaves, Belle asks, "What was she telling you in Bengali? And what does she mean that this place isn't authentic?"

I can tell she's upset, and with good reason. But I don't have any answers. I'm still trying to process everything my mother told me, her slanted logic. Leaving, she had turned to me, said something else. Maybe I misunderstood the Bengali words, but this is what they sounded like: *All this time I thought I was doing it for you. But I'd only been protecting myself.*

That night after Jona has fallen asleep I work on my painting. I paint over the man in white completely, then redo the foliage in that section of the canvas. When I'm done, there are only trees and grass, fallen bark, hanging branches—and behind them, a man-shaped gap of darkness you wouldn't even see if you weren't looking right. A man with his left arm arced high over his head, at once in the picture and absent from it, the final element the painting needed.

Later, I lie in bed, still high from the excitement of finishing, unable to sleep. As so many times before, my thoughts swoop and circle over my mother. How was she protecting herself by not telling me about India? What did she see—or think she saw—inside the coffee shop? And finally: if she drank the cup that was meant for me, the bad-luck cup, what would it do to her?

. . .

Years later, when I've begun dreaming again, dreaming with a vengeance as though to make up for all those barren, mud-brown nights, dreaming in neon hues and strobe flashes not only my own dreams but those of my mother and my daughter also, I will dream the inside of Java. By then there will be no Java and no Chai House either, and America itself as I had believed it to be will have ceased to exist, but this is what I will dream:

We are in an underwater café, filled with a deep, bottom-of-the-ocean blue. Everything sways and shivers in this space, and words echo like sonic booms. The table we sit at is made of coral—or is it porous bones? There's no one in the room except for my mother, Belle and myself. I turn to speak to them and find that they have turned into sea creatures. Belle waves her pink anemone tresses at me. My mother turns to me with her intelligent seahorse eyes. (And I? What am I? But I cannot see myself.) The manager swims in, but she is outside my line of vision, and I'm not sure what kind of creature she is. I see only her shadow against the wall where the kelp sweeps back and forth. It looms in the shape of a cloud or a net or the head of a hammer. The drinks we've ordered come floating through the water at us. The coffee is black as squid ink. I reach for it, but my mother is quicker. She takes my cup in her fragile seahorse hands and drinks. The color seeps into her, staining her like Shiva of the dark throat, who took in the world's poison to save it from destruction. But my mother, well intentioned though she is, is not as strong as a god. She begins to crack apart. Little bits come off her like branches of coral. She's trying to tell me something. The water grows turbulent, the booming is a huge echo in my ears, the manager smiles at me with her shark mouth,

her eyes are as white as toothpaste, her blond fin points at something on the undulating wall. It is a clock, with the number 2 positioned in its center. I know that it is a clock of days, set to move
backward. Next will come the number 1, and then 0. And then time
will run out.

13

Rakhi

I stand in a corner of the Atelier, wishing I could disappear. I've been to the gallery many times in the past for other shows, but it has never seemed so huge and cavernous, so empty.

"Belle," I'd whispered in dismay as I walked in earlier. "There's no one here."

Belle gave a patient, maternal sigh. "Naturally. The gallery doesn't open for another thirty minutes."

"What if nobody—"

"Have you ever been to a show where that happened?"

"This could always be the—"

"Spare me!" Belle said. She aimed a brilliant smile at Kathryn, who waved at us from the far end of the studio, and grabbed my arm before I could slink off to a corner. "Uh-uh," she said. "I want you to stand right here, where people will be sure to notice you as soon as they walk in. And I'd much appreciate it if you refrain from slouching. Quite ruins the effect I took hours to create." She adjusted my scarf, gave the back of my dress a discreet tug, handed me a glass of champagne, and went off to consult with Kathryn.

I shift nervously from foot to foot—no mean feat, considering that I'm wearing Belle's stiletto heels. I take a wary sip from my champagne glass and hold it in front of my body as though it were a protective device, and wish once again that I hadn't let Belle dress me for the occasion.

"No, no, and no," she'd said when I'd discussed my plans with her. "This is a milestone event in your life, and as your friend it is my moral duty to make sure you don't attend it wearing khakis and a sweater."

"Belle, all I have that's even halfway formal is a black granny dress from when we used to usher at the Zellerbach so we could see shows for free. You tore my other dress, remember? My Indian outfits are way too gaudy for this kind of event. And you of all people should know that I can't afford to buy anything right now. Anyway, I'm a painter, not a model. Why do I have to look good?"

"You just do. Take it from me. But not to worry—I have exactly the thing for you. It's lucky we're pretty much the same size, isn't it?"

So here I am, dressed in a black sheath of a gown with a slit up the side of one leg and spaghetti straps that live up to their name. My hair is swept up in a chignon, battling to escape Belle's pins and beginning to succeed. My eyelashes droop from the weight of Belle's mascara, and my lips are slathered with Belle's lipstick, which is aptly named Dragonette Crimson. The one thing in the ensemble that's mine is a gauzy Indian black-and-silver scarf Belle found in the back of my closet. "Perfect," she'd crooned, arranging it around my shoulders. "Just the right fusion of East and West!"

My parents have arrived. My mother, dressed in an elegant hand-embroidered sari in earth tones, beams at me, but Belle waylays her at the entrance. My father is dressed, amazingly, in a suit. I'm touched. The only other time he'd worn a suit was at my wedding. He waves shyly, but waits for my mother to lead the way. As I watch them cross the room, it strikes me that that's how he's always been where I'm concerned, happy to trail along behind her, letting her take care of whatever I need. One day I'd like to know what made them marry each other, sparrow and bulbul.

"Was your marriage arranged?" I asked her once.

She was startled into laughter. "Heavens, no! In fact, my people were dead against it."

"But why?"

She smiled that familiar let's-drop-it-shall-we smile.

Maybe rephrasing would work. "So, how *did* you marry him?"

"We met when I was visiting Calcutta—and fell in love." She looked surprised, as though she had forgotten this fact.

"What was it like?"

But she had regained her composure. "No different from what happens to other young people, I imagine," she said, shrugging. "Now, don't you have something better to do than waste your energy on things that are long over with?"

What she didn't know is how much energy I would expend later, trying to fill in the gaps. Trying to imagine, over and over, a man and woman, very young, meeting on the streets of a city I'd never visited. In my fantasies they looked at me, but their faces were not the parent faces I was familiar with. There were only two things I knew about them for certain.

1. What happened to them was not what happens to other young people who fall in love.

2. Whatever it had been, it was gone now, its place taken by something so different that even they would be baffled, if they allowed themselves to examine it, by the transformation.

"Congratulations!" my mother says, kissing me on the cheek. "Your paintings are just beautiful."

Of course she'd say that. She's my mother. I keep my eyes away from the walls. I know that the paintings are worthless and that viewers—if any do eventually come—will hate them.

My father pats me on the back murmuring something about being so proud. He's sober and holds a mineral water in his hand. I throw my mother a grateful look.

"You look beautiful, too! Very chic. Why, you're wearing my old dupatta." She touches my scarf lightly.

It had happened the day before my marriage. She'd opened an old trunk to take out a silver cup I used to drink from when I was a baby. It was valuable, and she wanted to give it to me for my children-to-come. But my eyes had been caught by the scarf, balled into a corner. I'd lifted it up and its silver threads had shimmered the way a web might, if spiders danced on it.

"Can I have this?"

She hesitated. Then she said, "This old thing? Why ever would you want it?"

Because it's from your other life, I wanted to say, the one that's magic, the one you won't let me enter. But I didn't want to spoil the moment. Besides, it wasn't all her fault. If I'd had the gift, the way she did, nothing could have kept me out.

She had handed the dupatta over, with a smile and a shake of her head. She did that sometimes, as though my actions were mysterious beyond fathoming. When all along it was she who was unfathomable.

All this I'd forgotten, the way we forget so many things without knowing what we've lost.

"Where's my granddaughter?" my mother is asking. I tell her that Sonny was supposed to drop her off at the studio before the show opened. But of course he's late.

"He probably has a reason," she says.

"Yeah, it's always the same one: me, myself and I."

My mother purses her lips. I know she thinks I'm too hard on Sonny. But then she doesn't know what happened that night. A champagne bubble of a smile forms inside me and bursts before it reaches the surface, leaving a bitter aftertaste. *Well, Mom, I guess I do have my own unfathomability, after all.*

All of a sudden the room is full of chatter and laughter. A few people are acquaintances, but there are many I don't know. I'm torn between the desire to eavesdrop and the fear that they might be saying my work is no good. Or—worse still—maybe they'll be discussing the weather or their holiday plans.

Then I spot him in the far corner, alone, looking intently at a painting. The man from the eucalyptus grove. I can't see his face from here, but I'm sure it's him. The build, the way he holds his body. The white jacket. There's a quietness around him even here, in the middle of this bustle.

I start toward him, but a whirling dervish hurtles into me, almost making me spill my champagne.

"Jona!" I kiss her runaway curls, which Sonny-the-delinquent-dad has obviously not thought to comb.

"Mom, you look great! And all your paintings are up on the walls! Cool! How many did you sell so far?"

I find myself grinning. "Do they look okay?" Some of my nervousness melts as I hug my daughter and take another sip of champagne. I'm glad that I arranged for her to come and share this special evening with me, even though Kathryn had expressed some concern at having a child present.

"Can I try some?" Jona asks.

"No, sweetheart. It has alcohol. Come with me to Auntie Belle. She'll get you some apple juice."

"Apple juice! Yuck. Yours looks much more interesting. Why can't I have just a little bit? Sonny lets me—" She sees my face and backtracks. "Only sometimes, of course."

I take a deep breath and hold on to my smile. Later, Sonny-boy. Later.

"So, how is it *Dad* was so late getting you here?"

"He couldn't find parking. Oh, there's Gramma!"

I start to say that he didn't need to find parking—all he had to do was drop her at the door. But she's gone. A terrible thought comes to me and, along with it, a prickling at the nape of my neck.

I turn slowly toward the entrance, and there he is, even though I have expressly not-asked him to come. He looks good, I'm forced to admit—far better than someone with his degenerate lifestyle has any right to look. That slightly tousled, boyish look, as though he just got out of bed, the full lips that remind me— much as I would like to forget—of how they felt on various parts of my body. Except he's not smiling that crooked, half-mocking smile that I've come to expect of him. He's standing there, lean-hipped in black pants and a form-fitting black silk shirt that shows off his muscles, and he's looking at me with dark sympathy. His look implies that he knows me more intimately than any other man ever will. That he can sense the little voice in my head that whispers, *You shouldn't be here, there's some mistake, you aren't good enough.* As though he, too, has heard a voice like that sometimes.

But that's impossible. Sonny has the sturdiest ego west of New York. If a little voice ever got inside his head, it would shrivel up and die quicker than a slug in a salt mine. Besides, I don't want his sympathy. I don't want anything except for him to stay away from me. Especially on this, the most important night of my life. (As I think this, there's an echo in my head, *the most important night, the most*—. When had I said those words before? Not remembering makes me angrier.)

And in my anger I stride toward him, forgetting my high heels. I stumble, and his hand comes out to steady my elbow. I see the smile in his eyes, his fingers burn my bare skin, his voice says, lazily, "Riks, you look gorgeous," and the composure I've worked so hard on learning since I left him vanishes.

My voice is shaking as I snatch my arm away and say, "Why did you come? To ruin everything for me as you've always done?"

It isn't what I meant to say. Amazing how quickly he can reduce me to this.

Around us, people pause their conversations to hear better. An unexpected look of hurt flashes in Sonny's eye, but it's gone so fast that maybe it was never there.

"Good evening to you, too," he says.

"Please leave," I whisper.

I think he's going to say something sarcastic, something I don't have the reserves to counter. But he only gives a slight bow and turns away, making me feel guilty and uncharitable and profoundly thankful.

He's at the door when Jona tackles him from behind with one of her hugs. "Sonny-y-y! I didn't see you come in. Where are you going?"

He kneels and whispers something in her ear.

"You can't leave! You haven't even looked at Mom's paintings. And you haven't talked to Gramma and Grandpa yet!"

I walk over and lay a firm maternal hand on her shoulder. "He has to go. He'll look at the paintings some other time."

"But I want him to look at them with me!"

"Jona, didn't you hear me? He has to leave. And I want you to go to Gramma or Auntie Belle and stay with them."

Jona looks from Sonny's face to mine.

"You fought with him, didn't you?" she says. "You told him to go away. How could you be so mean, Mom?"

I feel heat flood my face. "Jona," I say in my best don't-mess-with-me voice, "go to your grandmother."

"I bet Gramma won't let you send him away. I'm going to tell her right now. Gramma! Gram-ma!" Her clear child tones cut through the buzz of conversation. "Mom's telling Sonny he has to go away!"

All heads turn toward us. I want to sink through the floor. My mother comes hurrying. She whispers to Jona while Sonny tries to pry her loose from his arm. Jona's sobbing loudly. Over the heads of the crowd, which obviously finds this little drama far more riveting than my paintings, I see Kathryn's face, a death mask of disapproval.

No more shows for me at the Atelier.

Is the man in white watching, too? Somehow, that thought humiliates me most of all.

"Just leave," I hiss to Sonny. With my eyes I say, None of this mess would be happening if you hadn't decided to show up.

"I'm trying," he growls back. With his eyes he says, None of this mess would be happening if you hadn't left me.

"If Sonny goes, I'm going with him," Jona announces. "I hate you! I don't want to look at your horrid paintings."

"Good!" I say. I'm about to add, *I don't want to look at your horrid face,* but my mother puts a warning hand on my arm. She nods to Sonny, who picks Jona up and shoots me an unreadable look. (No, I take that back—I read it loud and clear. It's a look of triumph.) My mother walks me across the hall, past the curious faces and into the restroom. I expect her to tell me how shamefully I overreacted, but she merely suggests that I wash my face, repair my makeup, and breathe deeply. She leaves me alone with a row of faucets, all winking accusingly at me.

When I finally force myself to emerge from the restroom, bracing myself for stares and whispers and knowing smirks, I am amazed to find that no one pays me much attention. People are busy talking to each other, pointing at paintings, nodding. I walk over to Kathryn to apologize.

"No problem," she says, looking unexpectedly cheerful. "It seemed to pique people's interest. You know—Passionate Young Artist Confronts Her Dark, Handsome Past at Show Opening. You sold quite a few paintings after that little scene—more than I'd expected. Maybe I should insist from now on that artists invite their exes." She gestures and I see the bright red SOLD tags on the pieces.

The eucalyptus grove is tagged, too.

"Who bought that one?" I ask.

"Let's see—it was a man. Not one of our regulars. Looked Mediterranean—or maybe Middle Eastern. Isn't that great? That's your most expensive piece—and your most accomplished. Something about it I can't put my finger on—. Well, he must have a good eye for art."

My heart speeds up. "Was he wearing white?"

"I don't remember. There was a big rush right around then."

"Do you have his name? A credit card receipt?"

She looks at me curiously. "No. He paid in cash and said he'd be back to pick up the painting when the show was over. I asked for a phone number, but he said he was between numbers right now. I did write down his name, though." She opens a folder. "Emmett Mayerd. Unusual, isn't it? I hope I spelled it right. He was in a hurry to leave, so I just scribbled down what I thought he said."

Emmett Mayerd. I repeat the name to myself through the rest of the evening, through Belle's hugs and Kathryn's congratulations, through my mother's fingers cupping my face, her eyes proud but with a shadow in them. My father gives an exaggerated bow and raises a glass of cabernet in a silent toast. (When did he start drinking?) Emmett Mayerd rustles inside me as I ask my parents if they would like to stay overnight in my apartment. (They refuse, but maybe that's because, distracted by the possibility of Emmett, I don't insist as much as I should.) Would they like me to drive them down to Fremont? (Another refusal.) *I'll be fine driving,* my mother assures me. *Don't be such a worrywart.* Emmett stands by me as I wave my parents good-bye, turn down an offer to go clubbing with Belle, and drive to my place. He watches as I open the door to the too silent apartment. He is used to silence, Emmett. It is his element.

Emmett, I'm not as strong as you. I need someone tonight. Someone to share the excitement of the evening, the achievement and the upset, the feeling of deflation that I'm left with. Jona would have wrapped her arms tight around me, pushed her sweaty, demanding curls against my face, and kept me from thinking. But she isn't here. She's with her Sonny (*whom she loves more,* my little voice is quick to remind me) and I must face the truth by myself.

Seeing Sonny look at me in that infuriatingly kind way tonight broke open something inside me, some shell of denial I'd built around myself ever since I moved out on my own. All this time I told myself I'd be fine alone, I'm tough, I don't need anyone. But I'm not fine—and I'm not as tough as I'd like to believe I am. I want to be loved by a man who understands me the way Sonny did in our best days. I need him to love me until my whole body shakes with it.

Every time I exhale, I feel a little piece of my youth leaving me. Emmett, white shadow in a world of green, can you understand this? Can you be the man I want?

The phone rings.

I sit up, rigid with expectation. Could it be—? Why not? If he could be in the rain-filled grove, if he could come to the show and buy my painting of him (that shape made of emptiness that only he recognized), why couldn't he be calling me now? My hand trembles a bit—my voice, too—as I say hello.

"Riks," says a not-Emmett voice that I know too well, "we need to talk."

I'm disappointed, and angry at my foolishness.

"There's nothing to talk about, Sonny," I snap. "Not anymore. Please don't call me again."

But of course he does. The phone rings and rings, the answering machine comes on, I hear him say, "Riks, listen to me, it's important," I disconnect the phone. Then I go to bed, where I draw my knees up to my chest and shiver in spite of having turned the heat to high. Emmett has vanished (perhaps I'm too needy for his liking), and until I fall into uneasy sleep, I listen to my little voice. *Now that you've turned off the phone, what if Jona has an emergency?*

14

FROM THE
DREAM JOURNALS

Recently, they've been arriving when I don't expect them. This morning, for example.

She drives up in a car like a silver whisper and sits there for a long moment, comparing the address on her notepad with that on my door. Or maybe she's gathering the scattered petals of her courage.

When she does ring the bell and I open the door, she is beautiful and sad, like a princess from one of our old Bengali tales.

Maybe that's why, when she tells me her dream, I recognize it at once, though I haven't dreamed it myself.

In the dream—she's had it several times now—she is in a walled garden. There are golden plants all around her, flowers made of diamonds. A brook flows through the garden, with honey for water, and invisible birds sing so sweetly she thinks her heart will burst.

She pulls at the strap of her Gucci purse, looking down at her lap. She smooths out the silky fabric of her dress as she speaks. She has chosen pearls for her ears, her throat. This does not surprise me, for they are the gems of weeping.

As long as she is in the garden, she knows she will be safe. No one can get to her. Get at her. She hears them calling her name, outside. The voices are angry, angrier. But she doesn't care. She lifts her hand. A dragonfly swoops down to kiss it.

I read her story in her listless eyes. A husband who is so busy dreaming his king-of-the-mountain dreams that he doesn't know his home has turned into a desert. That the only solace his wife has comes from sitting in an unreal garden, listening to birds that aren't there.

You need to talk to him, I tell her. Make him talk to you.

She shakes her head. I tried. I don't care to anymore.

When did he stop sleeping with you?

She turns hunted deer eyes to me. How did you know?

I don't tell her that I know it through my own life, which is like hers turned inside out. We dream tellers do not speak of ourselves.

I forget, she says finally. It doesn't matter.

You need to find something—or someone—else to love. Or you'll go mad.

She looks at me.

Maybe I'm mad already, her eyes say. Maybe that's the best way to carry this emptiness.

Why did you come to me? Do you want me to explain what you saw?

No! Don't! I don't want it explained away. I just want to dream it again and again. Every night. I could bear the rest of my life then. If I knew for certain that when I lay down, I could go there. But it doesn't happen, not often enough. And recently, less and less. That's why I've come to you.

I sigh. It's a dangerous path she follows. But she will not accept any other help from me. And I can't turn down the entreaty in those eyes, the shimmer in them that could be mascara or desperation.

I bring her a bottle from my closet of shadows. One drop each night, I say, just before bed, in each eye.

She twists open the stopper. Smells the clear liquid dubiously.

You're sure? It looks just like water.

I nod. I don't tell her that I'll be sending my dreaming thoughts to her, too, to guide her across the threshold.

But it's such a small bottle—it'll be empty in no time. Can't you give me more?

I shake my head. It'll last longer than you think, as long as you use it right. When it's over, come and talk to me. Maybe you'll want something different by then.

She smiles her disbelief. Rises on unsteady stiletto heels. Without looking at them, she puts handfuls of dollar bills on the table between us.

I tuck most of them back into her purse.

Everything in moderation, I say sternly. But inside I'm telling her, Don't give up. The dream is not a drug but a way. Listen to where it can take you.

So many kinds of sorrow in the world. Sometimes I think I might break from it.

You'll be here for sure when I come back? There's fear in her voice, in the clutch of her perfect nails on the strap of her purse.

I say to her what I say to all my people, though this time I speak with a tinge of guilt.

My dear one. (She looks up at that, startled again. She'll never know how deeply I mean those three words, how deeply I am tied to her, now that she has come to me.) My dear one, as long as I'm alive, I'll be here for you.

15

Someone is pounding on the door of the apartment, calling her name. Someone rings the doorbell over and over until the maddeningly cheery chimes dig into her skull and hiding her head under the pillow can't save her. She drags herself out of bed, swearing, her head dull and throbbing as with a hangover. Unfair, this world where you can suffer a hangover without having touched a drink. (Half a glass of champagne, she figures, doesn't count.) She blinks hazily, wondering if it's Sonny, would he dare this final assault, but the voice doesn't fit. She considers not answering, pretending she doesn't exist. Maybe it wouldn't even be pretense. She feels a strange weightlessness as she makes her way to the bathroom, a sense of not belonging to the hands that splash water on the face that is bent over the sink. It is dark all around, or maybe her eyes have floated away. When she comes out of the bathroom, the voice shouting her name hasn't left, so she opens the door.

"God, Rikki, what's wrong with you?" Belle is sobbing as she pushes her way into the apartment. "Why didn't you open the door earlier? I thought something had happened to you, too."

She registers that *too,* a cold corkscrew of a sound that bores into her, leaving a narrow black tunnel in its wake. She mumbles something about being asleep. It isn't an unreasonable excuse. When she looks past Belle at the landing outside her apartment, with its small window, she sees the sun hasn't risen yet. Belle is wearing a short red dress. Surely that wasn't what she was wearing when she saw her last at the—where? With an effort she recollects the gallery, and then everything comes tumbling down on her: her parents, Jona, the paintings gallant and forlorn on the wall before the crowds came, the man in white, Sonny's disastrous entry and more disastrous exit. Belle's makeup is smeared, her eyes are swollen. Rakhi wants to tell her that she shouldn't have been driving when she was upset like that, she could have had an accident. Perhaps she does say it, but Belle doesn't hear, she's too busy talking and crying at the same time.

"I came home and there were these messages on the answering machine, like six of them, I almost didn't turn it on, I was so tired, but thank God I did, it was Sonny, he was calling from the hospital, he'd been trying you but you didn't pick up—"

Hospital. The word sinks into her with finality, a stone of a word.

"Jona?" Her body starts to shake. Belle is holding her.

"No, not Jona, thank God. But just as bad. Your parents. They got in an accident, going back. Your father's hurt bad. But your mother's—" Belle sobs so hard she can't complete the sentence.

But Rakhi doesn't need to hear the word, that sound like a fist striking flesh, to know what has happened.

. . .

At the hospital, where Belle has driven her, everything appears blurred, as though she's looking through glasses that are meant for someone else. Faces in uniforms and surgical scrubs float up to her, float away. They say things she can't quite comprehend. (What's there to say? Everything's been encompassed already in that one unsaid word. Its single syllable swings at her from time to time, making her flinch.) She follows a uniform down a passage to a room, a bed, someone lying in it, covered with a white sheet. Under the sheet, she can see the outlines of disconnected tubes, like the freeways of an abandoned city. Sonny is there, his eyes red-rimmed. She wants to pound her fists against his chest, shout that he has no right, that she has no tears left because he's cried them away. She knows he would grab her hands, hold her, murmuring like one does to a child or an animal. But finally she doesn't. It wouldn't change the thing she needs to change.

She doesn't look at the bed.

After a long time someone takes her to another room, another figure lying in another bed. There are bandages, a broken arm in a cast. This time the tubes are hooked up to a machine. He isn't conscious, so she doesn't have to talk to him. She's thankful for that. This surprises her. She hadn't thought she could feel thankful about anything again.

At some point, she finds that she is back home—she's not sure how—and in her own bed. There are two quilts covering her, but they can't stop her from shivering. She wants to ask about Jona, where she is, but all her words have wandered away and she's too tired to go searching. Belle gives her a couple of bright pink pills and thankfully she swallows them.

And then. The dreams that her mother had protected her from all these years, positioning herself between her and them like a fortress wall, crash over her.

16

Rakhi

I am in the kitchen that is no longer my mother's, boiling banana squash.

I've never cooked banana squash before, although it was a dish my mother was fond of making. She made it well and with deceptive ease. In her hands, it never turned into the disconcerting orange glob that stares at me from the pan. I add several spoons of mustard oil in an attempt to redeem it, and mix in salt and pepper. It looks just as unappetizing as before, only greasier. I sigh and place it, along with overcooked rice, on a tray.

I'm making the banana squash at the request of my father. He has also requested that I boil the rice until it turns mushy. He says his insides are too bruised to handle anything more demanding.

I'm quite sure there's nothing wrong with my father's insides. All his test results have turned out fine, and the doctors have told me there's nothing to worry about. But I don't point this out to him. Since the accident, I speak to my father as little as possible. I touch him as little as possible, too, but this is more difficult, since he needs my help with so many daily necessities until the cast comes off.

Sometimes I speak to my mother. I ask what she was thinking of when the accident occurred, how she could have been so disgracefully careless. I ask how exactly it came about.

I am angry with her, too, but it's a more complicated anger. I don't have words to articulate it. It is easier to allow myself to feel baffled.

No one is sure of what happened that night. But this much the reports agree on: she went off of Highway 580 where the road lifts itself up and curls lazily against the San Leandro hillside. She plowed through the guardrail and over the purple ice plant that covers the hillside, the car's nose pointed directly at the long, low flatness of the San Mateo Bridge, its floating fairy lights. Then the car flipped over. By the time the ambulances got there, she was unconscious. She died soon after reaching the hospital.

The reports say there were no skid marks, no sudden braking. Nothing to indicate that she'd lost control of the car—or that she'd tried to stop it from going over.

My father says he was asleep when the accident occurred.

I don't believe him. Somehow, he was responsible. I know it by the prickly coldness along my spine, the way my teeth hurt as though I've been sucking on something too sour.

"Talk to me," Belle said after she took me home from the hospital. "For God's sake, Rikki, talk to me. Cry, scream, do something." But every response I considered seemed clichéd. Meaningless. I knew I should save my energy for something more useful, even though I didn't know yet what it was.

I sat on the sofa in my apartment for a day and a night. From time to time I visualized the accident. Maybe my father had started an argument with my mother, distracting her. Had he grabbed for the wheel in his drunken state, sending the car over the edge?

When I was too tired to sit, I lay down. I ate what Belle put in front of me. I knew starving myself wasn't the answer. I closed my eyes and chewed, it was easier that way. I didn't recognize what it was that I ate. My taste buds had gone AWOL. When Sonny brought Jona over, I held her, but absentmindedly, as though she were someone else's child. Her hair was full of snarls, but this didn't agitate me in the usual way. She was very quiet. Someone must have told her what had happened, must have instructed her not to ask questions.

"I'm really sorry, Rikki," Sonny said. He knelt in front of me and held my hands in both of his. I didn't snatch my hands away. I would have, though, if I'd had the energy. What happened was Sonny's fault, too. If he hadn't shown up at the gallery and caused the scene, my father wouldn't have started drinking. He could have driven home. Then they wouldn't have had the accident. And even if they did (I couldn't stop myself from thinking this, though I hated myself for it) perhaps he would have died instead of her.

My whisper voice raised its serpent head to remind me that I, too, was to blame. I could have stopped my parents from driving home. I could have insisted that they spend the night with me. But I'd been too busy fantasizing about the man in white.

Now that my mother is dead, the man in white has faded into irrelevance, along with words like *romance* and *excitement*, *mystery* and *adventure*. I can't even dredge up his name from the muck of memory. Fitting payment for my selfishness.

There's another reason why I didn't snatch my hands away from Sonny. For once he meant what he was saying. He had loved my mother, too, and he, too, was hurting. He used to say that she was his only true family. Don't be melodramatic, I'd snap at him. But I knew he really felt that way.

"I can keep Jona for as long as you want," he said. "You'll probably have to stay in the Fremont house until your dad's well enough to manage on his own—"

I stared at him. It hadn't struck me until then that I'd have to go back to that house full of my mother's absence to take care of the man who was probably responsible for her death. My face must have shown my horror, because Sonny asked if I was okay. A stupid question, which he normally would not have asked—whatever he was, Sonny wasn't stupid. A question that I normally wouldn't have suffered without a sharp retort. But we weren't feeling normal, none of us. I gave a silent nod and tugged halfheartedly at Jona's tangles. Behind me, I could sense Sonny and Belle, co-conspirators for once, exchanging glances.

"She shouldn't be left alone," he whispered.

"Don't worry," Belle whispered back. "I'll stay with her."

It didn't bother me to hear them refer to me this way. It was comforting to consider myself a *she*. As though I were a balloon floating at the end of a long, thin thread.

Before she left, Jona asked, "What are you thinking of?" As an afterthought, she added, "Mommy?" She'd wriggled off my lap a while ago, as though she, too, felt that the woman on the sofa—this floating *she*—was a stranger.

"Nothing," I told her. I tried to construct my face so it would project sincerity. This must not have worked, because she threw me a doubting glance and clutched at Sonny's hand, tugging him door-ward. Long after the door closed behind them, I could hear their voices in the corridor, hers high and agitated, his a placating murmur. Or maybe it was inside my head that I heard them. When the voices faded, I let my body do what it wanted. It slumped sideways onto the sofa, it closed its eyes. Even before I was asleep, the dreams started coming, spools of light and shape unraveling too fast behind my eyelids, the fabric ripping, making me twitch and cry out, making Belle rush over anxiously. Yes, all the dreams I'd been longing for. But in the morning, waking exhausted, I remembered none of them.

I'd lied to Jona when she'd asked me what I was thinking. Keeping one's mind on nothing requires self-control of a kind I've never possessed, not even under more conducive circumstances.

I'd been thinking of the funeral.

The funeral was held at the Valley View Funeral Home, a squat beige building off of a freeway. Someone had tried to beautify it by adding windows and a courtyard with a fountain, but it remained what it was: a place where people were forced to recognize how frail lives were, and how little we appreciated them until they broke. Sonny had made the arrangements. Although I hated the place, I didn't hold it against him. It was better than what I could have managed on my own.

I sat in one of the front pews with my scraggly little family, what was left of it: Belle and Jona and Sonny. My father was in the hospital, where they were still running tests on him because he tended to blank out from time to time. (I had two theories about this: 1. He was faking it; 2. It was a result of guilt.) There was a covered casket up front, an overpowering scent of flowers. They could have been gardenias, I wasn't sure. My mother had disliked strong scents. At first I'd thought of complaining, having them re-moved. But then I figured it didn't matter to her anymore. A hushed, churchy music was being piped through the intercom. We'd invited a mere handful of people—my parents didn't have much of a social life. If there were relatives, I didn't know of them. The priest from the Indian temple gave a brief speech about how my mother had been a virtuous wife, mother and homemaker, and an asset to the community. (It was obvious he knew nothing about her.) Sonny spoke in a choked voice of how much she had meant to him, how she'd guided him through tough times and loved him even when he hadn't deserved it. Belle wiped her eyes as she talked about my mother's generosity. And then it was my turn.

I had decided to say a few words about how my mother gave me a sense of myself, how she never pushed me, like so many mothers do, to live out her dreams of success. It wasn't profound in any way, and I would rather not have spoken, but I felt obligated. I couldn't shake off the feeling that my mother's spirit was hover-ing above us somewhere, listening in.

But when I reached the podium and turned to face the audi-ence, I was so taken aback that I couldn't remember a single word I'd planned to say. The hall was full of people. When had they all filed in, so silent that until this moment I hadn't been aware of their presence? I didn't recognize any of them, but I knew at once who they were. People my mother had helped over the years, people who were connected to her by their dreaming. Perhaps that is how they knew to be here now.

Maybe I was dizzy from not having eaten that morning, but as I stood at the podium I saw that the faces of all these people were similar in some way, as though being touched by my mother had made them into relatives. There was—in the look in their eyes, in the way they held their heads, or rested a chin on a hand, or clutched a tissue in a fist—something that reminded me of my mother. From now on, I would know them by this sign wherever I ran into them—at a farmers' market, a BART station, on the seashore. But I knew also that I would never see them again.

I wanted to say something to them, something consoling and meaningful, for they were my mother's true family, her orphans. Their grief was more legitimate than mine. But what could I tell them? They knew her better than I did; they knew her in her essence. Until now I'd held on to the hope that someday I would know her in this way, too—when I was old enough, when I was wise enough. But as I stood there in the mortuary hall, I realized that it was never going to happen. My mother's secret self was lost to me forever.

I stood there, frozen into silence by this fact, until Belle came up and led me back to my seat. She held me tightly when I started to shiver. Later, in the crematorium, when a conveyor belt had fed the casket into the huge metal jaws of the furnace, she tried to make me talk about what I was feeling. But how could I tell her that what ate at me more than my mother's death was my exclusion from her life?

On the way back, Belle drove while I balanced on my lap the square urn the manager of the crematorium had handed me. She tried to get me to cry, but I didn't feel like crying. Instead, I wanted to ask if she'd been as surprised as I to see all the people who'd come to the funeral. But I was afraid. What if she said, What on earth are you talking about, Rikki? What if she said, What people?

. . .

$\mathcal{I}$ plump the pillows and help my father sit up in bed. I place the tray of rice and banana squash on his knees. I pour him a glass of juice. He asks me, hesitantly, if I'd like to sit down. As always, I say I'm busy. He should ring the brass bell I've placed on the nightstand when he's done.

"Have you eaten?" he asks. I incline my head briefly, a gesture that could mean yes or no. There's a fading yellow bruise on his left cheekbone that gives him the look of a boxer past his prime. I cannot remember a single instance in my life when I felt close to him.

I'm at the door when he says, "You're angry with me, aren't you?"

I don't answer.

"Don't be angry," he says.

What a ridiculous request, as though it were possible to will away anger. But even if it were, I wouldn't. I'm grateful to my anger; it fills up the pitted hollow inside of me.

"We need to talk," he adds.

"I don't feel like talking," I say. I grab the door, ready to shut it behind me.

"You blame me, don't you? You think it was my fault, somehow."

I say nothing, but my mouth feels like I bit into a raw bitter gourd. I'm halfway through the door already. When I get downstairs, I'm going to call Sonny and ask him to arrange for a nurse, starting tomorrow.

"If you sit down," my father says, "I'll tell you what happened just before the accident."

My entire body stiffens. Even though I've vowed not to let him engage me in conversation, I find myself saying, "I thought you were asleep."

"I lied," he says, gesturing for me to sit on the bed.

He has me in his trap, and knows it. As a compromise, I pull a chair close to the door.

"How do I know you aren't lying now?"

And he, wilier than I'd credited him with being: "I think you're enough of your mother's daughter to recognize a true story when you hear it."

In this house of death what I dread most is when the phone rings. But each time I pick it up.

Today there's a woman at the other end.

"Are you the dream teller?" she asks. There's a catch in her breath, as though she's been running. "I need help."

I tell her that my mother is dead.

She is silent for a long moment. Then she says, "But you can help me, no? You're her daughter, she must have taught you something? I can tell you this dream I keep having, and you can tell me what to do?"

I tell her I can't interpret dreams.

"Please don't say no," she says. "I don't know anyone else to ask. I'm so scared. Please try, please?"

She's still sobbing when I hang up.

. . .

"It wasn't a complete lie," my father says, "when I told the doctors I'd been asleep. I had. But I awoke—and noticed your mother was going too fast. It surprised me because she was always a cautious driver, as I'm sure you know. I told her to slow down, but she didn't. I asked her what was wrong. She was staring straight ahead. I mustn't lose him, she said. I peered through the fog to look. There was a large black car ahead of us, I couldn't tell what kind, also going very fast. I told her to be careful, to watch her speed, but it was as though she didn't hear me. Who's in that car? I asked. Who mustn't you lose? You wouldn't understand if I told you, she said. But I'll tell you anyhow. He's my only chance to get back what I've lost. I squinted, trying to figure out who it was, because she sounded like she knew him. All I could see was a silhouette."

Later I would ask, *Do you remember the license plate?*

He'd shake his head. *Didn't think to look at it.*

Was he wearing white?

He'd wrinkle his brows, wanting to help. But finally he'd opt for the truth. *I'm not sure.*

"The fog grew thicker. I couldn't make out the black car anymore. I shouted at her to pull over, told her I would drive—I was scared sober by then. But she—like always—paid my words no attention. I wanted to grab the wheel, but I was afraid that would cause an accident for sure.

"When the bend in the freeway came up, she sailed into it without hesitation, as though it were the route she had intended to take all along. I think she was smiling."

17

All day she has been packing her mother's things, going through the bedroom closet, surprised at how little there is: a handful of T-shirts, two pairs of jeans, sweatpants for garden work, three cardigans, a stack of saris, some silver bangles. Surely there were other things her mother wore. She recalls a pink kurta embroidered with chickan work, a gold locket with a red stone embedded in the center. Where did they go? And the photographs. Surely there were family outings to the zoo, to Golden Gate Park, a boat trip on the bay. She remembers posing with her mother, arms around each other, the toothy smiles they'd later joke about. She remembers her father sneaking up on them with the camera and catching them with their mouths full of cotton candy. She throws a suspicious glance toward the bed, where he slumps against the headboard as though he could never have been that man. He's rustling the newspaper, pretending to read, but really he's watching the small, sad stacks she's placing in cardboard boxes and labeling for the folks from St. Vincent de Paul to pick up. Should she believe the story he told about the black car? The skin of his arm, chafed by the edge of the cast, looks pale and dry. She should massage some lotion into it, but she can't bear the thought of contact. She hadn't consulted him before she decided to clear the closets. She feels guilty about that for a moment, then pushes the feeling away. He isn't in charge, she tells herself with a new cruelty. Not that he ever was. Besides, these things are not her mother. There is no point in keeping them.

She goes through the kitchen drawers, unearthing old recipes, unused garden gloves, several pairs of embroidery scissors, a silk shawl. From the garage she removes shoes, raincoats, a box of expired coupons. She lifts out, from the bathroom cabinet, toothbrush, comb, hydrating lotion, mascara, concealer, glitter. (Glitter? Her mother?) She considers the bookshelf. Her mother loved reading books about distant places—Machu Picchu, the Andamans, the Antarctic—though she never expressed a desire to travel to any of them. She touches their spines lightly, trying to imagine what went through her mother's mind as she turned their pages. How defenseless things become when their owner is gone! She leaves the books alone, at least for now.

She has saved the sewing room for last, partly from a reluctance to intrude on her mother's private space, partly from a hope that here, perhaps, she will find a clue to the mystery of who her mother was. (Is it excessive, this hankering inside her? Her mother would have had little patience with it. Ridiculous! she would have said, with some asperity. Didn't you live with me for eighteen years? What more can there be to know?)

When she opens the door, the room smells of cinnamon peel. But then she takes another, deeper breath, and there's no smell. Did she only imagine the spice odor? She's losing faith in her senses, their ability to evaluate accurately the world around her.

When she slides open the closet door, she notices that her hand is trembling.

Inside the closet it is disappointingly ordinary. Extra quilts, old clothes, rags for housecleaning. Catalogs for ordering seeds. But she remembers a time when she sifted through such quotidian items to find a box—what had been in it? Vials? She delves into the sad smell of unused things, things that suspect they'll never be needed again. No box, no vials, but in the back under a pile of bank statements she comes across a framed photograph of herself and Sonny at their wedding.

In the photo they're standing outside the Hindu temple, he in a maroon turban spangled with gold, she in a green wedding Benarasi with a too large bindi on her forehead. They hold hands shyly, looking very young and very pleased with themselves. Grasping the photo, she lowers herself heavily onto the carpet, onto the spot where her mother spent so many unaccounted-for nights, and finds herself thinking of how much she hates caviar.

The caviar she is thinking of had been heaped in neat dark mounds over bread triangles and arranged on a silver tray. This tray was the first thing she noticed when the door opened, after Sonny had rung the bell several times and finally resorted to pounding. The tray bobbed up and down in the loud dimness of a hall crammed with bodies, moving toward her unsteadily, a drunken moon complete with craters. When her eyes got used to the dimness, she saw that it was carried by a pretty woman with dark hair. The woman wore a frilly white maid's cap and apron, but Rakhi could tell she was no maid, even before she turned away and Rakhi saw that all she was wearing underneath was a black string bikini. That would come later, though. Right now the woman was smiling and holding out the tray, arms extended, the tray trembling slightly, until Rakhi felt compelled to take a piece even though she didn't want to. And knew—even before they'd pushed their way into another, louder room in their effort to locate the host, a room filled with sweat and frenetic movement and surprisingly good music—that Sonny had been right. She shouldn't have come.

The host, whom they finally found in a corner sharing a joint with two women, owned the nightclub where Sonny worked. He was large, affable, and very loud.

"Hey, Sonny, my main man," he bellowed, handing the roach to one of the women and hugging Rakhi's husband energetically. "Great you could make it! Like the sounds? Maybe you'll spin some for us later, what d'you say? And who's this lovely lady? New girlfriend? Oh, your wife, right, right. Delighted to meet you!" He lunged at her, arms open in hug-stance. When she quickly retreated behind Sonny, he looked startled, then laughed. "Enjoy the party!" he said with a malicious bow.

Then they were at the bar, where Sonny got her a glass of wine and a whiskey sour for himself. She was still holding the piece of bread. It made her feel foolish, so she put it into her mouth. The black, congealed mass slid along her palate, making her nauseous. If she'd had a napkin, she would have spat it out. Later she thought she should have spit it out anyway. Just as she should have grabbed Sonny's arm before he could order a second drink and asked him to take her home, or at least to give her the car keys. He could have caught a ride with someone else. It would have been easy enough; he seemed to know everyone there, and judging by their enthusiastic greetings, every one of them would have been delighted to take him back—to his home or theirs. But she was worried about appearing rude, leaving so soon. Would his boss be offended? Would he take it out on Sonny, who'd just been hired on as the new weekend DJ?

And Sonny was having such a good time. She could see how he loved this crowd. (Why? They didn't appear particularly lovable to her. Their pale faces, lit jaggedly in green and blue by the pulsing lights, seemed at once sly and exhausted with the effort of having a good time.) She watched him backslap and high-five and cheek-kiss his way across the room, smiling with genuine pleasure. She didn't want to dampen that smile.

He'd mentioned the party—he was always meticulous about letting her know where he'd be—but he hadn't asked her to come with him. He was doing that more and more nowadays, going out alone while she stayed home with the baby.

It's part of my job, he told her. That's how I make contacts, get more gigs.

What nonsense, he said when she told him he was moving away from her. I love you just as much.

When she insisted on going with him this time, he didn't say no. But he hesitated.

I don't think it's quite your scene, Riks. I'm not sure you can handle it.

I'm a big girl, Sonny. I can handle more than you think.

There was that also. She didn't want to admit that she'd been wrong.

So she waited awhile, and then it was too late.

She places the photograph carefully on the carpet, as though it were covered with something more fragile than glass, and continues her search. Boxes of old bills. She would never have guessed her mother to be the kind of person who saves old bills. Skeins of embroidery thread to go with the scissors she found earlier. Cartons of videos, *Sesame Street* rubbing shoulders with *Abs of Steel in 30 Days*. (Had her mother wanted abs of steel? Had she spent hours on the worn carpet in front of the TV doing leg lifts and crunches to the rhythm of the instructor's nasal commands?)

It is only when she has given up hope that she finds the journals, tied together with a blue satin hair ribbon.

All the air has been sucked out of the room. She kneels in the resulting vacuum, head pounding, to undo the bowknot. A rolling sound, like a giant stone door being pushed open. Or closing. She's not sure if it's in this world, or somewhere else. (Is there a somewhere else? The seesaw of her life balances on that possibility.) She opens the first book, the second, then all of them, riffling pages, tearing a few in her haste, her frustration. They are filled with her mother's writing, the words in an alphabet she doesn't know how to read.

The party had grown louder, more crowded, and she had lost Sonny. She felt panic, dry and scaly, slither through her body.

Don't overreact! she scolded herself. You haven't really lost him—you just can't see where he is. She tightened her sweating palms into fists and followed the music to another room. Tubes of black light lent her skin a ghostly sheen. Bodies gyrated wildly, slamming into each other. A man smiled at her, his teeth glowing like neon. His skin, too—he wasn't wearing a shirt. He grabbed at her and tried to pull her onto the dance floor. She put her hands on his damp chest and pushed so hard that he went staggering across the room. *Bitch!* she heard him yell. She elbowed her way through the dancers to the turntables. Sonny was playing. Three records spun simultaneously, a fast Western song and, under it, a sound like waves, then some other music. Once she'd seen a group of Tibetan men in the subway, playing instruments that looked like long wooden trumpets. Was it that she was hearing? Sonny wore earphones. His head moved to the beat, a small, bobbing movement, and his eyes were far away. He didn't hear when she called his name.

She lies on her side, her back to the door of the sewing room, holding one of the journals. She isn't crying, though she wants to. Perhaps she has forgotten how. To get this close, this close. She hears her father's footsteps coming up the stairs. Since the accident, he moves lumberingly, lurching a little to the left, though there's no medical reason for it. She hears his footsteps pause outside the door. She hears him call her name. She holds her breath and wills him away.

. . .

She pushed her way back across the dance floor. She must have drunk the wine at some point—the wineglass was no longer in her hand. She was holding another kind of glass. It, too, was empty. Who had given it to her? What had been in it? Where was her purse? The air was blue with smoke and fear. She saw a door opening onto a balcony. Maybe if she could get there, she could breathe. But the balcony was full of couples. There were threesomes, too. The moon was pocked and concave. A man and a woman stopped touching each other and turned to her. Wanna join us sweetheart?

But the footsteps don't resume their usual shuffle toward the bedroom, the bed that is his, entirely and forever. He calls her name again, his voice rising a little on the last syllable, as though it were a question. Then he opens the door.

Without turning she says, "Please go away."

"I can't," he says. "You need to talk to someone."

Not to you, she thinks.

"I know you don't want to talk to me," he says.

If I wait long enough. If I wait long enough without making a single sound or movement, he'll go. He has to.

"You didn't eat anything all day," he says. "Here, I made up a plate for you." He advances into the room.

Don't come in here, into her space.

"I think maybe you should go back to Berkeley," he says. "I can manage on my own now. Being here is not good for you. It's making you more depressed."

Jesus. My mother's dead. I have the right to be more depressed.

"She wouldn't want you to be this way," he says.

What the fuck do you know about what she'd want? What the fuck does either of us know?

"You probably wish I had died instead of your mother," he says. "I do, too."

She's shocked into looking at him. She hadn't thought he'd know. Wily old jackal. Or maybe it's just her, being naïve, like Sonny had said when she'd tried to speak to him about what happened to her at the party.

Her father smiles, if you can call something that sad a smile. "But I didn't die, and we both have to accept that—and deal with it." He takes another step toward her. She can feel the uncertain heaviness of his tread. A board creaks.

"You found her journals," he says.

She was back inside the house of smoke and music. She wasn't sure how much time had passed. The night was a blur, filled with things she didn't remember, or had forced herself to forget. Her lips felt swollen, as though someone had kissed them roughly. Her throat burned. She was in a narrow passageway. She had found her purse. It seemed very heavy, dangling from the crook of her elbow. Had someone put something in it? It was too dim in the passageway to see.

The music had changed. African drums, and a woman keening in Irish. It was interesting, but it wasn't Sonny's.

Now she was in a long, narrow room filled with silk cushions. People were sitting around a low, lacquered table. There was a mirror, lines of white dust. She knew what that meant. Sonny looked up at her. His eyes were red, like a night animal's. But how would she have known that, in this room lit only by candles? Hi sweetheart come on in.

She isn't sure which of the following actually happened, and in which order: She rushed at him, shouting. Hands pulled her down before she got far. Whoa sweetheart, here's something to calm you down. She hit him, sending the white dust flying. Arms wouldn't let her go. There were lips. Fingers on the buttons of her dress. She could feel each silk thread separately on her skin before it slid off. Later she would find a long scratch along the underside of her arm, crusted with dried blood. He offered her the mirror. She took it and lowered her face to it, because what else was there to do. Someone pulled her down on a cushion. There were hands everywhere. She cried out, Sonny, Sonny, help me, but he was busy smiling at someone else. Someone led her out of the room. Someone called a taxi. She was laughing. She was crying. She was very, very thirsty. She drank what someone put into her hand. She put her hand into Sonny's pants pocket and found the car keys. She drove home, careful not to speed, flexing her legs to keep them from cramping. She didn't throw up until she was parked in the driveway. She remembered to be thankful that Jona was staying with her mother. The only fact she's sure of is this: at some point that night, she looked up at the sky. It was empty, the moon had been eaten up. She knew then that she had to leave him.

Her father bends, strokes the cover of a notebook as though it were a face. "I can help you read them," he says. The words hang in front of her, gossamer-winged as a fishing lure. "If you want."

18

FROM THE
DREAM JOURNALS

Lesson 62: The Tale of
Neehar the Unfortunate (An Excerpt)

. . . and the elders saw that in Neehar the gift was strong, stronger than they had seen in their lifetime. Her body glowed with it, as if formed of phosphor, and there was distance in her eye, as though she were looking into the vastness of time. This made them afraid, for they knew the stories of other such gifted women, and what had become of them. They held a council and decided that they would share with Neehar the first nine levels of skill but keep from her the tenth and most powerful. It did no good. When Neehar dreamed, all secrets were laid open before her, even secrets that the elders themselves did not know. Thus Neehar grew stronger than the leaders of the council, but she was young and willful, and did not know how to use her power.

When the training of the novices was ended, the elders, in a last attempt to save Neehar, asked her to remain with them in the caves and become a teacher. They promised that with time she would be given the leadership of the council. But to Neehar a life among old women in the depths of a mountain's fastness seemed small and suffocating. The power that burned in her was restless to be known. It called to her to taste of the world and all that lay in it. She left the caves, but unlike her sister novices she did not settle in a town, as was the custom, and tend to its inhabitants. Instead she traveled through the land, reading the dreams of all who asked her. Though she had been warned that dream tellers must be secret in the practice of their craft, she scorned such caution.

In full sight of the crowds that gathered wherever she went, she would place her hands on the temples of those that came to be helped, and tell them the meaning of their dreams. There was no dream so complex that she could not unravel it, no problem so deep that she did not have its solution. It is said that each day she saved a thousand lives and reputations, predicted victory and good fortune, gave hope to the despairing, and warned the luckless of disasters that lay in wait. But in the trance of seeing, with a care for nothing but the truth, she often spoke aloud of things that should have been whispered into the dreamers' ears. Thus families were sundered, allies turned into enemies, and men and women in shame left their homes and were never seen again. In this way she angered many, though none dared to harm her, for it was believed that she had spirit protectors. People claimed to have seen a great gray wolf following her as she left one village at dusk for another, and some said that when she rested at midday, an eagle spread its wings above her head to shield her from the sun.

A year passed, or a decade. Neehar the Unfortunate told more dreams, and more, working day and night without pause, for the power that burned in her had taken control and was not willing to sheathe itself. She grew gaunt and hollow-cheeked, and her eyes, sunken in their pits, glowed like coals. She became known as Neehar the Ember-eyed, and men grew afraid to approach her. But this did not matter to Neehar. By now she could look at a person's forehead and tell if he had a dream worth reading. If he did, she told it to him whether he wished it or not. News of her doings traveled to the caves, and the elders sent a message reprimanding her for flouting the laws of dream telling and ordering her to come back. But Neehar did not obey. Perhaps it was no longer in her power to return.

It was in this time that Neehar began to read the dreams of the dead. Perhaps she did so because she had read the dreams of all the living who resided east of the river Kaveri. (Strangely, she who had broken so many laws observed this one ordinance: that dream tellers should not cross water.) Or perhaps the dead, with their brains cooled and stiffening and their eyes sealed, presented a challenge she could not resist. She went from home to grieving home and kissed the newly dead on their foreheads, or sat with their heads in her lap, not caring if relatives protested against her coming. People who had the ability to see such things said that a current of white would leap from the forehead of the corpse to her forehead. After a time she would open her eyes with a sigh and say, "Ah, so it is." But she never spoke of what she saw.

Only once, at the home of a mother grieving for her drowned baby, she touched the young woman on the cheek and said, "See, there is no need to weep." The woman grew quiet and dried her tears, but later, when asked what she had seen, she could only remember a sweet scent, as of lotus flowers.

Then news came to Neehar that the great saint Vishnu-pada

had announced that he was about to leave his mortal embodiment. She went to his ashram, where all his disciples were gathered, and asked the ascetic if she could touch him as he died. Vishnu-pada looked at her with compassion and said, "Child, the secret that you seek is not to be known this way. It is only by looking inward that you will find it." But he gave her permission.

It is said that when Vishnu-pada died, Neehar sat at his head, her fingers touching his skull. And when his spirit left his body, it passed through Neehar and exited from her head in the form of a shaft of lightning. Neehar fell to the ground, and for three days she remained unconscious. When she came to, she no longer spoke, though she laughed or cried often. Some said that the shock of such a powerful spirit passing through her frame had driven her mad. But others claimed that the light in her eyes was one of serenity. Be that as it may, from that moment onward, Neehar the Unfortunate did not tell a single dream. She sat by the Kaveri for days without moving, staring at the water. If the villagers brought food, she ate sometimes, but often she left it untouched. It seemed that she no longer needed such sustenance. When she disappeared—some say it was a few weeks later, some say it was years . . .

Questions:

1. What did you learn from the story of Neehar that might help you in your work as dream interpreter?

2. Why is she called "Unfortunate"? Do you agree that she was indeed so?

3. What is it that Neehar was searching for? What is it that you are searching for?

19

Rakhi

We're crossing the San Rafael Bridge in Sonny's silver BMW, Sonny, myself, Jona and my mother, heading toward the Marin Headlands. Sonny is driving. Jona sits in the back, looking out at the bay and humming, under her breath, that song again, those words I don't understand. My mother is in the back seat, too, Jona's arm looped around her burial urn. The urn is wrapped in a towel because Sonny says it is illegal to scatter ashes on state property. I am occupying, reluctantly, the front passenger seat, where Jona has insisted I sit. ("Only adults are allowed to be up there, Mom. It has an air bag," she stated virtuously. But I suspect she has a more devious motive.)

When Sonny and I were still married, whenever we drove somewhere, Jona made us place her car seat so that she could see us both. From her vantage point in the back she would instruct us from time to time, a small, insistent Cupid. *Mom, hold Dad's hand. Dad, kiss Mom.* I wonder now if it was anxiety that drove her, if she sensed something that I didn't know yet. Can children smell trouble the way animals do? An earthquake about to happen, tectonic plates getting ready to separate? *Mom, move closer and put your head on Dad's shoulder.* I feel the old words hanging between us like unfinished business, though they shouldn't. Our business was finished long ago, and this isn't even the same car. Sonny must have bought it recently. I wonder what happened to his Viper, about which we used to fight from time to time. (I felt that his refusal to trade it in for a "family car" was symbolic of his reluctance to be a family man.) Maybe he's kept that, too, Sonny-the-chameleon, who can be anything he wants. But I'm not about to ask. He wants to waste his money, it's none of my business.

According to Jona, my mother is not inside the urn but sitting on the back seat beside her. She adds that her grandmother has described to her exactly where she wants her ashes scattered. She trusts Jona to do it right, but she wants to come along for fun.

I wasn't going to encourage Jona by commenting on any of this, but Sonny asks, "Can you see her?"

"I don't need to," Jona says with disdain. "I know what she looks like."

The urn is surprisingly small, surprisingly heavy, made of a dark metal I don't recognize. It clinks when we move it. Those are the teeth, Jona states. She speaks with a calmness that I find admirable and gruesome.

Jona cried for her grandmother continuously for the first few days after the accident, then stopped all of a sudden. She says my mother has told her not to waste energy on such an unprofitable activity. I refuse to believe her, though it sounds like the kind of thing my mother would say. Am I jealous that my mother would choose to appear to my daughter and not to me? Jona says that her grandmother is going to stay near her for seventy-seven days; then she has to go. She says each day her grandmother teaches her one wise thing.

My father is not with us. I'd been sure he'd want to come. I'd dreaded the thought of having to drive him from Fremont to Sonny's house. In a car, there's no place you can escape to. In a few minutes, you could be suffocated by conversation.

I've resumed speaking to my father because he's translating the journals. A payment of sorts. But our talks are painful, stuttery, like learning to walk after your bones have been broken. The journal he's started on—we think it's the earliest one, because the cover is worn, falling apart. But we have no way of knowing. The books are not dated, and the entries, he tells me, meander from subject to subject. The one piece he's translated so far, a list of meanings for things you might dream of, made little sense to me. I was disappointed there wasn't anything personal about my mother in it. My disappointment made me suspicious. I wondered if my father was leaving out things he didn't want me to know.

When I asked my father if he wanted to accompany us, he said he'd rather not. I should have been relieved; instead, I was angry. Why not? I asked. He said scattering ashes was too final; he wasn't ready for it. I walked out of the room in the middle of his sentence. I wanted to slam the door but I didn't because I needed him—and hated the fact that I did.

We drive through the Marin Headlands. The late afternoon is beautiful in that foggy, Northern California way, budded poppies appearing suddenly through mist like orange periods. We pull into a couple of empty parking areas close to the cliff edge, but each time Jona shakes her head. I'm about to make a sharp, motherlike remark when she yells excitedly at us to stop. Sonny parks the car illegally on a narrow embankment and we scramble up the scrubby hillside, heads lowered against a strong wind that has started up. At the cliff edge, the ground falls away dizzyingly. Below, the Pacific hurls itself against black, gleaming rocks. My eyes are drawn to the sloping red cables of the Golden Gate Bridge, and beyond it, to the silver city, glowing against the day's late grayness. If I'd died, I, too, would want my remains to become part of this land, this water, because there's a way in which the geography of one's childhood makes its way into one's bones.

Then I think, perhaps this is how my mother felt about the landscape in which she grew into girl, woman, dream decipherer. Would she have wanted us to take her ashes there?

I don't even know where she was born.

Jona unscrews the lid of the urn and throws out the first handful. Sonny follows. There are tears in his eyes. I'm surprised and envious. When I'd left him, he'd shouted and threatened, begged and sulked. But he hadn't cried. What had my mother meant to him that he should cry now? And stitched into that, another question: what did my mother mean to me that I cannot?

Then it's my turn. Gingerly, I put in my hand and touch the rough, gritty dust. I can't stop a small shiver from going through me. Less than a month ago, she had cupped my face in her hands and told me how beautiful I looked. Lives and cars—how quickly they can flip over.

I throw the handful of ashes out as far as I can, but the wind blows most of it back at my face. Dust in my nostrils, making me cough. At least now some of her is in me.

.   .   .

We drive back to Oakland in silence. Jona has fallen asleep in the back seat. I feel drained, though when I try to figure out why, I come up only with unsatisfying clichés. Sonny stares ahead into the dusk, chewing on his lower lip, an old habit. Hosts of unspoken longings hang in the air, invisible as stars in daytime. I can't quite grasp them, can't say, *This is what I want for my life.* In the driveway, he invites me to stay and have dinner with them, but I say no. I start toward my old Taurus, waiting in the driveway, then hear footsteps running behind. Jona catches hold of my sleeve. Mom, she says, I want you to see my paintings.

I haven't been inside the house—his house now—since the night I left, carrying her in my arms. To anyone else I would have said no. She tows me behind her like a rudderless boat. There are dried streaks of tears on her cheeks. Who has she been crying for?

This is the only house I ever loved.

There's something I want to show you, Sonny had said as he drove very fast along the temperamental roads that lead into the Oakland hills. But you have to close your eyes.

What are you up to now, you crazy man? I'd said, laughing. But I did as he said. We liked playing such games then.

When I opened my eyes, the house was in front of me, like a woman kneeling with her arms open. There was a weathered wooden gate with a metal bell hanging from it that you had to ring. When you entered the courtyard, you smelled sage and lavender. Moss, cobblestones and a front door with a small stained glass window set in it. You could open the window from inside to see who had come to visit.

I fell in love even before I walked in and saw the scarred rafters, the large window through which San Francisco glittered on the northwest horizon, the wisteria draping the balcony. Living beside the interstate in Fremont, I'd never believed that houses like this existed. No. What I hadn't believed was that people like me could live in them.

Sonny smiled when he saw my face.

It's yours if you want it.

You're joking, I said. We can't afford a place like this.

Don't worry about it, Riks, he said, and kissed me.

I let the kiss enchant me, I let the house wrap me in its charm. I had questions, but I told myself they weren't important. I obeyed him and made myself forget. All these mistakes I made on that day, which I believed to be the happiest in my life.

I walk up the staircase to Jona's room, a tiny doll's house of a room with a window ledge wide enough for a mattress. I had it built so she could wake to a view of bridge and water, could fall asleep to the sun setting over the Pacific. I put in the skylight above the bed so she could look up at the redwood tree that spreads its branches over the roof. I put in—but enough of that! It isn't my house anymore. What use to remember the care I'd lavished on it?

On the paneled wall are Jona's new paintings, the ones she's done since my mother died. They all depict fires. Some are simple wood fires; others show homes burning. Still others show birds with women's faces diving into flames. One is a painting of the earth glowing like a coal, chunks of it breaking and flying off like meteors.

They scare me.

"What do they mean?" I ask. "Why did you draw them?"

She shrugs. "Just wanted to. Do you like the colors?"

I do like the colors. Lemons and purples and greens—not what you'd expect of a fire, but when you see them, you know they're perfect. She has true talent, my daughter. I tell her that.

I wonder what Sonny makes of the paintings. Does he think (as I do) that they're her efforts to come to terms with my mother's death, that body she is descended from, burned to ash?

At least she isn't drawing any more pictures of Eliana. I guess I should be thankful for that.

I come downstairs to find the table carefully laid for dinner: a real tablecloth, blue willow–pattern china, a vase of lilies, covered dishes. In spite of myself, I'm touched. I can't remember the last time someone decorated a table with such care just for me. It would be churlish to leave now. Besides, I owe Sonny. He's been unusually considerate since my mother's death, taking care of Jona, bringing her over to Fremont to see her grandfather every other day, helping me handle the complicated paperwork that accompanies tragedy. I don't know what to make of it. Maybe he's still in shock.

We sit down. Sonny uncovers each dish with a flourish. A grated-carrot salad seasoned with cilantro and lemon juice, a rice-and-chicken-kurma casserole. Jona carries in glasses of mango juice. I stare at the dishes, which look surprisingly good—and suspiciously familiar. I hadn't known Sonny's repertoire extended past hamburgers.

"I fixed them this morning," he says. He looks almost shy as he waits for me to take my first bite.

As soon as I do, I know.

"They're my mother's recipes!" I glare at him. "How did you get them?"

"I asked her." Seeing my face, he adds, apologetically, "Just a few simple ones—"

I'm so angry I could explode. "You had no business asking her for them!" My anger is really aimed at my mother. How could she betray me like this? If anyone has a right to those recipes, it's me! How could she give them to him—to *him*, Sonny-my-rival, whose favorite recreational activity is ruining my life? "You never even set foot in the kitchen all those years I was married to you," I say bitterly.

"People change," he says. "Why do you have such a hard time accepting that?"

"You haven't changed! You always tried to worm your way into my mother's good books, to win her over to your side, to—"

Anger flushes Sonny's face. "That's the real problem, isn't it? You can't stand the fact that your mother loved me. You never could. You've always wanted to control everyone in your life, what they do, how they think, who they love. That's why you left me—because I wouldn't let you control my whole existence."

I draw in an outraged breath. "That is such a lie—" But then I see Jona watching us, her eyes moving from face to face, her forehead furrowed with anxiety. Her lower lip trembles. I control myself and push my chair back.

I'm exhausted, I say, addressing myself carefully to Jona. I have to get back to Fremont.

"You shouldn't drive if you're exhausted," Jona says, pronouncing the word carefully. "Why don't you stay here? You can sleep in my room." She looks from me to Sonny. "You don't have to talk to Sonny if you don't want to," she adds.

Sonny holds up his hands in truce, his eyes amused. "Jona's right. You shouldn't be driving. Exhaustion and temper, that's a bad combination. Stay over. I promise I'll stay out of your way."

That's the other thing about him that used to drive me insane. He'd be livid with anger one moment, creating the biggest scene, making me furious as well—and the next moment he'd act like nothing had happened. The worst part was, he expected me to snap out of my bad mood (the bad mood *he'd* put me in) equally rapidly.

Well, it didn't happen then, and it isn't going to happen now.

"No, thanks," I snap. Suddenly I *am* exhausted—and irritated with them both. I want them to leave me alone to sort through my confusions. I grab my purse and start for the door.

They abandon their half-eaten dinners and follow me, identical worried expressions on their faces.

"Mommy, be careful," Jona says in a small voice. I can tell she's thinking of that other night drive, the one that changed all our lives.

Suddenly contrite, I kneel down and give her a hug, feeling the fear in her shoulder bones.

"I will," I say. "I'll be very careful."

And I am. It is foggy tonight, too. The freeway lights have yellow aureoles around them. Cars loom up and fade away like sharks in cloudy water. Luckily, there isn't much traffic. I'm on 880 south, an ugly freeway if ever there was one, but straight as a gash. In thirty nondescript minutes, I should be in my father's house.

I'm still stewing over the fact that by having her recipes Sonny now possesses a part of my elusive mother, leaving even less for me. To console myself, I think of the journal, something I'm determined Sonny-the-snooper will never lay his eyes on. I hope my father has finished translating another entry by now. He's slow. He tells me it's because they're more complicated than they appear to be, that they use a lot of archaic Bengali words that he has to struggle with.

I looked over his shoulder at the journal once as he turned the pages. The entries were fairly short. Written in my mother's neat, looped handwriting, they didn't seem complicated or archaic. Maybe he was exaggerating so I'd be more grateful.

"What are they about?" I asked, wishing I could read them without his mediation.

"A lot of different things," he said. "Lessons, stories from old books, famous dreams, clients, people she knew."

"Isn't there anything about herself," I asked, "about her own life?"

"Don't you understand?" he said, craning his neck to look at me. "That's what they're all about."

$\mathcal{I}$ feel its appraoch before I see it—like a heavy-metal vibration, an earthquake gathering its forces underground. I'm expecting a truck, one of those monster semis that are always jackknifing across lanes, spilling chemicals, holding up traffic for hours. But the car, when it appears, is slim and black, an ebony arrow whizzing past me. And though it looks nothing like the vehicle my father described, suddenly I'm certain it's the one my mother followed into the end of her life. I'm not able to see who's driving before fog shrouds it, but I catch a glimpse of the license plate. EMIT MAERD, it says, and then I'm left with the red pinpricks of taillights, fast receding into gray.

Am I going crazy, or is the world? Or maybe it's a dream I'm inhabiting, a déjà vu dream I've pulled up from somewhere. Once I heard my mother say that each of us lives in a separate universe, one we have dreamed into being. We love people when their dream coincides with ours, the way two cutout designs laid one on top of the other might match. But dream worlds are not static like cutouts; sooner or later they change shape, leading to misunderstanding, loneliness and loss of love.

I've known for a long time about dream worlds that don't match. But tonight, for the first time in my life, I'm having a coinciding dream. Somehow I've entered my mother's world. I must stay in it as long as I can.

I don't know when I speeded up, but I find I'm going fast—faster than my old Taurus is accustomed to. The car shudders in protest, but I can't afford to slow down. I've got to keep the black car in view. I've got to see who the driver is. (Was there a moment's gleam of white in that dark interior?) I'm not sure what I'm hoping for, if and when I catch up with him. If I make him stop. Answers?

I'm not even sure about the questions.

The black car changes lanes without warning, moving to the extreme right. At the last minute I realize that it's getting onto Highway 92. I swing after it, almost hitting a somnolent U-Hauler who honks furiously. My heart is thudding. I haven't traveled in this direction for some years, but I recall that the highway goes over the San Mateo Bridge and continues all the way to the Pacific. In the coastal hills it will turn into a dark, winding two-laner edged by treacherous drops. I should stop this ridiculous car chase and go back to my father's house. But I know I won't.

20

She approaches the bridge. On the other side of the tollbooth the fog is thick as sludge, but she has no time to worry about this because the black car is going through the permits-only lane. She follows even though she doesn't have a permit, even though she's always been the most law-abiding of drivers. (Will they take away her license? Will they make her do community service? But a part of her loves this recklessness.) Then she's in the slushy fog, navigating by feel, unable to see the railings that must be sweeping by her, dangerously close. Surely she will lose the black car now. But no, she sees the taillights only a little ways ahead. EMIT, she reads in relief and some puzzlement. Has he slowed down on purpose?

Along the flat, unending length of the bridge, so close to the water that she can hear the fat whisper of waves. Balanced on the highest point of the arc, where for a moment the fog parts and shows her the city, glowing as though on fire. But it is not a metaphor. She sees flames licking the TransAmerica tower. Can the dampness of fog warp itself into mirage, as desert heat does? The curtain falls, folding into it what she saw.

The black car is leaving the bridge, leaving the freeway. Here? In the heart of suburban Foster City, onto a road marked

Fashion Island, deserted because all fashionistas are in bed now? The signal light ahead turns red. The brake lights of the car wink three times in rapid succession, as though the driver is sending her a message. Then it roars into the intersection so fast that she realizes the driver has been playing with her all this while. It makes a fluid left turn and is gone.

She goes through the red light, too, amazed at how easy it is to keep breaking rules once you've started. Amazed at the jolt of excitement it sends through her. Was this how Sonny felt, and his friends, when—? She forgets the question halfway because she's looking down a long one-way road with no offshoots and no vehicle ahead of her.

Where could the black car have gone?

She drives down the narrow road. There's nothing else she can do, no place to turn. The lane is lined with buildings that look like warehouses. Through the closed windows of her car she smells salt, fish, rancid oil. Ahead, piers jut into water, cranes raise their rusted arms like prophets who have outlived their day. But there shouldn't be a port here, she knows there shouldn't. The streetlights are few and cocooned in fog. She waits for them to emerge and fly away. She drives onto a dock, turns off the engine. Water slaps hard at the pylons, a sound an angry parent might make. She thinks of how her mother (whose face grows indistinct in her mind) was never angry with her, not even when she failed and failed. Is it true, what Sonny accused her of, that she wanted to control her mother's life, whom she gave her attention to, whom she loved? She puts her head down on the steering wheel, squeezes shut her eyes as tightly as she can, grinds in with the knuckles. Perhaps pain will bring the tears that otherwise refuse to oblige her.

But no tears come. Only shooting stars, and her mother's voice, very clear, saying, *I want you to become a fox*.

The day comes back to her in all its detail, instant and whole and vibrating, though all these years she had forgotten it the way sometimes, if we're lucky, we forget events that humiliated us. But now she sees herself: eight years old, gap-toothed, dressed in a pink top and faded jeans, sitting next to her mother on the couch. Her hair is tied in two braids, her top is machine-embroidered with blue flowers, courtesy of Kmart, where her mother, innocent of the intricacies of American haute couture, often shops. The top is one of Rakhi's favorites, though after this day she will ball it up and hide it in the bottom of her drawer until she can throw it into a Dumpster. Her mother turns toward her with a smile and says the words easily, as though it were just a game they were playing. The girl knows it is no game, but she isn't worried or nervous, not yet, because she's certain she can deliver whatever her mother asks for.

I want you to become a fox, her mother says, so that you can learn to dream what the fox dreams. It is good to start with foxes, because they are intelligent and suspicious, and so their dreams are not unlike ours. Then you may learn to dream like birds, and snakes, and fish, creatures that are far more complex than we are led to believe.

The girl waits for instructions, but the mother gives none. She watches the girl for a while, then gives a sigh. Look, she says. I will demonstrate.

The girl can see the stillness that takes over her mother's body. Only the tip of her nose has the slightest quiver in it. And her eyes: they've turned moist and flecked with brown. In the light from the windows they shine like iridescent marbles. The girl waits for more: a musky smell, the reddening of hair. It doesn't happen. But it doesn't need to, because she can see that her mother has gone somewhere else. Even though her eyes are open, the girl knows that if she waved her hand in front of their beautiful opaqueness, her mother wouldn't blink. The girl begins to cry. She feels panic cramping her knees, her fingertips. It is not because she doesn't know where her mother has gone or that she fears she might not return (these, too, she feels) but because she, Rakhi, cannot follow. It is her first introduction to failure, her first awareness of herself as a separate, lesser being.

Later she will recall these movements, but only faintly, like a photograph seen through discolored glass: turning the car, driving up the one-way street, going in the wrong direction. (She's broken more laws today than in her whole lifetime.) The freeway sign looms suddenly from the fog as though she were in an old *Twilight Zone* episode. If she looked back, would there be nothing behind her? She does not look. She holds the fox memory inside her as she drives across the bridge to the Fremont house, the fog lifting with each mile. The minutes stream past the car window like clues she's failed to understand. At the front door she fumbles, dropping the key twice because the porch light isn't turned on the way her mother would always keep it when she knew Rakhi was coming home.

At the end of the failed fox episode, her mother had taken her by the shoulders and kissed her on each cheek. *It's okay*, she had said. *It doesn't matter.* Rakhi had been angry at her mother's disin-genuousness because of course it mattered. But tonight she sees what her mother was really saying. *It doesn't matter because I love you just the same.* Could this apply to all the other ways in which she failed? As she walks in darkness up the stairs of her parents' house (balancing on the balls of her feet so as not to wake her father) she carries this understanding inside her like a newly received gift she hasn't opened yet.

Later she will wonder: Is this why the man in white appeared to her, to bring her something old, something new, a crumb of memory, a sliver of understanding? Little enough, when placed against the great, gaping mouth of her loss. Yet significant.

(But her father *is* awake. He does not move from the bed, but the whites of his eyes shine in refracted moonlight as he swivels his head. He can hear her move in the sowing room, bumping into things. He can hear her drop onto the makeshift bed she's made there on the floor, an ascetic's bed, just a pillow on the carpet, a thin blanket for cover. But she's no ascetic yet, he knows this even if she doesn't, his daughter with all kinds of wants bubbling up inside her. He would like to come to her, touch her shoulder to indicate he understands more than she thinks he does, though not as much, perhaps, as she needs him to. She's overcome by exhaustion, he can tell by the way she tosses and turns, trying to get comfortable. By the way she doesn't hear the small crackle of the paper he has placed on her pillow, the next translated entry from the journal, which he has titled "Beauty and the Beast.")

21

FROM THE
DREAM JOURNALS

I never thought I would marry. I knew it was not allowed. The first question that the gatekeeper asked us novices before we were allowed to enter the caves was whether we were willing to give up all thoughts of husbands. And lovers too, she'd added drily. Some of the girls hesitated and were sent back home. I had no hesitations.

How little I knew myself, to think that I would not desire human loving. To think that my longings would be always in my control.

The interpreters I saw did not appear unhappy. This made sense to me. What I had seen of wifehood made it seem a drudge's life—all day at the beck and call of in-laws, husband, children. Wives worked endlessly and without hope of praise, though if things went wrong, there was always plenty of blame. The invisible life of wives, the one carried out in darkness in closed bedrooms, I knew little about. From what the elders let fall from time to time, that was a drudgery too.

Be thankful of the lot you have chosen, the elders said. Your body will always be your own. No one will invade it except your dream spirits—and to be invaded by them is a blessing.

Looking back, I question what I did not question then. How would they—women without men—have known of the joys of the flesh, the giving that is also a gift received? How would they have known the body's craving to be invaded by another body like itself?

But perhaps they did know. Perhaps that is why they spoke as they did, over and over, in the hope of keeping us from going astray.

My aunt, my first teacher in the way of dreams, told me this: One life is too little to be divided between the outside world and the inner one, the world of daylight and that of shadow. She said, A man's kisses will suck your life force from you. You will have nothing left to offer the dream god. And if then the god in anger leaves you, you will spend the rest of your life bereft.

If you turn from your husband to preserve your gift, he will resent that, for he will know he is not foremost in your life. Husbands do not like to know that.

Either way, she said, it is a path that leads to bitterness. With all my heart I wish you would not take it. But she said it sadly, for by then I had made my decision.

In the spring of my last year as an apprentice, along with twenty-four others who were judged ready, I was taken to Calcutta.

It was a trip we had waited for all year, had whispered about in the dark of our sleeping quarters after lamps had been extinguished. Calcutta, home to ten million souls, a place full of newness, of news from the world. It was the total opposite of the sleepy calm of our caves, our life that seemed so distant from everything. And we—no more than girls—longed for change.

It was to be a trip to further our education. Calcutta was full of dreams: not only the ones being dreamed by its present inhabitants but old, interrupted ones that hung motionless over the sluggish brown Ganga and colored the night with their confusions. We were to be tested on how well we could pluck these disembodied dreams out of the air and interpret them.

Dreams, the elders said, continue to affect the waking life, even after the dreamers are gone. We were to examine the patterns of these old dreams and determine their effects on the city's future.

Picture this: twenty-four young women getting off the train at Howrah Station, an elder ahead of us and one behind. We did not wear uniforms because dream tellers do not believe in external marks. Still, surely onlookers would have known that there was something about us that bound us together—a certain inward look, as though we were always searching, and unsatisfied.

But on this day we didn't look inward. Giddy with excitement, we ran from one end of the station to the other, and called to each other in amazed voices: look at that, how about this one, can you believe! We ate the too sweet old-woman's-hair candy the vendors sold, and wondered at the seriousness on the city dwellers' faces. How could they be so sad when they lived among such diversions? One of the elders bought a kaleidoscope, and we took turns looking through the shiny tube at the bright and changing patterns that didn't have to mean anything.

The years pass, I forget much. But I remember our visit to Victoria Memorial. Huge white anachronism of marble and brass and foreign pride where no one had slept in many years—how out of place in a city where so many crowded into a single room, a single bed. Where so many slept on pavements, with only the sky for a quilt. But in this variegated world there is a place for everything, even vanity. So the memorial stood in a huge green space surrounded by fountains, and the black angel on its dome balanced on one pointed toe and looked down with regal uncaring on a city it had once ruled. We walked into the largest hall, our footsteps echoing and hollow, and stared. Thrones and plantation chairs, crowns, robes encrusted with gold. A globe with RULE BRITANNIA etched across the equator. Seals the color of sunset affixed to documents that took or gave away things that weren't the signer's to give or take. In an alcove were muskets, army uniforms in scarlet, boots. Cannonballs with plaques below them telling the names of battles. Standing there, I couldn't breathe. Smoke festered around my head, I could smell voices from ancient nightmares. Someone asked for water. Someone whispered hoarsely of treachery, gates opened from the inside. Someone gabbled a prayer to Shiva that was cut off halfway through a word. Someone lay in a puddle of blood and thought on a childhood forest, the dark green of mango trees and shal. Someone begged someone else to kill him quickly. The voices made me dizzy. For the first time in my life I knew what hatred was. What kind of people, I wondered, would preserve such a place and make an attraction out of it? I would have razed it to the ground ages ago.

I must have looked unlike myself, for one of the elders stared at me. Then she motioned me over to a lady's ball gown, yards and yards of ruffle ivoried with age, a whalebone corset. Touch it with your mind, she signed, and I did. Straightaway I was plunged into a bedroom, a dim four-poster with a canopy of net to keep out mosquitoes. I was afraid, for I was living in a strange country, one I'd never wanted to visit. I longed for the gentle, rolling hills of home, the familiarity of daisies and daffodils, not these overlush vines that coiled around my house like snakes. I could not tell my husband my fears; he had already told me that he expected me to be brave and noble, as was proper for an Englishwoman. If I could not possess those virtues, he'd instructed me, then I must pretend them. So I lay under his weight at night, stranger that he had become since arriving in this land, and pretended. I tried not to think of the morning, when I must face the servants and give them orders and see them smirking as they whispered to each other about me in their strange, sibilant language. When finally I fell asleep I dreamed of snakes with tongues of fire.

Later the elder whispered, There are many sides to history, are there not? Most of them are never heard, except by those who know how to recover dreams.

She said, It makes it harder to judge, does it not?

Inside myself, I heard the young woman scream as men in turbans broke into the compound. I saw the sun flash on their bayonets. Once, twice, three times. Then the pictures were gone.

I did not answer the elder. I was upset with her for having divided me into so many parts, each in conflict with the other. I walked out of the dead palace. The other apprentices were silent, too, and some wiped angrily at their eyes.

But outside was the last of a beautiful sunset, orange against the black palm trees. The electric lights came on in many colors, making the fountains shimmer like a fairy display. Ice-cream sellers sang out *pista kulfi chahiye, pista kulfi*. The other apprentices pushed the dreams into corners of their minds, to be analyzed later. They pressed around the elders, begging to be taken to the cinema, to a Chinese restaurant, to the shops in New Market that sold lipstick and scented powder.

But I refused to let go of my agitation. I turned my back on them and walked into the garden filled with the smell of pink roses, flowers that women from a distant land had planted in their homesickness. I wanted to hate, but the flowers would not let me. Their petals were so soft, so easily broken. I knelt among them, and they were like entreating fingers on my arms.

When I opened my eyes, he was watching me. He sat under a tree, leaning against its massive trunk, and there was an ease about him that intrigued me. Living among dream interpreters for three years, I had grown used to intensity.

When he spoke, it startled me because I was not used to being addressed by young men, and also because what he said was so unusual.

Would you like to hear a song about flowers? he asked.

I nodded, and he sang. I did not understand the words very well—they were in a language different from mine. I didn't care. I liked his voice, rich and unself-conscious even when he forgot words and hummed to fill in the gap. What I didn't understand, I imagined, and thus it became a love song.

When the song ended, I knew I should leave without speaking. Already by looking and listening, I had disobeyed. Now I broke a third rule.

Sing me another song, I said.

This time he sang in Bengali about a woman whose eyes were as dark as those of wild deer, and he looked into my own eyes as he sang so that I felt like that woman. I knew I would break more rules to keep feeling this way.

The elders found me soon after and led me away, chastising me all the while. The other novices stared at me in mingled horror and admiration. I had to remain in the hotel room as punishment while they went to the cinema. One of the elders stayed to watch over me. As we recited the twenty-nine cardinal tenets together, I thought I saw pity on her face. Perhaps, like many experienced tellers, she had the gift of future sight.

I could see the future, too, though I was not experienced. I knew that tomorrow when the group went to the Kali temple, I would slip away and go to the address the man had given me, to the little room he rented on someone's rooftop. I would wait there until he returned from work. A storm would begin, and we would make love on the night terrace in the rain. I was not afraid of this. I was prepared to follow him wherever his destiny led us. I wanted his destiny to become mine, too.

Ah, but there were things I did not see.

They found me, of course—the elders had their ways—and the next day when he was away at work they took me back by force to the caves. They brought me first to my aunt (but was she really my aunt? I had begun to suspect otherwise) so that she could convince me.

It isn't too late, she said. You can still return to us. I'll intercede with the council to take you back, even though you are no longer a virgin. There are purification ceremonies. It is difficult, but it can be done. Come back, she said, or you'll regret your decision for the rest of your life.

But *regret* was just a sound without a meaning, buzzing like a fly in my ear. I was crazy with love, and I told her so.

How can you love someone you don't know? she asked in dismay.

I turned away, and though I had always respected my aunt, for a moment I felt contempt. What can a shriveled old woman teach me about love, I thought, about this dizzying excitement that runs through your body like electricity until you think you will die of pleasure?

But knowing what I know now, I would have answered her question in this way: Isn't not knowing the only way it is possible to love?

22

Rakhi

We're closing the store today.

Waking in the morning, I pulled the blanket over my head. A gesture from childhood, when I'd believed that if I remained in bed, hidden, I could escape from whatever unpleasantness hovered over the day. My mother would come and whisk the covers off me. My little ostrich, she said.

The difference between being a child and an adult: after a while, I throw off the blanket on my own. I roll up my bedding and place it in the closet, not exactly neatly but not untidily either. It's more than I would have done in my own apartment, an acknowledgment that it's my mother's space I'm inhabiting. In the bathroom I stare in the mirror, noticing new wrinkles, an age spot. I can hear my father puttering around in the kitchen downstairs. His cast came off the day before yesterday, and he's fixing his own breakfast. Good! The sooner he's able to take care of himself, the sooner I can get back to my own life.

My father calls up the stairs. Can he make me some scrambled eggs? No, I lie. I'm not hungry.

The real reasons:

1. I don't trust my father's scrambled eggs. In all the years of

living at home, I don't remember him fixing breakfast—or any other meal, for that matter. He did wash the dishes on the nights he was sober, but that scarcely qualifies as a skilled culinary activity.

As if to validate my thinking, there is a loud clang from the kitchen. Sounds like he dropped the pan. Maybe his hand isn't as strong as he thought it would be. I curb a pang, an urge to run down the stairs and sit him down and cook the eggs for him. He'll manage, I tell myself. If he dropped something, it'll do him good to bend over and pick it up. After all, that's what he'll have to do when I'm no longer with him.

2. I don't want to accept any favors from my father. I was forced to ask him to translate the journals; I didn't have a choice there. But I want to keep my debts as light as possible.

3. After reading the last entry he translated for me, I'm afraid I won't be able to stop myself from searching his face for the ruins of the young man my mother had loved so rashly. From asking, with my eyes, *What happened?*

When I come downstairs, I notice that he's set the table with two plates. The scrambled eggs, neatly piled into a serving bowl, look safe enough. He's also cut up some melon—my favorite fruit—and put out a loaf of French bread. If he dropped something, there's no sign of it on the kitchen floor.

"Have something," he says. "It's going to be a long day."

I give him a sharp look. I haven't told him about the store closing, haven't even told him how bad our finances are. I consider saying no again, but I'm suddenly hungry. And he's right: it'll probably be a long, hard day. I take several slices of melon, a wary spoonful of the eggs. They're surprisingly tasty. He pours us orange juice, his injured arm held at an awkward angle.

"How does it feel?" I ask.

"Better," he says, flexing gingerly.

"The eggs are good."

"Glad you like them. Can I give you some more?"

This is still the only kind of conversation I'm able to have with him, and he knows it. He must notice that since the accident I haven't called him *Dad*. Once in a while, when I've caught him unawares, I've seen the corner of his mouth pulled down with the weight of all the things he wants to say. But I'm not ready to unburden him.

I tell him I might be late coming back. He shouldn't wait up for me.

He follows me to the door, then says, "But I'm coming with you."

That's when I notice that he's wearing a clean pair of corduroys, a button-down shirt. He must have bathed early—his hair is damp, the comb markings clearly visible.

"No," I say. "I don't want you to." I speak slowly, as though to a child, trying to hold on to my temper. What makes him think he has the right to intrude like this into my life?

"Rakhi, it's going to be hard, closing down your store. Having someone there who cares for you may be a good thing."

"How did you know about us closing down?" My voice rises in spite of my efforts at calmness. "I don't recall discussing it with you."

"I overheard you talking to Belle. Maybe I can help—"

The words tumble out before I know it. "You've never helped me with anything in my entire life. And now you've started eavesdropping! Just because I'm forced to stay here with you doesn't give you the right to pry into my life like this."

He blinks as the words hit him. For a moment his lips move but no sounds emerge. Then he says, unevenly, "I didn't mean to pry. Maybe I shouldn't have listened. I did it because I worry about you. I always have. But until now your mother was there to take care of your problems. That's the way she wanted it, without any interference from me, so I let her. Maybe I should have insisted on doing more——. Well, it's too late to think about the past——"

I'm surprised, then suspicious. Easy for him to say that my mother's wishes kept him away from me. She isn't exactly here to deny it, is she?

"It is too late," I say. "And you're making me more late right now. So if you'll excuse me——"

I'm at the door when he says, "Rakhi, what's more important? Proving that you don't need me or not losing what you've worked so hard for all this time, your business—and maybe your daughter?"

I turn, stunned. How did he know my fears about Jona? And what else does he know?

"I can't guarantee that I'll be of any help, but at least let me try," he says.

I swallow what I'd been about to say—*If you really want to help, just take care of yourself so I don't have to be here*—and let him follow me into the car. What he said has hit me hard. Do I really have my priorities wrong, as he claims?

If my mother were alive, I would have consulted her, and she—always honest in such matters—would have told me. Now I must figure it out for myself. I chew on the inside of my cheek, thinking, as we drive to Berkeley in silence.

Belle is already at the store, dressed for hard labor in overalls and a sleeveless T-shirt, her hair bundled into a bandanna. But she isn't alone. Across the counter from her is a tall young Sikh, dressed in blue jeans and a traditional turban. At first I think he is a customer (an irony—we no longer have anything to offer customers), but then I see that they are arguing. Or, more accurately, Belle is holding forth while the young man listens. She gives my father and me a distracted wave as we enter but doesn't stop talking.

"I told you I don't want any of it. What am I going to do with it? What on earth were they thinking of, sending me this stuff! It'll all spoil. You'll just have to take it back."

Between them on the countertop there's a large box filled with packets and jars. I can also see produce: mustard greens, mulee, lauki squash. Her parents must have sent a care package.

"I told you," the young man says, "I've just come from Turlock, from visiting my folks. I'm not going there again until the end of the month." His accent, distinctly American, isn't what I'd expected. He must have been born here, like Belle and myself. I wonder at the turban—so many young Sikhs have chosen to dispense with it. It suits him, though, gives him a rugged, adventurous look.

"I don't care. Just take it away." Belle pushes the box at him. "I can't handle vegetable guilt on top of everything else today."

He raises a polite, inquiring eyebrow. "Vegetable guilt?"

"That's right. I don't know how to cook any of this—and my mom knows it. I can't figure out why she sent them—and right now, too, when I'm drowning in stress. Look at all these spices: cumin, red chilies, bay leaves. A whole bottle of chickpea flour. I've never used chickpea flour in my life." She pokes at a packet. "And this—I don't even know what this is."

"It's saunf," the young man says. "Foreigners call it fennel. Very good for digestion. People with bad tempers usually have digestive problems. Maybe that's why your biji sent it."

"Thanks for the lesson," Belle snaps. "Now if you would please remove the box and yourself from here—some of us have to work for a living, you know."

The man picks up the box. "I'll be happy to leave, believe me! I'll take the produce and use it myself. It's obviously wasted on you! It's a good thing your parents won't know how you treated their gift. They packed that box with a lot of love. But that probably doesn't mean much to you—you're far too cool to care about old-fashioned concepts like respect for your elders."

I brace myself for an outburst, but Belle looks taken aback. Only for a moment, though. Then she snatches the box from him.

"You think wearing that turban makes you better than other people and gives you the right to judge them?" she says. "You think you know all about me? Well, you'd better leave before I contaminate you with my coolness." She turns to me. "We need to start with the inventory. We're already late."

Belle has contacted a company that buys equipment from bankrupt businesses. They've agreed to look at our inventory and give us a price. If we agree, they'll send their van in a couple of days to pick up everything they want. We'll have to throw out the rest, I guess, or maybe give it to Goodwill. And then good-bye, Chai House.

Belle calls out the names of items, and I write them down. The espresso machine, the display trays, the spoons with roses embossed on the handle. I remember buying each item. My hand hurts. I realize I'm gripping the pen too tightly. My father has disappeared into the kitchen area in the back, where the stoves and ovens are, but the young man, surprisingly, is still around. When Belle climbs up to see what's stored in the attic, he steadies the ladder for her, although she pointedly ignores him. I feel a wrench as I add the rocking chairs to the list. I can't take them, even though I'd like to. Soon I'll have to move to a smaller place. And begin the long search for another job. My stomach curdles as I think of it.

Several hours and we've barely made a dent. Who knew we had so many little things: cookie cutters, melon scoops, teapots with silk cozies to keep them warm? I'm exhausted, dusty, hungry. Belle suggests that one of us run down the street for some fast food. The young man, who's been helping us fill boxes, offers to do it. I take out some money from my rapidly slimming purse, but he waves it away. "My treat," he says with a grin that makes him seem younger and less forbidding.

"Absolutely not," Belle says, chin squared in stubbornness. I can see we're in for another long argument, but then, from the door of the cooking area, my father clears his throat.

"I could fry up a few pakoras for you," he suggests hesitantly. "Make some cha, Indian style?"

Cha, that Bengali word again. I remember my mother using it, though I can't quite recall when. I'm about to refuse, but Belle says, "That would be great, Mr. Gupta. We have all this good Darjeeling tea we've been saving—"

"Not to mention a whole packet of chickpea flour," the young man adds, "destined never to be used in your lifetime—"

Belle draws in her breath for a suitable rejoinder, but my father, in his new incarnation as chef-cum-peacemaker, asks the young man to carry the box into the kitchen for him. We hear murmurings, the water runs, there's the sizzle of pakoras in hot oil.

Belle sits down in one of the rocking chairs and puts up her feet with a sigh.

"How's the job search going?" I ask.

She grimaces. "It's a soulless world out there, Rikki. No one wants people like us, with our enriching and impractical liberal education."

I sit there rocking. She's right—what am I trained to do? Maybe I could work as a maid in a hotel, or a waitress in someone else's restaurant. I guess I could clean houses, except if folks knew what my own apartment looked like, no one would hire me.

"Hey," Belle says suddenly. "Is that your dad singing?"

It is. He's singing one of his Hindi songs—it must be a well-known one, because the young man joins in the chorus. They make a good duo, though my father is obviously the lead singer. Interesting how when he sings his diffidence falls from him and a rich, pure melody emerges.

"He's good!" Belle says. "How come you didn't inherit either of your parents' talents?"

"Thanks," I say. It's the first time she's mentioned my mother without an accompanying somberness. It's the first time I haven't flinched when she's been mentioned. It's a progress of sorts.

"That other guy—he isn't too bad either," I say. "I wonder what his name is."

"Jespal."

"So you know him from before?"

"I've seen him around at community events back in Turlock. My folks talk about him all the time. Successful career. Keeps in close touch with his family. Plus a devout Sikh. What more could a girl want, as my mother is fond of saying."

"And what do *you* say, especially now that he's shown up at your doorstep, bearing gifts?"

"Yeah, chickpea flour and radishes."

"Things can only improve from there! He's obviously interested, to hang around after the tongue-lashing you gave him."

"Even if he is, I don't have the energy to respond. Besides, nothing could come of it. Do you see me covering my head and following him to the gurdwara every weekend? And he'd probably faint from shock if I took him to my favorite club."

The men bring in trays of steaming dishes. Tea, pakoras, a chutney to go with the spicy balls, which, my father informs us, he has concocted out of spinach, onions and chickpea flour. ("Known as besan to the initiated," Jespal adds, with an impudent, imprudent grin, to which Belle returns a dagger look.) It's a novel pleasure to be waited on in our own Chai House, and by men, too.

"How much sugar in your cha?" Father asks.

Now I recall when I heard that word before. My mother had said our problem was that we hadn't been able to make this into a real cha shop. It upsets me all over again to remember that she had thought we weren't authentic.

"Mr. Gupta!" Belle says as she crunches into a pakora. "How did you learn to cook so well?"

My father smiles. "When I was growing up, my parents were very poor. For a while there wasn't any money for me to go to school unless I earned it myself. So I took a job as an assistant in a snack shop. Someday when there's time, I'll tell you more about it."

"This tea is excellent," Jespal says. "Did you put in ginger? That's how my mother makes it, too!"

I sip my tea. It's rich and full-bodied and very sweet, with a slight kick to it that must be from the ginger. I have to admit it's far superior to the watery version with too much cinnamon that I'd drunk in other cafés and then served in ours.

Jespal exchanges phone numbers with my father before he leaves. He glances at Belle as though he wants to ask her something, but finally he doesn't. I watch my father pour another cup of tea for Belle, raising the pot high with a practiced hand to let the amber stream froth into her cup without spilling a drop. All the earlier weakness seems to have left his arm. He handles the cup almost tenderly, and I realize that he is enjoying this.

I'd always thought my mother was the mystery person in our household. But my chameleon father is turning out to have a few surprises in him, too.

"Girls," he says now. "If I may call you girls—? May I suggest that you leave the inventorying for the day?"

"We don't have the luxury, Dad," I say, my brief moment of well-being replaced by irritation. There he goes, interfering in my life again. "We don't have customers, and there's no money to pay the rent. Let's face the truth—we've lost the battle with the competition."

I glance balefully at the café across the street. Someone's standing outside, watching our store. For some reason, I can't see him—or her—clearly. Even though it's a sunny day, there's a shadow over the street right in that spot. Or maybe it's a smudge on our storefront window, which we've been too disheartened to clean in a while. But I don't need to see to know. It's the manager. Why is she standing outside instead of tending to her (or should I say *our*) milling clientele?

"I might have a suggestion or two, something to keep you from losing the store. It's a lovely space—" He says it with such earnestness that I hold back my retort.

"We've gone over every possibility already," Belle explains to him patiently. "We just don't have the funds to survive."

My father stares out the window. I wonder if he's looking at the manager, and what he's thinking. Had my mother said something to him about Java? But what could she have told him? They didn't talk much, and they never discussed the inexplicable. He was uncomfortable with what couldn't be verified by technology.

When he finally speaks, it isn't anything I'm expecting.

"I have some money," my father says. "Would you consider letting a new partner join your business?"

In the car we talk, but not about his offer. (Later I will wonder where the money came from, if it was my mother's life insurance. But surely not, surely he couldn't have received it so quickly.) I ask him about the journal entries.

"Is it hard for you to go through them?"

"Well, yes, it is. A lot of the time I'm struggling with the language. Some of the words—there aren't any English terms for them. I hope I'm able to do them justice."

"I didn't mean that. Does it—uh—bother you to read them? Sometimes I feel like we're trespassing, that perhaps we should just leave them the way they were, tied up, in the back of the closet—"

"You shouldn't feel that way. Your mother was a meticulous person. You didn't find those journals by accident. She left them for you. Maybe they're her way of telling you what was on her mind."

"From what I recall, she never had difficulty telling me exactly what was on her mind."

"Those were just the surface things, the things she needed to say to run your everyday life. But the important things—the ones that live in dark closets inside us—I think everyone has trouble speaking about them."

I didn't expect to hear of dark inner closets from my father— but now that I give it some thought, it fits. Perhaps that's where he disappeared to when he went on his drinking binges.

"Maybe leaving the journals behind is her way of comforting us," my father says. "Some of the time when I'm reading them, it's almost as though she's right here, talking to me. Some of the things she wrote surprises me, though. She remembers events so differently. How we met, for example." I dart a guilty glance at him, but he seems not to notice. "If it were anyone else, I'd say she'd just made that story up. But your mother—" He shakes his head, and I understand what he means. My mother was never one to make things up. Why would she? The world she lived in was more fascinating than any fantasy.

"Some of the time," he continues, "it's like reading a novel written by a stranger—I don't recognize anyone, especially myself. And the parts about the caves, and her—uh, skill—why, it's like one of those old tales I heard when growing up. Then she has those entries about clients coming to her for help. I can't believe that all of that went on right in my house." He sighs. "But they must have happened. At least in her mind." He gives me an apologetic look, and I know he's struggling with the same doubt that has plagued me. *Did she only imagine it all?*

But I'm not ready to discuss my mother's failing—if failing it was—with him. While I'm beginning to like the man I'm finding as I peel away that old label *father,* I have no doubt as to where my loyalties lie. I turn up the car radio to signal that our conversation is over, and the rest of the way we listen to Simon and Garfunkel on the oldies channel, singing about darkness my old friend.

23

They sit at the dining table late into the night, father and daughter, compiling lists, trying out ideas. Through their excitement they are dimly aware that this is a first-ever event. Before this, all their interactions took place in the presence of the mother, *through* her, as it were. She was their conductor, their buffer zone, their translator. She softened the combative edges of their words and clarified their questions, even to themselves. *I'll take care of it,* she whispered without words. *Don't you worry.* It was like making sounds underwater, the daughter thinks. Soft, rounded, beautiful, ineffective. Now that aquatic mother-medium is gone, taking all comfort with it, and her own words startle her, arrowing through the air with their new, harsh speed.

They have decided to transform the Chai House into an Indian snack shop, a chaer dokan, as it would be called in Calcutta. They're going to model it after the shop the father worked in so many years ago, with a few American sanitary touches thrown in. He'll teach Belle and her to brew tea and coffee the right way, and he'll cook the snacks himself. He lists them on a sheet of paper: pakora, singara, sandesh, jilebi, beguni, nimki, mihidana. The daughter stares at the list in fascinated misgiving. She doesn't recognize half the names, has tasted the others only occasionally. Can her father really transform himself into a chef extraordinaire and turn out these items from the mundaneness of flour and sugar syrup, chili, eggplants, peanut oil? Is he heroic enough to take on such a metamorphosis? But she doesn't wish to lose this brief moment of camaraderie, this floating together on the cloud of their shared dream. So she says, instead, "Tell me about the shop where you worked." And is plunged into her first Indian story.

I was only fourteen, he says, when my father lost his job. This was a great blow for our family, for though his job as a clerk in a government office was nothing special, it was the only income we had. Added to the problem was the fact that my father had developed a hacking cough—folks feared it was tuberculosis—and it kept him from finding a new position. He was always tired. The doctor advised us to move him to a place with cool, dry weather, Deoghar maybe, or Hazaribagh.

I remember that day in the doctor's office, my mother, embarrassed, whispering that we couldn't afford such an expensive move. The doctor, a young man, was sympathetic. My mother was a beautiful woman. I would soon learn that most men were sympathetic to her. He told her he'd give her the medicines for free. But my father needed more: clean air and bed rest and an ongoing, expensive diet of chicken soup and fresh fruit—things the doctor couldn't do much about. Nor could we. We could barely afford a basic meal of watery rice and chilies. Every night for a year my mother and I went to bed hungry so my father could have more to eat. We didn't let him know this, of course. He already felt he had failed us, and the doctor had warned us not to upset him further.

My mother found a job in a garment factory, where she spent twelve hours each day stitching quality shirts for men, handling rayon and dacron and polyster silk, materials her husband and son would never wear. At first she was thankful to get the job, but soon she found out that it had its drawbacks. It was strenuous work. The women were crowded into a hot warehouse shed with small windows and only a couple of wheezing ceiling fans. When all of them worked their sewing machines together, the sound was deafening. Many women lost their eyesight. They developed arthritis or chronic back pain or lung diseases from breathing in fabric dust. Some suffered from dizziness, and some told my mother that even at home, they kept hearing the dim roar of the machines. When they grew too ill to work, they were fired. There were always more women to replace them.

My mother observed all this. The money she was getting was not enough to run the household and take care of my father. Much against her wishes, she'd let me work at the tea shop down the street from our house, and she feared my studies were suffering. Even so, we could barely pay the rent. She knew we'd soon have to move into a smaller place with less light and air, and my father would die.

So when the overseer on her shift made her a certain proposal, my mother accepted. She began to work fewer hours and bring home more money. The overseer (I learned about him years later) often made her gifts of clothing (stolen from the factory) or food (he had a brother who was the overseer of a canning plant).

Did she appreciate his generosity? Did it make her grow fond of him? I don't know. She told my father she'd received a promotion. She had me cut down my hours at the tea stall so that I worked only a few morning hours. She was able to cook proper meals for my father and spend time with him. In the evenings as I sat at my desk, wearing a new shirt in the latest design and doing my homework, I'd hear their voices as they conversed. The low murmurings would fill me with contentment.

Such a precarious contentment could not last, of course. Time came for the overseer to retire and move back to his hometown. He wanted to take my mother with him. When she hesitated, he threatened to expose her to my father. My mother was faced with three choices. (She told me this much later, when I was on a visit home from the university.) To leave with the overseer—but to fashion her departure so that my father, who had by now regained his health, would think she was dead. This way he would continue to love her, and remember her as a virtuous wife. Or to dare the overseer to tell his story, and hope that my father would understand that what she did was for love of her family. Her third choice involved poison mixed into a drink—. But that's another story, and will have to wait for another day. You asked me about the tea shop, and I've digressed enough.

The tea shop was a small one—just a shed, really—at a crossroads, no more than a few wooden chairs and tables set in front of two large clay firepits. On the first Keshto, the owner-manager-cook, boiled tea all day in a large aluminum kettle. On the other, he would cook sweets, stirring the white granules of sandesh in a huge iron wok until they became a smooth paste, or squeezing the dough of jilebis through a hole in a cloth onto sputtering hot oil. Some days he would fry chili pakoras instead, their pungent smell reaching all the way to the bus stop, making passengers late for work because no one could resist stopping for Keshto's pakoras.

She leans forward, her eyes shining. Here is the kind of story she has waited for her entire life, has begged, cajoled, badgered her mother for—in vain. And to think it was waiting all this time inside her father, the drinker, the singer, the skeptic who never believed in dreams. The parent she always dismissed, although affectionately, thinking he knew nothing she'd have any use for.

Were they magical, she asks, the pakoras? Did they give special powers to those who ate them, or make them feel a certain way?

Not that I know of, her father says. People joked that their unique taste came from the fact that Keshto never changed the oil in his wok—nor washed it either.

Other rumors, too, floated around Keshto's shop. How late at night when the city slept the important criminal families of Calcutta would meet in the back of the shop to hand out payments—or collect them. There were seven important families, one night a week reserved for each of them. While Keshto, impassive as a stone Buddha, sat at his wok, stirring pantuas till they turned just the right golden brown, inside the shed they decided which of their enemies should live, and which should disappear.

And was it true? she whispers, reluctant to break the spell.

He shrugs, though there is a twinkle in his eye. Who knows? People love mysteries. If there isn't one, they're quick to make it up. The inner room was ordinary enough. Keshto's bedding was kept in there, though I never saw him sleep, and a painted tin suitcase that contained his few possessions. Ah, that suitcase! There were stories about that, too. In any case, the room was tiny—no more than six people could have fitted into it at one time. But some mornings when I swept it out, there would be torn scraps of paper, parts of names, some slashed across with red.

All I know for certain is that though Keshto was gruff toward most people and a hardheaded businessman, for some reason I couldn't fathom, he was kind to me. In the mornings after I had cleaned up the store, before I went off to school, he made sure I ate well. He wouldn't let me drink tea—he believed it stunted growth—but he gave me a full glass of milk and a choice of whichever snacks I wanted. And when I came back in the afternoon, he taught me his special recipes, sharing with me little secrets that gave them their special flavor. I learned that to make rasogollas that would be soft and yet not fall apart when boiled in syrup, one had to knead two spoons of sooji into the chhana dough. And that half a cup of oil added into the pakora mix would prevent the spicy balls from soaking up more oil when deep-fried.

She closes her eyes to hear better, but later she isn't sure if what she hears are his words or her own longing.

I learned to grind my own spices and herbs on a pockmarked slab of stone, to curdle milk with lemons and make fresh chhana of just the right consistency. The granules of my mihidana were orange as sunrise, and as addictive as an affair. My cauliflower-stuffed singaras were so crisp that customers whispered that the new assistant had outdone even Keshto himself. Keshto had been well known before, but now people from all over Calcutta came to our little shop to order food for weddings and funerals, house-warmings and sacred-thread ceremonies. Keshto and I worked late into the night trying to accommodate them, but still we had to turn many away.

By this time my mother was bringing home plenty of money. She asked me to quit my job at the tea shop so I could put all my efforts into studying for the entrance exam for engineering college. It was her dream that her son should become an engineer. I wanted to please her, so I agreed. But I couldn't stay away from Keshto. I would wake before dawn and slip out of the house, and when I got to the shop, though we never discussed anything the night before, he would have already lit the fires and set out the ingredients. We worked feverishly, in silence except for the few instructions he grunted from time to time. Our time together was short, as I had to be back in my room before my mother knocked on my door to make sure I was awake for school. In those days Keshto taught me the most difficult dishes he knew. We made rabri, where milk is boiled and thickened, cooled and poured, layer by slow layer. We made rasogollar payesh, which is two sweets in one, the fluffy white balls floating in a thick, delicious cream. We made dhakai parota, where the dough is cut and rolled in such a way that it forms thin, flaky layers that melt on the tongue. The week before I left for college, he taught me his special recipe for sandesh, the milk sweet for which Calcutta is famous, but he wouldn't let me write it down. He insisted that I learn it by heart, the way he had.

Before I went away, I wanted to tell him how much he meant to me, that I'd never forget him. In some ways I loved him more than my own father. But I've never been good with words, and Bengali is a language in which *thank you* is an awkward word. So I went off to college without saying anything and didn't return for a year, and when I did come back, Keshto's shop was gone, and a hairdressing salon had sprung up in its place. I asked around, but no one seemed to know what had become of him.

. . .

The story hangs in the night air between them. It is very late, and if father or daughter stepped to the window, they would see the Suktara, star of the impending dawn, hanging low in the sky. But they keep sitting at the table, each thinking of the story differently, as teller and listener always must. In the mind of each, different images swirl up and fall away, and each holds on to a different part of the story, thinking it the most important. And if each were to speak of what it meant, they would say things so different you would not know it was the same story they were speaking of.

But the sharing of the story has created something that stretches, trembling like the thinnest strand of a spiderweb between them. And it is this that makes the daughter tell the father (without looking at him, as she doodles on the pad where he has written the new menu of their tea shop) about her night adventure. She describes the black car she followed onto that rusted, Hopperesque dock, she tells of the water as it slapped blackly against the pier, the loneliness of that sound. She hesitates before she mentions the car's license plate, its impossible disappearance. But then she thinks of the story her father has told her, which is impossible in its own way, and writes down the letters from the back of the car onto the pad. *Emit Maerd*. Are they words from an Indian language, she asks? A name he recognizes? A mantra perhaps, or part of one. He shakes his head, staring, turning the pad around and around.

Are you sure it wasn't Amit? he says. Amit is an Indian name. Are you sure that it's the same name the lady at the art exhibition took down?

I'm not sure of anything anymore, she says. That's my problem.

Who knows, he says. It may be the beginning of a solution.

Look carefully. Were these the words on the license plate of the car my mother followed?

I'm sorry, I can't remember. Maybe it's a Middle Eastern name. Turkish, maybe?

They bend over the pad together, their heads almost touching, reluctant to relinquish this single, unsatisfactory clue. He plays with the letters, writing them down in random order, mixing them up, leaving out some and keeping others. It's when he gives up that they see it, in synchronicity. It's so simple they wonder how they had missed it for so long. Written backward, the letters spell Dream Time.

In bed she wonders about those words, what message they hold for her, if they hold any message at all. Is she reading too much into a quirk, someone's private joke? As she meanders toward sleep, her thoughts settle on her father's story, the vibrant, violent colors of the streets and the factory. The tea shop at once run-down and resplendent. The lineage of sweets. Now, finally, she has a way to bring it all into her own American life. She'll resuscitate the Chai House with the tastes and smells of the old country, with the whispers of stories learned by heart. Something else is being resuscitated—between her and her father, though she's not sure what shape it will ultimately take.

It is the first evening since her mother's death that grief hasn't been foremost in her mind. Even as she acknowledges this, the pillow beneath her head yields the smell of her mother's hair, and she is plunged anew into loss.

24

FROM THE
DREAM JOURNALS

When it became clear that I was determined to marry and move across the ocean to America with the man I met at Victoria Memorial, chaos broke loose at the caves. No dream teller had ever done such a thing—not in the living memory of the elders—and the shock of it cracked the sisterhood in two. The senior elders claimed that I should be stripped of my powers and turned out. It was clear that I had betrayed my art and my gift (and that, too, for a mere man). A funeral ceremony should be held for me, as ordained in the *Brihat Swapna Sarita,* for to them I was worse than dead. The other group, which included my aunt, felt I should be kept in the order so that the lore of healing I had learned should not fall to waste. They went to other ancient text, the *Swapna Purana,* to see what could be done to save me from myself. The two factions fought vehemently until the chief elder decreed that until my fate was decided, they were not to speak to each other. Bitterness and silence filled the caves where before only friendship had existed.

In my sorrow and guilt I thought to run away, believing that my going would restore peace, but my aunt guessed my mind and begged me to stay until the council came to a decision. I assented, for she was my first teacher, and this much I owed her. But later I wondered if it would have been better to have refused.

The meeting of the council (I thought of it as a trial) took days—or was it perhaps weeks? I attended some sessions; others were closed to me. At times I was asked to speak, at others ordered to remain silent while arguments were made for and against me. But perhaps it all took place in one afternoon, for time moves differently in the caves, and when I left to join my husband-to-be, less than a week had passed since we first met beside the roses.

I was sent to wait in my room while the council deliberated, and when I was brought back to the assembly hall, only the chief elder and my aunt were present. They told me I had three choices. The first was to remain in the caves with the elders for the rest of my life, and be a teacher. In doing so I would not suffer. This very night, with my permission, the elder would dream-walk into my memory and remove the man's image from there, so that when I awoke I would no longer remember him. This was the safest and happiest of the three choices, they told me, for it was clear that I had a wayward mind and the outside world would present me with temptations too strong to withstand.

My second choice was to give up my talent and live out my life as that most ordinary of women, a wife. Again, the elder would adjust my memory so that I forgot the caves and all I'd learned there. I would go to my husband blank as new paper for him to write on, and he would be happy, for (they said) it is the wish of all men to construct without interference the story of their wives' lives. This, too, was a safe choice, if not a happy one.

The third choice, of which they informed me reluctantly, and only when I rejected the first two, was this: I would be allowed to keep my powers, the lesser ones, so that I might help others in the world. In return, though I could live with a man if I chose to, I had to promise not to marry him. In the eye of the Great Power, then, my spiritual essence would not be joined to his. The door for my return to the sisterhood would thus not be closed completely in case I saw (as they hoped) the folly of my choice and wished to come back. But this was a dangerous choice, for it might go wrong in numerous ways.

It was this third I chose, though not with good grace, for it hobbled me with its many conditions. After, when my aunt tried to give me cautionary counsel, I turned from her angrily. Nothing would go wrong, I insisted.

I did not know that my choice would suspend me for the rest of my days between a world of inexplicable forces and the love of a man who insisted that such a world did not exist.

The night before I left for Calcutta, my aunt brought me a gift. It was a small cloth pouch the size of a fist. When I opened the drawstring, there was another bag within, and then another. I reached in and took out a pinch of the reddish powder that lay there. For a moment, I was confused. Was it sindur? I wondered. A gesture of conciliation from my aunt, a wish for my happiness in married life? But when I touched it with the tip of my tongue I realized it was not the powder brides wear on their foreheads. No. My aunt had given me a handful of earth.

It is from the walkway in front of the caves, she told me, ground that centuries of dream tellers have stepped on. You'll need it where you're going.

I did not ask her what she meant. I was angry with her still, and disappointed at what she'd chosen to give me at my going-away. It was not until later, when I found myself in California with all the dreaming gone from me, that I realized the importance of the gift.

In the beginning I was not worried. I needed time to settle, I told myself. I needed to get used to my new life. There was much in it that I found novel and charming: how to manage a household, how to please a husband. (It was important for me to please him because I'd displeased him deeply by insisting on a legal ceremony instead of a temple wedding. He complained that this made him feel we weren't really married.) There were dishes to try out, rooms to decorate. His lips tracing the lines of my collarbones at night. My hands feeling the corrugations of his spine, the smoothness of his thighs. But there came a day when these could not hold my attention, and when I looked in the mirror to apply sindur to my forehead, my face looked transparent, like a glass oval that was emptying out.

Dreams would not come to me in California because it was too new a place. Its people had settled there only a few hundred years ago, and neither its air nor its earth, the elements from which we most draw sustenance, was weighted yet with dreams. Yes, there had been older inhabitants, but they had been driven from the land, and in going had taken with them, along with their hopes, their ways of dreaming. They had left only tears behind, and curses that smudged the air.

At first I didn't know what to do with the earth in the pouch. I sprinkled a little in my garden, but though it made my dahlias and gardenias bloom, it did not help me dream. I mixed a pinch of it into my rice and lentils, but beyond giving me cramps, it did nothing. Finally I placed the pouch under my pillow.

That night my sleep was filled with the colors and scents of home—things I had never missed while there. I awoke with a sore heart. But the dreams I needed, dreams that went beyond my own small life—I could sense their presence, but they wouldn't come to me. My husband awoke with a headache, and a complaint that his sleep had been filled with terrible images, blood and rubble and dying animals.

I knew then what I had to do. The following night, when he fell asleep, I took my pillow to the living room and lay down on the scratchy carpet. Almost before I had closed my eyes, a dream descended on me. It spoke to me in a raven's voice, giving instructions. It told me whose dream I was dreaming, and where I must meet him the next day, and how to help him. I felt the power of the dream flow into me until my bones grew phosphorescent and my blood buzzed as though I were drunk. I awoke weeping. I knew now how much my link with the dream spirits meant. I couldn't give it up. I wept, too, because I realized the price I would have to pay—never again to spend the night with my husband. *Spend*. For the first time I realized the weighted accurateness of the verb, for dream tellers cannot squander their nights as ordinary women do. Never to hold the warm curve of his back pressed against me as we both drifted into oblivion. Never to wake and watch him still asleep, his hair tousled as a boy's, the corner of his mouth twitching in a smile that I could only guess at. The small intimacies of pulling the quilt cover over him on a cold night, of rubbing his shoulders when he moaned in a nightmare.

I knew he'd be angry when I told him my decision. I would make up for it, I promised myself. I would please him in bed, make his room (already I thought of it as not mine) spin with stars before I left it each night. I didn't know it would not be enough.

When I lifted my pillow and picked up the bag of earth, it felt lighter. I opened it with shaking fingers. The dust inside had diminished. It was as though my dreaming had used up a portion of it. My heart beat jaggedly as I looked at what was left. How many nights before it was all gone? And what would I do then?

25

Rakhi

We are going to reopen the shop tomorrow, on a Wednesday. It's not the best choice, says Belle, but it isn't the worst either. Wednesday is the day of the week named after Budh, the planetary deity of intelligence. Thursday, Brihaspati, would have been more auspicious—he is the wisdom planet, the teacher of the gods.

"Since when did you become an astrological expert?" I ask, half amused, half amazed.

"Jespal looked it up for me."

"Ah, Jespal!" He's been dropping by in the evenings to help with our redecoration efforts. Now it seems that's not all he's been doing. "Do I detect the blush of a rose on yon dusky cheek?"

"Quit teasing. It's important to have the planets on our side, especially when battling the dark forces. But I'm thankful it isn't Saturday. Shani can be a very destructive agent."

"Dark forces! Destructive agent! You look too intelligent to believe in such nonsense," my father says.

Belle's mouth falls open in outrage. I brace myself, but she pulls herself together. "Mr. Gupta," she says with a patience bordering on the saintly, "you know that's not true."

She must be growing fond of my father to make such allowances for him. It strikes me that I am, too.

"What's not true, that it's nonsense or that you look intelligent?"

I hide my smile behind my hand, but Belle is not to be deflected by paltry humor. "How could you not know, living with Mrs. Gupta all these years?"

"Ah, my dear, living with Mrs. Gupta was a most amazing experience, and a wonderful one. I wouldn't have given it up for anything in my life, but perhaps it wasn't quite what you've imagined it to be."

We both pause in our tasks—Belle polishing the countertops, I mixing red paint (the shop is to have a new name; Jespal has already scraped the old one off the storefront window). Of all his stories, this is the one we most want to hear.

My father has been telling us stories all week, while he tries out snacks and sweets on us. I'm rusty, he claims. Got to get in shape. But I suspect he just loves to feed us. I enjoy the snacks, but it's the stories I really crave. He has told us about his early days as a student in America, about the odd jobs he held to make money—a janitor in a hospital, a slot-machine repairman in a casino. About the people he met in these places. I would never have guessed that such a consummate storyteller lay waiting all these years inside my father. He prolongs the suspense until we're about to shake him; he makes us burst out laughing at unexpected jokes. My favorite stories are about his life in India. But so far he has not told us any stories involving my mother, though he does mention her—lovingly, ruefully—in passing.

From time to time my father sings as he cooks, mostly songs from the movies, though sometimes a haunting tune that sounds far older will wind like wood smoke through the store. They make me restless, these tunes, as though there is something inside my chest that wants to escape. There's a feeling like pinpricks in my fingers, a need to paint—something I haven't been able to do since my mother's death.

When I ask, he tells me these are folk songs that field hands sing in Bengal. He picked them up during school holidays when he visited his uncle, who was the subestate manager for the royal family of Nataal. I sense a story there. No, stories tucked within the envelopes of other stories, an entire post office worth of them, filling me with giddy anticipation.

But today my father tells us this is no time for lolling around, listening to foolish tales. Tomorrow's a big day. Flyers have been passed out via Marco and his friends, advertisements have been placed in the *East Bay Express* and *India West*. I've given in and let my father deploy Sonny as our publicist, and he's been talking up our new concept at the nightclub. We must be ready, my father insists. He needs to make another batch of gawja, those crisp diamonds of fried dough crusted with sugar. He wasn't satisfied with the consistency of the melted sugar last time. We assure him that the gawjas were delicious, but he shakes his head. Nothing less than perfection will do for our grand reopening, as he calls it. He assigns Belle the task of writing our new menu on the board. She asks if she should provide brief descriptions of the items, but he says no. No pandering to tourist types here, he adds sternly. This is a real cha shop. If people ask, you can explain. But you'll be surprised at how much they know already—and how much they can learn on their own. Jespal, who has just come in, is set to dusting the furniture. As for me, he shoos me outside to paint. The new name has to be dry by the time we open tomorrow. I comply, a little taken aback by his bustling, managerial manner. Is there no end to the personalities hiding inside my father's skin? Don't rush it, he warns as he disappears into the back room.

I trace the letters, then begin to fill them in. *Kurma House*. My father is the author of this name. He likes the pun, the idea of a word hidden beneath another word, to be revealed when the wind shifts, or when the viewer narrows her eyes. I pointed out to him that kurma is a dinner dish, something we don't plan to serve. He shrugged. We are artists, Rakhi, he said loftily. Must we be bound to literalities?

The heft of the brush in my hand, heavy with paint, feels so right. Even though this isn't the same as composing a painting, there are resemblances. The dip of the wrist as I tap it against the edge of the can, the curve of the arm as I trace the top of the *K*. I hadn't realized how much my body had missed such movements.

As I paint, my eyes stray to the inside of the store. Jespal has done a good job of cleaning the glass—it's almost as though it doesn't exist. He reads out items from a list my father has jotted down while Belle writes them on the board. From time to time their eyes meet and they smile shyly. Suddenly it comes to me that within the year they will marry. (Is this prophecy, intuition, or just a guess? How far can I trust it, I who am not my mother?) Watching them, I feel at once happy and lonely. It's not the loneliness of being without a mate, but something more primal. As though I were the only being left on this side of the glass, while the rest of the world—happy, uncaring—lived out its life on the other side. They were aware of my presence, they even waved to me from time to time, as Belle was doing, but they didn't know how it felt to be looking in, waving back, unable to cross over.

Is this how my mother felt when she left her community of interpreters and lost her ability to dream?

After his initial slowness, my father has made great strides in translating the journals. He tells me he has fallen into a rhythm, has become accustomed to my mother's style. I think he's as addicted to them as I am. That he searches them with the same hunger. We've come to an unspoken agreement not to discuss them. I fear it will make him self-conscious, defensive, now that so many of the entries are about their life together. But sometimes I can't help watching him with sideways surreptitiousness, trying to see him with my mother's eyes.

I'm halfway through painting when I experience that strange prickling again on the back of my neck. Why should this be? People have been watching ever since I started the lettering. Marco strolled over to ask what I was doing, Mr. Jamison from the art store came to find out what we were going to sell now, strangers waiting at the bus stop stared, trying to guess the words before they were completed. But this is different—there's a maliciousness to this gaze that goes through my clothes, through my skin, and into my spinal column like a needle of ice.

I look cautiously in the glass, but already I know. It's the manager, standing outside Java, smoking a casual cigarette. She isn't looking this way, but I can feel the intensity of her attention. There's a heaviness in my shoulders. My arm aches with the effort of holding itself up. My hand shakes, and when I try to continue, I smudge the *O* beyond repair.

"How's it going?" says my father from the door, making me jump and smear the *H* as well.

"Look what you made me do!" I say, hiding fear behind irritation. It isn't totally true, and he knows it, but he doesn't say anything in self-defense. He brings out a box of rags and dips them in thinner and helps me clean off the ruined letters. While I redo them, he stands beside me, arms crossed. I consider saying, *Don't watch, you're making me nervous,* but then I realize something. His presence feels calming, protective—as though he's a shield. I sense the malicious force hitting him and ricocheting away, unable to pass through. It gathers itself into a wave and hits him again, hard. I watch him carefully in the glass, but there's no sign that he feels any of it.

"Dad," I say, "don't look now, but did you see that woman outside the coffee shop?"

He turns to stare. My heart hammers and I grab his arm and jerk him back. "Didn't I just tell you not to look!" I hiss. I don't inform him of the thought that went through my mind like a lightning flash—if his eyes met hers, she'd turn him into stone, like Medusa, or enchant him, like Circe.

Such nonsense, he would declare—and wouldn't he be right?

He dips his head conspiratorially, looking at me in the glass. Whatever it is you're playing at, his good-humored expression says, I'm willing to play along.

"Your competitor, hunh?" he says with a grin. "But not anymore! We're about to do something totally different, something she can't match. You just watch, beti!" He gives my shoulders a squeeze. "I must inform you—rather immodestly—that I outdid myself with the gawja. Come in and taste some. It'll—as you girls like to say—blow you away."

He holds the door open. I go in. Behind me, tentacles of malice grasp for me one last time, slide off my skin. I nibble on the gawjas, which are as delicious as my father promised, and try to arrange my confusions.

This is what I end up with. It's by no means satisfactory.

1. If there is another level to existence, my father isn't aware of it.

2. His lack of sensitivity to it protects him from it in some way.

3. Or does his blindness place him in greater danger?

4. Can this level be called dream time?

5. Does the man in white belong to dream time, just as, in a different, darker way, the manager does? Is this the world to which my mother's gift allowed her access?

6. None of this is true; the only truth is that I'm cracking up.

"Rikki!" Belle exclaims as she comes in from the back room with a towering stack of paper plates. "I can't believe it! You ate the entire tray of gawjas! There must have been forty thousand calories in there, girl! Now you'll have stomach cramps and throw up all night and we won't be able to open the store tomorrow!"

I look down in horror at the empty tray. She's right. I can feel myself bloating up already. I'm probably breaking out in a rash, too.

"Girls! Girls!" my father says. He's smiling proudly at this evidence of his success, never mind that his daughter feels like an overinflated blimp. "My gawjas can't hurt you! Remember that song you used to sing over and over in your college days, driving us insane? Don't worry, be happy." He sings the refrain, sounding uncannily like Bobby McFerrin. "Everything's going to go perfectly tomorrow."

Tomorrow comes sooner than I think it will. I'd expected to lie in bed, awake with worry and anticipation, but my sleep is sweet and immediate and refreshing, like a mouthful of rasogolla syrup. I wake to a cool, clear morning, a sky like white oleanders. When I step out to the car, there is a bird in the maple tree, one I haven't seen in this part of the state before. It is large and gray, with bright orange mihidana eyes. It watches me intently, without any sign of fear. I run inside to get my father, but by the time we return, the bird is gone.

Could it be an omen? I ask.

What's an omen? he says.

I sigh. I don't want an argument between us today, but I know this: the universe does send us messages. The trouble is, most of us don't know how to read them.

It's at such times I miss my mother the most.

When we get to the store, the first thing I notice is a big banner over Java's entrance. ANNIVERSARY SELLABRATION! it screams in multicolored glittery letters. DOOR PRIZES! FREE FOOD!

I turn to my father in outrage. "That is such a lie! They've only been here a few months." But no one else seems to have noticed. Or maybe they just don't care. In front of the entrance to Java, people are milling around like sheep. Of the manager there's no sign. She's at the cash register, no doubt, gloating as she rakes in money that should have rightly come to us.

Inside, Belle is slumped against the counter, too despondent to be indignant. "She's outwitted us once again," she whispers. "What will we do with all the supplies we bought? And those sweets you made last night, Mr. Gupta? They'll all be wasted. All your savings gone down the drain, all your effort, just because you tried to help us."

My father looks a bit shaken, too, but he pats her shoulder. "Cheer up, Miss B!" he says. "Didn't one of your American heroes say, It ain't over until it's over?" He disappears into the back room. We can hear the banging of pots and pans, and after a moment, the sound of whistling.

Belle gives me a push. "Go in there and stop him. It'll be terrible if he makes more of those lovely things and there's no one to eat them."

But when I go in there, I forget what I've come to say, because there in a little alcove next to the big gas burner, sits the black-and-white photo of a young woman. I think it's my mother—but it's an old photo, from a time before my birth, and so I'm not sure.

Where had my father hidden it all these years?

In the photo my mother, if that's who she is, looks worriedly off to one side of the camera. I peer closely, hoping to catch a glimpse of the dream caves she wrote of in her journal, but the land around her is open and flat. What place is this? There's no grass, no trees, only tarmac under her feet and a blurred metal-gray shape far in the background. Then it comes to me. She's in an airfield, getting ready to board the plane that will bring her to the

United States. No wonder she looks anxious. She's about to leave everything she knows to follow a man she's met only a few times—a decision everyone close to her thinks of as a huge mistake. Maybe she's wondering if crossing the ocean will indeed cause her to lose her abilities, as she's been warned. And yet there's something else in her face—a determination, a strange joy. I realize I'm seeing something I never saw in my lifetime: my mother in love.

I close my eyes, trying to call up the face of the mother I'm familiar with. What was her habitual expression? Wry amusement at my follies? A guarded sympathy? But all I can see is the face in the photograph. Annoyed, I shake my head, trying to clear it. But the photo has taken me over. From now on, this is how I'll be forced to picture my mother, as a stranger younger than myself, and more hopeful.

If my mother could risk so much to follow her dreams, then as her daughter can't I take this small risk that faces me today? She had to take on her journey alone—I'm fortunate enough to have a friend and a father with me.

I don't tell my father to stop. Instead, I watch as he mixes a huge bowl of pakora dough, adds chopped onions, spinach, an assortment of spices. How lovingly his hands gather the besan flour, pour the warm water.

"Don't just stand there," he tells me. "Cut up the green chilies and throw them in." He tests the oil, starts releasing the first set of balls into its sizzle. Then the doorbell rings.

Our first customer!

"Just in time," says my father.

I rush to the front and find Sonny entering the store. Sonny, of all people! When we were married, nothing less than a natural disaster would have forced him out of bed before noon. When we started sharing custody, he had to hire a woman to get Jona to school, because he couldn't wake up on time.

"Oh, it's you," I say. "I thought it was a real customer."

"You really shouldn't get this excited when you see me," he says. "It's bad for your heart, now that you're getting on in years." He turns to Belle. "I thought I'd come and check things out. What's the matter? I was sure there'd be more people here."

Belle points glumly out the window at the SELLABRATION sign. Sonny lifts an eyebrow, which means he's thinking. After a moment he says, "Well, I'm going to start you guys off here, then." He orders a plate of pakoras and a box of sandesh to go, and saunters into the back room to talk to my father.

"Should we be charging him money?" Belle whispers to me. "After all, he is family, kind of."

I hesitate, not sure about ex-husband etiquette. It *is* decent of him to come by, especially after that dinner fight, which was more my fault than his. We decide we'll give him the pakoras for free but let him pay for the sandesh.

He comes out of the back room munching on a plateful of pakoras that my father must have handed him. "They're good! Didn't know Dad had these hidden talents. Want one?"

He isn't your dad, I tell him inside my head. He grins as though he knows exactly what I'm thinking and compliments me on the paint job. He jokes with my father about the new name, and tells him he expects to eat some real kurma next time he comes.

"Sure thing, beta," my father says. "I'll make a special order for you. Just give me an hour's notice."

He isn't your beta, I tell my dad inside my head.

Before he leaves, Sonny walks over to Belle. "You're looking even prettier than usual," he says. "What's up? Are you in love?" When she flushes, he laughs, a delighted, infectious sound. We watch him as he walks down the street, packet of sandesh swinging from his left hand, cell phone in his right, still smiling.

"I can see why you married him," Belle says. "He can really turn that charm on."

"And off," I say acidly as I watch him talk animatedly on his phone. "Probably calling his girlfriend," I add. "It's her turn to bask in five minutes' worth of Sonny's charm."

Belle looks at me with narrowed eyes. "And why should you care if he's calling his girlfriend? Riks, are you still—"

"I am not," I snap. "And don't call me Riks." I go over to the tables and wipe them down once again, though they are spotless already.

But I have misjudged Sonny. As the day goes on, several of his friends—musicians and fellow DJs—stroll in. I haven't seen them since I moved out. I feel awkward welcoming them into the shop, but they seem to have accepted the fact of our breakup with scarcely a blink. In their world, such things probably happen every day. Sonny must have called and asked them to show up. Several express interest in meeting the new chef, so he must have told them about my father, too. My father makes a dramatic entry from the back room, bearing aloft an emerald-green bowl of chutney, and impresses them by reciting the history of various dishes. The rice pudding, he says, is one of the oldest desserts of India, mentioned even in the Ramayan. It is what the gods sent to King Dasharath's barren queens to make them fruitful. He points to the laddus and informs Sonny's friends that they are made from the same recipe that Duryodhan's cook used in the Mahabharat to lure and poison his cousin Bheem—minus the poison, of course. I give him a suspicious look, but Sonny's friends love it. They order substantial amounts, leave large tips on the table. Jespal brings in a group of coworkers for lunch, and promises to come back after work with some more people. It's more traffic than our shop has seen in months, but I'm not happy. We can't run a business on the support of friends. Strangers—like the ones jostling to get into Java—is what we need.

But how to attract them?

After lunchtime the shop empties. Belle pokes around in the back room. I rearrange the plate of laddus and look out the window from time to time to check the crowd outside Java. It's still there. We've made only a small dent in the laddus, and some of the other desserts are still untouched. If a significantly larger number of customers don't show up by the end of the day, we'll be forced to do what Belle predicted—throw it all away.

My father, too, is looking concerned. He says he needs some fresh air and pulls a chair outside the door. When I leave to get the car and pick Jona up from school, I hear him singing under his breath as he massages the arm that had been broken. The words are not familiar, but the current of melancholy resonates inside me even after I can't hear him anymore.

At the intersection, I glance back and am surprised to see that he's talking to a man I don't know. The stranger is about as old as my father and, like him, Indian. I know this last fact not from his face (his back is to me), nor from his clothes (he is wearing blue jeans and a T-shirt), but by his gestures. My father, too, uses the same curving, insistent arm movements, the same dramatic bobs of the head. They are not gestures that Belle or I—or even Jespal, in spite of his zealous turban wearing—use. The rhythms of the body—how they separate people from each other!

The light turns green, the crowd surges forward and I follow, all of us with our identical, hurried, American gait.

I arrive at the school to find Jona in tears. She can't find her lunch box. It's a new one, she tells me, red and black, with a dragon stitched on top. It's special. We search her classroom and then the grounds, but there's no sign of it.

Finally, we give up and get in the car. I'm tired and frustrated, and Jona's still crying. I should have been back at the store an hour ago to relieve my father so that he could go into the back room and lie down for a while.

"We should have looked some more," Jona says. "Now my dragon will fly away and never return."

I don't mean to snap at her, we've spent so little time together lately, but the words come out before I realize what I'm about to say. "Don't be silly. That's not a real dragon. But you should have been more careful with the box."

"You're always scolding me," she says. "I wish Sonny was picking me up instead of you. *He* would have looked some more. *He* wouldn't have said I was silly."

I tighten my fingers on the wheel to stop myself from turning around and smacking her. How do children know the exact procedure by which a gentle, considerate parent can be transformed into a raging maniac?

I take deep breaths until I can control my voice. Then I say, "I wish your dad wouldn't buy you all these fancy things that tempt other people to steal them."

"You don't know that someone stole it," Jona says. "You shouldn't blame people until you have proof."

Where do they learn to talk like this?

"It could be under one of the maple trees in the other corner of the playground," she adds. "You didn't let me go there. And besides, Sonny didn't buy me the lunch box."

"Who did, then?"

"Eliana."

I swing the car over to the curb and turn off the engine. I turn around and look at Jona. The tears have left dirt streaks on her face, and for a moment I'm tempted to drop the matter. But no, this has gone too far. I can't let her confuse reality and fantasy anymore.

"Jonaki," I say firmly. "There is no Eliana. I want you to tell me who really gave you that lunch box. Or"—my voice shakes now, and not just with anger—"did we just spend an hour and a half looking for a lunch box that doesn't even exist?"

She stares out of the window.

"Jonaki, I'm speaking to you!" I'm shocked at this hard, loud voice that comes out of my mouth. I've never spoken to my daughter like this. But I can't seem to stop myself. "Answer me! Right now!"

Jona cringes back against the seat. "It's just like Eliana said," she whispers. "She told me not to talk about her to you. She said you wouldn't believe me, and that you'd be mad."

Her whispering voice, with a little break in it, goes through me like a knife. I close my eyes tightly. What in hell am I doing?

When I open my eyes, I see Jona looking at me from behind a lattice of fingers, her eyes large with fear.

"I'm sorry, baby," I tell her. "I really am. Things have been tough at the store today, but that's no reason to take it out on you. I'll buy you another lunch box if we don't find this one." I'll have to wait on the questions that fly around me like mosquitoes, waiting for the chance to bite. Such as, When and where did Eliana (if there is an Eliana) give Jona the lunch box? And if not, what is going on inside my daughter's head?

Perhaps Sonny has some of the answers. I'll have to catch him by himself, so I can ask him.

"Forgive me?" I say to Jona, smiling as best as I can. She nods, but she doesn't take the hand I offer, and when I drop her at the Kurma House before parking the car, she runs in without a backward glance.

The man walks into the store just as dusk is falling, and after a moment of confusion I see that he's the stranger my father was talking to earlier in the day.

We're getting ready to close up. A few people trickled in through the afternoon, but not enough, and enormous quantities of food sit inside the display counter, awaiting disposal. Belle's lipstick is chewed off, her hair stringy with defeat. My father's shoulders slump, and before he disappears into the back room I notice him limping, as he did in the first days after the accident. As for me, I'm mostly numb. I feed Jona and help her with her homework (I have plenty of time, after all), and she helps me clean the plate glass on which I'd written our new name barely twenty-four hours ago. I see the sweets—so caringly prepared, so carefully stacked—reflected in it and feel like crying.

The man asks for my father and, when he emerges from the back, talks to him in a rapid Indian language I don't know. My father answers him, though more haltingly. Both of them punctuate their speech with those emphatic, coded hand movements I'd noticed earlier. The language isn't Bengali, I can tell that much. I look inquiringly at Belle, but she shakes her head. Her parents insisted that she speak Hindi and Punjabi while she was growing up, but after leaving home, she made a concerted and mostly successful attempt to forget them both.

When the men finish their conversation, the stranger gives my father an unexpectedly graceful salaam and leaves. My father stares after him.

"What is it, Grandpa?" Jona asks. "What did he want?"

"It's the darnedest thing," he says. "He heard me singing this afternoon—humming, really—and stopped to listen. He asked me if I knew any other Hindi songs. I told him that I knew quite a few. He didn't say anything at that time, but now he came to ask if I'd be willing to sing for his friends if they came to the store. They all love songs from the movies, especially the old ones, and there's no place where they can hear them sung live. I said I'd be happy to. He said he'd go and get them. So, ladies—can we stay open a little longer?"

We agree. What have we to lose, at this point? An hour

passes. Jona dozes off. I'm beginning to suspect that my father misunderstood the man. Then there's a noise at the door, and a group of people around my father's age come in. Some wear Western clothes, and some are in kurta-pajamas, but what I notice most are their faces. Lined, unabashedly showing their age, they hint at eventful pasts lived in places very different from this one, difficulties and triumphs I can't quite imagine. The word *foreign* comes to me again, though I know it's ironic. They're my countrymen. We share the same skin color. I look from them back to my father's face. Does it hold the same expression? But I'm too close to him to tell.

The men order modestly: tea and jilebis. They take a few sips, a nibble or two. With awkward politeness—perhaps they're not used to talking to women they don't know—they tell Belle and me that everything is bahut achha. But their attention is not on the food. As soon as my father pulls up a chair, they begin to question him. Does he know the songs from *Anand*? From *Guide*? Could he sing "Gaata Rahe Mera Dil"?

And my father, who has sung only for himself until now (we had merely been backdrops for his vocalization) launches into the melody, his voice made truer by the hopes of strangers. The men nod their heads to the beat—clearly, they know the words, too, but they defer to my father's talent. After a few minutes, one of them takes a mouth organ out of a pocket, while another lifts a small, two-ended drum out of a bag I hadn't noticed. When my father starts on another song ("Sing us a gana from *Sholay*, Bhaisaheb!"), they accompany him, filling our shop with gaiety, causing Jona to sit up with a sleepy smile. They've forgotten our presence—even my father. The music continues for the next couple of hours, song after song, without break. When the tune is particularly catchy, two or three of the men get up and dance, their steps unhurried, unself-conscious, the bright handkerchiefs that materialize in their hands like magician's scarves rising and falling in slow motion.

When my father finally stops, out of breath, the men don't applaud. For them, what happened in this shop isn't a performance but a ceremony, something they were part of. Belle and Jona and I applaud, though. The sound of our clapping fills the room, echoing from behind us, and when I turn, I see other people. Did they notice the music makers and come in to see what was happening? Sonny's here, too, come to take Jona home. He gives a piercing whistle and calls out something that I don't understand. The men break into smiles.

"Last call for food," Sonny yells as the crowd begins to disperse. "Here's your chance to try Bengali snacks freshly made by one of Calcutta's greatest chefs!" I don't think it'll work, but a number of people wander over to the glass cases. We end up selling more than we'd expected. We still have to give away food to Marco, but when we lock up it's with a curious sense of accomplishment.

"Well, Dad," Sonny says as he follows us out of the store, carrying Jona, "maybe you're on to something."

My dad gives a cautious shrug, but he's smiling.

Every evening the men come back to make music. If my father doesn't know the song they ask for, they good-naturedly request a different one. (But my father's learning, too. Sonny has brought him more tapes, and even a karaoke machine so he can practice at home.) Word of our soirees must have traveled, for one day an African American comes in with a tall, carved drum, and a flute player who looks like he's from South America. A week later there's a hippie with a braid and a tambourine. The men eye the African American's shaved, gleaming head with curiosity. Some stare at the mermaid tattoo on the hippie's bicep. But they shift around and make room for them, and nod approvingly when they hear how the new instruments add timbre to the songs. A small but regular audience gathers to hear them. They're music lovers, not big eaters, but our business starts to pick up.

"I'd never have imagined people would be interested in listening to old-time Indian songs," Belle tells me. "Why, most of them don't understand a word they're hearing."

She's right. There are a few South Asians here, but our audience is mostly a mix of various races.

"I guess good music crosses all boundaries, like good food," I say.

But I suspect that the listeners keep coming back because they're drawn, like me, to the old men. There's an enigma about them—where they've come from, why they left those distant places. What they've had to give up in order to survive in America. Watching them pulls us out of the cramped familiarity of our own lives into a larger possibility, *once upon a time, in a land far, far away.* It's what I'd wrestled my mother for, even as she'd insisted that the only magic lay in *now.*

But what comes across most powerfully as they make music is their joy at discovering, like an unexpected oasis tucked into an arid stretch of dunes, something they thought they'd never find here in America. It's a pleasure to watch their pleasure.

With business stabilizing, we rehire Ping to handle the easier morning shift. My father, buoyed by his dual success as chef and singing star, starts driving himself to the store. I return to my apartment. Jona goes back to time-sharing her parents.

I'd expected to be delighted to be back home, but I'm surprised to find that I'm lonely. For all my irritation with him, I miss my father and our brief nighttime exchanges. He's been too busy to progress further on the journals, and this, too, fills me with impatience. And though I'm delighted to have Jona with me, I guiltily admit that I've grown unused to shaping my day around the demands of a child's presence. Being with her makes me restless. I miss my mother more when she's around. When she throws a tantrum or stares at me with new pigheadedness, I want to call my mother for advice. A grudging respect for Sonny stirs in me, for all those days he took care of Jona without boast or complaint.

My painting has reached a standstill. Even Jona with her fiery scenes is doing better than I am. Two more paintings have sold at the Atelier, but I don't feel the surge of excitement I thought I'd experience. I feel detached from the work I did before—as if it were painted by someone else, and not someone I particularly admire. There's a static feel, particularly, to my paintings about India. As my mother would say, they're not authentic.

I want to create something new, something different and magical, only I'm not sure what it will be. I can't replicate the treescape with the man in white, I know that much. Some things you achieve in art are a one-time deal.

Give yourself some time, Belle says. You've been through so much recently.

How can I explain to her that each day that passes without painting has a hollowness to it, a sense of waste?

I'm dreaming every night, but I remember nothing. It's as though there's a wall inside me, constructed (but by whom?) to protect me from something too painful to bear. My dreams take place on the other side of this wall. I wake in the morning with vague recollections of color, whispered laughter, smell of food or beaches, a sense of loss. I'm convinced the two are related, my not-painting and my not-dreaming. But I don't know how to break down the partition, and in truth, I'm afraid.

I worry about these things only in fits and starts. Mostly, I'm busy and grateful at the unexpected turn in the fortunes of Kurma House. Our audience continues to grow. An Asian woman has joined the musicians. She wears a black cape and plays a samisen. I haven't had time to wonder how our rival across the street feels about our success. Maybe my father is right: I shouldn't think of her as a rival anymore. At Kurma House, we're doing something unique that she could never imitate. She has her space, mine.

Late at night we turn off the lights, lock the shop and walk down to the parking lot. Sometimes Jespal is with us. Or Sonny, if it's one of his nights off. But mostly I walk between my father and Belle, carrying a sleeping Jona. My muscles ache satisfyingly. The streets are empty at that hour, for Kurma House stays open longer than all the other businesses around here. Sometimes my eyes are drawn to the unlighted square of Java's window. Is it darker than elsewhere, a squid-ink darkness, seeping out to touch us? I'm being fanciful. If I rubbed my eyes and looked again, it would be a window just like any other. Besides, why should I be afraid? I get into my car and wave good-bye to my father and my best friend. A warm expansiveness comes over me, a sense of many blessings. I send a kind thought to the blond manager, wherever she may be, and start with my daughter for home.

26

She wakes in the middle of the night, the dream already un-raveling around her, wisps of pulled-apart syllables, patches of fading color. She wakes to the jangling of the phone and feels her heart thudding dully, weighted down by the déjà vu of dread. She wants to burrow into her bed, ignore the noise until it goes away, but she remembers how such reluctance led her into tragedy once before. Had she not disconnected the phone that night, would she have been able to reach her mother before her death?

Such are the questions that come to her in the dark. To silence them, she picks up the phone.

It's Sonny. This does not surprise her. She is surprised, how-ever, to find that she isn't angry. At some other moment, she'll have to think about the meaning of this. Right now he's telling her that Jona has a fever.

"I gave her Tylenol and lots of water, and her temperature went down a little, but she's crying and asking for you." He ends the sentence on an upward note, as though it were a question, which it is.

In response to that unspoken question, she gets in the car. Driving through the late-night streets, she repeats her daughter's name, Jona Jona Jona, like a charm. Children always get fevers, she knows this. But loss has made her fearful in a whole new way. Her old companion, the whisper voice, elbows its way forward. *You weren't with her when she needed you—what kind of mother is that?*

But beneath all this is another woman who watches for a black car. What will she do if it appears? Would she be able to keep going on the road duty has mapped for her? There's a strange attraction to the thought of swerving from all the problematic roles of her life (insecure mother, needy friend, blocked painter, stumbling businesswoman, blind dreamer, grudging daughter, possessive ex-wife) into an unknown space, an unforeseen being. But the universe, which only gives when it wants to, chooses not to tempt her tonight.

Once again at the heartbreak house. He's left the door unlocked, a habit they used to fight about when they fought about things, before she chose to leave because her life was not long enough to spend it trying to make him like her. Yes, that's what they really fought about, she sees that suddenly, like the phosphorous flare of a match. For the first time the absurdity of that strikes her. *I wouldn't have liked it if he wanted to remake me in his image, would I?*

"I'm here," she calls as she enters, mostly to remind herself that she doesn't belong in this house, that her arrival must be announced and monitored. She follows his muffled reply up to the master bedroom. It's hard for her to step across the threshold into a space where (she knows this the way once-wives know such things) Sonny has brought other women. Then she sees Jona curled up on the bed, flushed and shivering under a quilt, and forgets lesser things.

. . .

*H*ours have passed, cold water brought in bowls, wet wash-cloths applied to the child's forehead. The child sweats and shivers alternately, hugs her mother rib-aching tight, pushes her away, fretting. She asks for water but when it's brought flails out with her arm, sending the tumbler flying. The Tylenol works for a while, the fever falls, then spirals up dangerously. The parents (fused into that role by anxiety) discuss taking her to the emergency room, but at this the child cries so bitterly, cheeks splotching with panic, that they abandon the plan. Finally the mother fills the bathtub with cold water and gets in. Only as the water soaks them does she realize she's still in her clothes. The father hands her the child, the small body hot and limp and listless. She gives a cry of protest, then settles against the familiarity of her mother's curves. The mother holds her and rocks, crooning. They make a strange tableau, this waterlogged madonna and child, their skin puckering as the minutes shiver past, their fingers shriveling like grapes. Finally, the child's body cools enough for the father to wrap her in a bath towel and take her back to bed. The mother rises to her numbed feet, grasping the edge of the tub with stiff fingers. She peels off her wet clothes and dries herself as best as she can on the hand towel hanging on the rack. She remembers this towel—it is part of a set she bought at a basement sale in their student days. She remembers how pleased she'd been coming home, holding them up for his inspection and praise. The towel is old now, its edges fraying, the maroon threads that smell of his aftershave coming loose. She wonders why he hasn't replaced it. Didn't notice it, probably. Men are like that, their man eyes always focused elsewhere, never on what's in front of them.

She reaches behind the door, where his robe hangs on its usual hook. The hook, too, has a history: her fingers recall peeling off the protective backing, the smell of the adhesive, the day bright with—but enough with the memories! She's here because she's needed by her daughter, that's her only reason, and she's not going to let late-night nostalgia nudge her toward believing otherwise. Still as she pulls on the robe (a thin silk kimono already slipping off her shoulders, most impractical for cold Bay Area nights, and who bought it for him, she'd like to know) she can't stop fragments of images from flashing in her head. That disastrous party, the drink in her hand, the several drinks, the woman in her mock-waitress outfit pressing caviar (had there been something in it?) on her, arms pulling her down, mouths she didn't recognize, her shouting Sonny's name, a blue bruise later on her thigh, the sense of falling upward, out of her body. Once again she has the sensation of watching a film dragged too fast through the projector.

She'd tried to talk to Sonny about it a week later. That was when she could finally bring up what had happened without break-ing down. Even then it was hard; she kept running out of breath, her mouth grew dry and her face was hot as though it was she who'd done something shameful. He'd frowned and said, "But are you sure? I can't believe anyone there would attack you. Maybe you got confused—do you think you might have taken some-thing—? Maybe without knowing it—?"

His dismissal of this terrible thing that had happened to her as a bad drug trip infuriated her. They had a fight, he stormed out, and she never got to what she'd really been trying to say. That the worst part of the night wasn't the assault but the fact that he hadn't been there to rescue her from it. She'd called to him for help, and he'd failed her.

She never brought it up again. Soon after that, she moved out.

But now, with the uncertainty that she's felt since her mother's death, she wonders, What really did happen that night? Could she, indeed, have been confused? Are events and occurrences—indeed, history itself, which she always thought of as solid and dependable—no more so than molten lava? Is reconstructing a story an endeavor doomed from the start?

All this flashes through her as she walks to the bed. And yet he should not have disbelieved her. He should have been more sympathetic, should have investigated, questioned, punished whoever was responsible. He should have been the protector she had expected a husband to be or, failing that, suffered in her suffering. But he didn't. He went back to that club of his and made beautiful music as though she had never spoken.

"Mom," Jona says in a hoarse smoker's voice, "I want you to lie down with me. Put your head on my pillow." The girl's eyes are a little clearer, and in thankfulness the woman obeys, though once she had promised herself she'd never lie in that bed again. The bed creaks under her weight. The sound is like a rusty chuckle, the house that she had abandoned laughing to see her pride brought low by parenthood.

"Now you," the child orders her father. "Lie down on my other side. Here, put your head on my pillow." When he does, she takes their hands in hers and links them over her chest. She gives a sigh so deep they can feel her rib cage heave with it. The woman lies there, awkward and silent but not daring to let go because finally the child seems to be resting. She keeps her eyes carefully away from the man's; with every nerve in her body she's aware of their interlocked fingers. They haven't touched except by accident since the night she moved out. What is he feeling? What is she feeling?

The child's heartbeats are less frantic now, her breath comes easier. Yes, she's sleeping, though it's a fitful sleep, eyes darting beneath her lids. Perhaps it's contagious, perhaps relief makes the parents relax—or maybe they're just exhausted after the night's ordeal. In any case, their eyes close, and they, too, drift into sleep.

She is dreaming. But she knows it isn't her dream. Not since she was little has she dreamed in those bright, finger-paint colors. It's Jona's dream, and she's dreaming it because in sleep their heads have shifted so that all three are touching. (Is Sonny dreaming this dream, too? But no, that man has no dreams inside him, only a cacophony of sound.)

In the dream they are on a hillside, a woman and child. She guesses them to be mother and daughter. She is not sure if she's seeing Jona and herself—their backs are to her, their silhouettes fuzzy in the predawn. It is a beautiful scene. There are wildflowers by their feet, poppies and lupines getting ready to open. The sun is coming up—they can see the glow, the edge of the hill growing brighter. They wait for it eagerly, holding hands. But when the sun appears, its light is too harsh, a white chemical beam. Too late the woman realizes that something is wrong. She barely has time to push the child down before the light hits her hair. And then she's gone—just like that—vaporized. The girl is left on her knees, alone and crying.

The mother calls out in her dream, trying to warn the girl, but she's only able to make a strangled, meaningless sound. The light is going to hit the girl any instant now. But no, the sun seems to have paused in its climbing, and instead, from the other side of the hill, a different woman comes into sight. Backlit and beautiful, with long brown hair, she walks toward the child, and when she reaches her, she extends her hand. The dreaming mother creases her brow—there's something familiar about the woman, the flowing, gauzy skirt, the flowers woven into her hair. The child looks up, uncertain, her tears forgotten for the moment. And in that moment the mother knows that the woman is evil—no, not evil, that's too simplistic a word. But she'll take the child and change her, transform her into something her own mother didn't intend for her to be, and that's a violation, isn't it? She makes one last supreme effort and cries out, pushing the rage out of her throat, and with that cry she wakes up. Her scream still hangs in the air, though, anguished and prolonged. Then she realizes it's Jona screaming.

"No, no, no," her daughter cries, her eyes still closed, flinging her body from side to side. "Someone help! Help them!"

The father, jolted awake by the screams, stares dazedly. So the mother must put aside her own agitation (strange how deeply that dream, coming after so many blank nights, shook her; strange how vividly she remembers each detail, after so much forgetting). "It's okay, baby," she must say, gathering the child to her, kissing her back into this wakeful life. "It's only a dream," she must say, though she knows this is not true. It's only a dream if you don't know the connection between the moon and the sun, between water and air, between fullness and annihilation.

Days later, the child will say, "It was terrible, Mom. They hurt so bad. They were so scared. I really wanted to help them."

"I know you did, sweetheart," the mother will reply. "I did, too."

The child will look at her questioningly.

"I dreamed the same dream," the mother will explain.

"Can people do that?"

"Not always. Maybe it was because you were so sick, and I'd been so worried. It made a special bond between us that night, I guess, when I lay down with my head on your pillow. It was so sad for that child to be left all alone—I really felt for her. I guess I was imagining you in her place—"

"But, Mom—"

The mother rushes on, propelled by the weight of what she has wanted to tell someone for years. "You were so upset when you awoke, your temperature started going up again. I was really scared. I wanted to buy that dream from you, like my mother did with me. I even took the coins out of my purse. Did I ever tell you I used to have a nightmare, the same one, over and over, until your grandma bought it from me?"

"I did, too, Mom! I dreamed the exact same thing before I got sick, only it wasn't so clear. But—"

"Then I remembered what happened when she bought it. Somehow it stopped me completely from dreaming. All the years of my growing up. And I thought, I can't do that to you. Even if they're painful, I have to let you have your dreams. Did that nightmare come back again, after that?"

The child nods, her face pale. "It still does, every few days. But, Mom, there aren't any girls in my dream. There's a burning building, with people trapped inside, but they're all adults."

That is how the mother learns that what she dreamed wasn't her daughter's fear. It was her own.

27

FROM THE
DREAM JOURNALS

The morning after we were accepted into the caves as novices, we received our first lesson. It was delivered by Elder Samyukta. Later we would realize that this was by design. She was one of the milder dream teachers, less intimidating than Elder Simhika, with her fierce mane of silver hair, or Elder Samahita, who had the habit of stopping newcomers in the dimly lit corridors of the caves and examining them with her steel-blue eyes.

In her simple cotton sari, Samyukta looked not too different from the mothers many of us (but not I) had left behind. She put us at ease by asking if we had slept well, and if we had had enough to eat at the morning meal. But when she began her talk, her voice deepened, and she looked at us as though she saw things we did not know about ourselves. We realized then that living here, in these caves that were in the world but not quite of it, would change us beyond recognition. And some of us—including myself—were frightened and focused all our attention on holding back tears. Thus later, when I finally realized how vital this first lesson had been, I could remember only parts of Samyukta's speech. I will set them down below as best as I can.

All of you, she said, are blessed because you possess the gift of dreaming, but unless you know what the dream is, whence it comes and what its purpose can be, the gift is useless.

Erase from your mind all the notions you hold about dreams. They will only impede you in your path.

It is true that oftentimes a dream is stitched together from images thrown up by an agitated mind, worries that surface when the body is still. But those are the dreams of ordinary beings and need not concern you, though much of your life will be spent in explaining them.

Sometimes you will be given a warning in a dream, which you must convey to the person it is meant for, a person whose mind is too thick for the dream spirit to pierce. This is a more difficult task—for often such a person will not want to hear what you say—but it is still not your main purpose.

The dreams that are most important come from another reality—you might call it another *time*, for want of a better term in our limited speech. This is the *time* of the dream spirits. I lack the capacity to describe it. All I can say is that even an instant of being in that time will transform you the way the philosopher's stone transforms base metal into gold. But I stumble ahead of myself.

As you progress in this path, you will realize that each of you has a guardian spirit. If you are fortunate and careful, the love between you and this spirit will grow into a great and wondrous thing. Through dreams the spirit will tell you who you truly are, although it might have to speak many times before you learn to listen. Unless you observe a life of service and compassion and cultivate the six treasured virtues, you may never learn this skill. But when—no, if—you finally hear, you will see the intricate web of love that binds existence together, and you will never need anything else in order to be happy. The more fortunate among you, blessed by the dream, will live long in the world after, and help many souls. But for others the message will come at the moment of death, and will be inseparable from it. For those who need extra guidance, a messenger may appear at the time. Do not lose him or her—it will be your last chance to grasp the truth of the dream time.

Many years have passed since Samyukta's speech, and since I left the caves in disgrace. I think of her words from time to time (the fragments I am left with) and grow dejected. I've tried to live a virtuous life, but unsuccessfully, caught as I am between two worlds that define virtue in opposed ways. I've often been impatient, and angry, and restless. I've regretted the choices I made and blamed them on others. Worst of all, I have not loved anyone fully, not my husband or child, not the suffering souls that have come to me for help. Try as I might, the core of my heart remains moldy and desolate. Even the dream spirits have not been able to fill it. My only hope is the messenger—will he ever come?

28

Rakhi

The fever is gone, but Jona is still too weak to go to school. Sonny wants her to stay at his house, and though part of me bristles at him (Sonny-the-controller), I have to concede that it's more practical. This way when he goes off in the morning to do whatever it is that DJs do when they're not performing, I can come over and keep Jona company. By the time I have to leave for the Kurma House, Sonny will have returned.

The morning after the fever, I wipe Jona down and change her sweat-crusted clothes. I put baby powder on her the way I used to when she was little. When I bend over to kiss her forehead, she asks if I will move in with her and Sonny until she's well enough to go back to school, *please, Mom.*

It's hard to refuse when she's been so ill. I hate myself for it. But if I weaken and give in, the result will be disastrous. Being in this house when Sonny is gone is difficult enough. Being here when he's around will bring up too many painful memories—even if he wants me here, which I doubt.

But most of all, I don't want to give Jona false hopes about the two of us getting back together.

I say no, bracing myself for tears, but Jona doesn't insist. She turns on her side and closes her eyes, as though she hadn't really expected that I would say yes. There's such resignation in the curl of her back that a pang goes through me.

Am I making a mistake? I guess I'll know only later. Up close, it's impossible to read the foreshortened angles of one's actions—which are the right turns, which will lead to sorrow.

Did my mother make the wrong choice in deciding to come to America with my father? Reading her journals, I begin to see what she hid from us so craftily: her regret, her longing for community, her fear of losing her gift. Ironic that her ability to tell dreams stayed with her; it was love that she lost—the love for which she'd crossed the forbidden ocean. I had always thought of my mother as a serene person. Now I see that this was only because she denied sadness, which she considered a useless emotion. She survived by making herself believe that loneliness was strength. I begin to understand why she kept her face resolutely turned to the future. It was too painful to think of the past. Except in the journals, she cut that part of herself out of her heart.

Reading, I feel a great pity welling up in me—for her and for us. Because existing in this way exacted its price. Her discontent worked its way under our skin, living there undetected like a low-grade infection. In my father's case, it would erupt from time to time in his drinking bouts. My disease was a subtler, more chronic one. It expressed itself in my endless sallies toward knowing her, as though by gaining that knowledge I could make her mine.

My life is not as dramatic as hers, nor my choices as momentous. But I know this as well as it is possible to know anything in this shifting, shadowed world: if I got back together with Sonny for Jona's sake, sooner or later I'd resent her for it. And that would be much worse than the disappointment she's suffering now.

This Friday Jona has recovered sufficiently to go back to school, but I decide to keep her home one more day. One day for us, mother and daughter, to shrug off worry and exhaustion and enjoy ourselves. When I ask her what we should do, she tells me she wants us to paint together.

As I set her up at the table with her watercolors, I can feel my heart tightening as though someone has pushed me to the edge of a cliff. I consider telling her I have nothing to paint with. But she'll catch me in that lie: she knows I always carry a portable easel and a canvas in the car. Reluctantly I fetch them, and we begin. Rather, I stand at my easel and watch my daughter paint, eyes narrowed, head tipped to one side, so engrossed that she forgets my presence. I envy her as she mixes reds and oranges and blacks, as she applies the strokes with a bold, unwavering hand. As objects take shape on the paper, I see that she is painting—once again—a fire. I watch uneasily. What is this obsession with burning? But soon I'm distracted by how much she's improved. She must have practiced a great deal in these last confusing months. With her grandmother dead and her mother overwhelmed, painting must have given her stability. A way to express her emotions. I observe the care with which she delineates details. The windows of the tall building gleam in the light from the flames. They are filled with people, palms flat against glass, mouths open in a silent scream. The sky, too, is full of fire. It's hard to wrench my eyes from the strangely magnetic quality of the painting.

My own canvas is still blank. Even after the vivid dream that came to me in Sonny's bed, I haven't been able to paint. God knows I've tried, staying up nights, even after returning bone-tired from the Kurma House. I've stared for hours at the canvas, trying to find a subject. But everything I loved to paint before—a Calcutta train station, fishermen on the Ganga, the Belur Math at sunrise—seemed tired. Or perhaps it was I who was tired of them. I needed a new field, a new style—I just didn't know what.

Maybe I, too, should paint my dream. I sketch in the line of the hill, the two figures standing with their backs to me. I mix white and yellow for a dawn sky, a deeper yellow where the sun would be rising in a little while. No use. Even when I use my best techniques, I can't seem to put life into the painting. The mother and child stand stiff as wooden cutouts; the wildflowers are lined up in regimented rows. The anguish I felt in my dream, the sense of loss and fear—I just don't know how to convey that, no matter how I slash my strokes or pile paint on paint. Finally I take a turpentine-soaked rag and wipe off the canvas.

Sonny comes whistling in the door, carrying a bag of groceries, but when he sees what I'm doing he breaks it off. He offers to carry my art supplies to the car. No thank you, I say, but he follows me out anyway.

"I'm sorry the painting isn't going well," he says.

I want to tell him it's none of his business. But I find myself blurting out, "What if I can't ever paint again? What if my talent left me when my mother died?"

He puts out a hand as though to touch me, then drops it. There's understanding in his eyes, and sadness. "I feel that way sometimes, too. It makes you want to die, doesn't it? But it'll pass. You have real talent, Riks. I know it."

I don't believe him, but I want to hold on to the small comfort of his words. When he invites me to stay and eat, I don't say no.

Jona decides we are to have pancakes for lunch. ("Sonny and I will make them, Mom. You just watch.") They put on aprons. Jona fetches the ingredients and Sonny measures them, looking decidedly domestic. *It's just an act,* says my whisper voice. *Deep down he's still Sonny-the-hell-raker.* Still, I'm impressed. The father-and-daughter team cooks the pancakes to the accompaniment of much laughter. (*Making a mess of the kitchen in the process,* my whisper voice points out primly. It's not my kitchen, I point out in return. I don't have to clean it.)

We eat our pancakes topped with fresh strawberries and cream—that's what was in the grocery sack. (My whisper voice purses its lips. *So impractical.*) Jona pours us orange juice. There's a smudge of flour on her nose; pleasure flushes her cheeks when I tell her how delicious the meal was. Sunshine floods the kitchen, loosening my muscles. I feel warm and fuzzy and pleasantly full. I could commit to doing this every once in a while. Even if we can't be a happy family 24-7, we can be it in bits and pieces.

Then Sonny says, "I've been working on some new music that I'm really excited about. I'd love to have you come to the club and hear it."

"Yeah, Mom," Jona adds. "You should go. It's really cool."

My serenity takes a nosedive. "How do you know?" I glare at her, then at Sonny. "Have you been taking her to the club?"

Sonny puts on his injured face. Jona rolls her eyes. "Mom! He brings his CDs home for me. The new ones, you know, the ones he's been recording." She pushes out her chest. "I'm the first one who gets to hear them! They're really good."

I stare at Sonny in surprise. "You didn't tell me you were recording music," I say, feeling unreasonably hurt. He shrugs and smiles but doesn't offer excuses. Why should he? I don't keep him informed of every little detail of my life.

"It would be great if you came," he says again. His smile is as seamless as silk. But I, who know this man better than any other woman does (ah, the ego of the ex-wife), locate a telltale pulse beating in his temple. It's costing him to extend this invitation to me.

Yet I can't say yes. Whenever those images come crashing down on me—smoke and sweat, arms grabbing for me, hands holding my head, forcing my lips open—there's always Sonny's music in the background, throbbing in complicity. Can I ever hear it freshly again? All that anger and hurt that I'm working so hard at getting rid of, I can't risk them surging back.

"I can't do it right now," I say, pretending casualness. "Too much going on. Maybe later—"

Jona glares at me. I can read her thoughts. Meanie. We were having such a good time and you had to ruin it.

"No sweat," Sonny says, his tone as casual as mine. Does he guess my real reason, or does he think I don't consider his music worth my time? Either way, he's angry. I can tell because of the way his eyes change color, turning darker. I wish I could put an arm around him and explain my refusal, but I'm too prickly a person for that. I say my good-byes to Sonny and a Jona who stares frostily out of the window.

29

Rakhi

Business is brisk at the Kurma House. Our busiest time is in the evening, before the music starts, with a flurry of take-out orders afterward, but we're getting a decent lunchtime crowd, too. The cooking is becoming too strenuous for my father. Though he loves it, sometimes I catch him massaging his broken arm. Belle and I help as much as possible, but we're needed out front, to attend to customers. If business continues this way for another month, Belle says, we'll hire a chef's helper. Jespal, who's here most evenings, jokes about applying for the job.

"It's more fun than my engineering projects, and I love the perks," he says.

"Like what?" Belle asks.

"Free food, great live music, and the company of you two beautiful ladies."

I hide my smile. It's quite clear which of the beautiful ladies he really comes to see. Often, after closing, the two of them drive off into the night—a development, I fear, that Belle's orthodox parents hadn't quite intended.

This afternoon when I come in, the Kurma House is quiet. The lunch crowd has left. Ping has cleaned up already, so I let her go. I can hear my father whistling in the back, but Belle isn't here yet. This surprises me. She's always here before I arrive.

"You don't have to come in so early," I told her once. "Ping can manage lunchtime. You always stay till closing, anyway."

Belle scrunched up her forehead. "I feel more comfortable if I'm around."

"Honest, Belle, you're getting to be like one of those neurotic mothers who believe disaster will strike her child as soon as she looks away. If it weren't for Jespal, you'd probably move in here!"

She let that one pass.

The shop is full of the smell of singaras. I peek into the back room and see that my father has already cooked the cauliflower-potato stuffing and laid it out on a large tray to cool. Oil is heating in our largest wok over the big gas burner. Now he's rolling out the thin dough that will make up the skin.

"Hey, Dad," I say. "How come you're going to all the trouble of making singaras—and so many of them, too? Is it a special occasion?"

"Sometimes we should just make special things, no?" he replies. "Who knows if we'll be around when special occasions finally arrive." He glances at the photo in the alcove, and suddenly I wish my mother could see us like this, helping each other. Not much surprised her—but seeing my father in an oversize apron would have. Maybe it would have made her laugh.

I try to recall how she used to laugh, but I can't. Everything about her is receding into mist.

My father sighs, then resumes rolling. He must miss her even more than I do. I make a mental note to drop by with Jona next weekend. Maybe I can get him to tell us some more India stories.

It strikes me that he hasn't had one of his drunken binges since my mother died.

"And as for making so many, I don't know. I just had a feeling this morning. I can always freeze the extra ones."

"I'll help you stuff," I tell him.

He eyes me with uncertainty.

"Don't worry! I've done them with Mom. And don't try to take that heavy wok off the fire by yourself, okay?"

He frowns. "I can manage." He's as stubborn as I am.

I cut a circle into halves, the way my mother did it, form each half circle into a cone, fill it with the mix, moisten the top and pinch it closed. It's a tricky maneuver. I set each one down on a floured tray, and wait. A well-stuffed singara, she once told me, doesn't topple over. I am gratified to see that mine are staying put. I flash him a grin of triumph. He grins back.

The door chimes. "Sorry I'm late," Belle calls as she rushes in, out of breath. "Rikki, I've got to talk to you! Mr. Gupta, please excuse us for a few minutes."

I leave the singaras, intrigued. Belle isn't the secretive type. In fact, she's embarrassingly frank in front of my father, whom she's taken to treating like a favorite uncle.

She pulls me into a corner of the store, looking at once excited and nervous. "Riks, what am I going to do!"

"You could start by telling me what's going on."

She takes a deep breath. "Jespal asked me to marry him."

I give her a hug. "That's wonderful. Congratulations!" Seeing the expression on her face, I add, "Don't tell me you weren't expecting it! Maybe it happened a bit sooner than I thought it would, but I could certainly see it coming. Aren't you happy about it?"

"I'm not sure," Belle says. "I'm crazy about him, and I know he's attracted to me. But I didn't think he was serious, not in this way."

"Why not? He strikes me as a serious kind of guy. Husband material, unlike the disreputable young men you generally tend to gravitate toward."

"Maybe that's the problem. Sometimes I think we're too different. He's so traditional. Like with his turban. Did you know, he really does have long hair under it. It goes halfway down his back, like that man in *The English Patient*, remember? The first time I saw it, I freaked out. Though now I must say it's kind of sexy."

"Well then, what's the problem? You think his turban is sexy. He probably thinks the same about your pierced navel and your pink hair—"

"The name of this color is Burnished Burgundy, I'd like you to know. But seriously, you can't build a marriage on sexiness."

"Oh, child, I am delighted to see that thou hast finally drunk of the well of wisdom. This isn't quite the tune thou wert singing even two months ago."

"That's your problem, Rikki, levity at inappropriate moments. In a serious relationship people have to think alike. He believes in living according to the Granth Sahib: physical purity, discipline, putting the family first, being a respectable gurdwara-going member of the community. Rules my parents pushed down my throat every day of my life until I escaped to college!"

"He doesn't seem like the kind of guy who'll push anything down your throat—"

"He probably won't. But those values mean the world to him. He didn't just accept them because he grew up with them. He thought about them and struggled against them, but finally he was convinced they fitted him better than Western ways. And me— well, you know me! We'll disagree on everything—and after some time, we'll get tired of compromising. That's what I'm afraid of. I don't want us to end up hating each other."

"So what did you tell him?"

"I told him I'll give him an answer tomorrow. That's why I need your advice, you having been a married woman and all that."

I give a dry laugh. "Belle, I'm not exactly the best person to give advice. Look how my marriage ended up!"

"And why *did* it end up that way? You never would tell me. Was it something Sonny did? Or was it what I'm talking about: ir- reconcilable differences?"

I think back on that night at the party, the blurry terror, the reaching out for help into a void. Was that the beginning, or the end? All those years I'd been in love with him, Sonny-my-savior. Except that what I'd been in love with was an image I'd painted over my eyes so I wouldn't have to see.

"It's complicated," I say. "I don't think you'll have the same kind of problems. But since you have all these doubts, why not ask Jespal to wait a while?"

Belle sighs. "He doesn't want to. He's keen to settle down, start a family in a couple of years. His parents are getting old, and they want to see a grandchild before they die. He loves me, but if I'm not serious about our relationship, he feels there's no point in continuing."

"Whoa! That's quite an ultimatum! I can't imagine you with—what's your preferred term? Rugrats? A passel of snot- nosed brats? Not to mention the in-laws! Can you handle it?"

She makes a face. "I don't know. I find it quite terrifying to contemplate. And yet when I think of breaking up with him, all the independence in the world doesn't seem worth it."

"Belle, I don't know what to—"

The doorbell chimes. When I see who's walking in, I forget what I was about to say and gawk instead. It's the manager from Java. She isn't wearing her uniform, though. Maybe it's her day off. Instead, she's dressed in a shimmery skintight dress that looks like it belongs on the set of *Star Trek*. It shows off her sculpted muscles to advantage and brings out the lights in her hair, which looks silvery today. Her teeth sparkle as she gives us a smile.

"Hope I didn't interrupt something? I thought I'd return your visit."

Belle recovers first. "Delighted to have you here! Please sit down. Would you like something to drink? Maybe you'd like to try an Indian sweet?" She gestures to the display case.

"Complimentary, of course," I pull myself together to add.

The manager walks regally to a corner seat by the plate-glass window. She gives me a measuring look as she seats herself, crossing her legs elaborately. Her short dress rides up to reveal thighs that look like they've never heard of cellulite. She glances at the display, wrinkles her nose elegantly. "I'm not a desserts person. I prefer food with a bit of a kick to it. I smell something cooking in the back. Maybe I'll try some of that—if you'll tell me what's in it. I'm finicky that way. Better still, maybe I could talk to the chef?"

I can't tell what her plan is, but I know I don't want her to meet my father.

"Sorry," I say. "Chef's busy." I consider adding that our ingredients are a cultural secret, and it's fine with me if she doesn't want any. But she's a guest in our store. So I say, "It's a vegetable mix wrapped in dough and fried. Comes with a dip—"

"I think I could handle that. I hope you didn't mind me asking, but foreigners sometimes put—uh—unusual ingredients in their food. And, oh yes, I'd like a cup of good American tea, if you have any."

"I think we've just been insulted," Belle whispers. "Except it's too funny to be insulting. Did she really say 'good American tea'?"

"I'm glad one of us thinks it's funny," I say. I go into the back, where my father has finished frying a batch of singaras. He makes a questioning face.

"Tell you later," I say. I put a singara on a plate and walk over to the refrigerator where our chutneys are kept. The tamarind one comes in three versions: hot, hotter and incendiary. I put a spoonful of the last kind on the plate. That should give her enough of a kick.

When I take the plate over, the manager waves a hand. Her nails are silver, too. "Do sit down," she says. "You don't seem too busy right now."

"There's always work," I say defensively.

"Ah yes, always work of one kind or another," she says. "It's the same with me. But evenings now, that's your busiest time, isn't it."

It's not a question. She's been watching us.

"You get some strange people in here," she adds.

I make an effort to hold on to my temper. "I guess it all depends on what you consider strange."

"I guess it does," she agrees with an ingenuous smile. "And the music—if you can call it that. It's really—loud."

Is that what this is about? Has she come to complain about the noise? "I don't see how it could be that loud," I say. "It's just a few people singing and playing instruments. We don't even have a mike."

"Ah, but you don't know how it sounds from the other side, do you?" she says, smiling sweetly. "That's the problem. One of these days, it could land you in a whole heap of trouble."

Is she threatening to lodge a formal complaint?

"We'll handle the trouble when it comes to us," I reply. But despite my bravado, I'm worried. Is there a city ordinance against musicians in cafés? I must check up on it.

"I have to go get some things done," I say. "Belle will bring you your tea."

"Tell her not to bother," she says. "I have more than I wanted."

I'm trying to think of a clever rejoinder when the phone rings. It's Ping.

"I forgot to tell you," she says. "There's a package. I think it's for you. I put it in the back room, on one of the shelves."

"Who brought it? And what do you mean you think it's for me?"

"I'm not sure who brought it. I found it on one of the chairs when I was cleaning up. There wasn't any name—but someone had written 'For You' on it. I opened it—there were art prints inside. I figured you must be the one they're for. Though I don't know why someone would just leave it on a chair—"

I want to rush to the back, but first I ask, "Who was sitting at that table?"

"Let me see, two or three people came in at different times.

It's the table near the window, you know, one of our popular ones. There was a woman, and two men, I'm pretty sure."

"Can you remember what they looked like?"

"The woman was quite pretty. She wore a loose cotton dress. The men were just regular, nothing special. They all ordered coffee—"

"Did the woman have long, curly hair?"

"It fell over her shoulders—I didn't see how long it was."

"And the men—" I swallow and continue. "Were either of them wearing white?"

"I think the one who came in last had on white pants. But any of them could have slipped that package onto the chair. It's only because I pull out the chairs to dust them that I even saw it—"

It doesn't mean anything. Berkeley is full of women with long hair and loose clothing and men wearing white.

As I'm thanking her, I hear a loud clang from the back room—something metallic falling—and a shout from my father.

"Rakhi," he yells, "quick, bring the other fire extinguisher!"

I drop the phone. In my panic I can't remember where we keep the spare extinguisher; then I locate it standing in a corner, covered with cobwebs. Belle has already run to the back room. I follow.

It's a scene of chaos. The wok is on the floor, oil spilled around it in a dark circle. Some of it must have fallen on the gas burner and ignited. Flames are leaping everywhere, some as high as the ceiling. My father's vainly trying to douse them with the extinguisher we keep next to the stove. I struggle with my extinguisher, trying to figure out how to make it function. It's industrial size, big and bulky and hard to manage, but finally, thankfully, it starts to work. I join my father in spraying, though it doesn't seem to make a difference. The flames lick my face hungrily, hotter than I imagined they would be. Is this what Jona dreamed about, us being trapped in here, burning to death? The flames are hotter now, sheets of them flaring out to grab us. Was the dream sent to her to warn me? Belle has filled a pan with water. She throws it on us, but it evaporates from my skin almost immediately. She fills another, throws it again. I'm coughing from the smoke. Is my daughter a dream teller, then? I yell to my father, *Give up! Run!* But he refuses to hear. He continues to spray though his aim is erratic with fatigue.

When I've almost given up hope, the fire begins to die down. We spray with renewed vigor, Belle throws more water and after a few minutes we're left with charred shelves, a blackened ceiling and walls, and a messy goo of oil and spray and water on the floor.

We walk shakily to the front of the store, which is empty now. When did the manager leave? My face stings as though slapped, smoke burns my throat and my legs are ready to collapse. But before I have a chance to sit, there are sirens outside. A group of firemen burst in, dragging a hose. We direct them to the back. They spray some more to make sure the fire is completely out, but there isn't much for them to do. An ambulance has arrived, and the paramedics treat my father and me for minor burns and cuts. The lead fireman fills out a report and tells us to contact our insurance company. He chastises us for not leaving the building right away. It was foolish and risky. You're lucky that room was mostly cement and brick and not wood, he says. Otherwise you'd be burnt to a crisp by now. Until the back is fixed up and a safety inspection done, he says, we can't cook in there. Before he leaves, he reminds us again, sternly, of how lucky we were.

We collapse at a table, Belle and my father and I, a bedraggled trio. I don't feel lucky, and judging from the looks on their faces, neither do they. I'm in shock at the speed with which disaster can strike—though I should know that already, shouldn't I? I consider telling them about Jona's dream, the fires she's been painting. But I don't think I can handle their responses right now.

"Thanks for calling the fire department," I tell Belle. "That was quick thinking."

Belle wrinkles her brow. "But I didn't call them! I should have, but I guess I panicked. Remember, I was with you all the time, throwing water on you guys, trying to keep you from catching on fire? Not that I did such a great job." She runs a light finger over my cheek, which feels blistered. "Your eyebrows are singed," she says.

"Who could have called them, then? The back room doesn't have windows. None of the neighbors could have seen—" I break off as a sudden thought comes to me. Could it have been the manager of Java? Surely not. She'd be delirious with delight if the Kurma House burnt to the ground with us inside. But I can't think of any other possibility.

A customer comes in to ask for coffee, and Belle has to tell him we're not open. We watch as he crosses the road and goes inside Java.

"You'd better put up the Closed sign," Belle says. I do as she says, feeling defeated.

We spend the rest of the day cleaning the back room. With a

pang, I throw the tray of ruined singaras into the trash. By the time it turns dark, we've cleared away the worst of the debris. But we'll need professional help to fix the rest. I cringe to think how much it'll cost.

I searched among the shards for my mother's picture, but I didn't see it anywhere. It makes me uneasy, that missing photograph. But I don't ask about it. To ask would be to make its loss—and the bad luck attached to this loss—real.

When we're done, I ask my father the question I'd been holding off because I didn't trust my temper. "What happened?"

"I'm not sure. I was taking the wok off the fire—I know, I know, I should have called you to help, but you were talking to a customer—and it's not like I haven't done it before. But this time suddenly it turned over. It was the strangest thing! My wrist must have given out." He sighs. "I can't tell you how sorry I am."

I must be too tired to get angry, because all I feel is depression. What bad luck that this had to happen just as we were finally getting ahead. Apart from the repair costs, our insurance is bound to go up. We lost a lot of supplies in there, too. And if we close, even for a few days, it'll destroy the momentum of the evening gatherings. People will find other things to do, and we'll never get them back.

Belle calls to me from the corner where the manager was sitting.

"Look at this," she says.

It's the singara I gave the woman, now squished shapeless. With the red chutney poured over it, it looks like a tiny, run-over animal. It's clear she didn't eat any of it. Compared to the destruction in the back, this is minor, but it makes me shiver. There's such malice behind this small act of wastefulness.

Could she have had something to do with our fire? Could she have wished it into being?

I shake my head to clear it. I'm looking to blame someone else because I don't want to lose the precarious closeness my father and I have achieved for the first time in our lives.

"Throw it away," I tell Belle, "even the plate." But she's already doing that. My head throbs. I think longingly of my bed, which I'm going to hit as soon as I take a double dose of aspirin.

As I'm about to lock up, my father says, "We'd better all go to your apartment, Rakhi. It's the closest."

I stare at him blankly. "What for?"

"To take our showers, of course." Under the soot that splotches his face, he looks resolute. "You do have a washer and dryer in the building? Belle can borrow an outfit from you, but this is the only set of clothes I have with me."

"What are you talking about?"

"We've got to get back and reopen before the musicians get here."

"Are you crazy?"

My father blinks at me. His expression indicates that he considers himself quite sane.

"Didn't you hear the fireman?" I shout. "We've got to close down until the safety inspection is done."

"I didn't hear him say that." My father squares his shoulders. "He said we can't cook in the back. And we won't. You've got machines out here to fix tea and coffee, and I put enough snacks in the refrigerator this morning to last us for tonight."

"Dad, don't you know when to quit?"

"We'll leave the exhaust on—that should clear the air.

Tomorrow I'll fix a couple of easy items at home and bring them with me. We'll take it from there, beti."

"You *are* crazy," I say. I turn to Belle. "Tell him he's crazy. We can't open tonight, in the middle of this mess. Not tonight, not tomorrow, not ever. As far as I'm concerned, we're done."

Belle looks uncertainly from my face to his. "Maybe Mr. Gupta has a point," she says. "We could try his plan, just for this evening—"

"I refuse to be a part of this farce. What will we tell the customers? Assuming that they'll hang around long enough to hear anything we have to say."

"We'll tell them the truth—that there was an accident," my father says. "They've had accidents. They'll understand."

"I don't want them to understand," I say. Bright streaks of pain slash across my eyes. "I want a handful of aspirin and some peace and quiet. You two can do what you like. Just don't involve me in it. As of now, I'm out of this partnership."

I toss the keys at Belle and walk away, leaving them staring after me.

30

FROM THE
DREAM JOURNALS

From the time she was little, Rakhi was fascinated with me. She put up with her father's attempts at amusing her, but it was for me her face would light up, and after a while he stopped trying. Do all girls go through such a phase of mother worship? Having had no mother myself, I didn't know. Only, for her it wasn't a phase.

From her playpen, Rakhi would watch me for hours at a time. Unlike other children, she didn't ask to be picked up or played with. She was happy just to watch. She observed me as I cooked or cleaned, as I sat with my eyes closed, sifting through the dreams that jostled demandingly in my head. When I spoke to clients on the phone, she listened, head tilted, black eyes unblinking, as though she understood everything I said. It made me uncomfortable. I began to go into the master bedroom to make my calls, even though being faced by the bed I no longer slept in made me uncomfortable in a different way.

She grew. Soon, I knew, she would start asking questions. I prepared my words. When I told her what I did, I tried to make it sound ordinary. But she'd already decided it was the most glamorous work in the world. By association, I was the most glamorous person.

It worried me to see my daughter idolizing me this way. There was so much she didn't know about me, that I couldn't tell her. My mistakes, my betrayals, my cowardices. Sooner or later, she was going to find them out, and then she'd feel betrayed, too. I wanted to stop that from happening, but how? I who advised so many people on their problems had no idea how to solve my own.

Rakhi was so upset she wouldn't eat. Wouldn't speak to me. She thought I wasn't teaching her to interpret dreams because I wanted to keep my gift selfishly to myself. (She was more accurate than she guessed. I *was* selfish, only in a different way.) Even her father, who seldom commented on household matters, asked what was going on. I should have told her right then what I'd surmised from the beginners' exercises: she had no talent. But it felt too cruel. Blinkered by love, I reasoned that I might be mistaken. To try once more couldn't hurt. And so that night, against my better judgment, I asked her to sleep with me in the sowing room.

I made Rakhi lie on my pillow so that our heads touched. I told her to close her eyes. This much I remembered from what my aunt had done when she had appeared like lightning in the dreariness of my life. Next, she had reached into me and touched something that lay sleeping. But I didn't know how to do that. It was something dream tellers learned in the last month of their studies, and I had left before then.

In the slums where I grew up, people had been afraid of me

because I seemed to know secrets about them, their hidden thoughts. It afforded me some protection in that place where orphans were used in cruel ways. I was thankful for my ability, but I didn't give it much attention. Now I realize I must have been reading the dreams of those who lived around me.

When Rakhi was little, I'd play a game with her. Can you guess what I'm thinking of, I'd ask her the morning after I'd had an important dream. I'd place her in my lap, look into her eyes, hold the dream in my mind and will her to tap into it. She'd touch my face, play with my hair. Finally, she'd grow fidgety and slide off my lap, and I'd be left with a mix of disappointment and relief.

I should have heeded those failed attempts. Instead, as we lay on the floor, our hair tangling together, I decided to try harder than ever before to break through the barrier between our minds. I closed my eyes. I was acutely aware of my husband in the next room, brushing his teeth, getting ready for bed. Did he wonder what we were doing? I heard his footsteps moving toward this room and stiffened, but the steps paused and went back as they always did. Rakhi was asleep already, her breathing shallow and effortful, as when someone climbs a steep staircase. Out of habit I probed her mind, but there weren't any dreams. She hadn't dreamed since the morning I bought her nightmare from her. I flinched away from that thought, that attempt to cure gone wrong. To be cursed by blankness each night as one slept! But perhaps if I succeeded in this venture, if I could funnel some of my ability into her, she would forgive me.

I shut off all outer sounds. I focused my attention on my awareness, that power that allows me to receive the dreams of others. After some time, it appeared as a speck of light in the center of my chest. I concentrated some more, and felt it begin to move. With effort I directed it to where my forehead touched Rakhi's. I visualized her awareness as a similar speck and called to it. I had never done anything like this before. At first I could not sense it; then I felt a warmth against my skull. In a while something began seeping into me. I could see it now, skittery and faint, bobbing next to me. I invited it in. The two lights began moving into my chest region. They were floating along a narrow corridor. Was it an artery? But perhaps they'd entered an inner landscape that had nothing to do with my physical body. As they went deeper, scenes flickered on either side of them as on a cinema screen.

Women in ragged saris crowd a footpath. They're waiting to fill water at the street-side tap. There's pushing and shoving because soon the water will be shut off. An unfilled pitcher means no water for cooking, nothing for the children to drink. The stronger women push to the front of the line. One roughly elbows a thin girl out of the way. She loses her balance, falls. Her clay pitcher drops to the pavement and smashes to bits. She stares at it, horrified. It will earn her a beating from the family that has kept her, grudgingly, since her mother disappeared. She turns her head and looks directly at me, and the force of her fear and anger strikes me like an explosion . . .

In darkness, an older girl follows a woman dressed in white. Only the stars shed a little light around them. Shadows shaped like animals lurk at the edge of the unfamiliar path. The girl wears a white sari, too—clothing she is not used to. She stumbles sometimes as she hurries to keep up, but she is afraid to ask the woman to slow down. What if the woman changes her mind, tells the girl she made a mistake, tells her to go back? They go on, the night doesn't end, nor the path. The girl imagines the caves they are making for. Inside her heart, the caves are the color of fog, mysterious and beautiful. A sudden rustling in the undergrowth. She turns a startled head, and I see that it is the same girl. Her face is charged with excitement. But already there are shadows in her eyes, because reality can never match up to the pictures in our heads . . .

Colors and shapes tumble as inside a kaleidoscope. The spot of light next to me flickers like a lamp in the wind. Ahead of us is another scene: a one-room flat, a rickety table with a kerosene stove on top of it crowded against an old settee. There are piles of records, an old turntable. This time, too, it's night, but an urban night. Light from a streetlamp makes its way through the small barred window. It fades before it can reach the mattress in the corner, where a young woman lies. A man—I see only the back of his head—is kissing her. We move closer. Tiny pearls of sweat stud the curve of his naked back. The woman puts out a hand to stop him, but he whispers something and it falls away. He pulls away her white sari and bends to kiss her breasts. She shuts her eyes in a shocked ecstasy that is not unlike pain. Her emotions crackle through me like an electric charge, and I realize what I chose not to know until now: she is myself. These are moments from my life that I had banished from memory. But like much that is banished, they didn't leave. They went underground. And now, somehow, my daughter's dreaming them.

Things I've kept so carefully from her all these years. Things she must not know.

I throw myself between her and the scenes that line the corridor, push at her to go back. But something stronger than me sucks us further in. What force has us in its grip? Pictures flash at us, huge and mesmerizing. They mix past and present, history and hope, truth and desire. In the caves I interpret a dream so excellently that the other novices rise to their feet in admiration. I follow the sounds of a flute from an old palace into a garden, and find a man who will change my future. I watch my expression the night I decide to run away from the caves. My face the night I decide to run away, again—this time from . . .

No! She mustn't see that.

I gather all my powers to push Rakhi back into her own body—but I can't find the flicker of light that is her awareness. Where has it disappeared? Down which corridor of my subconscious is it roaming? Panic fills me, causing my own light to waver and grow faint. What if I can't find her and send her back before her body awakens? I imagine her vacuous face, her limp limbs following me through the rest of her life. And I, bearing her within me on and on, a pregnancy without end . . .

But such wild imaginings pave the way to disaster. I force myself to be quiet so I can sense her presence. Heartbeat after heartbeat—the only measure of time in this space—passes. Nothing. Perhaps it is impossible to differentiate oneself from one's own blood?

How long do I wander down the twists of my inner alleyways, searching? Do I hear my husband knocking at the door, *Are you two all right in there?* I have no power to speak, to tell him he must not interfere. Does someone take my head on his knee, run a cool hand over my forehead? But I must focus inside, where the darkness is pulpy like pitch. Finally, when I've dropped both movement and hope, I feel the smallest prickle of otherness. I glide after it into an underwater tunnel. The memories are dim here, old as the crumble of pollen from a dying flower. Hands holding a child to a breast, smell of a woman's perfumed hair, a voice calling her away. Do her feet falter as she turns to look at her baby? Am I that child? Or that woman? The light that is Rakhi weaves drunkenly. I grab her, begin to draw her back. She doesn't resist. Perhaps she, who always hungered to know about me, has learned more than she can digest. We rise to the surface, the solidity of bone. With the last of my strength, I push her into her body.

In the morning it will be as though none of this ever occurred. Except that I will rise with a migraine and vomit in the downstairs bathroom all day. My husband will retreat into a bottle. And from time to time, as she goes about her daily business—doing homework, chatting with a friend on the phone—Rakhi will pause and look at me with puzzlement, trying to recall something important, something she has already forgotten.

31

Rakhi

They don't leave me alone, of course. Belle drives my father to my apartment. They're waiting at the door by the time I park the car and drag myself up the stairs.

Before I can explode, Belle says, "We won't do anything you don't want, Rikki. We won't even mention the shop. Let's just relax and have some tea, okay? We've all had a hard day."

"I'll make some special cha," my father adds. "You go get the aspirin, take a shower if you want."

I give them a distrustful glance. They sound like they've rehearsed this. They gaze back at me with innocent, sooty faces. I have to admit that the idea of one of my father's special teas sounds good.

By the time I come back, having washed my hair, the apartment is full of a minty fragrance. My father hands me a cup, and I sip gratefully. It's an unusual mix of herbs and spices, light yet energizing.

"Kashmiri cha," my father says. He doesn't explain where he got it.

I put up my aching feet and drink another cup. Then I notice what he's wearing.

"Dad! What are you doing in my old robe?"

"Belle found it for me. She's gone to the basement to put my clothes in the washer. That girl is a gem, I tell you."

"So you're going to go through with your crazy plan," I say.

"It's not so crazy. I just don't want to give up so soon. That's what that manager wants, no?"

I stare at him. Does he, too, think she had something to do with the accident?

Belle comes rushing in. "We've only got an hour, Mr. Gupta. Rikki, can I borrow some clothes from you? And can you go downstairs in twenty minutes and put your dad's clothes in the dryer?" She's in the shower before I can respond.

"We have nothing to lose," my father says.

"We'll look ridiculous. People will turn around and walk out."

"I don't think they will. In any case, I'm willing to look ridiculous. It just may keep us from closing down."

"I don't want our customers to stay out of pity for us."

"Sympathy is not a bad thing. But I'm not going to try to change your mind. You do what you want."

You do what you want. That's what my mother used to say when I went to her for advice. She'd tell me what she thought, then she'd add that phrase. That slight pulling back, that indication that ultimately her life was separate from mine. It always made me want to do what she'd suggested, as though by following her advice I'd bind her to me.

Does my father, sly Ananzi, know this?

"Oh very well," I say grumpily. "I guess I'll come along and help." I heave a loud sigh to make sure he realizes what a huge sacrifice I'm making. But inside I feel a stirring of elation. We aren't giving up, and that itself is a small victory. Who knows, maybe my crazy father is right. Maybe we can navigate around this disaster instead of crashing into it and drowning.

"Thank you, beti," he says formally. Then he breaks into a triumphant grin. "Better get dressed, we don't have much time.

I once heard my mother say, Calamity happens so we can understand caring. I refused to believe it. The calamities in my life were *caused* by the failure of caring, I felt. But after the fire at our store I begin to glimpse, just a little, what she might have meant.

I drag my feet as I follow Belle and my father to the store. Even before we reach it, my elation has faded and my doubts are back full force. It's useless, all this effort we're making. It would be smarter to call it quits and start over with something different—preferably in a place far away from Java and its witchy manager. Only my father's shoulders, sagging under his still damp shirt, keep me from turning around and fleeing.

I grit my teeth as Belle unlocks the door of the shop. It takes all my willpower to step into the smell of smoke and disaster that will not go away no matter how much Summer Rain deodorizer we spray. I start the coffee machine, busy myself with routine activities, stay in the background, where I won't have to answer questions. Still, I cringe each time a customer comes in and scrunches up his face at the odor, and my father begins another explanation, another apology for the meager snack supply.

I'd expected irritation from the customers, at best a brusque shrug of the shoulders suggesting they'd put up with the inconvenience—but just for today. Some do respond that way—and several people walk out—but more are sympathetic. A few share their disaster stories with us. Bad times are like visits from the in-laws, one man says. They seem like they'll never leave, but they do—and better times are bound to follow! Someone recites an Urdu ghazal about loss and heartbreak, and how good friends and happy memories can get us through them. Someone else interprets the words for Belle and me. (By now, they've gauged the depth of our language deficiencies.) They order lavishly from our depleted menu, so that by the end of the evening we've made a decent amount of money.

"But more important," my father says as we lock up, "we didn't give up and close down. That's what most people would have done."

I give him a sharp look to see if "most people" means who I think it does, but he isn't making a dig at me. There's a wide smile on his tired face. I remember how my mother, in her journal, referred to him as a good soul.

In the next few days, our customers help us take stock. What is it we need to fix most urgently? They check among themselves to see if anyone has skills that can help us. It turns out that there are two construction workers in the group. They offer to come in and do the repairs for a minimal charge on their off days. I can do the repainting. Jespal says he's good with putting up shelves. One of our customers who works at Home Depot says he'll buy supplies for us at discounted rates. Someone's cousin owns a home-inspection company. He'll come in when the repairs are completed to give us an okay.

I'm surprised and pleased, and then dejected. Even if they do all they're promising, it'll take us months to fix the problems. Can we limp along for all that time?

Our customers are more optimistic. Don't worry, they say. (Disaster has made them less hesitant about addressing me.) The shop will be in mint condition before you know it. Meanwhile, we'll keep coming. Whatever food you can manage to make, we'll buy. And we'll sing and play and keep your spirits—and ours—up. We're all brothers and sisters here, after all, bhai-bahen.

Even those who aren't Indian nod at this.

I appreciate their sentiments, but don't quite believe them.

This is my fatal flaw, as my mother often informed me: I'm suspicious and pessimistic, quick to think the worst of people. "Not that you have reason to be that way," she'd say.

I'd bristle every time she said that. I'd remind her that I had a whole list of reasons, headed by Sonny-the-cross-I-have-to-bear. What I didn't point out was that I hadn't always been this way. (She should have known it, as my mother. She would have known it if her attention hadn't always been pointed elsewhere. Until the party, I'd believed the best of everyone, particularly my husband. It was not suspicion but trust that undid me that night.)

But now that she's gone, I can see things from her perspective, too. When I think of the people she helped, I have to admit that my problems are minor ones. Her journals have given me glimpses: illness, murder, suicidal depression, schizophrenia. Sometimes at night, I worry about her dream people, whether they've been able to find a new interpreter. After I send a good thought to Jona, I send them one as well.

Even in death, my mother has proved to be right. Our customers are starting to help us, just as they'd promised. It's excruciatingly slow—they can come here only in between their other jobs—but it's costing us much less than I feared. We had to argue with them before they'd even accept any payment. The results are not five-star, but they're serviceable, and done with affection. As my father reminds me, it's not as if this was a five-star venue to begin with. Meanwhile, business continues. We've lost some of our more finicky customers, but it isn't enough to put us under.

After the fire, other changes occur. One evening a few people ask if they can put together a small stage for the musicians. It would help some of them if they could sit cross-legged. We'd still keep chairs for the guitarist and the drummers. The stage could be dismantled after the evening's performance, if we wished.

After a hasty consultation in the back room (with me resisting as usual), we agree to give it a try. Soon two low wooden platforms, draped with a patchwork quilt, are set up in a corner. Bolsters that someone's wife has covered with silk are arranged on them. (I hadn't thought of the musicians as having families. They seemed so complete in themselves as they made their music. But recently I'm seeing children running around, teenagers taking over on instruments while their parents break for tea.) Someone puts an enameled box filled with breath-freshening masala on the counter. And as if that's a sign, people begin to bring in other things—a Tibetan bell, a small Persian rug in jeweled colors, an African mask, a woodcut from Afghanistan, a jade figurine, a beat-up mirror that looks Russian, with carved metal doors you can open and close. I can't guess the value of these items, but it's clear that they're precious to their owners, who carried them all the way to this country from their past lives.

No one ever speaks to me about these objects. I find them in little piles behind the stage when I clean up at closing time. (We've stopped dismantling the stage at night. It doesn't seem worth the effort, especially as it's become a popular seating area for our daytime customers.) I'm ambivalent about the gifts. At times I'm deeply honored, at others I'm exasperated at having to find space for them in the store. I'm afraid that people will keep bringing in things until the place is crushed under their weight. Already I've had to remove several of my own decorations to accommodate the new items—even my painting of bathing elephants (though recently my fondness for it had been somewhat reduced). My Kurma House (but was it ever mine?) is suffering a sea change, growing into something very different from what I had envisioned. I feel as if I'm losing control. But when I calm down, I find that I quite like the creature it has become, this many-chambered nautilus. One day I take my paintbrush and add a word to the window: *International.* Soon after that, by some unspoken consensus, our customers decide that the Kurma House has everything it needs. From that time on, I never find another gift.

"I don't like the way we do business," my father says, "charging our customers for each little thing they order, keeping track of every paltry pakora and jilebi. Can't we ask them to pay a minimum amount and eat what they want? Like a buffet?"

I bristle with objections. They're big men, many of them, with the healthy appetites of men who work with their hands. What if they take "All You Can Eat" as a challenge, a matter of machismo? We could go bankrupt, I fret to Belle.

"I'll set out the food in warming trays and put a large bowl on the counter for payment," my father says. "People can pay at the start of the evening and help themselves whenever they want."

I can feel my frown solidifying into a permanent fixture on my face. "You mean you won't even check to make sure they're paying?"

"Honor system," says my father. "Makes everyone feel trusted, and doesn't disturb the musicians."

I frown. "Is this how you did business in the tea shop in India?"

He bursts out laughing. "Are you kidding! Customers there would have robbed us blind."

"Then how come—?"

He shrugs. "But now we're in a different country, with different people. We can't just follow old ways. We've got to be flexible, no? This feels right to me."

It doesn't feel right to me. I fear that our customers who are immigrants will not understand the honor system. I fear that the others can't be trusted. But at the end of the first evening, I discover, with some embarrassment, that we've collected about as much money as we usually make, and gone through a similar amount of food. In the next few days, I watch carefully and find that if people want several helpings, they put more money than we'd asked for in the bowl. They do it silently, not making a big deal of it.

"But why?" I ask my father one night as we walk to the parking lot.

"It may be that Kurma House International has become more to them than just a place to pick up something to eat. Maybe because they helped rebuild it, they feel it's theirs. They don't want to lose it. So they're doing their bit to ensure we stay in business."

Was this what my mother had hinted at when she'd spoken of a unique attraction? Had we, willy-nilly, managed to create what she'd wanted?

"I'm so ashamed," I confess. "I didn't really trust them at first."

"You find it hard to trust people, don't you?" he says.

His tone is uncannily like my mother's. Startled, I glance at him. But his eyes are his own: kind and happy and a little tired. For a moment I'm tempted to tell him about the party that changed me. But the moment passes.

"The honor system was a good idea, even if I say so myself," he adds with a chuckle, then gestures toward the darkened windows of Java. "Bet *their* customers don't feel the same way about them."

"I guess not," I reply. I chuckle to keep him company, but there's a tingle of uneasiness inside me, as though I'm overlooking something important.

32

It is silent in the apartment, and dark. The woman comes from the shower, the ends of her wet, curling hair soaking into the thin material of her robe. She turns on a lamp and sits by the small oval of yellow light with the package on her knee. It is actually a large manila envelope, stained and grimy from the fire, forgotten for all this time. Only today a workman rescued it from the back room, from under a pile of rubble. She does not recognize the smudged handwriting, but the message is clear: *For You.* She tells herself not to hope too much, but she can feel the blood swirling in her head. She has been waiting so long for a sign.

With trembling hands she tears open the envelope, discards the bubbled plastic, the cardboard protector sheets. She is left holding five photographs. She lays them on the coffee table. They are photographs of paintings—all by Indian painters, though she is not sure how she knows this. Neither the subject matter nor the style is Indian in any traditional way, though one of the compositions places words from an Indian script in the midst of geometric shapes. She cannot tell if they are photos of the actual paintings, taken in a studio or a gallery, or images of images taken from books. It doesn't matter. They are clear enough, and—her throat grows dry with excitement—like nothing she has seen before.

The first is an abstract landscape in flesh-pink and chalky yellow, with startling insertions of blue and red. There is a river, emerald green, flowing by cliffs where flowering shrubs hang. There is a triangular shape that could be a temple or a rock. But what strikes her most is the energy behind the lines, a sense of a hidden presence. She stares awhile, mesmerized, then turns the photograph over, hoping for a further hint: a name, a title. But the back is blank. The backs of all the photos are blank. She is left with only her imagination as guide.

The second painting is a dark submarine blue. A woman's torso is submerged in this color. Light and shadow play over its curves, its absolute, held stillness. Petals, the waxy white of plumerias, float on a current across it, catching for a moment on the island of the breast, the rounded promontory of the hip. Could the blue represent not ocean but night, the current of dreaming? What kind of expression would the woman's face hold, if Rakhi could see it?

The third painting has a background of neon yellow. A many-armed purple being with a moonlike face floats above a nest of serpents. Is he (she? it?) a god or a human? Or the representation of an idea? Her breath is caught by the strident juxtaposition of color and shape, the brilliant jewel eyes, the surprise of the composition, like a twist in a complex plot.

The fourth painting pulls her into the dark circle at its center, a black hole, magnetic, inexorable. She saves herself from falling by holding on to the border: squares made up of geometric shapes, richly textured rugs. Crosses, arrowheads, concentricities in earth colors. She did not realize a triangle could fill space so beautifully.

The final painting is made up of two parts, side by side. The left gives her the sensation of bending over and peering into a blue-green well, spheres within spheres, like ripples. At the very center, where one would have expected darkness, a brilliant white light. The image on the right is that of a closed door with an arch above it. (Or is it a sacred shape she cannot fathom, a lingam, a stupa?) Blacks again, blues, pale greens. At the top of the door, that same light. When she closes her eyes, she can see brightness branded into her lids.

She'll never know who sent her these paintings, but she has no doubts as to why they were sent. They've exploded the boundaries she had put around what art must be, and given her possibility. They're Indian—but in such different ways! All this time she's been putting boundaries around that word, too, what it can mean. Why, that word encompasses her just the way she is, with all the gaps in her education, all her insufficiencies. She doesn't have to change to claim her Indianness; she doesn't have to try to become her mother. Things are breaking down inside of her. She waits to see if she can build new, satisfying shapes from them.

33

FROM THE
DREAM JOURNALS

In the third year of our training, we were put in the care of
Elder Jahnavi, a bent-backed woman who could walk only with the
help of a staff. We paid her little attention when we first saw her.
Among the more flamboyant elders, she appeared as muted as a
night-blooming flower in daytime. But when she addressed us, we
knew at once that we were in the presence of power.

Jahnavi's expertise lay in the study of dreams out of history
and myth. She would ask us what they meant, and what they revealed about the nature of dreaming and its relationship to our
waking lives. We spent many afternoons in the dim sand cave as-
signed to her, examining dreams that, correctly interpreted and
faithfully followed, had transformed lives and nations. Others, ig-
nored, had brought about ruin. The dream of Sage Narad who
turns into a monkey, the dream of Markandeya and the flood, the
demon king Ravana's dream of defeat and death, sent to him in
warning—they all come back to me, though the years have eroded

their details. But I remember the dream of Tunga-dhwaja in the forest as though I saw it yesterday.

Yes, deliberately I say *saw,* for in Jahnavi's presence we were able to dream these ancient dreams again. We would lie down on the soft floor of her cave and close our eyes, and the dream would appear to each of us, though each saw it differently, based on the level of her understanding, and colored by her desires and fears. One of my sister dreamers had a sweet tooth, and for her, every dream celebration had a golden bowl filled to the brim with kheer. Another feared scorpions. In her dreams disaster took the shape of a scorpion bite. And I—but I will write of my own weaknesses another time.

Here is the story of King Tunga-dhwaja:

The king is a fearsome warrior, a conqueror well aware of his reputation. He is also a lover of the hunt. And on this day, accompanied by his nobles and his huntsmen, he rides into the forest that borders his palace. It is a good place for finding boar and tiger and deer—though Tunga-dhwaja considers deer too easy a target and will go after one only if nothing else is available.

But this day, despite the efforts of his beaters, not a single animal appears. The disappointed king is ready to return to his palace when he sees in the distance a white boar, that rarest of creatures. He rides after it—he cannot resist—entering deeper into the forest's darkness, leaving his companions behind. Engrossed in pursuit, he does not notice how the forest is changing its nature, how the trees have grown foreign, how the flowers release a heavy, mesmerizing fragrance into the air. Until the boar disappears behind the trunk of a tree, vanished inexplicably, and an exhausted Tunga-dhwaja realizes he is lost. He dismounts. He is not afraid—he has been in worse situations. In the morning his huntsmen will find him. If not, he will retrace his tracks and find his own way back.

As he rests under the tree, the king hears a sound as of many people moaning. When he looks to the side, he notices a group of dwarfish wildlings dressed in tree bark performing a primitive worship. He strides over to ask if they can lead him back to his palace, but they do not seem to comprehend him. They have set leaf bowls filled with porridge in front of a stone they have decorated with flowers—and suddenly he realizes how hungry he is. He asks for some porridge, but the men—though surely they see that he is a king, their king—pay him no attention. They continue to pray. When, angrily, he reaches for a bowl, they stop him, and in sign language indicate that the food must first be offered to the stone god. Then they will share it with him.

But the king refuses to wait. Sword in hand, he pushes them aside and takes what he wants. They do not protest. They merely watch him, eyes glinting under their matted hair. When he looks up from eating, they have melted into the trees.

The king pays them no mind. They are smaller than him and have no weapons. He sleeps, and when he wakes it is day. His horse is gone. He curses the woodsmen, who must have stolen it while he slept, and sets off on foot. An experienced tracker, he retraces his steps easily, reaching the edge of the forest by late afternoon. There is his palace, its crystal dome gleaming in the sun! He makes his way to the gate—and is stopped by the guards.

"Beggar!" one of them cries, holding up his spear in the king's face. "Where do you think you're going?"

"Beggar?" shouts the enraged Tunga-dhwaja. "Don't you

know your king? I'll see you buried alive within the hour, with thorns at your head and feet, as payment for that insult."

The guard is about to strike him, but the other guard, an older man, holds him back. "Brother," he says, "it is not proper to take offense at the words of a madman. Has God not punished him enough already?"

At this the king looks down at himself and sees that his kingly garments are gone, that he is clad in tree bark, that his hair is matted. Looking up he sees that the banner flying from the palace dome is not the familiar three green elephants on a ground of red, but a new one, silver lightning against a field of blue.

"What is the name of your king?" he whispers to the older guard.

"Why, it is Aniruddha, the righteous one," says the guard. "All love him for his mercy. You are in luck, for today is the prince's birthday, and the royal family will appear on the palace steps to give alms to the poor." Seeing the stricken look on the king's face, he adds, kindly, "I will take you there, if you like."

Tunga-dhwaja follows the guard to the steps. He does not recognize the king, but the queen—she is his own dear wife, and in her arms she carries his son, a child of three. Surely she will know him!

He rushes toward her, calling, "Wife! Wife!" But she stares at him in distaste and without recognition. He is intercepted by guards, and it is only by the king's command that he is spared a severe beating.

"Throw the madman out," the king orders, "and see that he never returns."

Sprawled in the dust outside the city gates, in a world that is and is not his own, Tunga-dhwaja realizes that this calamity has occurred because of his behavior toward the woodsmen and their deity. He returns to the forest, resolving to beg their forgiveness. But though he wanders for many days, he does not find them. Finally, filled with despair, he decides to drown himself in a forest lake. When he has waded in up to his neck, he senses a movement out of the corner of his eye. It is the white boar.

The boar leads Tunga-dhwaja back to the clearing where the wild ones—he guesses them to be sages—are performing their worship. Everything appears the same as on the fateful night when he was here last. But perhaps it *is* the same night, perhaps the boar has taken him back in time? In any case, Tunga-dhwaja knows what he must do. Weeping, he prostrates himself before the stone and, when the ceremony is concluded, humbly accepts the blessed food. He lies down beneath the same tree where he had tethered his horse a lifetime ago. At first he is too agitated to fall asleep—but sleep he must, for he knows that only through a dream can he change back to who he was. At last oblivion drops its merciful shroud over him, and in the morning he finds himself dressed once more in his royal hunting clothes, his horse grazing close by.

The king leaves the magic grove, finds his anxious companions and returns to his palace, where all is as it was before the hunt. The king, though, is a changed man. No longer arrogant, he lives out his life prayerfully, ruling his kingdom with justice and mercy. He is especially kind to beggars and madmen, and upon his death his subjects mourn the passing of Tunga-dhwaja the righteous.

34

Rakhi

The phone rings in the morning, in the middle of my efforts at painting. Efforts, because even though the photographs had showed me exciting new directions, I hadn't internalized them yet. I still didn't have a subject I felt passionate about. I'd started a landscape and a still life and abandoned them both. I was now trying for a portrait of Jona in an abstract style, but the colors clashed, the composition lacked energy and the figure in the center didn't possess my daughter's spirit. When I hear the phone, I'm so glad to be interrupted that I pick it up on the second ring.

It's Belle. Instead of apologizing for calling during my painting hours, she tells me to turn on the TV.

"But Belle, you know I don't like to watch—"

"Just turn it on, Rikki!"

"Which channel?"

"Doesn't matter. Any of the main channels will do." She sounds as though she's coming down with a cold. "Hurry! I'll hold on."

I see the explosion and think I've caught the middle of a sci-fi film, or one of those gruesome disaster movies that people are so inexplicably fond of. I'm about to change the channel when there's a rapid arc of a movement on the screen, followed by another soundless blast. It takes me a minute to process what I saw: a plane crashing into a tall building that looks familiar, looks just like the one that exploded. The scene comes on again. I become aware of the newscaster's voice telling me that the World Trade Center has been hit by terrorist planes. As if on cue, the skyscrapers begin to crumple in on themselves. The scene changes to show the Pentagon. It has been hit, too. I see smoke, shattered walls, people screaming in terror as they run. A briefcase falls open and scatters papers all over the street. The camera zooms in on a woman's high-heeled shoe, lying on its side.

There's a sick feeling in my stomach. My legs are trembling so much I have to hold on to the wall as I stumble back to the phone. "Is it really real?" I whisper.

Belle gives a hiccup of a sob on the other end.

"How can something like this happen?" I say. "Who would want to do something so terrible?"

"I don't know. I don't know, Rikki. I'm so scared. I was getting ready to go and open up the store, but I don't think I can manage it. There was another plane with hijackers that went down somewhere in Pennsylvania. Who knows how many more they've planned—" She gives another sob, sounding more like a little girl than a woman.

And with that I remember my daughter.

"I've got to go get Jona from school," I cry.

"Rikki, I'm scared. I called Jespal, both at work and at home, but there was no answer. Where can he be?" She's weeping in earnest now.

I think fast. "Belle, I want you to come over here. I'll leave the key for you under the doormat. It'll be better for me, too, to not have to be alone. Don't worry about Jespal just yet. He may just have stepped out. You can call him from my phone. He can come over also."

"You're right," she says in an uncharacteristically meek voice. "I'll come over. I shouldn't worry just yet."

How sadly easy it is to convince people of what they want to believe.

The streets are curiously empty as I drive toward the school. Perhaps everyone's inside, watching TV, mesmerized by those towers disintegrating in slow motion, over and over. I turn on the radio. So far, four planes have been hijacked. All four were destined for California. Flights across America have been canceled. The stock market has closed. The president, his wife, and the vice president have been moved to an undisclosed location. I peer upward nervously as I listen, though there's nothing in the sky except a few bay gulls.

About two blocks from the school, pandemonium has broken loose: lines of cars locked in a traffic jam, drivers honking at one another as they try to find parking. A mother abandons her minivan in the middle of the road and runs into the school building. Drivers stuck behind her begin to yell, and a man shakes his fist and shouts out an obscenity.

I finally find parking and make it to the entrance, only to be stopped by the vice principal. She entreats me not to disturb the children by pulling Jona out of class. They're perfectly safe here, she insists. It's more traumatic for them to see their classmates being taken away without explanation. "Most parents are too distraught to discuss what's happened in a calm manner," she says.

"You'll just scare the children more. And what are you going to do with them? Take them home to watch the news with you all day? They don't need that."

She's probably right. The children don't need that. It's us, the parents, who need them with us so that we can touch their small, sturdy bodies and heft their weight in our laps, so that we can nuzzle their necks and comfort ourselves with their smell, that one familiar thing in this world turned unrecognizable.

"I'm sorry," I say as I push past her. "I have to have my daughter."

In the car I force myself not to turn the radio on, even though I'm anxious to hear the latest update. First I must tell Jona what has happened—how, literally, the sky has fallen since I kissed her good-bye just a few hours ago. How do you explain to a child that someone deliberately slammed a plane full of people into a building full of people, three times in three different places? That this might be the beginning of a planned terrorist attack across America? What do you say when she demands to know why people would kill themselves just so they can hurt people they don't even know?

By the time I reach my apartment's parking lot, I still haven't found the words to talk about the attack. I'm thankful that Jona hasn't asked me why I took her out of school—but I'm surprised, too. She's been gazing out the window all this time.

"Jona," I say. "I have to tell you about something really bad that happened today. It might upset you and scare you, but you do need to know."

"I already know." She says it in a flat voice without turning to me. "The buildings exploded and burned. People died. Some of them jumped from windows. They were screaming. We couldn't help them."

My heart pounds in agitation. I should have been the one to break this traumatic news to my daughter. "Who told you this? One of the teachers? A parent? Did they turn on the TV at your school?"

This time she does look at me. Her face is expressionless, and that frightens me more than if she were hysterical. "I saw it in my dream. Don't you remember?"

It all comes back to me: her sweaty head pressed against mine in her fever bed, Sonny's hand and mine, intertwined, riding the uneven rise and fall of her chest. Her restless dreaming, and my own, and how I thought, with mistaken complacence, that they were the same.

And that is how I learn two painful facts in one morning:

1. There are people out there who are willing to do whatever it takes to destroy us—even kill themselves. That's how much they hate America—and they want us to know it.

2. The gift I've longed for all my life has passed over me and lighted on my daughter. Only it's not a gift but a terrible weight she'll have to carry from now on by herself. Much as I want to, I can't help her with it.

We're sitting in front of the TV, Belle, my father, Jona, Jespal, Sonny and I. We know we should turn the machine off, shouldn't watch the replays over and over, the towers flaming and crumbling, crumbling and flaming. But none of us can gather the energy to press the power button. We see clips of firefighters heading into the blaze; we see the buildings collapsing under the weight of their own rubble. Ambulances wail as though they'll never stop. Thousands of people died in the towers. Some of them called home before they jumped. We see the ruined walls of the Pentagon through smoke. Police cars. The hijackers were armed with box cutters, we're told. Mayor Giuliani comes on: *Stay calm and stay indoors—unless you're south of Canal Street.* A man in a uniform claims he'd filed reports stating airport security was too lax. President Bush comes on, vowing revenge. We look at them all, then at each other in disbelief. How could this have happened—here, at home, in a time of peace? In America?

A new broadcast is woven into the replays: a street somewhere in the Middle East where people are dancing and handing out sweets because the American devils have finally got what they deserve. Men in turbans and black beards clap their hands and chant slogans. Children are waving miniature paper flags. There are women in the crowd too, in long black burkhas, their heads covered in shawls, faces gleaming in sweaty satisfaction. One of them shouts, *Let them learn what we live with every day.* The words are translated at the bottom of the screen for our benefit.

The scenes of devastation in New York had been terrible, but this broadcast upsets me differently. It makes me want to drop a bomb on these people and end their hellish celebration. But then, as I watch it come on a second time and then a third, I start getting scared in a whole new way.

"Idiots," my father says. "They shouldn't keep showing that at a time like this." He rises unsteadily to his feet, switches off the

TV and takes Jona off to play Chinese checkers. And as though his action had released us from some kind of spell, we all get up. Belle and I go into the kitchen to make sandwiches. I'm surprised to discover that I'm ravenous. We all are. Belle says it's from the relief of being safe. We decide that we'll switch the TV on once every hour for updates. Belle says she's going to bake a cake, and I bring out a sweater of Jona's that I've been working on desultorily for the last several months. Jespal says he wants to go back to work just so that he can feel halfway normal. "I'll come see you in a few hours," he tells Belle. "You going to be at the Kurma House?"

"I guess so," Belle says.

"That's not a good idea!" Sonny says sharply. "You should keep the store closed today."

I've had the same thought, but I don't like his tone. Sonny-Know-It-All. Maybe because I'm already tense, anger flares up in me. "Why?" I ask.

"Can't you see?" his tone implies that I had better not enter any IQ contests. "It's not safe."

"Maybe Sonny is right," Belle says. "I don't want to go *any-where* today. Not even home. Rikki, can I sleep here tonight?"

I nod. But I'm not done with Sonny. "And why isn't it safe?"

He gives an impatient sigh. "Are you really that dense? People would think you didn't care about the folks who died, about America being attacked. They'd think all you cared about was making money."

He knows exactly how to get under my skin. "You mean to say every business in this country is closed today?" I say, my voice rising. "That closing is the only way we can show we care? What about the fact that it might be good for the country to keep running as normally as possible, and not allowing everything to come to a standstill, which I think is exactly what the terrorists want—"

Sonny shakes his head tiredly. "Let's not make this into a sparring match, not today. I'm just telling you how the average man on the street would react. I'm just telling you what would be a safer course of action."

There's truth to what he's saying, but it only makes me angrier. I look at Belle, then Jespal. They look away. It's clear they agree with Sonny. I clench my teeth. I'm even more determined not to give in. But as I try to figure out a plan of action, support comes from an unexpected quarter.

"We can't close the shop," my father says. "Especially today. For a lot of our customers, it's their only meeting place. If we're upset and worried, so must they be. We owe it to them to stay open so they can come in and talk about what's happened, draw support from each other. Maybe we can help them deal with the shock."

This is my chance. "You're absolutely right, Dad," I say. I give Sonny an angelic smile. "We'd be providing a valuable community service." I turn to Belle. "And don't you think we'll feel a lot better off if we're busy doing something useful, rather than sitting in front of the TV listening to a bunch of experts conjecturing about what terrible thing's going to happen next?"

She looks uncertain, but finally she nods.

"I think you're making a mistake," Sonny says to my father before he leaves. He doesn't speak to me. From the way his eyebrows are jammed together, I can tell that this time I've really managed to annoy him. I count it as a small victory on this day of defeats.

35

FROM THE
DREAM JOURNALS

The story of Tunga-dhwaja was a perplexing one, because unlike the other stories we studied with Elder Jahnavi, it contained no obvious dream. Discussing, we wondered if the king had dreamed the entire story from the time he fell asleep in the forest till he awoke there the second time. Was it a warning dream, heeding which he escaped an ominous fate? Yet that was too easy a solution. It negated the king's suffering and undercut the magnitude of his transformation.

"You are right," Jahnavi said. "That is not the answer. Think again."

After more thought, we decided that the forest was a magical dream space. What the king did there called down a curse upon his waking life so that people were no longer able to recognize him. The curse could only be negated by a reparation performed in the same dream space.

"You are getting closer," Jahnavi said. "But you're fixing your attention on the wrong things. You're trying too hard. Forget all you have learned about interpreting. Unfocus your eyes. Then maybe the real picture will appear before you."

But we did not know how to unfocus.

At the end of a week of waiting, Jahnavi took pity and gathered us around her. She drew a diagram on the sand floor, two ovals connected by a tube. She added small squares along the circumference of each oval. A few squares had thicker outlines than the others. She looked at us hopefully, but we had no idea what it meant.

"The story of Tunga-dhwaja," she explained, "is important because it illustrates a rare yet pivotal occurrence in dreaming." She pointed to one of the ovals. "Think of this as waking time, and the other oval as dream time. The connecting tube is called the gateway, and allows us to pass from one time to the other. Under normal circumstances, the oval of dream time is always in motion, so that whenever you pass through the gateway, you enter a different door"—here she pointed to the squares—"and thus experience a different dream. The oval of the waking state moves, but with infinite slowness. Thus, throughout a human's life span, he or she will reenter the same door, and experience the same story, which we have termed reality. Now do you see what happened in the case of Tunga-dhwaja?"

"He upset the balance between the ovals somehow," one of us ventured.

"Yes," Jahnavi said. "Usually when the balance is upset, the oval of dream time comes to a halt, and people dream the same story over and over. But the king's problem was unique. By angering the sages in the forest he speeded up his waking time, so that when he returned to it, he entered through a different door into a different life. Here, he paid for his earlier arrogance by being reduced to the lowest of the low."

"But why did that happen?" I asked. "All of us do what we shouldn't, from time to time, in our dreams. But we aren't pushed into other lives in punishment—"

"It is because, in the magical forest, the king had entered a transforming dream." Here Jahnavi pointed to one of the thickly outlined squares. "Transforming dreams are rare. They come to a human once or twice in a lifetime, or perhaps not at all. What we do in these dreams transforms our natures and affects our waking lives in powerful ways. In most cases, the dream erases itself from our consciousness once we have dreamed it, and we can do nothing to change its effects. Tunga-dhwaja was fortunate in that he remembered, and even more fortunate in that he could reenter the same transforming dream, where he was forgiven. Otherwise he would have been trapped in his new life, and doomed to spend his days as a beggar."

That night I lay on my pallet in the sleeping hall and contemplated what Jahnavi had said. The tale of Tunga-dhwaja was meant to caution us, but it filled me with exhilaration. To think that there existed, just beyond our perceptions, different realities! To think that they might become available to us—to me, even! That I might slip, by virtue of something I did in a dream, into another life, and become a new person, possessed of talents and joys I could not even imagine at this moment! The law of reversal had transformed Tunga-dhwaja from a king into a beggar. Couldn't that same law transform me—an orphan and a novice, a beggar girl of sorts—into a queen?

As I thought this, a strange discontent took hold of me. Until now I had loved the caves. I'd blessed the day I'd been accepted here to become a dream teller. It had allowed me to escape the hopelessness of my life in the slums. It had opened for me a world I'd been ignorant of, had stirred within me powers I'd barely guessed at. It had given me a reason to live. But today the darkness of the sleeping hall pressed upon me with a heaviness I'd never felt before. The curved roof of the cave was like a hand held over my mouth, suffocating me. It might be years before the elders decided I knew enough to go out into the world to practice my craft. By then my youth would have passed away, and what beauty I possessed, and along with them, my hopes for happiness and adventure. A great despair filled me as I thought this. I gathered all the power within me into a dream-seeking wish. I knew the elders would be furious if they found out, and not only because of the dangers involved in wishcraft. The dream chooses the teller, they had told us over and over. The teller must not choose the dream.

I felt the wish leave me the way a powerful bird takes off for the sky, beating its vast wings, confident of its destination. I was filled with elation. Until that moment, I hadn't believed I could accomplish such a complex task. But—I would learn this later—it wasn't a bird wish I'd sent forth. It was a boomerang, and it would recoil upon me in the way I least expected.

What did I want from my transforming dream? I wanted it to take me into a new world, one unshackled by the rules that guided every moment of our lives in the cave. I wanted reckless passion. I wanted adventure. I wanted a man who'd be willing to kill himself for my love.

Did a transforming dream come to me that night? I was no Tunga-dhwaja; in the morning I remembered nothing. All was as before, except the discontent that had been a grain of sand in my eye had grown into a ball of iron in the pit of my stomach. It continued to grow in the weeks before we went on our trip to Calcutta. It unbalanced me.

Transformation is an erratic phenomenon. It strikes people in different ways. Tunga-dhwaja's change was like a tower cracked open by lightning. My own would be slower, subtler, more insidious—a rodent gnawing at the roots of a banyan. But it had begun.

36

Rakhi

For a long time after we open, no one comes into the shop. Most of the businesses around us are closed, and the street appears abandoned. Even the homeless people have disappeared, leaving the streetlamps to throw shivery pools of light on empty pavements.

"Maybe we should go home," Belle says again.

"Let's wait a little longer," my father says, "until the time our musicians usually come in." He disappears into the back room, and when I look in, I see him sitting in front of the empty alcove where my mother's photograph used to be.

The door chime rings, but it isn't the musicians. It's Mr. Soto, the owner of the Mexican restaurant next door. It takes me a moment to recognize him—I've never seen him without his chef's hat and apron. I hadn't realized he was bald.

"You planning to stay open?" he asks.

I nod.

"Wouldn't do that, if it was me," he says. "I only came in to make sure everything was locked up safe, with the alarm turned on. I'm going home now. Too many angry people around—"

"But why would they do anything to us?"

Mr. Soto shrugs. "Angry and scared—that's a dangerous mix. People don't think much when they're like that."

I peer out the window at the deserted street. Then I notice that the lights are on in Java. I point. "She's open."

"Si. You seen what she's put up?"

I peer out. A big banner hanging from the storefront proclaims, PROUD TO BE AMERICAN.

"She's quick, that one," Mr. Soto says with a grin that's more a grimace. "Can't blame her this time, though. I myself—" He gestures with his chin toward his store, and I see there's a large American flag taped to the inside of his window. Under it a sign in red, white and blue reads GOD BLESS AMERICA.

"They're selling them on the corner of University and Shattuck," he informs us as he leaves. "You should get one before they run out."

Belle and I stare at each other. The look on her face mirrors the disbelief I'm feeling. "Is this California, year 2001," I ask, "or is this Nazi Germany?"

"Maybe Mr. Soto's right," Belle says. "Maybe we should put up a flag, too. To show solidarity, you know."

"Belle, I don't have to put up a flag to prove that I'm American! I'm American already. I love this country—hell, it's the only country I know. But I'm not going to be pressured into putting up a sign to announce that love to every passerby."

Belle doesn't say any more, but I can see the disquiet in her eyes as she places a tray of cookies—that's all we're serving today, along with tea—on the counter.

.   .   .

The musicians arrive in ones and twos, looking stunned. No families accompany them today. Instead of kurtas and loose pants, dashikis and fez hats, today they're dressed in jeans. T-shirts. A 49ers cap. They incline their heads in greeting, then sit silently, their cups of tea untouched in their hands. I turn on the portable TV and we watch President Bush, who has been flying around the country in a military plane all day to keep himself safe. He vows to root out terrorists—not just the ones responsible for today's tragedy but all terrorists, everywhere. It seems a task as impossible as those described in Jona's book of fairy tales. I wonder how he plans to go about it. A stern newscaster announces that a certain Osama bin Laden is the mastermind behind this plot. A picture of him in white robes, with a turban and a beard and black fanatic's eyes, flashes on the screen. The picture fills me with uneasiness, though I can't put words to it.

"What will happen now?" one of the men finally asks. There's a moment of silence; then everyone starts speaking at once. I pull on my father's sleeve, and he translates for Belle and me as best as he can. People wonder why the terrorists launched this awful attack, what the government will do in response, how this will affect our home countries, and what will happen to us all. They talk of people who are dead now, some of whom they knew. Folks who began this day by brushing their teeth and drinking their coffee, waving good-bye to their families, taking the subway to work. What did they feel when they realized they were going to die? Jespal—when did he come in?—comments that this is bound to change the lives of everyone who lives in this country. And Sonny—I'm surprised to see him sitting near the door—says in a harsh tone, in English, Some people's lives will change more than others.

When the voices fall silent, one of the old men begins a low chant, a drawn-out mourning song, or maybe a prayer. The rest bend their heads. Perhaps they're remembering other tragedies. The chant grows louder. More people join in, swaying back and forth, clapping to keep time. Though I don't understand the words, there's something about this sharing of grief that comforts me. When the chant ends, the men file out silently. We don't thank one another.

After the fire, when I'd tried to express my gratitude for their kindness to our customers, they'd been awkward, uncomfortable. My father had had to explain to me that giving thanks is not a common practice in India.

"Then how do you know if people appreciated what you did?" I'd asked.

"Do you really need to know?" my father had asked back.

The two things happen almost simultaneously.

1. There's a loud crash, a crack appearing like magic in the storefront glass, bisecting the *M* with its shiny curvature.

2. Four young men burst into the shop.

Belle and Jespal are straightening chairs, I'm about to pour the leftover tea (no one drank any) into the sink. My father's putting away cookies. Sonny is sitting in a corner with Jona, playing finger games that make her giggle. We all stop what we're doing and stare at the men.

They're ordinary enough—tall, close-cropped, one blond, three brown-haired. They wear jeans, just like our departed customers. One has on a leather jacket. Two carry baseball bats, one a chain wound around his hand. The fourth one—I don't know what he carries. His hand is in his pocket.

They're shouting something. I can't understand them because they're all talking at the same time. Or maybe it's that my brain refuses to function right, like my shaking hands. There's tea all over the floor. Sonny pushes Jona behind the counter. Belle grabs her and presses Jona's face into her stomach so Jona can't see what's going on.

Sonny raises his hands in a pacifying gesture. He's trying to talk to the men. Do they want money? He gestures to the cash register.

One of the men shoves him out of the way. "We're not thieves, shitface," he says, his mouth a crooked line of distaste. "We're patriots."

"We've been watching you and your terrorist pals," another one says. "Celebrating, huh?"

I'm ashamed of how scared I am. My throat feels like it's closed up permanently. But I've got to try to explain that they've misunderstood. It's our only hope. "We weren't celebrating," I make myself say. My heart pounds so loudly I can't hear my voice.

"Shut up, bitch," the man with his hand in his pocket says. He nods and one of them brings down his baseball bat, cracking the glass counter. There are cookies all over the floor. My father manages to step back just in time, or the bat would have broken his hand. Jona is crying, and so is Belle.

"Stop!" Jespal says. "We haven't done anything wrong. Those men in here—they were mourning. We're Americans, just the way you are. We all feel terrible about what happened."

Two of the men grab him. "Looked in a mirror lately?" one

of them spits. "You ain't no American! It's fuckers like you who planned this attack on the innocent people of this country. Time someone taught you faggots a lesson."

"You're crazy," Jespal yells. He struggles free for a moment and manages to hit one of them in the face. His turban comes undone. Belle is screaming.

"You shouldn't have done that," the man with his hand in his pocket says. Except now his hand is outside, and it's holding a switchblade. Two of the men begin to drag Jespal outside. Sonny starts forward, but one of the men holds up his baseball bat with a grin. The man with the switchblade cuts the telephone line with a flick of his wrist. "Stay inside and no one else gets hurt," he says as he leaves, closing the door with exaggerated care.

I'm rummaging frantically in the drawers, looking for something to fight with. The only thing I can find is a bread knife. I'm not sure I have what it takes to use it, but I grab it anyway. Sonny emerges from the back room with a metal pipe, and my father carries a length of wood. Belle holds tight to a struggling Jona with one hand while she upends her purse on the countertop. At one time she used to carry pepper spray. I pray she still does.

Jespal is doubled up on the pavement, his hands protecting his head. "Let's put our mark on him, boys," someone shouts. "So his little pals will remember us every time they look at him." One of the men swings the chain, and I can hear the soft thwack of metal hitting flesh. Sonny runs forward with a yell, and the man turns. The chain whips toward Sonny, catches the metal pipe. For a moment I'm afraid it'll get wrenched from his hand, but he manages to hold on. He thrusts the end of the pipe into the man's chest and the man goes down with a surprised grunt. But a different man's behind Sonny now, hitting out with a bat. I shout a warning as I run toward him. I catch a glimpse of my father helping Jespal up, then I hear him cry out. One of them aims his bat at my knife hand. I pull back, but I'm not fast enough. Hot pain shoots up my arm; the knife goes flying. He's moving toward me, a murderous look on his face. I back away. I hear Sonny yell, "Watch out, Riks!" But it's too late. Someone's got me in a choke hold. I hear him laugh in my ear. Sonny's rushing at us, an intent look on his bloodied face. He lunges with the pipe. My attacker curses, his arm loosens, I can breathe. Now two men are coming at Sonny together. I grab one, a fist strikes the side of my head, and I learn there's truth to the saying about seeing stars.

I must have passed out for a few moments. When I come to, groggily, I'm lying on the pavement. The man with the switchblade is kneeling over Jespal. Someone's holding Sonny with his arm twisted behind his back. He's yelling for help, but of course no one comes. The man raises his knife and Jespal screams.

Then I hear sirens, and a moment later I see flashing lights as a police car comes around the corner. The men are yelling. They let go of Jespal and Sonny, pull up one of their companions who's sitting on the ground, holding his head, and jump into their car—an ordinary-looking car, except it's got an American flag tied to the antenna. Will I ever be able to look at a flag without remembering this moment that I can't believe is happening, this taste in my mouth like copper, which later I'll discover is blood? Then they're gone.

The police car screeches up to the pavement, and the officer leans out the window. *Get inside and lock the door,* he yells. There's something familiar about him. But before I can work out what it is, he's gone, too, sirens screaming. We're left on the empty street to take care of ourselves the best we can.

Belle runs out of the store. In her hand is a cell phone. Thank God she was able to call the police! Jona follows her.

"Daddy, Daddy," she cries as she hurls herself at Sonny. My head's still throbbing, and bright yellow dots swim in front of my eyes, but I manage to drag myself over to them. Sonny's cheek is bleeding a lot. I pull out some Kleenex and try to stanch it.

"It's a flesh wound, I think," he says. "Could have been worse."

When I think of how much worse it could have been, I throw my arms around him.

"You know I love it when you do that," he says, with a laugh that's half a cough. "But my ribs are an unromantic lot, and they're complaining!"

"Are they broken?" Jona asks anxiously.

"Let's hope not," he says.

Belle is tending to Jespal, who has a cut under his right eye. His other eye is swollen shut. One of his arms hangs at an unnatural angle—but overall he, too, is lucky. My father sits on the edge of the pavement, massaging his arm. He looks as if he's in shock. He slurs his words as he says someone might have hit him on the head, he can't quite recall.

Sirens again—it's a different police car this time, with two men in it. One of the policemen asks what happened, jots down notes, tells Belle to drive Sonny and Jespal to the emergency room.

"If you're not feeling too bad," he tells me, "I recommend you go home with your little girl and the old gentleman. It's a mess at the hospitals tonight, all sorts of craziness going on."

When he asks me to describe our attackers. I find that I can't come up with many details. They were so ordinary—men I'd pass on the street without looking at twice. It's the same with their car—I can't even remember the color. Except for the flag, which is absolutely clear in my mind, everything else has blurred into mush.

"But your colleague who got here first saw them," I say. "He'd know what they look like. He may even have caught them by now—he took off after them right away."

The policeman stares at me. "This is the only police car that was sent here."

"Can't be! It was because of him those men took off. Otherwise they might have killed us."

His companion shakes his head. "The dispatcher would have told us if she'd already asked someone else to come here. Besides, they wouldn't have sent two cars to the same place, not tonight. Too many people calling for help."

I watch their taillights recede through the light fog that's settling over the empty street. The September night has turned chilly. Belle has left for the hospital. I help my father to the parking lot, where my car waits alone. Jona holds tight to my other hand. What kind of stain will a night like this leave on her? A wild bird shrieks somewhere. We all flinch. But it's not the night that is frightening, nor its birds, however wild they may be. There's nothing out there that's worse than human beings.

I pull out the sofa bed for my father and settle Jona in her room, where I'll sleep with her tonight. When Belle drops Sonny off, I tell him he can have my bed.

"Wow! Never thought I'd hear you say that, Riks!" he says.

"I can tell you're feeling better."

He gives me a lopsided grin. One side of his face is bandaged. When he moves, I can tell he's in pain. But at least he doesn't have any broken bones, not like Jespal, who's going to be in the hospital for several days. The doctors are worried about his eye, too.

I offer to make Sonny some chamomile tea.

"That wimpy stuff does nothing for me. I'll have a couple of your sleeping pills instead. You do still take them, right?"

I bring him one. That man knows too much about me for his own good.

Afterward, I stand at Jona's window, too wound up to sleep. I look out at the darkness, the still sky with its untouched stars. In my room, Sonny is tossing and turning, trying to get comfortable on a strange bed. I look at my reflection in the glass—the brown skin, the Indian features, the dark eyes with darker circles under them, the black crinkles of my hair. It's familiar and yet, suddenly, alien.

You ain't no American, one of the men had said.

He's a racist idiot, I tell myself.

Is that so? my whisper voice gibes. *And how many others in this country would have agreed with him today?*

But if I wasn't American, then what was I?

Sonny calls my name, breaking the chain of my thought.

"What's wrong?" I ask from the door. "Does it hurt?"

"Yeah, but that's not it. I was wondering—" He hesitates. In the dark I cannot see his expression. "I was wondering if you'd sit with me for a little while."

I'm about to plead tiredness, but then I change my mind. Some things are more important than old grudges. I sit on the edge of the bed, and he takes my hand and holds it. After a while, he says, "It's a strange thing, facing a man who wants to kill you. It's never happened to me before."

I remember the look on his face, savage and focused, as he swung his pipe at the man who was choking me. I hadn't known Sonny could look like that. It had shocked me, but then I'd been glad, and that also had shocked me.

He lets out a sigh that is partly a shudder. "I was ready to kill him, too, you know."

"I know," I say. I consider thanking him for saving my life. Instead I give him a small push. "It's uncomfortable sitting on the edge of the bed," I say.

He moves over to make space for me, and when I lie down, he puts his arm around me with a different kind of sigh. I place a cautious arm around him, too, trying to avoid his bruises. It surprises me how easily our bodies fit into each other, as though they remember. He nuzzles my hair lightly. I can tell he's thinking.

After some time he says, "So many people lost so much today."

I nod. I think of the people in the towers and in the airplanes, who lost their lives. The people grieving tonight, who lost their loved ones. Leaders and decision makers, who lost belief in their invincibility. And people like us, seeing ourselves darkly through the eyes of strangers, who lost a sense of belonging.

So much hatred unleashed in the world today; where will it end?

Perhaps it's to counter that hatred that I kiss Sonny. Perhaps it's because death brushed by us so closely, and because I'm thankful to be alive. Perhaps it's the simple comfort of having someone hold you on a day when certainty has slipped through your fingers and shattered on the floor.

I let his fingers undo the clasp of my brassiere and cup my breasts. I let them wander over my body, and I push myself closer to him. I have to help him off with his clothes. As I touch him and feel him grow hard, I murmur his name in his ears, as though he might have forgotten who he is. When he comes, arching against me, crying out, not *Riks* but *Rakhi*, I feel I've reclaimed a tiny sliver of myself.

37

Days pass, seeming like weeks. Weeks pass, seeming like months. A month passes, and it seems like yesterday all over again. She wakes in the night at the smallest sound, checks the chain on the door, the window latches. She wishes for a transforming dream, but all she gets is blackness, like being buried under rubble. One day she goes to work to find that someone has painted TERRORIST in red letters over the name of their store. Paint has run down the stem of the final *T*, pooling thick and rubbery on the windowsill. It takes hours to scrub off. They do not replace the glass in the storefront window but only patch it up with duct tape. Belle says there's no money, but they all know the real reason. It might happen again.

Sonny brings in copies of e-mails that are being circulated by Indian organizations. The notes caution them not to go anywhere alone. (There's no risk of that, she thinks wryly. She's too afraid to attempt an excursion.) Don't wear your native clothes. (What native clothes? she wonders, looking down at her pants.) Put up American flags in prominent locations in homes and businesses. (But this she cannot bring herself to do.) Pray. (When she listens to the president's military plans, she feels a need for prayer, but she doesn't know toward which deity, American or Indian, she should aim her supplications. Who should be forgiven, and who saved.) She grows almost accustomed to suspicious glances on the street. A couple of times people cross over to the other side so they won't have to walk near her. How is it, she wonders, that one can become, overnight, both so frightening and so vulnerable?

The attack on Kurma House International was written up in the local papers. They received a large number of letters after that. Most were from strangers who expressed sympathy and outrage. A few anonymous notes spouted invective, and one person sent a large manila envelope with a Ziploc bag filled with turds.

They reopen the store the night after Jespal gets out of the hospital. They seat him in a corner, his arm in a sling that glows very white. Rakhi joins in Belle's jokes about how his dark glasses make him look like a celebrity in disguise, a turbaned Elvis, but her mouth is dry with fear. She finds herself flinching every time someone she doesn't know comes up to the counter. People she's never seen before tell her how sorry they are that she's had such a terrible experience. They want to shake her hand. They declare that they welcome her presence in their community. She tries to be appreciative but only ends up resentful. They make her feel like a guest.

I was born here, she wants to tell them. How can you welcome me?

The musicians don't discuss what happened, though she notes the way they crowd around Jespal in a protective knot. He can't see too clearly with his left eye yet. The doctors are waiting to see if it'll get better on its own, or whether they'll have to try an invasive procedure. (Invasive, now that's an interesting word. Her mind meanders into the many ways such a word might be used.) He still wears a turban. (Would it qualify as his native dress, or his chosen one?) For the reopening, he's picked one the color of banana leaves. Seeing it wound around his head makes her at once proud and anxious. One of the musicians pounds his fist on the table, swearing. But Jespal shakes his head in his usual mild manner, and soon after that they begin a song.

When closing time comes, the men hang around, pretending to be busy, packing and repacking their instruments. They wait outside until the store is locked up, and stroll behind Rakhi and Belle to the parking lot, chatting casually with her father. They watch the women get in the cars and start the engines. Their solicitousness makes her want to laugh and cry. They do this each night, until she grows used to the ritual, until she finds it comforting and companionable. Some days she forgets how it began.

She invites Sonny over and cooks for him—something she'd vowed she'd never do again. But there's a warmth to being in her small kitchen, Jona and him and herself crowded around the countertop, chopping green onions, sautéing chicken with ginger. They don't attempt to make love after that traumatic night. (When she thinks back to how they'd clung together in bed, trying to help each other remember who they were, she's not sure whether to be glad or mortified.) But they do sit together sometimes after Jona falls asleep. They try to stick to talk of their everyday lives, but can their everyday lives be separated any longer from the search for terrorist cells, or the president's bluster about the axis of evil? Sonny tells her that he feels guilty about making music while so many continue to die. She tells him how her neighborhood has changed. The Pakistani women barely come out of their apartments. The Afghani men take turns rounding up the children of their community and driving them to the neighborhood school, although it is only two blocks away. Sometimes they sit wordless in front of the late-night news and watch bombs being dropped on a country halfway around the world, the elegant plumes of smoke rising above the fires.

"We don't even know what's really happening out there," he says. "I feel like a pet dog being fed tidbits to keep me quiet."

Reporters interview American soldiers, many in their teens. Some look nervous, but everyone who's on camera declares that he or she is ready to die for America. Rakhi feels her guts twist. Their faces are so naked, so unknowing. She wonders what they'll look like by the time they come back home.

One night she finds herself thanking Sonny for saving her life. The words come more easily than she'd thought they would, perhaps because the dead and the dying have been on her mind so much recently, so present in her living room. Or maybe it's because she's not Indian enough. She expects him to be embarrassed, to shrug it off with an *It was nothing*. But he must not be Indian enough, too, because he takes her hand and says he's happy for what little he was able to do—this time at least. She recognizes the words as his apology for that long-ago night at the party, his failure to rescue her. She touches the calluses on his fingers, wondering how he got them. His fingertips are square and neat, with the nails cut short so he won't scratch the records. She is surprised at how distant the party seems, how dwarfed by newer, larger calamities. But as these new calamities recede, will that night regain its dark power over her? Sonny's fingers smell faintly of wild thyme. But when he asks if he should stay the night, she shakes her head.

She doesn't want to extend a facile forgiveness only to take it back later. He asks her again to come to the club to hear him. She doesn't say yes or no. She bends forward a little to allow him to kiss her cheek before he leaves.

One morning Marco comes into the shop. When she sees him, she realizes that he hasn't been around for a while. He looks shrunken, like a carrot left too long in the refrigerator. She gives him a sack of onion pakoras. He holds them in his rough, cracked hands with the chewed-off nails and shifts from foot to foot.

"What is it, Marco?"

"I was there the night those men broke into your shop and hurt you folks," he said. "I was sleeping behind the flower lady's stall, but the crash woke me. I saw everything." He scuffs the floor with the tip of a torn sneaker. "I was too scared to come and help you."

A wave of pity rises in her. "Don't fret about it," she says. "I would have been just as scared."

"She was there that night, too," he says. "I seen her. The café was closed by then, but I seen her in there."

She stares at his face, knowing at once to whom he's referring. She doesn't know if he's telling the truth, or if he merely believes he is.

His eyes are watery and red-veined, darting everywhere. "She was standing at the window looking at you guys. She stood there for a long time, until the policeman came."

Later Rakhi will imagine that scene, even though she doesn't want to. Coming to her at night, when she's about to fall asleep, it will jerk her awake. In her mind, the manager stands in the darkness inside Java with her face to the cold glass of the window, her palms pressed so hard against it that they turn white. Her eyes shine with a green chemical glow, and the force of her hatred leaps across the empty street and powers the chain that's swinging at Sonny.

"She isn't there anymore," Marco says. "Did you know that?"

Rakhi did not know. She's been struggling too hard to keep her head above water to think about Java. But today she makes a point to stroll by the café. Indeed, the place has a new manager, a middle-aged, bucktoothed man, plump and hearty. When questioned, he will confess he doesn't know what happened to his predecessor, where she disappeared to.

Can a person be vaporized by the deflected force of her own hate? Rakhi is left to wonder.

She takes out her easel, the first time since September. She closes her eyes and doesn't fight when the images deluge her. Crash of a glass cracking, fear like slime tracks up her arm, how she couldn't clean it off for a long time afterward, no matter how hot she ran the bathwater. She starts painting them in: a Sikh man shot at a gas station because someone thought he was Middle Eastern; terrified women peering from behind curtains that look like burkhas; Jespal's turban unraveled like a river of blood; his eye the swollen purple of a monsoon sky. The background is a collage of faces striped red, white and blue. A fist waves a flag so mammoth that if it falls, it'll suffocate them all. The birds have disappeared, their places taken by airplanes. Some crash into buildings. Some drop bombs as easily as insects drop their eggs. She paints in a GOD

BLESS sign, she paints in tablas, bamboo flutes, violins. Kicking feet, swinging chains, cookies swept off a counter and ground into the floor by boot heels. Knives fly across painted space like the props of jugglers—but they're deadly real. A police car glides through the broken night under a gouged-out moon. When she stands back to look, the colors and shapes come together in a rush that makes the hairs on her arms stand up. She gives it the only name possible: *You Ain't American.*

When she finishes painting the policeman, looking over his shoulder as he speeds away into a vortex of dark brushstrokes, she realizes that she has given him the face of the man in white. Is she remembering accurately? She recalls a tingling as she'd looked at his face—had it been recognition, or merely relief? Or merely a wish to find a savior whom she knew?

Tomorrow, she decides. Tomorrow she'll go to the eucalyptus grove. Maybe among root and bark she'll find some answers.

38

FROM THE
DREAM JOURNALS

In the caves they told us that when dream tellers work in their sleep, they each throw out a thin, invisible thread, as a spider might, from their navel. This thread reaches all the way to Swapna Lok, the world where dreams are born. Through it, the dreams that the teller needs to know travel back to her. When a teller dreams alone, the thread is thin and weak, easily broken. But when tellers live close to one another, their threads combine to form a powerful rope that can bear the weight of even the most difficult dream. This is why dream tellers should not travel too far from their community.

I said nothing, but inside myself I doubted. These are just tales, I told myself, made up to keep us close to home, under the elders' control.

Why did I doubt what all my fellow novices accepted? Perhaps, unknown to myself, I was already preparing to leave.

Much later, when I told my doubts to my aunt, she sighed. I read that sigh to mean she was tired of my rebelliousness. Perhaps she regretted bringing me out of the slums. I had, after all, caused nothing but trouble.

But it was a sigh of exasperated love. (Since becoming a mother, I too have learned that sigh.) There is proof, she said. But asking for it is like asking to know that a glass dish is breakable. You'll be convinced, but there'll be no putting the pieces back together.

I listened with only half of my impatient mind. Riddles, riddles, I thought. Why can't you just tell me what you mean?

Years later my daughter would say the same words to me.

But some things can't be told that way, I know that now. They can only be approached stealthily, from behind, like wild birds. And even then they catch your scent and take flight before you throw your net of words over them.

My ability to dream may have weakened even in Calcutta, once I married, but in those early, dancing days I wasn't paying attention. I was full of another kind of dreaming, for which sleep is not necessary. It was only in America, its nights stagnant as the Sargasso Sea, that I was forced to face the magnitude of my problem. Sometimes I would feel a thin, sickly tendril pushing itself out of my body. But when it found nothing outside to connect with, it shriveled and fell back into me. For a while, the bag of earth my aunt had given me staved off my despair. But each time I dreamed, there was less in the bag. And one night it was gone. With it the dreams, too, went.

How can I put into words the emptiness of being without my dreams after I'd tasted them again, after I'd used them to help people? I couldn't eat, I couldn't sleep. All day I paced up and down the threadbare carpet of the apartment, trying to think of a remedy. I knew no dream tellers in America. Perhaps there were none in this land that believed technology to be the cure for all ills?

Even if I could have given words to my problem, I could not speak them to my husband. He didn't know I was a dream teller. I'd intended to inform him of it before we married, but at the last moment I shied away. Many people feared the dream tellers, many thought us unnatural. What if he did, too? I could not risk losing his love, I who had given up so much for it. I told him that my family was against our marriage, and that I'd left them for that reason. I told him I did not want to speak of them again, it was too painful. He respected my wishes and showered me with tenderness to make up for the love he believed I'd lost. How could I tell him now that he'd poured out his heart after a lie?

Besides, he did not have the power to help me. He had problems of his own. We had little money, so he was forced to work in addition to taking classes at the university. He came home each night exhausted, uncertain that he could make it in this new country that had glittered so beckoningly in the beginning. Still, he was a kind man, and he could see I was unhappy. He tried to distract me by taking me to restaurants, or to the movies, or to the seashore for the weekend—entertainments we could ill afford. They did no good.

In the weekly paper I read about a psychic who would, for a fee, answer questions about your future, offer solutions to your problems, and reconnect you with lost loved ones. My heart twitched like a beached fish that senses water nearby. I took twenty dollars from my husband's wallet without his knowledge and called her for an appointment. But when I heard her voice on the phone, raspy from too many cigarettes, too many unslept nights of her own, I knew she couldn't help me.

My days grew unbearable. I could focus on nothing but my lost ability to dream. I'd never paid my gift much attention before, but now my life seemed unlivable without it. In my misery, I blamed my husband for my loss. I quarreled with him for the slightest of reasons. The bafflement in his eyes only made me angrier. Thoughts of suicide filled my brain like rain clouds till everywhere I turned I saw only blackness.

It was at this time that the snake came to me.

I will not describe our meeting; some things should not be set down in a book, not even a book like this that no one might see, written in a language that few in this country can read. But this is what I learned from him: each time I had sex with my husband, or even slept in the same bed, my powers—already weakened by being so far from the caves—dwindled further. Soon they would die out altogether. If I wanted to remain a dream teller, there were two things I had to do—and soon.

It is your choice, the snake said. He glistened at the periphery of my vision, a raindrop on an ear of maize. He was the only thing of beauty in my dim and suffocating existence. I couldn't bear to imagine him gone.

It is your choice, he said. But I knew I had no choice. I had to break off all ties with my husband. And I had to find a way to get back to the caves.

39

Rakhi

All night I can't sleep. My brain feels hot and perforated, my eyes itch as though I'm coming down with an illness. Thoughts thud through my head like a herd of elephants. Random things my mother had said to me. *Using a hair dryer kills your brain cells. Don't go to bed holding on to a grudge.* Snatches of Sonny's old music, and pushing out from behind the notes, his new music that I haven't yet heard. A recipe for coconut chutney that my father made last week, down to its last detail, though I dislike coconut. Lists of clothes Jona was growing out of, household items Belle would need if she got married, security measures the U.S. airports should have taken. But these are not my real thoughts. My real thoughts are the ones I'm staving off by filling my mind, as fast as I can, with unnecessary chatter. When the light behind the blinds is the color of melted butter, I give up on rest.

Jona's with Sonny, so I'm free to go to the eucalyptus grove whenever I please, but I keep delaying. I make breakfast, take a shower, throw a long-overdue load of clothes into the washer. I'm reluctant to go, afraid that the man in white will not be present. If he isn't, I have no other way of reaching him.

Or is it that I'm afraid he'll be there?

. . .

$\mathcal{I}$'m hoping the grove will be empty, but it's unusually crowded for a weekday. People are taking advantage of the sunshine, the mildness of this November noon. Students amble along the path, children run squealing after squirrels, dogs pull their owners along as they explore smells, lovers sit on fallen tree trunks, exchanging kisses as lovers have always done. A family has spread a tablecloth over fallen pine needles for a picnic. I peer over their blond heads to see falafel and salad, pita bread, pureed eggplant. How can everyone look so happy? Is there a magic shield around the grove that filters memory from the minds of those who enter here? Or is this how humans survive, shrugging off history, immersing themselves in the moment? If so, it's a skill that has passed me by.

I go to the hollow at the heart of the grove where I last saw the man in white practicing his Tai Chi. There are no signs of him, but it's quieter here. I sit on the ground, leaning against a fallen tree. There's a ragged circle of sky overhead where the tops of the eucalyptus haven't quite met. I look up at that. Inside me the thoughts I've been battling wait like submerged rocks in a river. Even one of them can make me sink if I crash into it. Immerse yourself in the moment, I tell myself. The brittleness of dry twigs under you, the scratchy bark behind your back. The sky is very pale, white rather than blue. It pulls at my chest until something pops, like a cork. And as though they were waiting for just this moment, the thoughts rush out. On TV a week ago, a preacher declared that homosexuals and abortion-rights advocates must bear the blame for the terrorist attacks: they angered God and caused his wrath to descend on America. Jona awoke crying. I was afraid to ask her why. She told me, anyway. She had dreamed of a frozen cave filled with bodies. I couldn't say, like other mothers might, *Don't worry, it's only a dream*. The weight of her gift pressed on my chest like a slab of ice. I received e-mails saying no one should go to the malls on Halloween, that another major attack was planned on that day. Many of the waiters in the World Trade Center were undocumented workers. We'll never know who they were, or their families. Other e-mails advised me to stock up on garlic and oil of oregano—they were antidotes to anthrax. A week after the towers fell, police found a pair of hands on top of a building nearby, bound with plastic handcuffs. On board the USS *Enterprise*, a sailor held up a bomb on which was printed, HIGH JACK THIS FAGS. Some nights I'm afraid to go to sleep. What else in the world will have broken by the time I open my eyes again? Other times I want only to sleep, dug deep into the ground like a badger, the cool, comforting mustiness of earth, which never changes, against my skin.

Often I find myself contemplating death. Until recently, I'd experienced it only as a theory. But now it had swooped into my life like a great gray owl, taloned, eyes shining through the night. It terrified me, but it was beautiful, too. Was that why some people rushed toward it in a frenzy of unfathomable joy, calling it the Savior of the Faithful?

And what about her, the woman closest to and farthest from me, who lived her life trying to save others and ended it driving her car (with her husband in it) over a hillside? It was no accident, I've grown sure of that. What transforming dream did she enter, that last night of her life? What was she seeking, for which death seemed the only gateway?

. . .

A dragonfly has lighted on my hand, large and metal-blue, with transparent gauze wings. It balances on my knuckle for a moment, its wings shining, the black beads of its eyes. I haven't seen many dragonflies here. I feel curiously honored that it has chosen me for its way stop. I sit very still, hardly breathing, until it lifts off and spins toward the sky. I watch till it vanishes, and when my eyes come back to earth, I see the man in white.

He is in the hollow, in his usual place, but today his practice is different. He balances on his right leg, pulling the left leg back with his arm. His right arm is pointed up at the sky. His eyes are focused on a point on the horizon. Slowly, he extends his leg behind him, still holding on, until it is stretched taut. It's a beautiful, powerful stance, perfectly balanced. I can't take my eyes from it.

After a while, he relaxes his leg, brings it down to the ground, repeats the stance on the other side. I recognize what he's doing as a yoga posture, though I don't know the name of this particular one. I marvel, as I did earlier, at how naturally his body moves through the steps. I know I couldn't do it.

He's finished with the asana now. Before he starts another one, I stand up. The blood pounds so hard in my head that I grow dizzy. But inside me I'm sure, with a certainty I haven't felt in a long time, that if I don't take this opportunity to talk to him, I won't get another one.

"Hello," I say.

He turns, and I see that he is much older than I'd thought. His body had moved like a young man's, but his face is weathered and lined. It is hard to tell his race—his skin is brown, but his eyes are a startling green. Is he the same person I saw last time, on that rainy morning? Perhaps many men come to practice in the grove. Several may wear white, at least some of the time. Perhaps the person I've titled *the man in white* exists only in my imagination, to be superimposed on other people when my subconscious feels a particular need. And with this last doubt I'm so embarrassed, I'm ready to apologize and leave.

"Hello," he says, eyes crinkling in a smile. I like his eyes. They're attractive, but not in a sexual way. Though there's no sign in them that he recognizes me, they hold me as a wave holds a swimmer. They make me want to stay awhile, even if he isn't *my* man in white, even if he knows nothing about my mother's death.

I take a deep breath. I have the sensation that we're engaged in an elaborate, dancelike game. The outcome of our encounter will depend on how well I play it. But what are the rules?

He waits, at ease, for me to speak.

A hundred questions crowd my mind. Do you drive a black car? Are you a policeman? Does your license plate say Emit Maerd? Is that your name, and what does it mean? Did you know my mother? Did she follow you over the edge of a freeway?

I say, "Is that yoga you were practicing?"

This time his smile brings a shimmer to his face. Somehow I've asked the right question.

"Yes," he says.

"Would you show me an asana?"

"I will," he says. He looks at me, brow creased, as though making a decision.

I follow him to a different, larger clearing. There are people all around us, but it doesn't matter. Walking beside him, I feel as though the two of us are inside a bubble that no one else can break into.

"Do what I'm doing," he says. He stands with his legs together and raises his hands above his head, stretching them all the way. He touches his palms to each other. I follow. The movement is simplicity itself, but new to me. I feel a slight tingling in my fingertips as I stretch.

He moves his legs apart, then turns to the right, pointing his front foot ahead. Bends the right knee and lowers his body. His left leg is stretched out behind him. He gazes upward at his joined palms.

I try to do the same, but my left leg, unused to stretching and bending in this manner, begins to wobble. I lose my balance and have to bring my arms down to prevent myself from falling.

"Don't be embarrassed," he says. "Try it again." He puts his hands on my shoulders and turns them. He pulls on an ankle to position my legs correctly. He draws my arms all the way up and brings the palms together.

"Look up," he says.

I stare at the white aperture in the sky, but this time I'm not dizzy. I feel the warmth from his palms passing into my hands. Between the sky and myself hangs a spiderweb. Stretched between two eucalyptus branches, laden with silver dew, it is the most intricate thing I've ever seen. *To think that it was there all the time,* my whisper voice says, *only you'd never noticed.*

He has let his hands fall away. I stand alone, balanced, and for a split second I have the strangest sensation, as though I were a dewdrop on a web that I can't see, a web huge beyond imagining. The man in white is another dewdrop. Right now some force—

wind, gravity, planetary influence—has brought us near each other. In another moment it might push one of us away, to slide along a webbing and end up in another city, another country—even another dimension. This is how it is all the time—people go skittering out of our lives, never to be found. But they're all still somewhere on the web.

Then my legs give way, and I have to grab his hand to keep from falling.

When we stop laughing, he says, "This is one of my favorites, a variation of the Warrior. A regular practice of it leads to balance, poise, vision and fearlessness—not to mention strong legs and a straight back."

I grimace. "I certainly need all of the above."

"We all do," he says, and he looks at me with great kindness. He nods in farewell, then wheels his bicycle—an old blue ten-speed that had been leaning against a tree all this time—out of the grove and passes from my sight.

I keep my encounter with the man in white a secret, though at times I'm sorely tempted to discuss it with Belle. But she would think I was foolish. ("I can't believe it! You wasted your time with him practicing a *yoga posture* when you had all these important questions to ask? For Christ's sake, Rikki, you aren't even interested in yoga!") I wouldn't be able to explain to her how I felt when he joined his palms over mine, as though they were petals on the same flower. Or my notion about the web.

Words are tricky. Sometimes you need them to bring out the hurt festering inside. If you don't, it turns gangrenous and kills you. That's how it had been between me and Sonny, why we couldn't move on with our lives—together or separately—until we talked. But sometimes words can break a feeling into pieces. That's how it is with my grove episode.

My mother had tried to teach me this. Once when I was pesteringly insistent with my questions, she said, "Everyone breathes in air, but it's a wise person who knows when to use that air to speak and when to exhale in silence." I wouldn't lay claim to such wisdom—but perhaps I'm learning.

I try the Warrior posture from time to time. I'd hoped it would transform me, make my weaknesses fall away, but it isn't so. Yet sometimes when I'm practicing, in front of a half-finished painting in my cluttered living room, or out on Sonny's deck, in the blue shade of the jacarandas, I feel something loosening inside, some coil of distrust, some need to be in control. Energy flickers in my fingertips, and my whisper voice curls up like a cat and closes its eyes.

I never saw the man in white again—maybe because I didn't need to. Something in me had been satisfied by our encounter. I would never know what mysterious link, if any, connected him to my mother, whether he was indeed the long-awaited messenger of her journals. But somehow for the first time I could accept this not-knowing. There would always be mysteries about the people I cared for, enigmas central to their lives, that I would be unable to decipher. That was all right. Love worked its slanted way along other paths. Maybe the man in white, whom I will hold inside me next to Jona and my parents, Sonny and Belle, had come to tell me that.

40

FROM THE
DREAM JOURNALS

Once I had made the decision to leave, I was no longer depressed. There were too many things to plan. The first was to collect enough money for a ticket without my husband's knowledge. For that, I had to get a job.

I approached my husband with some anxiety. The first lie I'd told him had been for both our sakes; this one was for me alone. Could I look into the face I loved (yes, still) more than any other person's and do it? But it was easier than easy. My voice was steady as I said I was lonely, that work would keep me occupied, that the extra money would help with our expenses. He agreed at once—he'd been worried at my black moods—and inquired among his Indian colleagues. (I cannot call them friends. We'd been too busy trying to survive our transplanting to make friends.) In a few weeks—a miracle, considering I had no work permit and no skills—I was given a job.

I worked in an Indian grocery—in the back, where no one would see me. I measured dals and spices from large sacks into plastic bags, sealed them and attached appropriate labels. Some would have considered it a tedious job, but I was comforted by the simple, repetitive nature of my task. It pleased me to apply the seal in a straight line, to attach the label to the exact center of the packet. All the while I imagined the day I would buy my ticket with the money that lay accumulating in a shoe box under our bed. (I would have enough in three months.) The day I would take the Ride-A-Van to the airport and step onto an Air India plane bound for Calcutta. Things grew blurry after that. I presumed I would catch a train to the village that lay closest to the caves. Then I would make my way on foot. This part caused me some disquiet. I remembered rumors about how the caves were hidden so that, though all could leave them at will, only the elders knew how to enter them. But I resolved not to worry. The snake had invited me back, had he not? Surely he would make things clear when the time came.

The owners of the grocery paid me a low hourly wage. It was much lower than the legal rate, but I didn't hold it against them. They undertook a certain risk in hiring me, and they were kind in their way. They gave me a good number of hours each week, and in the afternoons, when the owner's wife took a lunch break in the back, she always invited me to eat with her.

Perhaps it was guilt, or perhaps it was that I knew I'd soon be gone, but during this time I tried to do everything my husband liked. I cooked his favorite dishes. (I was not a good cook, having had no experience in the caves, but I tried.) I accompanied him each evening to a nearby lake to feed the ducks, an activity that bored me but that seemed to give him pleasure. And when he wanted to, which was almost every night, I let him make love to me.

I cannot pretend that I did it only for him. He was an attractive man, and I did love him—just not enough to give up my dreaming. I had always enjoyed sex. Even my fear that it was making me lose my gift hadn't totally taken away the sharp, gasping pleasure of the act. Now, the secret knowledge that I was leaving added the sweet ache of transience to our lovemaking. If I felt uneasiness, a sense that I shouldn't be doing this, I refused to heed it. I'm giving up everything, I told myself. Surely I deserve a few memories to take back to my chaste, caved life. I slept dreamlessly during this time. I didn't care. Soon there would be little other than dreams in my life.

Two weeks before I was to leave—I had called a travel agent and reserved a ticket by then—I fainted at work while pulling a large sack of lentils to the measuring area. The owner's wife heard the clatter—I'd fallen on a stack of aluminum spice boxes—and came running. She wiped my face with a wet towel and rubbed rosewater on my temples to revive me, then touched the dark circles under my eyes and pronounced that I was pregnant.

"It can't be," I cried, horrified.

"Have you been taking precautions?" she asked.

From my face she must have seen that I didn't know about precautions. She nodded. "Well then, that's what happens. I should know—I had five before I insisted on getting my tubes tied."

She waited for me to say something, but I was incapable of speech. She made me sit down and gave me a bottle of mango juice to drink. (Even in my state of shock I registered her generosity. The mango juice was imported from India, and sold for a dollar a bottle.)

"Don't be scared," she said kindly. "It'll all turn out okay.

You can't imagine how much happiness a child can bring you, how it'll change your life."

No, I wanted to cry. You're the one who can't imagine how a child will change my life. But I said nothing. What was the use? I sat there and drank the too sweet mango juice and used all my willpower to keep from throwing up.

For seven days I agonized over what to do about the pregnancy. I complained of not feeling well and slept apart from my husband for seven nights—and he, trusting soul that he was, did not question me. Each night I begged the snake to come to me, to help me decide. Each night I wept, muffling my sobs in my pillow, when he did not. Even now I wonder why he stayed away. Was it punishment for what I'd done, or was it because it was too late?

At the end of the seven days, I made my decision. First I discarded the possibility of abortion. (Yes, I confess it had been in my mind. If the snake had asked me to do it, I would have obeyed. But the snake had abandoned me, and all I had to depend on now was my own powers of navigation.)

Next I let go of the possibility of return.

For a time afterward I pretended that my decision was an altruistic one, something I did for my unborn child, but I knew it came out of fear. I was afraid the elders would not accept me back into the caves—even if I was able to find them. We had parted in bitterness. They'd warned me that once I left, they owed me nothing. And now, with the visible reminder of my transgression growing inside me, surely they would shun me. Had the snake not done so already?

What would happen then? I couldn't bear to go back to a life in the slums. I couldn't punish my child with the dual curse of poverty and fatherlessness that my own mother had burdened me with.

At the end of the seven days I told my husband of the pregnancy. He was overjoyed. He did not concern himself too much with my quietness. No doubt his colleagues told him that at such times women grow temperamental. When I would not share his bed, he accepted it, thinking it to be a temporary matter. When I told him I no longer wanted to work at the store, he said it was better that I stay home and take care of my health.

As the baby grew within me, I paced the apartment from morning to night because I couldn't bear to be still. But I was no longer agitated. One is agitated only when one has hope, and I had none. My life in India was over. I didn't care how the rest of my days here unspooled themselves, how tangled they grew.

But on the day the baby inside me kicked for the first time, I felt a different kind of movement, too. It took me a moment to recognize it: my old power, stirring once again. Diminished perhaps, but still alive. Who knows how such things work? At first I wouldn't believe it, I was so afraid of disappointment. Then I was filled with a sense of reprieve. And also a new fear. No matter what happened, I must not lose it again.

I noticed that on the days I remained most silent, the power was stronger. On those nights the dreams of strangers came to me, and directives as to how I should find them. I began to make phone calls again, to get responses. I helped one person, then a second, then more.

I decided that I would speak only when necessary, and never

of my past. To speak of something is to dissipate it—and I had already squandered so much. Happiness as ordinary people know it was not for me. But perhaps I could glean satisfaction from the practice of what was left of my gift.

I wished to be a good wife, but that was impossible. I did not dare to sleep with my husband again. I was convinced that if he touched me in desire, I would lose the faint power I'd regained. I could not explain this to him. Words had become a rare commodity, to be hoarded. Besides, he would not have believed me. I took care of him in every other way, cooking, cleaning, ironing, sitting beside him on the worn plush sofa at night, ready to listen to whatever he might say. But he grew morose and would not speak. He wanted only what I could not give him: my body, to which my soul was yoked. I prayed he would stop loving me and turn to someone else—it would have made life easier for us both—but he couldn't. He had webbed himself in me, and the only escape left for him was into the periodic oblivion of drink.

I was not a good mother to Rakhi. I loved her, but not fully. To love someone fully is to give up selfhood, and I could not risk that. She knew this. Perhaps that is why she constantly longed to understand who I am, to become who I am. I did not have the power to give her the latter, even if I wished such a fate on her. If I gave her the former, it would have destroyed me.

And so I attempt these journals, for the written word is different from the spoken. The spoken word vanishes, frost in sunshine. The written word endures, its black frieze like ironwork in palace windows. But I am hampered by my lack of craft. Thoughts rush through me and disappear, memories. I can express only a fraction of what I feel. The rest is lost, like spores scattered by wind. I do not read over the fragments I've written. I'm afraid I will tear them up.

I write this for you, husband, child, to read when I am gone. Perhaps you will be baffled by my ramblings. Perhaps you will hate me for my confessions. Perhaps you will understand a little of what I could never explain: who I was and why, what gods haunted my dreams, and what serpents.

She stands in the long line waiting for the doors to open, fidgeting with her purse, with the piece of paper on which Sonny had written down directions. It is a windy San Francisco night, and here, south of Market, gusts blow torn strips of newspaper from unlit doorways to catch against the legs of the club's patrons. But *patron* is too formal a word, she thinks, for this variegated group, mostly of Indian origin, though people have brought friends of other persuasions. Their hairstyles range from punk-dyed to shaved to crew cut to curls cascading over the backs of designer tops. Some wear baggy, oversize pants and caps turned backward; others have come gothic, in black capes and blood-red lips. Underneath coats she glimpses tiny gold-embroidered sari blouses, worn over capris, or transparent dupattas wound over bustiers. Pierced, tattooed, painted, hennaed, bindied, they seem to belong to a different nation, their speech casually peppered with terms she does not know. She can't remember coming across Indian Americans of this kind, either in Fremont or Berkeley. Perhaps they're a new nocturnal species? Or are they masters of camou-flage who have been in front of her all along, in grocery stores and banks, hospitals and college campuses?

She would have felt mortifyingly out of place among this crowd, except that Sonny had instructed her how to dress. In her embroidered Gujarati vest, calf-length black skirt and old ankle boots, she blends in sufficiently that no one spares her a second glance. Not that they pay much attention to one another, either, though she guesses many of them to be regulars. Perhaps that's what it is to be young, she thinks. You're so consumed by the energy boiling up inside you, by all the things you have to have *right now* in your life, that you don't have time to look at anything—or anyone—that isn't a fast lane to what you want.

She is surprised to find herself liking them. There's a camaraderie in their non-attention. A confidence that the people standing in this line, with their ten dollars clutched in their hands, are culturally superior to the barbarian hordes who are spending their Friday evening elsewhere—at some yuppie discotheque, perhaps, or watching a Hindi movie on a too large TV in a too ornate suburban family room.

It had taken all her courage to tell Sonny that she'd like to come hear him DJ. When he'd told her that he played his most creative work at Must-Must, the end-of-the-month desi party in the city, she'd almost backed down. She'd imagined a riotous crowd, her expectations fueled by leftover terror from that other party-gone-wrong. She knew she had to come, though, or else there was no possibility of laying those memories to rest. Now she marvels at how patiently people stand here, chatting with the bouncer, exchanging quips with a couple of homeless people who are trying to cadge beer money out of them. Still, she's careful not to meet any eyes, not to smile.

Sonny had offered to bring her with him, but she'd refused.

She'd told him she wanted to experience the evening authentically, just as any other clubgoer would. But the truth is, it was a test she set herself. Since the assault at the Kurma House, she'd been too afraid to go anywhere alone at night. Things she'd hardly noticed before—a group of people waiting at an intersection, footsteps behind her as she walked to her car, someone asking her if she had the time—loomed in her mind, throwing out monstrous shadows. Just thinking about them made her breath fast and shallow.

Tonight, taking the BART train across the bay, she was caught by claustrophobia when the train dived underground and the windows turned black. The faces of the men in the car—there were three, one dozing, two listening to headphones—took on a predatory aspect. In the flickering light, their mouths were thin slashes. Harsh frown lines cut into their foreheads, angry shadows filled up the hollows under their eyes. Were they watching her covertly, trying to guess where she was from? She sat there wondering which one was most likely to attack her. Fear crept upward from the soles of her feet, turning them numb. She took a deep breath and forced herself to open the journal she'd brought with her.

Halfway through the final entry, she'd read about the abortion that might have been, the matter-of-fact words her mother had chosen. *If the snake had asked me to do it, I would have obeyed.* She read them over, once, twice, again, until the words blurred and fused into a string of nonsense syllables. Here was confirmation for what she, with the blood's devastating intuition, had suspected all her life: She was less important, was an obstacle, a burden. With all the strength in her shaking hands, she had thrown the notebook across the room.

But then she'd thought of her father, how much harder it must have been for him to read it. To learn the reasons his wife had stayed with him all her life and realize that those reasons didn't include him. To let his daughter learn them, too. *I loved him,* her mother had written, *just not enough.* In some way that was worse than not having been loved at all. It would have been easy enough for him to skip those lines, to pretend they weren't there. Instead, he'd put aside shame and picked up truth and continued translating because his daughter had asked him to.

And her mother. As her anger ebbed, and her self-pity, she saw that for her mother it had been the hardest of all. To strip herself of silence, that lifelong armor. Had she hesitated, bending over the notebook, biting the end of her pen? Had she imagined how they'd hate her, the husband and daughter she'd abandoned even as she decided to remain with them? Each word she'd set down in the journals was a gift and a wound. It could be healed only by being read. Thinking of that had made her pick up the notebook and smooth its crumpled pages, the binding that was coming apart. With a dark gratitude, she'd kept going till the end.

In the train she turned to one of the first translations her father had done. She read the same page over and over.

The dream comes heralding joy.
I welcome the dream.
The dream comes heralding sorrow.
I welcome the dream.
The dream is a mirror showing me my beauty.
I bless the dream.
The dream is a mirror showing me my ugliness.

I bless the dream.
My life is nothing but a dream
From which I will wake into death,
which is nothing but a dream of life.

In her panic she was incapable of deciphering the meaning behind the words, but through them she heard her mother's voice, calm, pragmatic, a little exasperated at her daughter's tendency to drama. It held her until the train came to a jolting stop and a machine informed her that she had reached the Embarcadero. She emerged from the train on shaky legs, but all in all, it was a victory.

She identifies herself to the woman who is stamping hands at the entrance, as Sonny had asked her to.

"Wow!" the woman—a girl, really, very thin, all in black with frizzy hair and huge eyes made up Cleopatra-style—exclaims as she jumps up from her stool. "You're DJ Sundance's woman! He told us you'd be coming." Despite Rakhi's protests, she presses her ten dollars back into her palm. "We can't take money from you!" She offers to escort her downstairs to Sonny. "He's just the coolest. We all think he's terribly talented." She gazes at Rakhi reverently, as though some of his talent must have seeped into her. When an embarrassed Rakhi assures her that she'll be able to find her way by herself, the woman calls out, in a disappointed voice, "Enjoy the evening." The words send a frisson of uneasiness through Rakhi.

The club is cavernous and dimly lit, and she pauses, back pressed against a wall, to orient herself. Video images flicker on the opposite wall, washing over each other in monochromatic red—

the ruins of some colonial building, a lake, a woman drinking from a green coconut, a cobra, a mushroom cloud. The redness makes her feel as though she's entered a different space. *Dream time,* she thinks, as she wends her way through crowds of people. She had no idea so many people were in here already. She thinks of the long line still waiting outside. How will they all fit in? *And in case of a fire, or something worse, how would we all get out?* But she hasn't come here to worry. The club has survived for this long without her trying to solve its problems, she reminds her whisper voice.

Now she hears music, though it must have been playing all this time. She's always been more of a visual person; she doesn't know much about music and has been curiously reluctant to learn. Once she told Sonny, There's a special charm in listening to something you don't fully understand—like hearing a foreign language. You're not distracted by what the sounds are supposed to mean. You can let them drop all the way down inside you. That's what she does now, and as she does, she realizes she's hearing Indian instruments, though they don't sound anything like the classical music CDs she sometimes listens to. Nor do they have the raw folk quality of the music produced by the men at Kurma House. She pushes her way to the low stage in the front of the room, and sees a man and a woman on tablas. Next to them there's a saxophonist—ah, that's what she's been hearing, the drawn-out molasses of notes weaving dexterously in and out of the insistent drumming, changing it into something alien and mesmerizing. A few people are dancing, mostly by themselves, eyes closed, but the majority are listeners. They sit cross-legged on a concrete floor that looks extremely uncomfortable, rapt and swaying. She'd like to stay longer, taking in the various expressions on their faces—a painting is taking shape in her mind, another collage—but she sees the stairs disappearing underground, and follows them. Behind her she hears a woman beginning to sing classical vocals, a single vowel, *aaaa*, raised and lowered, broken into syllables, pulled out in a single, shivering note. Soft, then powerful, then soft again, the sound lodges in her, oddly familiar, a déjà vu of cultural memory she hadn't expected to find here.

The cellar is awash with a blue protean light punctuated by the pulse of strobes. It makes her think of a poem she'd read a long time ago about Bavarian gentians, about the afterworld. At first sight it seems as though a thousand people are crammed in here, all dancing. She spots Sonny right away, drawn to him by some inner radar. He's in a corner behind a set of tables, earphones around his neck. Surrounding him is a plethora of complicated-looking equipment. Records spin on two turntables in front of him. From time to time he puts on the phones and adjusts something on a CD player. He hasn't seen her yet. She likes that. It makes her feel invisible and powerful to watch him while he's unaware. A dreadlocked woman sits on a stool next to him, beating on a set of African drums. A man is bent over another turntable. From where Rakhi stands, it looks as though he's scratching at it, making it stop and start. She'd have thought it would create a disruptive cacophony, but that's not the case.

She realizes she's holding her stomach muscles tight, waiting to be wrested into the dark spiral of memory, she's been so sure that hearing Sonny play will do that to her. But the sounds around her meld together to make a music unlike anything she's heard before. It's on edge, slightly off-key, weaving together disparate elements—she hears a moment of guitar, then a bass throbbing, then something that has to be computer generated. A woman's voice swoops in, singing *chhaiya chhaiya*, then flies away again, and what's left behind, a magnetic roll of drums and words she doesn't understand, a folk beat that she recognizes from the Kurma House, snags her and pulls her onto the dance floor—she, who hasn't danced in a lifetime! *Floor* is a misnomer, though, because people are dancing everywhere—on the stairs, in front of a video screen flashing pictures of other dancing people, on a low stage at the other end of the room. People bob up and down on stools at the bar. They're dancing alone, or with a partner, but mostly dancing in groups. A boatman's song from an old record her father loves comes on, but in its present incarnation it's mixed with electronica and voices in another language. The singer's voice, honey with an undercurrent of grit—*o majhi re*—disappearing into the background melody and emerging from it, is a surprise, every time.

She finds herself among a group of people who are dancing bhangra. Their fluid shoulder movements remind her of the men in her store. Though here the dance is speeded up tenfold, mixed in with break dancing and belly dancing and other kinds of dancing she doesn't know the names of. They're intimidatingly talented, and watching them she wants to retreat to the safety of the bar. But the rhythm is so catchy, so carefree, she can't resist bobbing her head and swaying from foot to foot. No one's looking at her anyway. So perhaps it doesn't matter that she's not a good dancer, that she's not doing any of the fancy moves, that she can barely keep time. A few minutes, she thinks. Then she'll head for that bar stool.

Now the group opens out to form a circle. They're playing

some kind of a dancing game. As the others clap and whistle, a woman dressed in zari-embroidered pants and a leotard top spins into the middle, dancing with her eyes closed, her arms high, hair whipping her face as she moves. She whirls so fast that she loses balance and stumbles into the people who make up the circumference. Rakhi flinches, but the onlookers have caught her. They spin her back into the circle, laughing and cheering. She does this a few more times, then exits, and a young man with braided hair takes her place. Rakhi watches as he, too, spins with eyes closed, stumbles, is steadied and returned to the center. Others follow. She can't take her eyes off them. There's so much fellowship here. Perhaps it's induced by alcohol and adrenaline, but still! To go out blind among strangers, trust them to bear your weight, to not hurt you, to keep you, in fact, from getting hurt—could she dare such a thing after all that has happened?

She doesn't know how she finds herself inside the circle. Did she take the first step, or did someone nudge her in? In any case, she's here now, turning around and around. Almost at once she feels dizzy, nauseous. What foolishness! She's much too old for something like this, she'll probably sprain an ankle any second. And as she thinks this she stumbles, her arms thrown out, rigid with fear, her eyes flying open. But someone's caught her already. It's a woman in a loose dress, flowers woven into her long brown braid. She's wearing a coronet of feathers. *Eliana?* Rakhi whispers, *Is that you?* but the music erases her question. The woman winks at Rakhi (in assent, or merely goodwill?) and pirouettes away. Other hands hold Rakhi steady, then release her into the circle. Someone cries, *Go, girl!* She finds herself rotating, eyes closed, except this time she's not so afraid. She spins to the circumference, is held and spun back, once, twice, three times. She's astonished to feel herself smiling. With each revolution, she's increasingly a part of the music, part of the scene, and as she dances to the darkness inside her eyelids and feels the sweat sprout on her skin and the beat throb through her, she's suddenly, deeply grateful.

She dances her way toward the DJ area, pausing at the bar to pick up a drink, something sweet and strong she doesn't recognize, but this doesn't worry her. She's beginning to understand, a little, what the club scene means to Sonny. It's not just the excitement and glamour, the money and easy popularity, as she'd accusingly thought. But to make a roomful of people lose themselves to the mood and become one with the sound! To throw up their arms to the sky and never want it to stop—the music that you've created from random bits and castaway pieces and made it sound like no one thought it could. To make people shed suspicion and the memory of pain. Why, it was a little like being God!

She likes how the music surprises her as it moves from ethnic to techno to drums, drums, drums. It's okay not to know what's coming next; she trusts it'll be good, or at least interesting. Small chunks of fear break off her and float away. There's much more inside, but it's a start. She's lighter with each shrug of her shoulders, each swish of her hips. It's like walking on the moon. All right, she admits it, some of it's from the drink, which she's holding out to Sonny, and that's okay, too. He smiles at her, his teeth a neon flash in the black light, takes her glass and raises it in a wordless toast. A ray of light catches the liquid, flashes like strawberry satin. Dancing, she knows this can't last. Tomorrow she'll be back to her usual curmudgeonly self. (She must be tipsy, even to think up such a word!) But she's content to enjoy this moment, this transient mote of glitter-dust on the web of the world where Sonny and she have touched orbits once more. She dances back to the center of the room, its nexus of energy, feeling his gaze like a silk dupatta on her shoulders as she goes.